The Campus Killer
Book 1 of the Detective Ryan Series
By Andrew Hess
Published by Phoenix Entertainment and Development 2015

Table of Contents

<u>Chapter 1-CK</u>

It was the calm before the storm. The town of New Paltz slowly buzzed as move-in day quickly approached. A new crop of freshmen were in the middle of orientation. They had dreams of what college life would be like. It was their first taste of freedom, their chance to meet new friends, and the opportunity to make memories that would last a lifetime. Other students were set to return to their day-long lectures, late night cram sessions and, of course, lots of parties. But there was one man who was chomping at the bit for the fall 2006 semester to begin. In fact, he planned on making it the most memorable year ever. Some may call it a bloody good time.

Everyone knew him as a geeky looking junior. His stocky size plastered down hair, and oversized glasses only enhanced that image, but all of that was about to change. A much needed transformation was about to turn his world upside down.

It started with a shopping spree. Bags tugged at his wrists as the student climbed three flights of stairs to his studio apartment. A black number fourteen had been inked at the top of his white paint-chipped door. Sweat dripped down his forehead as he struggled to unlock his sanctuary.

He managed to get inside just as the plastic handles from the bags began to rip. They were thrown onto his unkempt bed next to the red comforter that had been rolled into a ball earlier.

Shit, it's hot in here. He rushed to the windows to open them. It hadn't been humid when he left that morning for the galleria. But by midday, eighty-five degrees made his apartment feel like a sauna.

There wasn't much to his place. The landlords purchased the house and rented each room out to college students. Room fourteen was large enough for them to convert it into a studio apartment. The bathroom was a small closet where they had installed a toilet. The stove was a notch above using an easy-bake oven with a brick wall sitting behind it to hide the fumes. There was nothing about the apartment that felt comfortable, but the landlords had at least provided some furniture. There was a black metal desk which sat next to the entrance. It was perfect for his TV and to do some homework. They left him a corkboard hanging over an old wooden dresser, and a small card table with matching chairs that rested on a sloping floor.

I need to get out of this hell hole. That was the perfect way to describe the house on Oakwood. The New Paltz heat; the loneliness; the feeling like nothing will get better gave him a sense of what being in hell would be like.

"Can this place get any hotter?" he asked himself.

"Did you hear the weather for tomorrow?" a woman called out from the hallway. Her voice was a complete shock pulling the man's attention to the door.

The woman standing at the entrance to the studio apartment was his neighbor from across the hall. She was petite with short reddish brown hair which fell to the middle of her neck. Her blue denim short-shorts and white tank top nearly had the man drooling. He looked her and down before settling on her green eyes.

"Hey, Jess; how's it going?"

"It'd be better if we were allowed to put air conditioners in our rooms." Beads of sweat glistened on her chest as Jess began to fan herself with her hand. "They said it's going to be ninety tomorrow.

Great, he thought. "I'll probably spend the say sitting under the cold water in my shower." He glanced over at the closet-sized shower with frosted glass doors. It was difficult to move around inside of it. The idea of sitting there for hours was almost as unbearable as the hot humid summer days in New Paltz.

Jess let out a laugh and walked towards the bed. "Looks like someone went on a little shopping spree." She touched the broken bag handles to look inside. "What'd ya get?"

The sound of the plastic being moved caused the man to snap his head in Jess's direction. He quickly moved to the bed to move his neighbor back. His body shielded the bags from her view.

"It's just a few things before the semester began." His voice was shaky and nervous. He didn't need Jess snooping around and ruining his plans. "You know; new clothes and books. I figured it would be best to get them out of the way before the school store opens the *gates of hell*." He tried to make his voice sound evil with the last words he spoke.

"Yeah, those long lines are a nightmare," Jess laughed. "I tried finding this semester's books online, but only two of my classes had them listed."

"I guess you'll be down there with the rest of the animals."

Jess didn't seem pleased with her neighbor's response. Her lips pursed together as she narrowed her eyes at him. Then, her face seemed to relax. She inched closer and moved her head from side to side, inspecting him.

"There's something different about you."

The man's paranoia seeped through the cracks in the wall he put up. He questioned if Jess noticed something in the bag to make her think he was up to something fiendish.

Did she see the black mask and gloves in the bag?

Jess snapped her fingers with a smile. "I know; you got a haircut." Her hand reached up to examine her neighbor's much shorter brown hair that had been spiked up with gel. "I like it a lot. It really brings out the green in your eyes."

The comment took the man by surprise. He wasn't used to getting compliments and didn't know how to respond. So, he said the first thing that came to his mind.

"But my eyes are hazel." He wanted to kick himself instantly for feeling the need to correct Jess over something as trivial as eye color.

"They've always looked green to me. Today, they seem brighter than usual." Jess stared into his eyes a little longer.

"W-what are you doing for dinner?" he stammered.

The question seemed to snap Jess back to reality. She glanced at the nearby clock on the wall. It was a quarter past three.

"Shit, I'm going to be late. I'm supposed to be at work in fifteen minutes." She ran across the hall and opened her bedroom door. Jess grabbed a backpack before locking up. "I'm sorry," she called out. "I'll see you tonight when I get back."

The man watched his neighbor flee from the house. His lips curled into a smile at the thought of hanging out with her. She was the only girl in town he wanted to go out with. Even one date with Jess would mean the world to him. He was certain his new image would help win her over.

Quickly, he closed the door to his apartment and stood in front of a long mirror. The man staring back at him had a hot new hairstyle and had lost twenty pounds during the summer. It was all part of his plan.

"Time to get rid of the geek," he said sternly to himself.

He reached into the first bag and pulled out a small blue box. The large glasses were cast aside as two contacts were placed in his eyes. They filled with tears instantly, which turned his hazel eyes into the shade of green Jess claimed to have seen earlier.

There was nothing but confidence beaming back from the man in the mirror. It was something he attained from a seminar. The flyer had been taped to the fridge. The bottom of the paper had a broken picture frame lying on the ground with a black and white photo of a man with glasses in it. The same man stood over it dressed in an Armani suit with a super model looking woman holding onto his arm. The bold caption read: **Find the Success You Want.**

It was a rainy Thursday afternoon when he found the flyer. The man had just exited the Lecture Hall and found it posted on the bulletin boards. It came at the perfect time. A few days earlier, he had been dumped by his girlfriend ending their three year relationship. She was the same girl who had convinced him to transfer up to New Paltz for his sophomore year. She'd complained he wasn't the right man for her. She wanted someone with confidence; someone who could treat her right; someone who had ambition and passion in his life. None of that described him until the day he'd found that flyer.

He ripped it down from the fridge. "I don't need you anymore." It was shredded into tiny pieces and thrown into a tall beige trash can next to the sink.

The man's eyes glanced back at the calendar. There were two dates circled in red. The first was marked August twenty-third; the first day of school. The other had a bullseye over the date September first. He placed a finger on the mark and smiled before walking to his desk.

The drawers let out a high-pitched noise as he opened them. The sound was worse than nails on a chalk board. It sent a chill down his body causing him to open the drawer enough to fit his hand inside. He pulled out a small, wrinkled piece of paper with four names written in black ink. He stared at them intensely.

"Vengeance will be mine." The man rolled his chair to the bed and sifted through the new clothes. "I think it's about time Mark Thompson makes his debut."

<u>Chapter 2-CK</u>

September first, 2006, was a day no one in New Paltz would ever forget. The first week of school was over. A local party at a house on South Oakwood signaled the official end of summer and welcomed the students to a new school year. It was a celebration marked for the first Friday of the fall semester, one all returning students looked forward to.

Mark Thompson attended the party last year with his then girlfriend and some friends. He'd tried to enjoy himself, but he was thought the music was too loud, it was too crowded, and he wasn't a fan of the selection in beer. It turned out to be one of the worst nights of his life.

A year later, Mark Thompson eagerly sat in his new Civic down the road from the familiar ranch style home. He wore blue jeans with a black tank top and a matching button-down shirt which was left open. It was his premiere night; designed to debut his new look and set a trap for his first victim.

He had a spectator view from his parking spot watching cars drive up and down the block searching for a place to leave their cars. More students appeared rounding the corner from campus. None of them mattered. There was only one person he wanted to see. Mark refused to get out until he saw her.

Music blasted loudly from the house as another group gathered on the front lawn. He saw a small thin woman with long black hair. Mark clapped his hands and rubbed them together excitedly.

"She's here," he whispered.

Mark scrambled out of the car and hurried up the block until he arrived at the beat up looking house with peeling white painted rails. Bursts of music filled the street every time the door opened behind the wannabe bouncers. A six foot three inch monster flexed his muscles through his tight black t-shirt while blocking the entrance. He stood in back of a smaller red-headed man who sat on a stool with a metal tin on his lap.

"Money and ID," the red-headed man said.

"How much?" Mark asked while handing over his license. The picture didn't match his new image. Using the real ID was a risky move, but he knew no one would remember his name or his face.

"Ten bucks to get in. You get one red cup for the keg. It's in the backyard. We've got dollar shots in the kitchen." The man barely glanced at the license before handing it back. A blue band was placed around Mark's wrist. "He's all set; enjoy!"

Mark nodded to indicate he understood, but nothing the men at the door said mattered to him. Mark wasn't there to drink like the rest of the students. There was only one thing on his mind, revenge.

More than forty people crowded around the house. Many of them danced around the living room to the deafening music. Their red cups were held tightly in their hands with the contents spilling over the sides. Beer dripped onto Mark's sleeve. His head turned towards the culprit. His eyes flashed with anger.

Don't do anything stupid, he reminded himself. *You're not here for her.* His focus returned to scanning the darkened room for his victim. He was halfway through to the kitchen when he noticed a handful of girls grinding on each other with a circle of men gawking at them like lions stalking their prey.

Every few steps intensified Mark's hatred for parties. Flashes of the previous year brought up the horrible memories. He needed to get out before they overwhelmed him and cause him to throw away all he had worked so hard to obtain. His new image was perfect for blending into the crowd. One minor freak out would draw attention and everyone would know who he was on campus.

Maybe this wasn't the best idea.

At last, Mark made it to the kitchen. A group of students stood around a rectangular table playing flip cup. He knew it was a get drunk fast type of game where either the players competed one on one or in teams. They would race to down each cup of beer and attempt to flip the cup over onto the opening by only using a finger and the edge of the table. Mark was sure his target would join in the fun. He had seen her participate in the drinking game a couple of times during the last year. He casually made his way around the table to check each person, but none of them was the girl he was looking for.

This is a fucking waste of time.

Mark was about to leave the party when someone exited the backdoor. It allowed him to see another large group of people standing around drinking. He remembered the red head saying the keg was in the backyard.

She has to come out there at some point.

He carefully slipped out the door and avoided any direct contact with anyone. They may have been drunk, but Mark was sure someone would remember a man lurking around, especially a guy who wasn't drinking.

He moved to the back of a line of guys waiting for the keg. They were held up by a crowd gathered around a rail thin woman as she was lifted upside down. The keg spout was inserted into her mouth as another man pumped the beer.

Mark tried to hide his delight. His victim was already on her way to being drunk. *It's party time!*

The woman was put down moments later receiving a thunderous applause at completing her keg stand. Mark overheard someone saying she was the first chick to do one that night. It wasn't some incredible feat or something for her to boast about to her friends. The guys at the party looked at her as their first easy lay of the night. Watchful eyes were on her, waiting until she was too drunk to care who took her to bed.

Mark knew how those guys thought. A former housemate had used the same approach to get what he wanted on several occasions. But no one was scoring with her tonight. She belonged to Mark Thompson.

The girl pushed past Mark on her way back inside the house. Her black ponytail brushed against his chin as if taunting him to go after her. She was within inches of his grasp. He could have found a way to get her alone, but there were too many potential witnesses, and his revenge needed to be done in private.

Mark followed his victim into the house, a place he didn't wish to return to. He remained in the shadows watching her; noting how much the girl drank; who she hung out with, and when she decided to leave the party. A few times her eyes locked onto his, but she never made any indication she knew him. His makeover was already deemed a success. It was the perfect disguise. None of the people he encountered knew who he really was or where they knew him from.

"Hey, it's getting late," one of the girls shouted over the music. Mark noticed it was one of his victim's friends. He inched closer to hear where they were going. "We should get back to the dorms."

He watched the girls down the contents of their cups before putting them down on a table. He followed them from a distance with a sadistic smile on his face. He made a quick dash to his car and retrieved a backpack from the trunk before walking briskly to catch up to his victim and her friends.

Mark was now facing the part of the night where so much could go wrong. His target was on the move with a small group of girls. He couldn't get too close, and he needed to be hidden from view. One wrong move could alert any one of them, and they would hurry off to get help or call the police. The only thing working in his favor was their level of intoxication.

The trio of girls stumbled back to campus until they reached a small brick building. Mark Thompson watched as his victim held onto a nearby rail while her friends clung to the glass doors in a desperate attempt to keep their balance.

"You should come up with us and stay here tonight," the taller girl said with her eyes half closed.

"Yeah, stay here," the other friend repeated in a high-pitched tone.

"Nah, I can make it to my dorm," the target advised. She pointed blindly to a cluster of trees near the pond. "Do ya wanna meet for brunch tomorrow?"

"Suuuuurrrrreeee," the taller girl slurred. "We should be there like elevnish." Her voice made it sound more like a question than a statement.

"Okay, sounds like a plan."

"Bye, Rachel," the girls called out as they entered the dorm.

Mark waited for his victim to move away from the doors before taking a single step. He watched the girl hold out her hands as if she were stepping onto a tight rope. She turned back to wave goodbye to her friends. Little did she know it was the last time she would ever see them.

Mark maintained his distance down a paved path. He saw the pond to the left. The moonlight bounced off the top of the water. It would have been the perfect setting for a romantic or peaceful stroll, but that was not his intention. His original plan was to throw her in the pond. Rachel, his soon to be victim, was. Rachel, his soon to be victim, was drunk enough to throw in the pond, but Mark needed to be ensure his success. It was possible someone could find them if she managed to cry out for help. There was the option to hold her under the water, but then Mark would get soaked and his mistake could leave behind evidence. No, there was no way Mark was going to change the plan. There were too many variables unaccounted for, and he had worked too hard to let the night go to waste.

They rounded the bend. Rachel wasn't far from her dorm. Another two minutes and she would be at the backdoor about to escape. Mark clutched the strap of the backpack around his arm. He quickened his pace, gaining speed as he rammed his shoulder into Rachel. He knocked the girl off the path and into a nearby tree.

"Watch where you're going, asshole," she snapped.

Mark quickly grabbed her arm to make it seem like he was helping Rachel. Hearing her voice bubbled his anger within, something he needed to push down. His grip was already tight on her elbow. He feared if he squeezed too much, he might break one of her bones.

"Sorry bout that," he tried to mumble. "Guess I didn't see you." Mark kept his eyes half shut trying to make it look like he was drunk as Rachel.

"Then, maybe you should open your eyes." She ripped her arm away from Mark and stumbled back up the path. "Fucking asshole," she said loudly.

That was the second time Rachel referred to him in a derogatory manner. The first time came back to him in a way which blazed his head. Mark's mind let the memories of her butting into his relationship. His ex told him stories of Rachel giving her relationship advice even though she had didn't have a man of her own. He flashed on her moments of being bossy and controlling; instances of her forcing his ex to change plans to accommodate her. There were conversations where he felt Rachel talked down to him, as if she were better than everyone around her. And he remembered she never took responsibility for anything she did wrong. Every bit of hate consumed Mark as he stared at Rachel walking away from him.

You're about to pay for it all.

He reached into his back pocket and pulled out a pair of black leather gloves, the same ones Jess almost found earlier. He slipped them on and stared down his victim. It was the moment of truth. There was one last chance to back out, but his hatred would only fester until he made a rash decision.

This is it; now or never.

He took off at a jog until he reached Rachel. In one quick motion, his right hand cupped over her nose and mouth while the other pinned Rachel's arms behind her back. She was too drunk to fight him off. Her arms flailed momentarily before Rachel's body went limp. Mark slowly lowered her gently to the ground and stared at her unconscious body.

Now to figure a way to get her inside.

He had hoped to have it done closer to the dorm, but his emotions got the better of him. Mark had no other choice; he had to move Rachel before they were seen. He picked her up into his arms and carried her up to the large gray building. She weighed ninety pounds soaking wet, but felt like he was lugging around a sack of bricks for a quarter mile.

Mark set her down behind the dorm. He took off the backpack and unzipped it. Three large bottles of alcohol stood next to each other. He pulled each one out with the intention of using them to end Rachel's life. His finger slid along her lips until he dipped it inside her mouth.

"Open up, sweetheart. The party is just getting started."

Mark pried Rachel's mouth open and poured the first bottle of liquor down her throat. Its contents reeked of rum as it slid down the sides of her cheeks.

Rachel gagged and coughed after the first bottle emptied. Mark could tell she wanted to throw up. She attempted to roll onto her side, but Rachel was too weak to move.

"Come on; have another drink."

Mark pinned his victim down with his knees as he unscrewed the top of a vodka bottle.

"Help," she tried to cry out, but Mark shoved the opening into her mouth and poured more liquor down Rachel's throat.

"Just keep drinking like a good girl and everything will be over soon." Mark stroked her hair gently as he watched the last of vodka drain. "There, that's a good little bitch."

Tears streamed down Rachel's face. "Why? Why are you doing this to me? Why can't I see anything?"

Mark held a finger to her lips. "Just one more; I promise." He opened the final bottle. The smell of tequila filled the air. "Drink up,"

He waited until the final drop was gone before putting the bottles back inside his bag.

"What did you do to me?" Rachel cried out. "Am I dying?"

"No, but you're about to."

Rachel's eyes flashed open. She was hit with the realization that the guy she ran into was slowly killing her. She wanted to stop him. She wanted to call out for help, but it was too late. The alcohol had taken over her brain rendering her useless.

Mark reached into her pants pocket and groped around until he found Rachel's ID. He grabbed her arms and hoisted Rachel onto his shoulder.

"Time to get you into your room."

Mark used the ID to unlock the backdoor and brought Rachel inside. The door closed silently behind them, signaling the end for his first victim.

Chapter 3-Ali

The sun broke through a small opening in my blackout curtains. It was as if the sun took over the role of my mother urging me to get out of bed. I could still hear her voice every time I tried to sleep in late.

Come on, Ali; it's time to get up. You have the whole day ahead of you. It wasn't even seven yet and I was awake.

"No, I don't want to get up," I whined to myself.

I was used to getting up that early, but not on a Saturday, and not when I was off for the first weekend in months. It instantly reverted me back to a child who refused to get up for school. I wrestled with the sheets trying desperately to find a spot on the bed where I was comfortable enough to fall back asleep and not have a ray of sunshine hitting me in the face.

I tossed and turned for another fifteen minutes while continuing to relive my younger days of growing up on a farm in Glen Falls, New York. My mother would guilt trip me and my sister, Amanda, into helping our dad work in the fields all day by reminding us they didn't have a son to do the yard work. To this day; I never understood how that was our fault, but our mother always made it seem like it was until we agreed to help.

I couldn't wait to get out of the house. I was the daughter they relied on the most. I worked on the farm, helped my mom cook, I cleaned the house when my parents weren't around, and I was charged with keeping my little sister in line. Once I graduated high school, I was free and clear to do what I wanted. It came as a shock to my folks when I decided to move down to Poughkeepsie for college. A few years later, Amanda made a similar move by getting accepted into New Paltz.

Our parents never understood why we felt the need to get away from them. Maybe it was because they held onto us too tightly. Yeah, that had a lot to do with it. Another factor was my desire to become a cop. I grew up watching tons of police dramas and reading detective novels. I had a dream of being one of those hot shot cops working high profile cases, solving elaborate crimes no one could figure out, and putting the worst kinds of criminals behind bars. That was never going to happen in Glen Falls. There was little to no crimes happening in that town. I think the worst I heard of was shoplifting or car accidents. There was nothing that screamed out newsworthy to me.

I spent several years on the force; patrolling the Kingston and Saugerties areas. My big break came when I was thrown on a bank robbery case in Newburgh. There were three of them to be exact. Local police were baffled by the thieves getting in and out of the buildings without any cameras catching sight of suspects' faces. I probably wouldn't have known where to find them if it wasn't for their own stupidity. One of the perps stole an expensive watch from a bank manager and had the brilliant idea of pawning it. Many criminals use pawn shops to sell stolen goods, mostly because there wasn't a way to track down the seller. The robber made one big mistake; he took the watch to a shop one of my friends owned.

I was given the tip, and I stupidly went without backup. The suspect took off when my squad car pulled up in front of his apartment.

"Freeze, police," I called out.

The suspect took out a gun and fired a shot at my head. The bullet ricocheted off the roof of the car just missing me. I had no choice but to return fire. I squeezed the trigger twice. The first missed but the second clipped him in the leg. I later found out the other bullet had hit an innocent bystander; critically wounding her. She had died later from complications.

Just the thought of that woman dying caused high anxiety. It was something I lived with every day of my life. I constantly replayed the moments in my head wondering what I could have done differently. Not calling for backup was my first big mistake. I also should have informed my boss about the lead and strategically planned how to take in the suspect. Maybe if I had been smarter, that woman would still be alive.

The shooting resulted in my probation, but I was still permitted to consult with the other officers on the case. The arrest and interrogation of the suspect led to the capture of the remaining bank robbers. They were tried before a jury and convicted on all counts. They were each serving three consecutive fifteen year sentences.

"Good job, Officer Ryan," other cops on the force told me.

It was great to hear them praise me for a job well done, but no one wanted me to be their partner. I was viewed as a liability; a wild card; someone they couldn't trust. Very few saw me for what I was; persistent or someone who would take necessary measures to solve the case. There was one person who believed in me, Lieutenant Esposito. He urged me to work hard and keep my nose clean. Once my probation was lifted, I applied to be a detective with the Ulster County Police Department. I got my wish six months ago, and now, I was his problem. I don't think the lieutenant realized what he got himself into when he promoted me.

Those memories continued to replay in my mind until I finally gave up on going back to sleep. I had a weekend to myself and all I could think about was work.

Well, I might as well start the day.

I decided to stick to my morning routine. I started every day with a morning run across the Walkway Over the Hudson. Depending on my mood, it was a three to six mile run over a bridge connecting Ulster and Dutchess County. It was a peaceful jog to watch the sun rise over the river. I didn't generally see anyone when I was running the route, but I was sure I wasn't the only one who took advantage of the serenity..

It took me close to an hour to get out of bed this morning. I finally decided to pull my legs over the side and let my bare feet touch the soft carpet. I reached for my gray and pink sneakers, but only found a pair of black pumps from the night before.

Damn, I left them in my locker.

Yesterday, I had gone into work right after my morning run and washed up there before my shift. I went in earlier than usual so I could get out sooner for my date. Now, I regretted that decision. My running gear was still in my work locker, which meant I would have to go to the station on my day off to retrieve them. I had spent so much time there as of late; I was beginning to think I lived at my desk.

I went to the dresser and pulled out a pair of black sweatpants and an orange tank top. Other than my missing running shoes, I was set to go out for my morning jog. Unfortunately, it wasn't the ideal outfit to walk into work wearing. I grabbed an oversized t-shirt to throw on over the tank top. I could already tell it was a bad decision as it trapped the heat the moment I went out to my car.

I drove from my house in Highland to the station on Route 299. The Shift change had already happened and the Saturday morning officers were heading out for the day. A muscular six-foot tall man with rugged good looks sat across from my desk. My partner, Officer Rodney Johnson, stuck out like a sore thumb. He was a former bouncer for a few bars and clubs in Poughkeepsie. That life was given up the moment he met the love of his life five years ago. That was when he made the decision to make a better life for them.

Rodney sat up straight in his chair once he caught sight of me. He didn't know about my date, and I wanted to keep it from him. Rodney was a great partner and even better friend, but he was also overprotective as if I was his little sister. He knew I was off today, so I expected an interrogation the moment I came by to say hello.

"Well, if it isn't my favorite partner, Detective Ali Ryan."

I moved closer and patted his arm. "Rodney, I'm your only partner. I mean, the only one who could put up with you." I looked at him with a serious look; my eyes narrowing at him before breaking character and laughing.

He gave a hearty laugh. "Okay, but that doesn't mean you're not my favorite." Rodney turned back to his stack of paperwork. "So, what brings you in? I thought you were off today."

"I forgot my running gear last night. Trust me; I don't wanna be here any longer than I have to."

Rodney's eyes lit up. He knew I cut out early yesterday, but I never let him know why. "Did you have another date with Mr. Hot Stuff?" He looked for me to confirm. I smiled and turned away. "I knew it," he said loudly. "You never cut out on your shift unless there's something big going on. So, tell me; how'd it go?" Rodney's eyes squinted as he searched for answers I didn't want to give up. "Out with it, detective; or else I'll take you to interrogation to make you talk. By then, the whole station will know your business."

"Okay; fine; I'll tell you." I brought a chair over and sat next to Rodney. "First off, his name is Matthew. He took me to a nice restaurant and a show in Manhattan." I couldn't help but smile as I remembered my wonderful night out.

"Oh, I know *that* look," Rodney said.

"What look?" I replied innocently while trying to wipe the smirk off my face. I folded my arms over my chest and stared my partner down.

"You like this guy; don't you?"

"Yeah, so what?"

Rodney had a twinkle in his eye. He patted my shoulder. "I guess it's time I sit him down and have a talk with Mr. Hot Stuff."

"Whoa, what talk?"

He leaned back in the chair cracking his knuckles. "You know; the one where I tell him if he breaks your heart, I'll break his legs."

"Stop; you'll scare him off."

At times, I wondered if Rodney's job was to bring law and order to the streets of Ulster County, or if he was the station's comedian.

"Okay, but if he hurts you-"

"Trust me; if Matthew breaks my heart, I'll break his face so no other woman can enjoy that man candy. You can have whatever's left of him." We both laughed at my comment. "Come on; I have to head down to the locker room and grab my bag before the lieutenant finds out I'm here."

"Yeah, he'll either put you to work or blow a gasket the moment he sees you here on a day off."

Rodney escorted me to the locker room where we briefly talked about the show I saw with Matthew. He promised to keep all comments to himself, which I didn't think was at all possible. I went to the women's side and retrieved my bag. I had just put on my running sneakers when I heard a door slam against the wall above us. It was the lieutenant's typical scare tactic to make everyone stop what they were doing and pay attention to him. He did it almost daily, but somehow it still made everyone flinch.

I hurried up the stairs and kept out of sight while I watched our five-foot-two lieutenant stand on a chair in front of his office. I could tell his fiery Columbian temper was flaring, and he was looking to take it out on any officer caught in his sights.

"What the hell is everyone still doing here?" the lieutenant snapped at the gathering crowd. Somehow his voice echoed around the station as if he spoke into a microphone. "I guess no one listens to their radios anymore."

The officers mumbled their apologies while bowing their heads to avoid his gaze. I had a clear view of the lieutenant, and he seemed like he was looking for someone specific to target.

"Johnson," the lieutenant called out.

"What's up, Lieu?" Rodney asked.

"I need you to get down the New Paltz campus immediately. There was a reported overdose in the dorms."

There was what?

I dropped my duffle bag causing a loud thud. Every head in the station turned towards me. The crowd had mixed expressions ranging from shock to annoyance to the dreadful look every cop has when they have to tell someone their parent or child died.

"Ryan, what are you doing here?" the lieutenant questioned.

"I came to get my running gear out of my locker." I took a few steps forwards still focusing on what he said to Rodney. "Who overdosed at New Paltz?"

"We don't have the victim's name." The lieutenant glared at me. His eyes lowered to the bag next to my feet. "I see you have your gear. You should head home, detective; it's your day off."

No, he wasn't going to dismiss me that easily. "Which dorm was it?"

His eyes told me not to keep pushing my luck with the topic, but I had to know what happened and who the student who died was.

"It's none of your concern. You're off this weekend. I suggest you go home and enjoy your time away from this place."

My heart was pounding violently in my chest. He was purposely withholding information from me. He knew my sister went to school there and that she lived on campus. I had to know the truth.

"Which one?" My voice was stern and demanding. I stood firmly with my hands on my hips caught in a staring contest with my boss. He showed no signs of budging. "Fine, I'll have to go down there by myself."

"You better not set one foot on that campus, detective, and that's an order." His eyes darted to Rodney. "Officer Johnson, go to Esopus Hall." I grabbed my bag to run for the door. "Ryan, where do you think you're going?"

His boisterous voice brought me to a halt. Rodney rushed to my side and pressed a hand to my shoulder.

"I'll make sure she's okay," he whispered before hurrying out the set of double doors. I was about to run after him, but I knew the lieutenant had me in his crosshairs.

I turned to face him. "I'm going to visit my sister," I snapped. "You can't stop me; I'm off the clock."

The lieutenant stepped down from the chair and pushed his way through the crowd of officers staring at us. "Fine," he sighed. "If you wanna go see your sister, then I'll bring you there. But you better not go near that crime scene. Is that understood?"

"Yes, sir," I replied. "I just want to make sure Amanda is safe. Once I know she's okay, I'll go back home. You have my word."

The lieutenant let out a chuckle. "Yeah, like that means anything."

Chapter 4-Ali

My heart continued to race while I sat in the passenger seat of the lieutenant's car. It was beating to the point where I was afraid I was on the verge of having a heart attack. The lieutenant appeared just as nervous. His hands tightly gripped the leather steering wheel while his foot pressed firmly on the gas. We sped through the normal Saturday morning traffic passing cars that sat bumper-to-bumper at a red light.

"I'm sure she's okay," the lieutenant said sympathetically.

"Thanks," I mumbled. It was the only word I could say without bursting into tears.

Everyone at the station knew Esposito as a hard ass; a man who was stressed and overworked. We also saw him show glimpses of his human side, too. This was one of those times. He knew there was no amount of threats or suspensions that would keep me away from campus, especially after learning the OD was found in the same dorm as my sister. He wasn't going with me to prevent me from finding the crime scene. He was escorting me fearing the same thing I did; the student was my sister.

I helped navigate the lieutenant through campus. There were half a dozen security vehicles, New Paltz branded police cars, and ambulances. I noticed two men dressed as medics standing in front of the glass doors smoking cigarettes. I shoved open the passenger side door and stormed up the path.

"Why aren't you inside with the victim?" I said while restraining myself from ripping their heads off.

One of the men took another drag of their cigarette and blew the smoke in my face. "Who the fuck do you think you are?"

"I'm a detective with the Ulster County Police Department," I snapped in return. I ripped the cigarette from his fingers and tossed it into the street. I was filled with so much emotion, a part of me considered putting it out on his face.

The medic looked me over and laughed. "Funny, you don't look like a cop." His foul-smelling breath invaded my personal space. The man was itching for me to knock him out.

The other medic stepped in and pushed his partner aside. "I'm sorry for this jerk, Ms-"

"Detective," I corrected him. "My name is Detective Ryan."

"By the time we arrived, the girl had been gone for a while. Her body was already cold before we had a chance to work on her."

"Is she still in her room?"

"Yeah, the M.E. hasn't arrived yet."

"Thanks," I replied.

I glared at his asshole partner before marching towards the front doors. Another officer stood guard; one I didn't know. His arms were folded in a tough guy stance with an expression begging me to try him. I reached for my back pocket in search of my badge. When I found nothing there, I remembered I was still wearing the clothes for my morning run. The officer was bigger than me, but I stared him down like I was a running back about to make a game winning dash into the end zone. My left foot was about to take the lead in charging the officer, but a firm hand closed on my shoulder jerking me away from the front doors.

Lieutenant Esposito braced himself by holding onto my arm. He was gasping and wheezing heavily as he pulled out an inhaler.

"I swear; you're going to be the death of me."

"I doubt it, but I have given you plenty of gray hair," I responded with tense humor.

He pursed his lips as he glared at me. "Keep it up, Ryan, and you'll be transferred to corrections and forced to do cavity searches for the next year."

Nope, that didn't sound like a good idea to me. I decided it was best to keep my mouth shut. I let him lean on me as we moved towards the officer blocking the door. The lieutenant flashed his badge.

"She's with me," he said. "Where did they find the girl?"

"The body was discovered in her room on the third floor," the officer replied. That news made my heard sink into the pit of my stomach.

I leaned against the door feeling nauseous. The lieutenant placed a hand on my shoulder. "Are you okay, detective?"

My eyes were glassy as a single tear broke free to run freely down my face. "That's Amanda's floor," I managed to croak out.

My legs felt like jelly. My hands shook with fear as the lieutenant ushered me into the building. For the first time since joining the force, I was afraid of what I might find at the crime scene.

The first-floor lounge had plush gray and purple couches lining the walls with wooden tables scattered around the common area. It was just as I remembered the day I helped Amanda move in. Chills ran through my body as we moved towards the elevator and stood in front of the cold steel doors.

What the hell is taking so long?

It took over two minutes before I heard any movement, but it felt like an hour had passed. The red number slowly ticked from three to one. The high-pitched ding let me know the elevator doors were about to open. A petite young girl with hair the color of the night sky exited. I stared at the girl as she moved towards me.

"Amanda," I gasped while throwing my arms around her. I hugged my sister tighter than I ever had before. "Thank God you're alive." She tried to squirm away, but I didn't want to let her go.

"What the hell is going on? There are police everywhere." She glanced over my shoulder at the lieutenant. She had to know there was no way for me to answer freely.

"I see you found your sister," he told me. "You have ten minutes to drop Amanda off at her room and meet me at the crime scene."

"You want me on the case?"

"You wanted it; now it's yours." The lieutenant boarded the elevator and disappeared behind its closing doors. In that moment, I realized why Rodney was sent there first. The lieutenant wanted to ensure the victim wasn't my sister before letting me take over the investigation.

I led Amanda to one of the nearby couches. "Look, I don't have much time. We received a report of a girl dying from an overdose or alcohol poisoning on the third floor of this dorm."

"And you thought it was me?"

"They mentioned the New Paltz campus, Esopus Hall, and the third floor. What was I supposed to think?

"W-who was it?"

"I don't know. We just got here and my intention was to find you first. I'm headed up there in a minute to check it out." I grabbed Amanda's hands. "You need to stay in your room and don't open the door for anyone unless it's a uniformed officer, Rodney, or me. Do you understand?"

"But you said it was-"

"I need you somewhere I know you're safe. Promise me you'll stay put." Amanda nodded her head profusely. I hugged her again before going back to the elevator.

I was relieved to know my sister was okay. I would feel even better once she was back in her room with an officer standing guard. The elevator brought us up to the third floor. There weren't any uniformed cops patrolling that area. I escorted Amanda down the corridor and watched her enter her dorm room.

"Stay put," I reminded her.

"Okay," she replied like a teenager being pestered by her mom.

As much as I wanted to make sure my sister stayed true to her word, I had needed to locate the room where the body was found and focus on the investigation. I hurried to the other side of the third floor. Yellow crime scene tape had been attached to the doorframe. A large black man stood inside of the room with a notepad in hand.

"Wait for me," I called out. My sneakers squeaked across the tiled hallway floor.

Rodney stared at me from the doorway shaking his head. "Ali, you're not supposed to be here. The lieutenant will have my ass for it."

He stopped me from entering the room. "What are you gonna do; arrest me?" I grabbed the crime scene tape, but my partner blocked me.

"I will if I have to." Rodney reached for his handcuffs and dangled them in the air. "Who knows; you might like it."

I could feel the heat rising in my cheeks as they burned with embarrassment. I stood on my tiptoes to get a better look at the room, but my partner was too damn tall to see over him. I ducked down and noticed a pale thin woman sprawled out on the bed.

"Any ID on the vic?" I asked.

Rodney put a reassuring hand on my shoulder. "Relax, Ali; it's not Amanda." His voice was gentle and supportive. His all business tone gone and replaced by a friend who had my back.

I patted his hand gently. "Rodney, I know. I found her downstairs a little while ago. She's back in her room waiting for you to question her." I glanced inside the room again. "Are you gonna tell me who the victim is or do I have to pretend to be a mind reader?"

Rodney steered me away from the room. He checked the hallway to make sure the coast was clear. "Look, I shouldn't be telling you this."

"But you're gonna because I'm your favorite partner."

"You're my only partner," he reminded me. He leaned to search the hall again. "According to the roommate, the girl is Rachel Walker. She's a junior who lived in Brooklyn before moving up here for college."

"Cause of death?" I could see Rodney struggling to comply with the lieutenant's original orders while being a good friend to me. I could have let him dance around the two a little longer, but I decided to let him off the hook. "It's okay; he sent me up here to look over the crime scene."

Rodney grabbed his radio to call it in. Within a minute, he had the confirmation needed to give me access to the crime scene.

"The victim died from what appears to be a combination of alcohol poisoning and choking on her own vomit. The medics said her airway was blocked with it and had been that way for hours."

"Do we have any confirmation on how much she drank?"

"A little thing like that," Rodney said. "It shouldn't have taken much to get her drunk. She's ninety pounds, if that."

I entered the room and surveyed the surroundings. It should have been an open and shut case. We had the cause of death; nothing seemed suspicious, but something in my gut told me to give it a closer look.

"Go ahead," he told me. "I know you want to review to put that Ali Ryan stamp of approval on it."

I gave Rodney a half smile before turning my attention to the victim. There was no time to waste. The crime scene had already been contaminated before anyone could make an official ruling, even if it was an accident. There was no telling what the roommate touched since Rachel entered the room.

The lifeless body of a young twenty-one-year old girl was sad to see. Thin was a poor way to describe Rachel Walker. Ninety pounds was really stretching. My estimate had her pegged at eighty to eighty-five pounds. Her bones were visible underneath her skin, which had questions flowing through my mind.

I nudged Rodney. "Let me borrow your notepad." My eyes searched the room as I noticed pillows scattered on the floor. "Did anyone move these?"

"The roommate claimed to have found them like this when she came in last night."

My partner's statement provided a bit of insight. Rachel Walker must have been the first to return to the dorm room. I needed to examine the body. I stepped over the pillows and stared at the young woman's face. Her coal black hair was still tied back in a ponytail. Rachel's chin was pointed at the ceiling indicating someone had performed CPR. I looked back and saw the roommate's bed hadn't been made. She must have woken up and noticed something wrong with Ms. Walker.

Did she try to resuscitate Rachel, or was it a medic or was it someone else? My eyes continued to search the room. I looked under the bed, the closet, and the garbage. "Did the medics or other officers report finding any liquor or beer bottles?"

"No one mentioned anything to me," Rodney replied.

"Then, how'd she get back here?" I turned towards my partner who had an annoyed expression on his face. "That wasn't a rhetorical question."

"Come on, Ali; it's a simple case. The girl died from drinking too much and choked on her own vomit. Let's call it what it is and move on."

I wasn't going to let it go. There were questions which needed to be answered. Her parents would want to know what happened to their daughter. I would want someone to tell me everything if I had a child who suddenly died.

"Think about it, Rodney. Rachel is way too thin, and she drank enough where we believe she had alcohol poisoning. She had to be somewhere close by to get back here on her own."

An officer overheard me and poked his head into the room. "I don't know if it helps, but they usually have a RA or a RM watching the front doors at night."

"Thank you," I replied. "Can you find out who it was and where to find them? I want to question whoever was on duty last night." The officer was about to leave, but I stopped him. "Do you know if anyone questioned the roommate yet?"

The officer pulled out his notepad and flipped it open to his notes. "I spoke to her. The roommate's name is Nicole Sherman. She claimed to have returned to the dorm around two this morning and found Ms. Walker in bed already. She woke up and noticed the victim unresponsive. She immediately called 9-1-1."

"Stupid college girls," Rodney muttered as he cupped a hand to his face. His head shook from side-to-side.

"Officer Johnson," I snapped.

"What? They are," he said defensively. "Those girls knew they were going out last night. How do you not check out your roommate when you get back to the room?"

"Maybe she was too drunk to notice," the other officer chimed in from the doorway.

He had a valid point. The roommate could have been too tired or too drunk to check on her friend. There had been many times when I was in college I came home on the verge of blacking out. College kids had an act first think later mentality, but it seemed that was something that bothered Rodney. His eyes glared at the officer as if to say *who asked you.*

"When I worked as a bouncer, I saw a lot of things. Girls would go to a club with a group of friends to get trashed. Some were a hot mess and were kicked out before they hurt themselves or passed out on the floor. I witnessed a lot leaving the bars and clubs hours later without their friends. They were hanging all over some random guy they'd apparently just met. It killed me I couldn't step in to stop those girls from making bad decisions."

I clapped my hands together excitedly. "Rodney, that's it." His story sparked a theory of how Rachel Walker made it back to her room. "I will bet anything she either met someone at a party or knew someone there who helped her get back here."

I climbed over the pillows and examined Rachel's body again. Her clothes were still intact. She wore a black v-neck blouse. It was a little wrinkled, but I didn't notice any rips or stains on it. My eyes searched the rest of the victim's body to her legs. She had tight blue jeans on, but I noticed something off immediately. There were dark green and brown spots on the knees. I suspected she fell at some point in the night, most likely on the way home.

There was a look of concern from Rodney. "What's the matter?"

"Something's not right." I asked the officer outside for a pair of gloves before returning to the victim. I rolled Rachel Walker onto her side and noticed the bed was still made. "If you came back after a night of drinking, what is the first thing you'd do?"

The officer stared off into space. "I guess I'd probably grab something to drink and climb into bed."

"But how would you do it?" I asked.

Rodney and the officer shook their heads trying to piece together what I was asking. 'I guess I'd kick off my shoes and pull the covers over my head."

"Exactly," I replied to the officer.

"I'm not following, Ali. Why does that matter?" Rodney asked.

"Drunk people who call it a night typically want to curl up in bed, but our victim was found lying on her back with her shoes on." I pointed to the black ballet flats on the bottom of Rachel's feet. Grass and mud were caked to the bottom of them. "The bed is still perfectly made. I don't know a single person, who was as drunk as we suspect our victim was, who could get into bed without making some sort of mess or creases in the blanket or sheets. Someone was with her last night, and that someone helped her into the bed."

"You don't know that for sure," Rodney replied. "We both know drunk people do weird shit all the time. She was probably too far gone to care about the shoes or the covers."

"Yeah, but-"

"But nothing, Ali," Rodney growled. He was set in his belief this was an accidental death due to bad decisions from both the victim and the roommate. "You're reading too much into this investigation. The girl drank too much and choked on her vomit; case closed!"

He could very well have been right. I was sure the official cause of death would reflect his thoughts, but I knew there was more to the story. We owed it to Rachel Walker to find out what really happened, even if it was an accidental death.

"Look, you're entitled to your opinion, but I'm still the lead on this case. I want to catalog the bedding and her clothes. We need a thorough search of the room and a full set of tests run on the victim."

Rodney already looked exhausted from my list of orders. "Weren't you supposed to be off today, or rather this weekend?

"You should know by now; I'm never off duty."

<u>Chapter 5-Ali</u>

Rachel Walker's shoes were placed into an evidence bag while Rodney surveyed the room again with the officer. I decided it was time to speak to the roommate to see what I could learn from her. I walked down the hall to the study lounge where another uniformed cop stood guard. Rodney called ahead of me to let them know I was going to interview the only person who could give us some insight into what happened. The officer opened the lounge door with a keycard and allowed me to enter.

The girl inside looked up at me with her tear-stained chubby face. Her long black hair was perfectly tied back. Even though she was wearing pink and white pajamas with matching fuzzy slippers, the roommate appeared well put together. In my mind, she was either a perfectionist or she was hiding something.

"Morning," I said s I closed the door behind me. I pulled one of the maroon chairs up to the table and extended my hand. "I'm sorry for your loss, Miss-"

"Sherman; Nicole Sherman," the girl replied as she reluctantly accepted my hand. She avoided my gaze as I tried to get a read on her.

I introduced myself as I took a seat. I had a few questions to ask the roommate with hope she could tell me anything which could bring closure to the investigation. We knew nothing about the victim other than her name and the probable cause of death. I needed to take a little time to find out what I could about our dead college student leading up to the moment her roommate discovered the body.

"What can you tell me about Rachel Walker?" I asked somberly.

"We met about two years ago during freshman orientation. By some miracle, our dorm assignments made us neighbors, but neither of us liked our roommates."

"Why not?" I questioned.

Based on my time in college and the stories my sister told me; switching rooms was a common thing in the dorms. Freshmen typically change more often than sophomores because it is their first time living on their own and forced to be with a stranger. As they develop friendships within the dorm, students ask for a change to be with someone they are more comfortable being around. I assumed Nicole's response would fall in line with my thoughts, but I wanted to hear her confirm it.

"Her original roommate was messy and mine was very loud. I couldn't sit in my own room to study or do homework. She blasted the T.V. or music every day. Rachel was a bit of a neat freak and had anxiety over her roommate leaving the place a mess all the time. It took us two and a half months to arrange the switch. We felt a world of relief once we moved in together and set up the room just the way we needed it." Talking about Rachel caused Nicole's eyes to well up again. I could tell she genuinely cared about her roommate.

"What was Rachel's major?"

Nicole wiped a tear from her eye. "She started out in the English department but transferred to psychology after our first semester. She loved learning about people and what made them tick. She was always trying to diagnose people."

"Was that something she did often?"

"Every day," Nicole laughed. "It was one of her favorite things to do outside of watching T.V. and movies. We spent plenty of afternoons sitting by the bond or on a bench near the Lecture Hall watching people walk by. I would try to read, but she kept observing everyone around us trying to guess what their deal was."

It was an interesting story. I could imagine other students feeling annoyed by some random girl staring at them and passing judgments to her friend. I know it would have pissed me off.

"Did Rachel have many friends?"

"She had a few, but not a lot of people understood her sense of humor." Nicole's eyes flickered to the door. I wondered if she expected someone to come walking in to pull her from the room, or if her mind was hoping it was all one big nightmare she would wake up from at any moment.

"Was she with any of those friends last night?"

She blew out a deep breath. "They all wanted to go to the Summer's Over Party on Oakwood." Something about that statement struck Nicole hard as new tears streamed down her face. She tried to wipe them away, but she couldn't fight them off. "I don't even think they know she's dead."

I flipped to an open page on the notepad and placed it in front of her along with a pen. "Please, write down their names and where we can find them. I'll see to it one of our officers breaks the news to them, so they don't hear it from the rumor mill."

I wasn't lying about wanting to help them avoid hearing it from other students speculating what happened. They deserved to know what happened to their friend. But I also wanted the names of the people Rachel Walker was last seen with so I could ask them some questions about last night.

Nicole took the pen and wrote five names on the paper along with their dorm names and room numbers. "I think that's all of them."

I watched as her tears dripped onto the table. I placed a hand gently on her shoulder as I wrestled the notepad from her tightly gripped fingers.

"I'll have one of the officers locate them immediately."

I opened the door and alerted the officer standing guard to take the list and track down the potential witnesses. He was being tasked with breaking the bad news to them before I had a chance to interview the girls. I glanced back at Rachel's roommate who was rocking back and forth in the chair.

She looked up at me with doe eyes. "Do you think I'm a bad person for not checking on her when I came back to the room last night?"

"No, things like this happen." I decided at that moment to turn the corner on my line of questioning. "How often did Rachel go out to party?"

"She never went out during the school week. Rachel held off until Thursday, Friday, and Saturday nights."

"So, she went all out those three nights?"

"Well…" I could see Nicole wrestling a thought in her head. She wanted to tell me something, but I was sure she was afraid it might get her in trouble. "Rachel would find ways to sneak a few beers into the room during the week."

"It sounds like Rachel drank pretty often. How much did she typically consume when she partied?"

"I-I never really counted. I know Rachel had at least one of two beers before going out, and then a few more once she got to the bar."

The roommate already established a pattern of behavior for Rachel consistent with binge drinking. Going to a house party could easily have caused her to lose count of how many drinks she'd had or make other stupid mistakes.

"Has Rachel ever brought a stranger back to the room after a night of partying?"

"No, never," Nicole replied.

"Has she ever needed help getting back to the room?"

"No. Why are you asking me these questions?"

"I believe someone helped Rachel get back to this dorm and put her in bed last night. I'm hoping they can tell us more about what happened leading up to their return to the room and how Rachel was behaving prior to them leaving."

Nicole sat with her mouth hanging open as tears streaked down her cheeks onto the pink and white pajamas. "Do you think this person could have prevented this from happening?"

"I don't know, but that's what I intend to find out."

<u>CK</u>

Mark hid in the bathroom on the third floor as police began to abandon the crime scene. Their hands were filled with larger brown paper bags and a smaller clear plastic one. He assumed they had taken items believed to be potential evidence. He was sure one of them had Rachel's shoes, which meant the plan wasn't as successful as he originally thought.

Mark had used the keycard to access the dorm early that morning to hear the piercing scream of Rachel's roommate as she discovered her friend lying in the bed cold and lifeless. He also wanted to hear what the cops thought hoping they'd closed the case as an accidental death. Seeing the evidence bags being carried out added a level of worry he wasn't expecting to face.

Only a few cops left with the potential evidence. Others were patrolling the third floor. A taller muscular black man was knocking on nearby doors. Mark heard him asking questions about their whereabouts from the night before. They were most likely trying to find anyone who remembered seeing Rachel Walker earlier in the night or right before she'd returned to her room. Little did they know the man they were looking for, the last person to see Rachel alive, was a mere twenty feet away standing behind the bathroom door.

Mark waited for the police to move onto the next hallway of rooms before making his escape. He couldn't run the risk of being caught hiding out in the bathroom. He didn't have a room in that dorm he could return to, and he had no excuse for being inside the Esopus building. He peered out the door to make sure the coast was clear.

"Hey, kid," an officer called out after catching Mark round the corner. "What are you doing out of your room?"

"Sorry; I didn't know it was against the law to take a leak." Mark tried to act like a bratty college student who felt the need to smart mouth a cop. Unfortunately, it drew more attention to him.

The cop stepped out from his lookout spot. His hand pulled his nightstick and pointed it at Mark's chest.

"I suggest you cut the attitude and get back to your room before you find yourself in real trouble, kid."

"Am I under arrest for something?" Mark waited for a reply. His attitude was about to get him in trouble for something other than the actual crime he committed. The officer didn't respond. Instead he glared at Mark, indicating he wasn't going to do anything. "That's what I thought." He took a step back. "Then, I guess I'm free to come and go as I please."

"Not until you've answered a few questions." The officer put his nightstick away. "Now, go back to your room before I personally escort you there." His fingertips touched the handcuffs attached to his belt.

"Whoa, questions about what?" Mark asked with his hands raised defensively. "I didn't do anything wrong."

The officer glanced back at the hall behind him and then down the hall where Rachel's room was located. There was sadness in the cop's eyes.

"I can't go into detail, but there was incident in this dorm resulting in a student's death."

Before the officer could ask the question that was on the tip of his tongue, Mark decided to bombard him with some of his own.

"Who died?" He bounced on the balls of his feet to see the yellow crime scene tape. "Was it one of the girls down the hall? How did they die?"

The officer ignored the questions. His mind was already focused on getting his own answers. "Do you know a Rachel Walker or Nicole Sherman?"

"The names don't ring a bell," Mark lied. "Why? Was it one of them?"

"Miss Walker passed away this morning in her sleep. We need to know if anyone saw her come home last night."

Mark pretended to be devastated by the news. "That poor girl," he said before shielding his face with his arm. His fake cough hid his malicious smile. "How did she die?"

"That's still under investigation." The officer took another step towards Mark. "Did you happen to see anyone going into or coming out of that room?" He pointed to Rachel's door that was marked with the crime tape.

"No, sir," Mark replied. He did his best to play the part of a concerned student, but he was running out of time. The cop was bound to ask for his name or what was his room number.

"Thank you for your time," a man said from around the corner.

The officer talking to Mark turned his head. It was the momentary distraction needed to make a quick escape. Mark re-entered the bathroom and exited the other door. He could hear someone shouting in the area he just used as a detour. He ran down the hall until he reached the study lounge. There were two women inside. The first was Rachel's roommate. The other was a tall, beautiful lady dressed in sweatpants and a t-shirt. Her long curly hair bounced off her shoulders while jotting down everything Nicole Sherman said.

Mark let out a smile. *You must be the detective investigating Rachel's death. It'll be my pleasure getting to know you.* Then he glanced at

Nicole and saw the tears running down her face. *I'll be seeing you soon, Nikki; sooner than you think.*

Mark raced to the other end of the third floor and down the stairs. He was careful to avoid running into any more cops as he fled from the building and into the beautiful sunny day. The sense of urgency diminished. He was sure no one else spotted him, and now he was free to casually walk around campus. It was the first time he felt calm and relaxed since moving to New Paltz.

He glanced back at the Esopus building and nodded. *Thanks for a night I will never forget.*

Chapter 6-Ali

I exited the lounge and walked back towards Rachel Walker's room where a uniformed cop was searching aimlessly down each row of rooms.

"Are you okay?" I asked. He glared at me in confusion. "Did you lose something?"

"More like someone," he growled. "I caught a boy walking around the halls. I tried to question him, but he was too busy being a wise ass."

I pictured the cop being one of those old men who shake their fist at kids calling them a whipper snapper.

"He's in college; what do you expect?"

"These punks think they can say and do whatever they want like lurking around a taped off crime scene."

My eyes shifted to the room down the hall. "Did you get his name or a description of the guy?" I was already feeling unsettled about this case. Hearing there was a student walking around close to the crime scene made me even more uneasy.

"No, I got distracted for a moment and he took off."

I felt my cheeks getting red hot again. This time, they were enflamed from trying to hide my anger. Rodney and I kept most of the officers at the dorm to maintain order. We'd wanted all the students in Esopus to remain in their rooms so we could interview everyone.

"Find him, now," I snapped at the officer.

Rodney exited a nearby room and poked his head around the corner to stare at me. "What the hell is going on out here?"

"There was a male student snooping around out here, and this genius didn't think to get the kid's name, description, room number, or why he was roaming the halls." I was furious and needed to compose myself before I ripped the officer a new asshole. I pinched the sides of my nose just under my eyebrows while taking a couple of deep breaths. "Please tell me you got something out of these kids."

Rodney shook his head. "No one saw her leave or come back to the dorm last night. Were you able to get anything out of the roommate?"

"Nothing useful," I replied. "Apparently, our victim wasn't well liked and enjoyed getting drunk at bars or parties. She also snuck alcohol into her room quite often." It almost seemed hopeless. If there wasn't anything substantial to indicate Rachel Walker's death was more than an accident, the case was going to close before we knew what really happened. There was at least one more person we needed to interview at Esopus before moving onto the friends. "Have you spoken to the RM who was on duty last night?"

"No, but I was told she was in her room waiting for us. She's a senior by the name of Bette Willis."

Rodney led the way to the RM's room. He knocked on the door and waited for the woman to respond. It opened a moment later showing a shorter curvy woman with hair pulled back and thick framed glasses.

She looked at me and then Rodney. "Hi, can I help you?"

I reached for where my badge should have been, but I groped the top of my sweatpants instead. "I'm Detective Ryan, and this is my partner Officer Johnson. May we have a word with you?"

Bette stepped aside and let us in. Unlike other dorm rooms, this one only had one bed whereas the rest typically had two or three. It had a smaller studio apartment feel to it. The only things missing were a stove and bathroom.

"The other officer told me you would be stopping by to ask some questions." Bette grabbed two chairs from her desk area and pulled them into the center of the room.

Rodney had his notepad out ready to jot down everything the RM had to say. "As we understand, you were in the lobby last night monitoring the front door." He paused to watch Bette nod in confirmation. "What time did you begin your watch?"

She took a seat on the bed across from us. "I came down around ten last night and stayed there until about three in the morning."

"During that time, did you see Rachel Walker return to the dorm?"

The redness in Bette's cheeks grew brighter. "No, there were only a few students who came through those doors between eleven and one."

I could sense there was something off about the RM. She was getting emotional quickly as if she felt a measure of blame for what happened.

"How many students came in between one and three?" I asked.

Bette buried her face in her hands as she began to sob. "I-I don't remember." I could feel my partner was about to make a comment, but I held up a hand to stop him. "I was doing my homework at the desk. When I finished, I read for a little while. I must have fallen asleep. When I woke up, it was a little after three. I ran up here and went back to bed."

Rodney wasn't able to hold his comments any longer. "That's wonderful; a girl died from drinking and you were in the lobby napping on the job."

"Officer Johnson," I snapped. His head turned towards me with anger in his eyes. "Outside, now," I ordered. I walked to the door and held it open for him.

"Ali, I'm sorry but-"

"But nothing," I interrupted. "You need to go somewhere and cool off." I didn't know what got into my partner, but he had been making several comments that made me think this hit him on some sort of personal level. "I'll finish the interview and will find you when I'm done." I closed the door as I re-entered the room. "I'm really sorry about my partner."

"It's okay," Bette whimpered. "He's right; I screwed up last night. I should've been awake. It was my job to keep watch for any students coming back to the dorm. I probably would have seen Rachel and got her help before she came up here."

The poor girl was blaming herself for something that was beyond her control. Yes, she fell asleep at her post, but that didn't mean Rachel didn't find a way into the dorm another way. From my observation, there were several entrances.

I gripped Bette's hand. "Was there anyone else in charge of watching the other doors?"

"No," she replied. "Everything is locked after midnight. The only way in would be through the front doors."

"So, if she came in later than midnight, she would have gone through the lobby." My statement caused Bette to tear up again. She was about to break in front of me. "Are there any cameras or a log of when the last time her card was used to access the building?"

I already knew Nicole Sherman returned to the dorm around two. She told officers Rachel was already in bed. With the doors locking at midnight and the RM falling asleep at one, that left a one-hour time frame where Rachel Walker got into the building and up to her room.

Bette shook her head. "The only camera is in the vestibule between the inner and outer doors, but nothing is recorded."

There were two other scenarios running through my head but I would need to speak to Rachel's friends to see what time they left the party and if Rachel went home with anyone else.

"You said the doors lock after midnight," I said. "Would that prevent anyone from exiting them too?"

"No," Bette replied.

"So, then is it possible Rachel came in through one of the rear entrances if someone was leaving at that same time?"

Bette sat up a little straighter. "Yes, it's possible."

That confirmation was all I needed to keep the investigation open a little longer. Rachel Walker didn't return to the dorm alone, and she most likely had help bypassing the lobby by having someone open the backdoor for her.

"Thank you, Bette. If you can think of anything else that might help us, please contact the station and ask for me. Otherwise, I'll be in touch if we have any more questions."

"I'm really sorry," she said. I knew it was her guilt over falling asleep pleading for forgiveness.

"This isn't your fault," I told her.

I patted her arm gently and handed Bette a tissue. Once I exited the room, I felt a weight lifted from my shoulders. I just had enough information to keep the case open.

I roamed the halls thinking over everything I learned so far. My wandering led me back to Amanda's room where the lieutenant sat outside in a plush maroon chair.

"Lieu, you're still here?"

"I made it my personal assignment to make sure you both followed orders. After all, the Ryan sisters are known to ignore everything people tell them."

I let out a light-hearted chuckle. He was right. I did my own thing, which is why the lieutenant made sure to bring me to the dorm instead of letting me go off on my own. Amanda had been known to follow in my footsteps quite often.

"Has anyone gone in to speak to my sister?"

"Your partner came by a few minutes ago." The lieutenant knocked on the door lightly. It swung open moments later. Rodney filled the frame as he exited the room. "So, did either of you find out anything useful?"

I took the lead in relaying the information back to the lieutenant. "The victim's name is Rachel Walker. She attended a party on South Oakwood last night. Her roommate, Nicole Sherman, claims to have returned to the room about two in the morning and saw Rachel in her bed already. The roommate provided a list of friends who are believed to have been the last people to see our victim alive. I put Officer Adams in charge of informing the friends of Miss Walker's death and to gather them to be interviewed."

The lieutenant clapped a hand against his chest. "You mean you actually delegated work to someone other than Rodney?"

"Why should we have all the fun?" I smiled tensely.

Rodney cleared his throat. "I have been interviewing most of the students on the third floor. According to the residents that knew the victim, Rachel was a constant party girl who usually hung out with the same handful of people."

"Her roommate corroborated those reports. Rachel had a habit of sneaking alcohol into the dorm and had three designated party nights; Thursday, Friday, and Saturday."

"Anything else?" the lieutenant asked. "What about the RM?"

"She was monitoring the main lobby until three this morning but fell asleep around one. She advised Rachel did not come through the lobby before she fell asleep. There are also no surveillance cameras covering the remaining entrances."

"So, we have no idea when our victim came back to the dorm or how she got up to her room?"

I saw Rodney shaking his head at me. He knew about my original theory of someone bringing Rachel back to the dorm. I knew he wanted this to be an open and shut case, but I couldn't let that happen.

"I believe the victim was brought up to her room by an unknown person between one and two this morning."

The lieutenant squinted as if experiencing the beginning of a migraine, which was something I was notorious for causing according to him.

"What are you basing this off of, Ryan?"

I presented the facts and speculation I uncovered so far. I noted Rachel lying in a perfectly made bed with her clothes still on including her shoes. I reiterated this was not a typical behavior of a drunken person climbing into bed. I made sure to speak on the position of the body lying flat on her back.

"So, you think someone was in there with her?" he asked.

"Yes, sir," I replied.

I could see the lieutenant mulling over my words and formulating more questions in his mind. "Did our victim have any known enemies?"

"Her roommate told me Miss Walker was a psych major who frequently pointed out other students' flaws. I'm sure there were several people who had their feathers ruffled over it."

The lieutenant began pacing up and down the hall bopping his head from side-to-side. "What is your case ruling, detective?" He wanted me to put my stamp on it; was it an accident or homicide."

"It's still pending, sir."

He stopped short and stared me down. The vein above his left eyebrow began pulsating after hearing my decision.

"Why?"

"There are a few key items we need to figure out before we close the case. How did she get back to her room? Did someone help her, and if so who? Did she come in through the front entrance or did someone open up a rear door to get her inside?"

The lieutenant nodded his head, but I knew he wasn't in agreement. I could already read his mind. He was ready to put an end to the investigation unless there was evidence presented to him to suggest it was a homicide.

"And what's your take, Officer Johnson?"

"I think we should find out what the friends know first and wait for the test results before making a decision."

Rodney went with the option to appease both the lieutenant and me. He wasn't saying I was wrong, but he wanted to hold off until we had more evidence and witness statements.

The lieutenant's lips curled into a smile as he patted Rodney on the back. "There's hope for you yet." He ushered him away from my sister's room. "Oh and, detective," he called out before tossing Rodney's car keys at me. "Make sure you gas up the car before bringing it back to the station."

I felt the growing need to speak to Rachel Walker's friends. Her roommate had provided the names of each one and where they lived. I wasn't familiar with the campus and didn't know where each dorm was located. I knocked on Amanda's door and saw she had changed into her jeans and a tank top.

"Hey, I need your help. What do you know about Rachel Walker?"

"Rodney already asked me a bunch of questions."

"I don't care; I need you to talk to me about her."

"Not much," Amanda replied. "We didn't really run in the same crowds and we didn't have any friends in common."

"Can you elaborate on the type of people she hung out with?"

"She had a small group of friends that always hung out together. All of them were party girls. You know; the ones that went to every party and hit up the bars all the time."

I knew my sister had been to her fair share of parties. She tried to act innocent, but I knew her better than that. "Did you ever run into Rachel at a house party?"

"A couple of times, I guess. I don't really notice other girls when I'm out having fun." She must have caught me with a grin on my face. "What?" she asked.

"So, does this mean you notice the boys?" I let out a laugh. "Does Sean know you've been checking them out?"

Amanda blushed and tried to hide it. "I wasn't checking them out. I was just…they were there…and I…"

I decided to wave off the question I asked and launched back to my original thoughts. "Did you ever see Rachel hanging around those guys? Was she flirtatious or did she play hard to get?"

"I don't know, Ali," she snapped. "What's with the fifty million questions? I thought she died from drinking."

"She did, but there is something off about the crime scene. The way she was found made it look like someone placed her on the bed instead of someone stumbling back to their room."

"Why would that matter?" Amanda asked.

I considered my theory and knew I was reaching for a reason other than a night of binge drinking gone wrong. "I just wanna be sure."

"Sure of what?" Amanda lowered her voice. "Do you think someone murdered her?" She laughed after saying it. "Come on, Ali; people drink too much all the time, especially in college."

"Maybe you're right, but I still need to talk to Rachel's friends before finishing up here. Can you tell me how to get to Capen Hall?"

"I'll walk you over there." We exited from the back of the building and walked down the path by the pond. "So, I have some questions for you, detective." Amanda had a smile plastered across her face. "What happened on your date last night?"

My cheeks suddenly felt like they were on fire. My mind returned to the night before. I pictured Matthew holding my hand while we walked through Manhattan.

"It was nice," I replied while trying to downplay how special the night was to me. I had to suppress the glow on my face. "We went to dinner and saw a show in the city."

Amanda slammed her fist against the palm of her other hand. "That's not good enough, detective. I want the facts." We both laughed at her impression of the lieutenant.

I stopped at the top of the hill. "Okay fact; Matthew took us out for a sushi dinner. Fact; we had a few drinks while we there. Fact; we had a great night, and I plan on seeing him again. Fact; my sister is too damn nosey."

"Consider it my inquisitive nature," Amanda joked. "I guess being around a cop all the time had your curious nature rub off on me."

"Fine, but next time you want to butt into my life, I want to see your warrant, or maybe I should have my attorney present."

My sister continued to pester me about my love life and a few other items causing us to laugh until we arrived at Capen Hall. It took us about ten minutes in total to arrive. I noticed a group of students already huddled together outside the old brick building. It seemed the campus was already buzzing over the presence of police and rescue vehicles showing up to Esopus.

"Wait here," I told my sister. The last thing I needed was for her to go wandering off or eavesdropping on my investigation.

I entered through one set of doors and pressed the buzzer for someone to let me in. A stocky male student opened the door and stuck his head out to greet me.

"Can I help you?"

"I'm Detective Ali Ryan with the Ulster County Police Department. I'm here to question a couple of the residents from this dorm."

"It's okay," another man called out. "She's with me." Officer Adams appeared next to the student and held the door open for me. "I managed to pull the girls into a closed off lounge area."

"Did you already break the news to them?" I asked.

"Yeah, they're not taking it very well." He escorted me up to the second floor where the girls were still huddled together on older armchairs. Officer Adams entered first and introduced me to the three young girls as they wiped the tears from their eyes.

"I know this is a very difficult time after hearing about Rachel, but I need to ask you some questions about her and about last night." I took their silent nods as their agreement to help. "How long have you known Rachel?"

Marci, a short, dark-haired girl with pale blue eyes looked at the others before turning back to me. "We met her at a party freshman year. She was there with her roommate who apparently was pissing her off. Rachel decided to ditch her and went off to get drunk."

I interrupted the story with a quick question. "Was this her first roommate or her current one, Nicole Sherman?"

Jodi stood up to pass out more tissue to the group. She was taller than the other girls. "This was a few weeks into the fall semester. I don't think she was hanging out with Nicole yet."

"Okay, then what happened?" I asked.

"She sat down at a table where I was playing king's cup," Jodi continued. I tilted my head to the side unsure of what she was referring to. "It's a drinking game where every card you draw has its own rule."

Lucy was the smallest of the girls. She was thin like Rachel with light brown hair pulled into a braid down her back. Her smile and far off look to her eyes made me think she was picturing the night as if she were reliving the night.

"Wasn't that the night Rachel did her first keg stand?" Lucy asked.

Jodi let out a chuckle. "Yeah, those smartass guys we were hanging out with thought it was funny to make every face card a minute doing a keg stand."

Marci smiled. "Yeah, and Rachel drew two of them. Man, she drank most of the guys under the table that night."

"So, Rachel had a history of binge drinking?" The girls looked at me as if I intruded on their reminiscing. It was almost as if they had forgotten I was there investigating their friend's death.

Jodi turned back towards me. "She wasn't like other girls. Rachel was small, but she could hold her own in a drinking contest one night and ready to take on the world the next morning."

"Has she ever been sick from drinking?"

The girls looked at each other and shook their heads. "No, not that we know of," Marci replied. "Rachel always seemed to know her limit."

Maybe she was off her game last night, or maybe someone convinced her to drink beyond her limit. My thoughts were pulling me towards something happening to Rachel rather than an accident.

"According to her roommate, Nicole, Rachel was out at the Summer's Over Party with you three last night."

"Just two of us," Marci replied. "Jodi was working at the video store until about two in the morning."

"And did you all leave together?"

"Yeah, we never leave anyone behind."

That was interesting. If they were together, then how did Rachel end up alone in her room? I took a few more notes as I dove into my next question.

"Do you remember what time you got back to campus?"

"Sometime after one," Lucy said.

"And did Rachel go back to her dorm on her own?"

"Yeah," Marci replied. "We walked back here and asked her to stay with us for the night. She refused and asked to meet up this morning for brunch, but she never showed."

"Do you know if she met up with anyone else on the way back to Esopus?" I asked. The girls shrugged their shoulders. It added a new disturbing element to the investigation. Rachel was able to get back to the dorm without help. She was coherent enough to make plans with her friends for the next day. Nothing seemed to add up. "Can you remember anything else about last night?"

Marci shook her head. "Most of it's a blur."

I wrote down my number for all three girls. "If you remember anything else, please call me right away." I walked out of the dorm and called the lieutenant to update him. "I just finished questioning the victim's friends. They don't remember much, but said Rachel walked with them back to their dorm before going to her own."

"So, there's nothing contradicting our initial report?"

"No, sir, but I-"

"But nothing, Ryan," he growled. The lieutenant increased the bass in his voice to let me know he meant business. "This case is closed."

"Wait, we're still waiting on the toxicology report."

There was a long pause. For a moment, I thought he was about to demote me down to a crossing guard for speaking against his decision.

He let out a deep breath. "You have until the report comes in to convince me; otherwise the case is closed."

Chapter 7-CK

New Paltz campus remained in a state of mourning. Rumors spread like wild-fire with students speculating on Rachel's death. There was even gossip it was more than just an accident. Many used the incident to get out of tests and homework saying they were close with Rachel and had great difficulty handling the loss. There was one person who seemed to be hit by the news the hardest, her roommate.

Mark knew Nicole Sherman was a perfectionist. He remembered her studying all day and night almost bringing her to the brink of insanity. She was early to class every day and made sure her homework was done the day it was assigned. But Rachel's death seemed to have changed her.

Mark snuck in and out of Esopus to stalk Nicole, but she never left her room except to make a trip to the cafeteria when everyone was in class. It was hard for him to keep tabs on her. He needed to resort to drastic measures. A simple webcam feed allowed Mark to spy on her. Nicole ignored calls and text messages. She remained in seclusion with her back to Rachel's side of the room. It had been stripped to just a bed, a dresser, and a desk remained. All of their contents split between police evidence bags and what Rachel's parents took back with them. It was as if she never existed.

Nicole glanced up to the pictures of her and Rachel on the wall from their various campus events and parties. There was a brief smile where she remembered all the fun times they had together. The girls were like sisters, virtually inseparable.

"Miss ya, sista," she said. The halfhearted smile faded as tears overwhelmed her. Nicole picked up the phone and called someone. "Hi, Brian; it's Nicole. I know we haven't talked since Friday, but I wanted to see if you wanted to get dinner tonight. I guess you're probably in class. Give me a call back when you can."

Mark remembered Brian. It was a guy Nicole was obsessed with since freshman year. He never seemed to give her the time of day. It wasn't until a few days before the party that he had spoken to her. Some flattering words sent Nicole into a tailspin of emotion as they set a date. It happened to be on the same night Rachel Walker died. There was no coincidence. Mark ensured Nicole was tied up with something she would never be able to turn down, a date with the man of her dreams.

Mark kept his eyes on the computer monitor anticipating his next move. Rachel Walker was only one piece of his plan. Time was running out on the next part. He needed to go after his second victim before his access to Esopus was gone.

Mark pulled open the creaking drawer. He dug his hand inside to pull out a small envelope. Inside was the list he made earlier in the year. A red line had crossed out Rachel Walker's name.

One down and three to go; he thought while holding his victim's student ID in his hands.

Mark stared at the list with an elated feeling. It had almost been a week since his first kill, and the police presence had disappeared from campus. He was sure they ruled Rachel's death as an accident, which meant he was in the clear.

There was a soft knock on his door causing panic to set in. He considered where to hide the list and the ID to ensure no one located it, but a couple of quick breaths calmed him momentarily.

"Who is it?" he called out.

"It's Jess," a woman's voice replied.

Mark placed the list back in the drawer and closed it up. The ID was shoved into his pocket. He hurried to the door and opened it to find his neighbor standing in front of him wearing another pair of jean shorts and a black tank top.

"Hey, what's up?" he casually asked.

"Not much; I was about to head out when I heard a noise coming from your room. Aren't you usually in class right now?"

Damn, drawer makes too much noise. He glanced back at the desk wishing there was a way for him to get rid of it. "Yeah, I forgot my text book and came back to get it." He grabbed it from the behind the door and showed it to Jess. "I figured it would be a pain to find parking again, so I decided to hang here until my next class.

"Oh, okay," she said with an unsure look. "I'm about to head over to campus to grab lunch before class. Do you want go with me?"

Mark had the intention of watching the monitor all day to spy on Nicole, but the offer to go out with Jess was too tempting. It was something he had wanted to do for months ever since she spent the night hanging out in his room watching movies with him.

"Yeah, that sounds great," he replied.

"Cool; just give me a minute to change my shirt." Jess darted back to her room and disappeared behind her open door.

Mark locked up his apartment and sat next to the landlord's version of a greenhouse. There was a smile on his face as he waited for his neighbor to re-emerge from her room. It was the first time he pictured a future without thoughts of getting revenge on the people from his list.

It didn't take long for Jess to re-appear. She had ditched the black tank top and replaced it with a white short-sleeve shirt.

"I'm all set," she said while slinging her backpack over her shoulder.

Mark walked next to his neighbor through the hallway and down the stairs. His hands grazed against hers twice. He considered making a small move to see if they were more than friends. Mark swiftly laced his fingers around Jess's. He was finally holding her hand. His eyes searched for a reaction. Jess seemed surprised, but she didn't withdraw from his grasp. Instead, they continued down the steps and out the front door.

Mark knew Jess typically walked to campus. They didn't live that far, maybe about a mile and a half from their destination. The hot summer day had already reached a humid ninety-two degrees. The thought of going on foot was not an option for Mark.

"Do you want to drive over?" he asked.

Jess nodded and followed him. "Hey, did you get a new car?"

Mark had hoped she wouldn't have noticed. He was usually flying under everyone's radar and ignored by most of the people in the house, but Jess seemed to pick up on everything new about him.

"Yeah, I just got it. My old one was always breaking down."

They jumped into the car and drove down the block to the stop light. Jess sniffed the air with curiosity. "Why does it smell like liquor in here?"

Mark had forgotten to clean up after his attack on Rachel Walker. He had been in such a rush to get far from Esopus, he thrown the backpack with the empties in the backseat. A few drops had leaked out and were now soaked into the cloth seat coverings in the backseat.

"Oh, I picked up a friend the other night and he spilled a drink back there. I keep forgetting to get it cleaned."

Jess seemed to accept the answer and played with the radio for the five minutes it took for them to arrive at the commuter's parking lot near the Lecture Hall. They exited the car and walked another seven minutes until they arrived at the Student Union building. They split up and searched for their choice in food before swiping their IDs to pay from their meal plan.

"Over here," Jess called out while signaling to Mark.

He hated she was drawing attention to him. The new look was to help him stay off everyone's radar. Even though no one looked at him, Mark was paranoid someone would associate his new image with his real name. His eyes flickered from each person until safely reaching the table Jess called him to.

"This place is mobbed today," he said.

"Yeah, we're lucky there weren't longer lines to get our food."

Mark looked down at his plain cheeseburger and wished he had taken the time to put more on his plate. Then, he looked at Jess's tray. It was a large salad with a vinaigrette dressing over mostly fruit and vegetables. Their eating habits were completely different.

"So, how are your classes so far?" Mark asked. It was an attempt to make idle conversation.

"They're okay," Jess replied. "The professors have been trying to teach, but a lot of people are playing up their grieving over the loss of that girl."

"You mean the one who drank herself to death?" he asked pretending not to have known Rachel Walker. "Didn't her roommate find her?"

"Yeah, that poor girl; I can't imagine what she's going through right now." Jess's display of sympathy for a woman Mark hated sent a spark of anger to his eyes.

"Can we talk about something a little less depressing," Mark interrupted. He realized his comment sounded insensitive, but he didn't want to hear people caring for Nicole Sherman. "I'm sorry; I just hate the idea of something like that happening on campus here."

"I understand," Jess replied.

The topic of conversation switched to the latest shows on T.V. and their plans for the weekend. It was another sore subject for Mark, especially since he didn't know when he would pursue his next target. He decided to lie and create a cover story in case he decided to pull the trigger on the next part of his plan. He told Jess about possibly going home for the weekend, but he had not made a final decision yet.

The light in Jess's face darkened. "Oh, I guess that should be fun." She seemed disappointed at hearing his plans. She quickly checked her cell phone. "Oh, I have to run to class." She got up and hurried off before Mark could say anything.

He let out a deep sigh knowing he had somehow messed up his lunch date with Jess. Hearing he was going out of town ripped the smile from her face and made Jess run out on him. There was nothing left to do but go back to his apartment to finish spying on Nicole.

Mark walked back towards the commuter lot and headed towards the Lecture Hall. He was about to go down the steps to the parking area when he saw someone who caught his eye. Nicole had ventured out of her room and appeared to be going to class.

I guess it's time to move forward with part two.

Mark watched her disappear into the building before running down to his car. He popped open the trunk to retrieve his backpack before hurrying up to a stone bench opposite the Lecture Hall entrance. A gentle breeze washed over him as he pulled out a book on abnormal psychology. Pretending to study out in the open was the perfect cover. Everyone seemed to scurry off to their classes leaving only a few students lingering around the area.

Mark used the time to plot his course of action. He unzipped the front pocket of his bag to retrieve a folded piece of paper. It was a schedule of classes for one Nicole Sherman. His finger traced along the Tuesday/Thursday courses to see his target was in her Women in Literature class for the next hour. He could easily take the time to break into the dorm room and prepare for the next piece of his plan, but there was no way of knowing if Nicole decided to leave class early. She could have been meeting with her professor to find out what she missed and planned to go back to her room after getting the information. He needed to sit back and wait to see what she did for the rest of the day.

As Mark sat on the stone bench, the doors to the Lecture Hall opened. It wasn't his target, but rather a forty-year old woman with short black hair that curved under her chin. The thick framed glasses rested on the edge of her nose. Mark recognized her instantly as his former psych professor from the most recent spring semester. He didn't want to chance her recognizing him. Mark held the book higher and hid behind it. He listened for her footsteps as they carried her further away. Mark slowly raised his head enough to peek over the top of his book. He was free and clear.

That was a close one.

Mark continued watching the Lecture Hall doors waiting to see Nicole re-emerge. When it hit the top of the hour, a group of students spewed from the entrance. Their smiling faces indicated they were a step closer to being done for the week, which meant their nights of partying were about to begin.

Where is she?

Mark searched the crowd hoping to lock onto his target, but she was nowhere to be seen. He had already spent more time than he wanted sitting around doing nothing. His impatience was reaching a boiling point. He wondered if Nicole took one of the basement exits which led to the parking lot. It was another path one could take back to the Esopus dorm.

I'm such an idiot. She could already be back in her room.

Mark shoved his text-book back into his bag and slung it over his shoulder. Just as he stood up, the Lecture Hall door opened again. The familiar sight of a chubby, dark-haired girl emerged clutching her books to her chest. Nicole's ravioli eyes pointed at the ground as she set off in the direction of her dorm.

Mark kept a ten-foot distance as he followed her. The flowery smell of her perfume was causing his anger to rise. It made him want to kill her the moment no one else was around. His eyes studied her movements while his brain thought of ways to end her life and dispose of the body. He was sure she was going back into hiding, but a sudden change in direction meant an abrupt end to Mark's plan of attack. She wasn't headed back to Esopus. Nicole Sherman was walking towards the Student Union, most likely to eat before continuing her day.

Mark's anger got the better of him. He closed in on his target, which drew her attention. Nicole came to an abrupt stop sending Mark crashing into her.

"Watch where you're going," Nicole snapped as her books toppled to the pavement.

Mark reached for her arm to help Nicole to her feet. "I'm so sorry; let me help you." He steadied his victim while picking up the fallen textbooks.

Nicole's eyes were fixated on Mark's face. "Were you following me?" Her tone was more accusatory rather than questioning.

Mark worried his mistake would result in her guard being raised. He tried not to seem like a danger. "No," he replied defensively. "Why would I be following you?"

She shook her head but kept focus on Mark's face. "Do I know you? You look familiar."

The question sent an icy chill down his body. He was moments from blowing his cover and knew Nicole had his name on the tip of her tongue.

"Sorry, I don't think we've met before."

"Are you sure?" Nicole took one last long look at him. "I swear; I know you from somewhere. What's your name?"

He extended his hand to Nicole with a plastered slick smile on his face. "The name is Mark; Mark Thompson."

She accepted his gesture; juggling her books in her arms as she placed her hand in his. "It's nice to meet you. I'm Nicole."

Mark felt repulsed he had to charm a woman he despised. It had been the first real interaction Nicole had since Rachel's death. It was something he needed to use to his advantage.

"Well, Nicole; it's been a pleasure meeting you." He forced a flattering smile. "I'm sorry again for bumping into you, even if it was a way for us to meet. Maybe we can get a bite to eat sometime."

"Yeah, I'd like that. What are you doing right now?"

It was an opening to infiltrate the target's life. It would be best to use the opportunity to set up a contingency plan, but he needed more time to work on a better cover before agreeing to go out with his future victim.

"I would love to, but I have to get down to the registrar's office and the school store. I just found out I'm about to get off the waiting list for one of my classes."

"That's great news; I guess." Nicole took out her phone. "Maybe we can exchange numbers and meet up this weekend?"

Mark was surprised to hear her eagerness to go out, especially when her dream guy took her for dinner and drinks six days earlier. He put in the number to his burner cell before hurrying down the path to a flight of stairs. He was off to the administration building but detoured the moment Nicole was gone from view. He took a longer route back towards Esopus. He took Rachel's ID from his pocket. A sinister smirk crept over his face.

Let's hope this still works.

<u>Chapter 8-Ali</u>

The precinct was quiet for a Thursday afternoon. I was coming back from another case I was asked to consult on after Highland was struck with a string of robberies. The lieutenant asked me to help out where needed, but he didn't assign me to it. I was fine with that decision. It gave me more time to focus on the Rachel Walker case, even though I was told to let it go unless there was evidence to suggest anything more than an accident.

When I got to the station, Rodney was hunched over his desk with a stack of folders and papers piling up around him.

I dropped into my chair across from him. "Is that *actual* police work you're doing?" I clapped a hand to my chest to add an over-dramatic effect.

"Yeah well, someone has to; not everyone can make detective and come in whenever they want." Rodney raised his eyebrow to indicate his bitterness. But then, I saw the corners of his mouth raise and he broke into a smile. He looked me over. "Something's off; you seem like you're in a good mood."

"Is that a crime?"

"For anyone else; no, but you're never in a good mood." He placed his hands on the desk and rose to his feet. He towered over me and had an intimidating feel to him. "So, are you gonna tell me why, or do I have to get it out of you another way?"

I wasn't about to give up the goods that easily. "It's none of your business." My eyes flashed to a file sitting on the desk. I reached for it, but Rodney's hand was preventing it from moving. "Come on; get off it."

"Tell me why you're in such a good mood."

"Well, I won't be if my partner keeps being an asshole." I struggled to get the file free, but realized Rodney wasn't about to let it go without a fight or until I told him what was going on. "Fine," I sighed. "I'm happy because I have plans to go out tonight."

"Oh really?" Rodney's voice went a little high before coming down to a sultry tone. It made what I said sound like my night would be all about getting laid.

Okay, I'll play your game. I placed my hands on the desk and went nose-to-nose with my partner. "Yeah, you know I do have a life outside of this place unlike *some* people I know."

"I have a life. It just centers around a wife and a kid."

"Yeah, Rodney; it sounds *really* exciting."

"You're just jealous because you're still out there trying to find Mr. Right and he's doing his best to hide from your crazy ass."

"How do you know Matthew isn't the right guy?" I asked.

"Oh my God; do you think he's Mr. Perfect?" Rodney decided to stop the low sultry voice and changed it to sound like a high-school girl who needed to hear about cute boy gossip. "Did you use the L word yet? Do you guys think you're gonna get married? How long will you wait to have his kids?"

I let out a laugh and retreated back to my chair. "You're such a jerk."

"Yeah, but you love me, Ali. Who else would make you crack up the way I do every day?"

Rodney was right. He was my rock and my comedic relief in life. But he was also letting his guard down just enough for me to pull the file out from under his hand.

"So, what are you working on?"

Rodney snatched the folder from my hands. "The lieutenant has me following up on the case where *that* girl died on campus from drinking."

"Her *name* was Rachel Walker."

I couldn't help but snap at him. Rodney was a great guy and a damn good partner, but sometimes his lack of filter caused foot-in-mouth syndrome. I had no problem putting him in his place. This time he stopped and stared me down with a *why do you have to be a pain in my ass* expression.

"The preliminary findings came in, and the lieutenant wants me to finish up the investigation."

"Why did he put you in charge of it? It was my case."

"He probably wants to make sure it doesn't stay open without a justifiable reason."

The lieutenant was right in trusting Rodney with the investigation if he wanted to ensure it was an open and shut case. I was more interested in learning the truth.

"What did the report say?"

"Nothing," Rodney replied.

"Don't give me that shit," I barked while ripping the file from his hands. "We need to know everything before making a decision on the investigation."

"Look, there's nothing out of the ordinary, and nothing contradicting the initial thoughts of Rachel dying from choking on her vomit. We cataloged everything in her room and anything that could be potential evidence. We didn't see anything out of the ordinary."

I sat down at my desk reading the file. I studied it intensely. They had everything listed from Rachel's clothing, her bedding, everything from her desk drawers, and even her garbage. There were text-books and course outlines which had barely been touched; notebooks with only a couple of pages used. Maybe I wanted there to be something to pop out at me; something to help me keep the case open; to find a way to give Rachel Walker's parents a reason for their daughter's death and not some stupid mistake. Nothing stood out. Every page of the report and interviews confirmed what we already knew.

I closed the file and left it next to my keyboard. "Did we get the toxicology report back yet?"

"No," Rodney replied. His head dropped when he saw my face. He knew what I wanted. "Let me guess; you wanna take a field trip to the M.E.'s office?"

I smiled. "You read my mind."

Rodney and I took my car out to a large white building on Flatbush Avenue in Kingston. In all the years I had been a cop, I never had to visit the medical examiner's office. I was surprised to see it was bigger than I expected.

We badged our way through the building to find a young woman sitting behind a large circular desk. The sun beamed off the cherry wood finish which caught our eye instantly. I sized up the girl. She seemed small, maybe five-three at best. Her soft golden-brown curls fell to the side of her childlike face. She looked like a fifteen-year old trapped in a twenty-three-year olds body.

"Can I help you?" she asked in a high-pitched voice.

I held up my badge and introduced Rodney and me. "We're here to see Dr. Wu."

The girl didn't flinch at the sight of our badges or even asked why we were there. It was as if she had been used to seeing cops come in asking to see the medical examiner to expedite their reports.

"Give me one moment to see if he's available." The girl grabbed the phone and placed a call. She placed it down and looked up at us. "The doctor will meet with you. Please, follow me." The young girl got up from the desk and pressed a button to unlock the glass door behind her. She held it open for us to enter. "Right this way," she said.

The receptionist strutted down the hall with her thick hips and round bottom swaying from side-to-side. I noticed my partner gawking at her.

I snapped my fingers in front of his face as the girl rounded the corner. "Hey, you're married; remember?"

"What? I didn't do anything."

"No, but I know that look," I whispered. "You were practically undressing her with your eyes."

"No, I wasn't," he quickly replied in a hushed tone.

I glared at him to let him know I saw through his lying bullshit. He was trying to deflect the guilt knowing he was caught checking out another woman.

"Relax, partner; I won't rat you out to Mia." I watched Rodney's shoulders slump as relief washed over him.

The girl stopped outside of a solid door with a small window. She swiped a keycard and pulled the handle. "You can go right in."

We entered the room. It was cold and dark. The lighting was muted but grew once the center of the room was reached. A thin man wearing a green surgical gown a paper hat and a white mask stood over a table working feverishly under a blinding spotlight. A large man was lying on the cold metal slab in front of the doctor.

"Excuse me, Dr. Wu," I called out as I shielded my eyes while moving closer to the table. "I'm Detective Ryan. I was hoping to have a moment of your time."

"One moment," he replied. Dr. Wu turned off the spotlight and walked over to the wall. With a flick of a switch, the rest of the lights in the room sprung alive. "How can I help you?"

I watched the doctor strip off the gown which had blood spattered all over the front of it.

"There was a young college girl brought in last week. I was hoping you could tell us what you can about her death. The name is Rachel Walker."

"Ah yes, this is the young girl who died from an apparent overdose." His words hung in the air, suggesting there was something more to the story. He moved towards a filing cabinet on the other side of the room. "Here we are. The toxicology report came in last night. There were no drugs found in her system, but her BAC level was a two point six."

"That's gotta be a mistake," Rodney blurted out. "There's no way the BAC was that high." He walked over to view the report. "I worked in the bar scene for years. She would've had to drink a few bottles of liquor or an entire keg for our victim to be that drunk."

"Her friends said she had a lot during the party, but never indicated she consumed that much alcohol." I recalled my interview of Rachel Walker's friends. They made it seem like she was alert and aware, at least enough to make it back to her dorm on her own. "How far could someone walk in that condition?"

"I doubt they would be able to stand let alone walk," Dr. Wu replied. "Especially someone as thin as this young woman."

"The victim's friends said they walked back to campus from a party. I saw where both dorms are located. There is at least a mile from either location to any houses away from the college."

"It would be impossible for her to have made it without someone carrying her. Are you sure no one drove them back to campus?"

"No, the girls said they walked to the one dorm, and then our victim walked back to her own building which was about a quarter-mile away."

"So, the test has to be wrong," Rodney added.

"Excuse me?" Dr. Wu stepped up to my partner. The size difference made them look like David and Goliath. "I have been a medical examiner for the last seventeen years. I have never made a mistake with any of my lab reports or in reading back the information."

I looked over the file, and the doctor was right; Rachel had an abnormally high BAC level. I never encountered anyone having registered above a one point five.

"I'm sorry," Rodney said. "It's just hard to believe she drank that much and made it back to campus with her friends." He paced around the room for another minute, and then turned back to me. "You mentioned the roommate claimed alcohol had been snuck into the dorm a few times. Maybe she dipped into a stash and drank the rest on her own."

"Where were the bottles?" I asked. "There was nothing found in her room. There was no one who recalled seeing her in or around that dorm the night she died. Plus, she would have needed to be in her room after consuming that much alcohol; otherwise she wouldn't have been able to get back on her own."

Dr. Wu grabbed another surgical gown and placed it on his body. "I can't help you figure any of that out but let me know if there is anything else you need." He put the file away before marching over to the wall to hit the light switch again. "If you'll excuse me, I need to get back to work."

Rodney and I exited the room and walked back through the corridors to the front of the building.

"We need to figure out what happened to Rachel," I exclaimed.

"You need to drop it, Ali. The poor girl died from drinking too much. If it wasn't for choking on her vomit, she was going to die from alcohol poisoning. You read it in the report."

I don't know why, but it was that moment which took my mind back to the cataloged list of items taken from Rachel Walker's room. There was something I didn't come across; something all college kids had on them.

"Did you or anyone else recover the victim's student ID?"

It was the one thing missing from the list, and it was the one key item Rachel Walker would have needed to get back into her room the night she died.

My partner stopped short. His eyes searched the sky for answers. "No, I didn't come across it. Come to think of it; I don't remember it being on the list of items either."

My eyes widened as we discovered the missing puzzle piece. It was the proof I needed to keep the investigation open.

"Rodney, her missing ID proves someone was with Rachel after she left her friends. She couldn't get into the dorm without it, and she definitely couldn't access her room without the card. Someone had to have helped her, and that person must still have her ID."

Rodney clapped a hand to his forehead. "Ali, that doesn't change how she died." He shook his head in disbelief. "Why do I get the feeling you're not gonna let this go?"

"Because you know I won't stop until I have all the facts."

He let out a sigh. "Fine, but when the lieutenant reams you out for this, just remember I tried to warn you."

It took an hour to get back to the station. Rodney and I had opposing views on the case and neither of us were willing to waiver from our stance. The best solution to avoid arguing was to ride in silence until we returned to the precinct. He held the door open for me and I nodded in gratitude. We marched back to our desks, but the temporary truce was disturbed by the sound of a wooden door crashing against the wall.

The lieutenant stepped forward. His eyes glared at Rodney and then traveled over to me. "Where the *hell* have you two been?"

Rodney and I case sideways glances at each other. Neither of us wanted to admit we were poking our noses into the Rachel Walker case instead of waiting for the official results to be sent to the station.

"We took a drive out to Kingston," Rodney began. "We were checking in with the M.E. about the New Paltz girl."

I could see the vein in the lieutenant's forehead pulsate violently again as he stared a hole through us. His lips pursed together so tightly; I thought he was chewing on the inside just to stop himself from screaming at us.

He gritted his teeth. "Get…in…my…office…now."

It had been a while since I made the lieutenant that mad at me. Rodney wasn't a typical recipient of the boss's anger. He looked at me nervously. I nodded and took the lead into the lieutenant's cramped office. I took the inside chair as Rodney closed the door.

My partner was the first to speak. "I just wanna say-"

"Keep your trap shut, Johnson; this has nothing to do with you." The lieutenant paced around behind his chair. "You were authorized to work the case until the tox screen came back on the victim." He paused as if there was a question being asked, but we all knew it was just prepping us for his next statement. "I know for a fact; we received the report this morning."

"Yeah, but-" I tried to reply. No matter what I said; the lieutenant was going to blow up at me. My only hope was to minimize the damage, but he wasn't even giving me that opportunity.

"But you figured it was better to go against my explicit orders?"

"No, sir; we were just following up with the M.E. to get their final ruling on the cause of death, so we can officially close the case." It was a bold-faced lie, and he knew it. Lieutenant Esposito had a good read on me and was able to tell when I was up to something.

"Fine, I'll play your little game, detective. Tell me; what did you find out from your field trip?"

I told him about meeting Dr. Wu and how he indicated no one would be able to walk, let alone stand, with such a high blood alcohol content level.

"I don't care how the girl got back to her room," he said while glaring at me. "It doesn't change how she died." That was becoming a common statement directed at me for the last week. "We know the cause of death. We know this was an accident." He pointed a stern finger at Rodney and then at me. "I want you both to write up a report confirming the findings and ruling the case closed, and I want it on my desk by the end of the day." His eyes focused directly on me. I could feel the heat from his stare. "Dismissed!"

Rodney and I scurried out of the office like scolded dogs. My partner pulled me aside before settling in our desks. "Why didn't you tell him about the missing ID card?"

I knew that bit of information had Rodney questioning the case. "He wasn't going to listen to us no matter what we told him."

"So, what are you gonna do about it?"

I batted my eyes playfully and pushed my shoulders inward as I rocked from side-to-side. "I'm gonna do my report like a good girl."

"Stop messing around, Ali. I'm being serious."

I grabbed the case files and headed to the copier with Rodney trailing behind me. "I'll investigate things on my own time; when I'm off the clock."

<u>Chapter 9-CK</u>

A cool breeze swept through New Paltz campus. It was the day most students waited for all week. They were done with class and it was time to party. But there were still a handful that scrambled to get through the final hours of coursework before they were free for the weekend.

Mark had been hoping for the right opportunity to strike against his second target. He had dreamed of it all week. There were several ideas to get rid of yet another thorn in his side, but none would have work until she left the room. Seeing Nicole outside of the Lecture Hall meant Mark had the chance he had been waiting all week for. It was time to make his move.

Mark followed Nicole's schedule. She was set for one early morning class at ten and another one at twelve-thirty. He wanted to rush over before she left. He traveled the same paved path by the pond up to the backdoor of Esopus. He reached into his backpack and retrieved Rachel's ID card. With one swipe, he had access to the building. Mark entered the rear stairwell and headed up to the third floor.

A small cluster of students dragged their feet as they sleep-walked their way out of the rooms and down the stairs. Mark rounded the first corner. His next victim sat on the other side of the wall. He wanted to burst through the door, knock her around a bit, and degrade her the way she had made him feel for the last year. But he couldn't; not yet. He had to be patient and wait for a few more hours to get his revenge.

Nicole's high-pitched voice echoed through the door. "Yes, mom; I know I have to just deal with my issues, but I need to come home. I need a few days away from here." There was a long pause. Mark thought Nicole's mother made an attempt to convince her daughter to stay put. "I-I just can't deal with this right now. I have class in a few minutes. I'll call you later."

Mark had a few seconds to come up with a plan to hide himself from his victim. He turned the corner and pretended to look through his bag for homework. He heard the door close. His face dove into the backpack, but his eyes peeked out over the zipper. He saw his victim rush off to class with books in her arms. Her peacock feather earrings stood out against her long dark hair. She walked by Mark, not even giving him a second glance.

Mark's eyes followed her until she disappeared into the stairwell. He pulled out the ID again and used it one more time. The low buzz permitted him access to the room where he claimed his first victim. He stared at what used to be Rachel Walker's bed, but now it was bare. She was gone just like all of her belongings, and now it was time to do the same to her roommate.

Mark turned his attention to the pink comforter on the second bed. He placed his gray backpack next to throw pillows before settling in at Nicole's desk. Her laptop was still open. It was something she had always done. She trusted her roommate well enough to let her use it whenever Rachel needed. The old habit remained, which allowed Mark to go on to begin setting up his victim.

Time to get to work.

He placed the leather gloves on his hands before pulling the wooden chair away from the desk. The pink area run curled up on the floor behind it. Mark sat down and began to set up the cover story. His fingers rapidly clicked the keys and the mouse to bring up web pages searching for suicide hotlines; how to make a noose; and counseling centers. After filling Nicole's search history with enough information, Mark set out to type up a note pretending to be his victim; explaining how she can't live with her mistake.

That should do it. Mark pushed the chair in and left the computer on, so it would eventually go into sleep mode. He fixed the area rug and relaxed for a while. *Now, we wait.*

Hours ticked away as the breezy day switched to a brisk cool summer night. The green luminescent numbers on Mark's watch read nine o'clock. Nicole's classes ended earlier in the afternoon, but she usually spent Fridays catching up with some of her other friends on campus. Targeting her on a day where she had plenty of free time was a risky move, but he needed to act fast before Rachel's student ID was deactivated. Thankfully, he knew Nicole's routine for staying away from her room when something bothered her. After classes, she met up with one friend for lunch. Then, she hung out at the library to do some studying before grabbing dinner with another one of friends. But based on the conversation with her mother, Mark assumed she was trying to stay away from the dorm room as much as she could.

Mark stood inside of Rachel's closet and peeked through the opening in the doors. Nicole's high-pitched voice could be heard in the hallway. It was getting closer causing Mark to panic.

She wasn't alone.

"Thanks for walking me back." Mark could hear her on the other side of the dorm room door. "Are you sure you don't mind driving me home tomorrow?"

"Yeah, it's no problem," a man said reassuringly.

"Thanks; I really need to get away from this place for a while."

There was a brief pause. Mark knew a thought was running through Nicole's head.

Was she considering asking the guy to stay with her for the night?

He didn't know what to do if the guy entered the room. He considered a two-for-one special, but he had no reason to kill the guy other than him being in the wrong place at the wrong time.

"I guess…just give me a call when you're ready to leave and I'll meet you out front."

Mark felt relieved. Nicole was pushing the guy away. She was set to walk into the room alone. The low buzz of the lock sprung the door open. A shadow of a girl walked around the room. The lamp next to the bed turned on as Nicole dumped her books onto the bed. She moved to her desk and turned on the computer. She opened the web browser to check her email. Her eyes flickered to the open application at the bottom of the screen.

"What the hell is this," she muttered to herself. She pushed the chair away from the desk. "Is this some kind of sick joke?"

Mark knew Nicole read her suicide note. He could almost feel her heart beating out of her chest as she wondered who broke into the room and was that person still there.

Time was running out. Nicole was moments from running out of the room to call a RA or RM over what she found. Mark couldn't let that happen. He waited until her back was turned again before slipping out of the closet. He held a thick brown belt in his hands. He gripped both ends tightly as he raised it above her head. Nicole looked up just as the belt pressed against her throat, but she was too late.

Mark pulled it with all of his strength, crushing his victim's windpipe to ensure she couldn't call out for help. Nicole's fingers ripped and tore at the belt to allow one breath, but Mark was relentless. He dragged her in front of a mirror; forcing his victim to see who was attacking her.

He was the man she ran into the day before, but he wanted Nicole to know who he really was, and how she knew him. He whispered his name into her ear as Nicole's arms went limp and fell to her sides. Her eyes were closed but her chest still rose with shallow breaths.

Mark stood over her unconscious body. "Well, that's one way to shut her up." He let out a soft chuckle as he retrieved his backpack. "You know; this wouldn't have happened to you if you weren't such a nosey little bitch.

A moment later, he had a recently constructed noose, one he had been working on all day while Nicole had been away at class. He quickly checked the hall to make sure no one was coming. Nicole was hoisted onto his shoulder. The noose clutched tightly in his left hand. It was time to end the life of his second victim.

Chapter 10-Ali

I ran around my bedroom looking for the perfect outfit to wear. I spent an hour checking my closets and dresser, but I seemed to be running out of time and options. The red glowing digits on the clock counted down the minutes until Matthew arrived at my house. He told me to be ready by eight, and it was already seven-fifty. Finally, I found everything I was searching for. I pulled on a pair of tight dark blue jeans; the kind that make men stop and stare as they clung to my body. I paired them with a frilly black blouse, which had a low-cut neck-line, perfect to draw Matthew's attention to where I hoped the night would go. Last, I grabbed a pair of black peep-toe pumps.

I checked my hair and make-up one last time before entering the living room. A pair of headlights beamed through the window and bounced off the mirror hanging over the mantle.

Eight on the dot; punctual as usual, I thought while checking the time on my cable box.

I almost skipped to the front door. There, on the opposite side, stood my six-foot-two gorgeous man. Matthew looked incredible in his black dress pants and light-blue button-down shirt. He curled an arm around my back and pulled me close. His lips pressed against mine. I was lost in the moment. My fingers ran through his short, thick, black hair.

"Hey there, beautiful," he said softly. A hint of his Puerto Rican accent slipped through.

My heart skipped a beat as I looked into his big brown eyes. I pulled him in for another passionate kiss. "Hello, yourself," I replied.

He took a step back and smiled. "We can stay in tonight; if that's what you want."

"That's a tempting offer, but I think we need to grab some food; preferably something Italian."

"I know just the place." He stuck out his hand and laced his fingers with mine.

Just the touch of his skin had me feeling like a giddy school girl. Every time we spoke I just wanted to know everything I could about the man, but he liked to be vague in responses.

"How was your day?" I asked.

"It was good," he replied. "It was pretty much a normal day for me. How was yours?"

"It was slow for the most part." I responded instinctively, but tried to force the topic back onto Matthew. "You know; you never told me what a typical day is for you." He had once told me he was a liaison for a major corporation, but Matthew always seemed to change the subject when I asked any more questions.

He reached for the passenger side door and held it open for me to get it. "There's really not much to my day. I go in around nine; make a few calls; meet with a few clients; and I'm gone by five."

He closed the door with a smile before walking around to the other side of the car. He got in and started the engine. We pulled out of my driveway and began our long crazy night.

Matthew pulled up to a large brick building on Route 9. If it wasn't for the sign saying Frank's Italian Restaurant, I would have overlooked it while driving. Inside was much different. There were various paintings lining the beige and gray walls. Matthew took the lead up to the podium where a young girl stood waiting to greet us. I looked at the hostess. I estimated her age to be around eighteen or nineteen. She could have easily been in her last year of high school or first semester of college. Seeing how young she was made my mind go back to Rachel Walker. My head kept spinning with questions, making me wonder if we were ever going to get answers for.

"Right this way," the girl said.

Matthew nudged me to snap me out of the daydream like state. I followed him and the hostess through a maroon curtain with violet butterflies on it. The large room was filled with customers. The walls were lined with wooden cabinets filled with glasses, mirrors, and rustic gold frames. It made me feel like we were walking through someone's home during Sunday dinner.

We were led to a glass door. The hostess pulled it open and escorted us to a small table overlooking Route 9. My eyes focused on the stop and go traffic next to us. My thoughts returned to the investigation. My instincts told me the decision to close the case was wrong. No one else saw it from my perspective. Maybe I was wrong. Maybe I was just looking for there to be something more to give the Walker family a reason for their daughter's death other than one night of making the wrong choices.

Matthew grabbed my hand from across the table. It ripped me from my obsessive thoughts. "Is everything all right?" There was genuine concern coming from his voice. "You've been very quiet and you've been staring off into space a lot."

"I'm fine," I lied. Seeing a college girl lying dead in her dorm room shook me to my core. The image haunted me every time I saw anyone who resembled Rachel or seemed to be around the same age as her. "I just have a lot on my mind."

The waitress came to the table carrying two plates. She set them down in front of us. I didn't remember ordering anything. Hell, this was the first time I recalled seeing anyone other than the hostess.

Matthew began cutting up his chicken as I stared at my dinner. "Are you sure everything is okay?"

"Yeah, I just don't remember ordering this."

"That would be because you were too busy staring out the window. I took the liberty of ordering the chicken caprese." I was surprised Matthew told the waitress what to bring me. I was even more impressed when he asked for the exact dinner I would have ordered. "Now, do you want to talk about what's really bothering you?"

"It's nothing; just an investigation I'm working on."

Matthew's eyes perked up. "What case?"

I wasn't permitted to divulge any information about an ongoing investigation, but the lieutenant did say the case was closed. Technically, I was free to talk to Matthew about it. I started with how Rachel was found in her room; how much alcohol was reportedly in her system; and how she supposedly made it back to the dorm on her own. Then, I told him how everyone was forcing me to close the investigation despite my protests.

"There are so many unanswered questions," I told him.

"So, what are you going to do about it?"

"Well, I can't do anything officially, but that doesn't mean I can't do some digging around on my own time."

"Ali, are you sure that's a good idea? Your boss told you to close it for a reason. Won't he be mad if you're poking around?"

"Yeah, he probably will, but I need to know we have all the facts. One tiny detail could change everything about a case. I just want to make sure we don't miss it."

Matthew patted my hand gently and smiled. "You seem like a really dedicated detective."

I thanked him and decided to finally put the case behind me so I could eat. I wanted to enjoy my date night with Matthew, but the low ringing from my bag wasn't going to let that happen.

I saw Rodney's name plastered on the screen. "This will only take me a minute." I accepted the call. "This isn't the best time, partner."

"Ali, you need to get down to the school." I could hear sirens blaring in the background.

"What happened?"

"A call came in a little while ago. Another body was found on campus. The lieutenant wants us to check it out."

"Who was it?"

"It was Rachel Walker's roommate."

I nearly came undone at the thought of another body being found dead on campus, especially considering the proximity to my sister.

Hearing it was Nicole Sherman, Rachel's roommate, shattered my restraint.

"What? How did it happen?"

"The RA found her hanging from one of the shower stalls. I just pulled up to Esopus a minute ago."

"I'm in Wappinger's Falls right now. I can be back in New Paltz in about an hour. Keep everyone away from the crime scene until I get there."

I watched Matthew wave the waitress over. "I think we need these wrapped up and the check immediately."

I hung up the phone and shoved it back in my purse. My eyes locked onto Matthew. "Remember saying that I'm a dedicated detective?"

"I heard everything, and I'm already a step ahead of you."

The waitress came back with two food containers and a black leather book with the check inside. Matthew quickly placed his credit card in it before handing it back to the waitress. We rushed to shovel our dinners into the to-go containers and placed them in a plastic bag.

"Hey, do you mind if I drive?" I asked with my hand stretched out.

There was hesitation in his eyes. I doubted Matthew had let anyone drive his car before. I could already tell he liked to be in control of things in any relationship. Boy was he in for a rude awakening.

"Y-yeah," he reluctantly said. His hands plunged into his pockets and pulled out the keys. He handed them over just as the waitress appeared with his card and a slip of paper to sign.

"Great, let's go," I commanded. I grabbed Matthew by the wrist and led him through the restaurant and into the parking lot.

I slammed on the gas the moment we were buckled into our seats. I was well versed in weaving in and out of traffic, speeding down Route 9, and knowing just how to time the lights perfectly to avoid getting stuck at one. I almost expected a Dutchess County cop to catch us as I drove twenty-five miles over the speed limit. I told Rodney it would take me an hour to get to the campus, but that was just to give me a cushion. I actually made it there in thirty-seven minutes.

I pulled the car up to the commuter parking lot across from Esopus. Police had the resident lot sectioned off to keep anyone else from getting up to the doors.

"I'm really sorry about this," I told Matthew as I pushed open the driver side door. He came around to my side of the car and wrapped an arm around my waist. He tried to kiss me, but I didn't have time for a proper goodbye. I definitely didn't have the restraint to push him away the moment his lips touched mine. "I'll call you tomorrow."

I hurried off at a brisk pace. I glanced back to see the look of disappointment etched across Matthew's face. I wanted to stay with him; to enjoy a romantic dinner; to be held in his arms. I wanted to see how our night would have ended had we not been interrupted. Unfortunately, duty called, and I needed to focus on the dead girl on the third floor.

It was like déjà vu. It was another day where I was called to a crime scene during my time off. It was the same dorm; the same floor; technically the same room. Nicole Sherman sat in a room across from me less than a week ago. And now, I was going back up to the third floor to investigate her death.

Rodney stood at the glass doors waiting for me to arrive. His head bobbed up and down as if he was checking me out.

"Well, don't you look nice?" Rodney joked.

I shoved my partner harder than usual. "Cut the crap, Rodney. I'm not in the mood to mess around. I had to cut my date short for this."

"Oh, so sorry to have bothered you, detective," he replied rather sarcastically. "I just figured you would want to personally investigate this one."

"You said the lieutenant wanted us to check it out."

We entered the building and waited for the elevator. "That's not entirely true. He called me to take the lead. I decided to involve you."

"Why…" I knew the answer before finishing my question. The lieutenant wanted Rodney on the case to ensure it was handled correctly. He feared I would take it as a link to Rachel's death and I would want to re-open it. He would have been right. So, I decided to change my question. "Where is she?"

"The victim or your sister?" he asked. Rodney put a hand on the small of my back as the elevator doors opened. He ushered me inside and pressed the number three. "Your sister is fine. I had an officer take Amanda to her boyfriend's dorm to make sure she didn't see any of this." He looked to me as if waiting for a pat on the back for a job well done.

"What about Nicole?"

"She was found hanging from a noose inside the bathroom across the hall from her dorm room. The RA stumbled on the body and immediately called for help."

"Who had access to the bathroom?"

"Everyone who lived in Esopus," Rodney replied. "But Nicole shared the bathroom with the RA and two other neighboring rooms." He took a deep breath. "I'm bringing you on just to look over the crime scene."

I tilted my head to the side replaying Rodney's last comment. I wasn't being put in charge of the investigation. He just wanted me to give my thoughts on it.

"Don't tell me this is already being ruled a suicide."

"Ali, she was found hanging from a noose in the bathroom."

The elevator doors opened, but I refused to move. I pushed my partner to the side. "If this girl was suicidal, why would she make an attempt on her own life in a public bathroom where anyone could have found her before she died?"

"Trust me; I know," he snapped while pushing my hands away. "Why do you think I called you? It's a little suspicious, so I wanted to get your opinion before bringing anything up to the lieutenant."

He was right to ask for my help. I was already thinking there was something off about Rachel Walker's death, and I already called this new crime scene into question. My partner and I needed to ensure their deaths were what they seemed, or else we had a homicidal killer on the loose.

Chapter 11-Ali

Students crowded the hall of the third floor trying to get a glimpse of what was going on. For the second time in a week, police patrolled Esopus keeping everyone away from a room near the rear stairwell. This time, it expanded to a larger section of the dorm.

"Out of the way; police coming through," Rodney called out as he led the way to the crime scene. "Everyone; go back to your rooms until further notice."

I trailed behind my partner trying to ignore the guys gawking at me. I heard a few cat calls as I passed by.

"DAYUM," one boy said drawing out each part of the word. "Yo, she's a cop?"

"How about you arrest me?" another boy called out.

I ignored them. I was used to being verbally harassed. As a woman, I hear guys making inappropriate comments. As a female officer, I get them more often. Some are just being sexist, who think only men can be an effective cop, and my role should be to get coffee. Those are the guys I purposely go out of my way to show them up. They are put in their place quickly, and they never make that same mistake again. Then, you have moments when people cross the line. One of the boys in the hall darted behind me. I could feel a hand grabbing my butt; copping a quick feel.

I snatched his wrist and spun around pressing my forearm against his throat. "You ever try that again, and the only thing that hand will ever be good for is to defend yourself against Big Bubba in the county jail. Do I make myself clear?"

The boy's eyes nearly popped out of his head as he nodded repeatedly. I removed my arm and straightened his shirt.

"Good, now go back to your room."

I was sure that warning was enough to scare the kid into never doing something that stupid again. Had I wanted to be a bitch, he would have been brought up on several charges including assault, assaulting a police officer, and sexual assault. His life would have been over before it ever had a chance to begin. I didn't want that to happen to him. I just wanted the boy to know he would face a world of trouble if he ever did that again.

"Ali, are you coming?" Rodney called out.

I heard a few more boys giggling at the remark, but this time there were a few girls telling them to grow up. I held back a smirk after hearing strong women standing up for one of their own.

Rodney stood at the end of the hall signaling me to follow him. Yellow crime tape sectioned off two sections of rooms. We ducked under it and turned into the open bathroom. Nicole's body was sprawled out on the black and white tiled floor. A short Asian man hovered over the body taking pictures.

"Dr. Wu, I didn't expect to find you here."

"Ah, Detective Ryan; it's good to see you again. I wish it was under better circumstances."

The feeling was mutual. "What do we have here?"

"A dead girl," he replied. It almost made me laugh to hear him state the obvious. "I hate to see someone die this young."

"Based on your observations, can you estimate a time of death?"

"I would place it within the last two hours."

"So, it wasn't long before we got the call?" Rodney asked.

"I'd say that's a good guess," Dr. Wu replied.

I turned to my partner and pulled him towards the door. "We need all students back in their rooms. I want everyone questioned."

"Are you sure that's necessary?"

"What the hell do you mean; is it necessary?" My partner called me down to the campus fearing there may have been more to the incident, and now he was questioning why we needed to interview all the students.

"Ali, her roommate died in the bed across from where she slept. It would be natural for our victim to be consumed with guilt that she took her own life."

Any other time, I would think the same thing. Even now, it was very possible Nicole Sherman was guilt-ridden over Rachel's death, especially if she believed there was a chance she could have saved her friend's life. It's *that* kind of guilt which could tear someone to pieces, even cause them to do something as extreme as taking their own life.

"Rodney, you called me here for my opinion because you thought there was something off about her death."

"Exactly," he replied. "I asked for your opinion; that doesn't mean I have to do as you say."

My eyes found the door at the other end of the bathroom open. I could see into Rachel and Nicole's room. Both girls were found dead less than a week apart.

Were these random occurrences, or did someone target these women? I inched closer to the body to get a closer look. "The lieutenant put you in charge of the case; have at it. I guess that means I'm free to go back to my date."

I turned on my heel to walk out of the bathroom. Rodney put a hand on my shoulder to stop me.

"Do you really think someone was behind this?"

I looked up at my partner. "Anything is possible, but I find her death very suspicious."

"I'll bite, Ali; what else is off about this case?"

It was a challenge; one I was ready to accept. I took a deep breath and began to examine the crime scene as if I was the lead investigator.

"Where was the body found?"

Dr. Wu pointed to the shower stall behind him. "She was hanging from that shower head."

I cautiously stepped around the body and into the stall. There was a small brown stool lying on its side. There was no doubt in my mind it had been knocked over just before the noose closed off Nicole's airway. I pictured her ripping and tearing at the rope as she struggled to breathe.

Next, I checked out the noose. It was poorly constructed and looked like it had been slapped together quickly, but not something done last minute. Whoever made it; put effort into creating the noose. It wasn't a spur of the moment decision. It was crafted for at least a day or more, which meant Nicole would have been planning to take her life for the last couple of days.

"There are a few things that don't add up," I began.

"Here we go," Rodney interrupted.

I chose to ignore his comment and launched into my review. "Rachel Walker died sometime early Saturday morning. Her roommate waited until almost a week later to end her own life. Why wait? Why did she let an entire school week pass before committing suicide?"

"Maybe the guilt kept building until she couldn't take it anymore," Rodney responded. It was a very plausible explanation, and he may have been right.

"But then, why wait until Friday night? Why do it in such a public place like a bathroom shared with about five other people? If our victim wanted to commit suicide, she had plenty of better options to choose from. She could have done it outside using the branches of a tree, the rail from the stairwell around the corner from her room, or even the banister that overlooked the first floor."

"What are you saying, detective?" Dr. Wu asked.

"The bathroom was probably the worst choice to make an attempt on your life. I already noted; there are too many people who could walk in and catch you doing it." I walked back and pointed to the noose and the shower head. "Hanging from this had a greater likelihood of something going wrong. The shower head isn't too high off the ground, it could have broken from the wall if there was enough weight pulling it down, and she could have pulled the stool back over with her feet had she changed her mind. At best; this was a cry for help gone terribly wrong."

Rodney scoffed at my statement. "So, does this mean you're giving up your homicide theory?"

"No, not yet," I replied. "There are a lot more questions begging to be answered, especially when combined with her roommate's investigation." I tiptoed out of the stall and stood next to Nicole Sherman's lifeless body. "Are we clear to move the victim?"

"Yes, I have everything I need," Dr. Wu advised.

I stared at Nicole and saw she was dressed in jeans, a t-shirt, and peacock feathered earrings. It was a little dressy for someone looking to end their life.

"Did anyone check her pockets?" I asked.

"No," Dr. Wu replied.

I plunged my hands into each pocket of Nicole Sherman's pants.

"What are you looking for?" Rodney questioned.

"If this was a suicide, there would most likely be a note." I pulled my hands out and sat back on my heels.

"Did you find anything?" my partner asked.

"No," I said with confusion weighing in on my voice. "She didn't even have her student ID on her."

Dr. Wu shrugged his shoulders and stared blankly at me. "Why would it matter if she had the ID on her?"

"Residents need their ID to access every room in this dormitory, including the bathrooms. If this had been just a cry for help, our victim would have kept the ID on her as a way of getting back into her room."

I further detailed my thoughts on Nicole's outfit. I pointed out she had on make-up and appeared to have either just come back to the dorm or she was about to go out. I was well on my way to proving there was more to this case than a simple suicide, but new evidence quickly derailed my theory.

"Excuse me, Officer Johnson," another cop called out from the bathroom door facing Rachel and Nicole's room. "I was told to let you know if we found anything. We uncovered the suicide note."

This was turning into a bad dream. I crossed the hall and entered Nicole Sherman's room. One side was bare; the other was organized and clean with everything in its place. The officer led us to the desk with an open laptop. The screen had an open application on it with a typed letter.

To whoever finds this;

It has been a week since Rachel died. I can't stand being here without her. She was my best friend and roommate. She was like a sister to me. It's my fault she's gone. I should have been with her the night of the party. I should have made sure she got back to the room safely. I should have checked on her before I went to bed. I can't live in this room anymore. I can't live with this guilt. Please, let my family know I love them, and that I'm sorry.

There was a tear in my eye. I couldn't believe the sweet young girl I met a week ago, the one mourning the loss of her friend, wrote this gut wrenching note. Her last words were typed up as an expression of her remorse.

Rodney put a consoling hand on my shoulder. "Ali, I…uh…" He was fumbling with the right words to say without saying *I told you so.*

I placed my hand on top of his. "I already know what you're thinking, partner. And for once, I think you're right."

<u>Chapter 12-Ali</u>

Rodney took me home that night, but I never went to bed. I tossed and turned for hours thinking about the two girls who had their lives cut short. I knew what both cases looked like on paper. It was easy for anyone to rule those investigations as accidental deaths or suicides. I just couldn't come to terms with it. Something in my gut told me to look their files over again. There was something we were missing.

I got to the station early the next day hoping to look at the reports again before the lieutenant reamed me out for putting my nose where it didn't belong. I had little to no time left before he closed both cases, and anything I dug up would be considered non-compliant with his orders.

I snuck in a full hour and a half before my shift. I hurried over to my desk. My focus was on making sure the lieutenant wasn't in his office or lurking around a corner. Instead, I ran into my partner who was walking with a bagel and cream cheese.

"Ali, what are you doing here so early?" He set the bagel down at his desk next to a steaming cup of what our station considered coffee.

"I'm just getting a jump start on the day."

"Really; because I'm pretty sure you're about to do something you're not supposed to." He sat down in his chair with a smile.

"I don't know what you mean. I just want to look over some case files and grab some breakfast before really sinking my teeth into whatever the day brings."

"So, this has nothing to do with the Rachel Walker or Nicole Sherman cases?"

Rodney knew me too well. There was no way to BS my way around the topic or to convince my partner I was there for any other reason.

"Fine, I wanted to put in a request to get Nicole's phone records leading up to last night."

"You know the lieutenant will have your ass if he sees you making requests on behalf of either case, right?"

"Look, I'm not ruling out the possibility of this being suicide. I just want to know who she spoke to during this last week. Did she call anyone? Did she reach out to anyone for help?"

"So, you want to ask for information on a case you're not assigned to, just to ease your mind?"

"I'm sorry," I replied. "Something just feels off about both cases, and I can't get them off my mind. I need to go over without interference from the Lieutenant Buzzkill. Maybe then, I can let them go."

Rodney pulled the top right drawer of his desk open and grabbed a file. He handed it to me. "You didn't get this from me."

I skimmed through the pages. I glanced up at Rodney and locked eyes with him in an irate glare. "Why were you hiding this in your desk?"

"Hear me out, Ali. I put in the request for it after I dropped you off last night. I knew you would ask for this. It's obvious you're not gonna let it drop. So, I'm doing what I can to help you stay under the radar or else the lieutenant will have your ass."

"Thanks, partner."

I sat at my desk with the file and reviewed the phone records of every outgoing call for the last week. I checked the numbers against a database and found some unexpected results. I called Rodney over right away.

"What did you find?"

"Nicole called the Student Health and Wellness Center twice in the last week along with a few numbers from Queens."

"I guess that ties in perfectly with the note we found. Can we close this case and let both girls rest in peace?"

I had to agree with Rodney. Calling the Wellness Center indicated she could have felt depressed almost to a point of having suicidal thoughts. I was about to tell him to go ahead and close the case, but the last number in the call log grabbed my attention. It belonged to Nicole's mother, Marissa Sherman.

"Fine, but let me talk to the victim's parents first."

"You wanna be the one to break the news to them?" Rodney seemed relieved; despite knowing I had an ulterior motive. "Good luck, Ali."

The hardest thing for any cop to do is to tell a parent their child is dead, even worse; to tell them they died from suicide. It was a call I took in another room at the station. I spoke to Nicole's parents briefly to let them know what happened. I asked to meet with them when they came up to the school. They told me they would be up in a couple of hours.

I arranged for Rodney and me to wait at Esopus in preparation for the Shermans to arrive. I sat in the study lounge down the hall from Nicole's room. It was the same one where I spoke to Nicole the morning Rachel Walker's lifeless body was found in bed. I sat down in one of the plush maroon chairs against the wall picturing students using the room for some peace and quiet. It seemed like a perfect place to shut out the world for a little while. Unfortunately, it had a different feel to it during the last week.

Rodney appeared outside the door. I heard the low buzz signaling the room was being unlocked. He stepped inside and allowed a couple enter. The husband was average height, maybe five-seven, with graying hair. The presence of his wife startled me. She was short and a little chubby. Her face looked exactly like Nicole but about twenty years older.

I stood up with my hand stretched out. "Mr. and Mrs. Sherman; I'm Detective Ali Ryan. You already met my partner, Officer Johnson."

Mrs. Sherman curled into her husband's chest while hiding her tears. Mr. Sherman grasped my hand firmly.

"It's nice to meet you, detective. I just wish it was under better circumstances." Mr. Sherman steered his wife towards one of the plush chairs at the table. "I'm confused. Why did you want to meet with us?"

I sat down at the table with my notepad in front of me. "I know this is a very difficult time for you and your wife, but I had a few questions. I figured it would be better to do it here rather than over the phone or at the station."

"What kind of questions?" His tone was cold and aggressive. His eyes narrowed at me while his chest rose and fell rapidly. I could tell Mr. Sherman was working himself up before I asked anything.

"Before this year, how often did Nicole call home?"

"I don't know; a few times a week," he replied.

"Has she ever been depressed or seemed down?" I felt it was a dumb question. Every kid goes through bouts of moodiness. Every college student has moments where they feel down about themselves, especially after they move away. But I needed to establish how Nicole acted on a regular basis prior to the last week.

Mrs. Sherman looked up. Tears streamed down her puffy cheeks. "She was always a happy child. She was our baby; our happy little girl."

"And how many times did she call you during this last week?"

Mr. Sherman shrugged his shoulders and deferred to his wife. He apparently wasn't the one Nicole spoke to when she called home.

"We talked every day," Mrs. Sherman replied. "Nicole was heartbroken over her friend's death."

"Would you go as far to say she blamed herself for Rachel dying?" I knew the question was out of line and was about to wreak havoc on their fragile minds but I needed answers, and pushing them was the only way I would get them.

Mr. Sherman's nose scrunched up with anger in his eyes. He stood up quickly. "My daughter had nothing to do with her roommate's death."

That didn't go the way I had hoped. "I'm sorry, Mr. Sherman. I didn't mean to imply-"

"Then, what *are* you implying, detective?"

I closed the notepad and sat upright in the chair. "I am investigating the mindset of your daughter leading up to and during the time of her death."

He inched closer. I could tell Mr. Sherman was ready to tear me apart if I said one more inappropriate thing about Nicole.

"Why? So, you and the police can exploit her on T.V. or use her as some sort of example of what can happen if you don't seek help when facing depression?"

I didn't flinch, but his words got to me. I kept my eyes locked on Mr. Sherman; watching to see if he made a move. My heart was beating a mile a minute.

"No," I replied while slowly rising to my feet. "It's because I am convinced this is not a clean-cut case of suicide." I winced the moment I made the statement. "I'm sorry; I shouldn't have said anything." I collected my notepad and headed for the door.

There was a moment of silence in the room before Mr. Sherman blocked my path to the exit. "Do you think someone did this to my little girl?"

My statement had its intended impact; forcing Mr. Sherman to consider there was someone else to blame for what happened to his daughter.

"I don't have all of the facts, sir, but I'm trying to find out everything I can about Nicole's final day and moments leading up to her death."

Mrs. Sherman grabbed my wrist and tugged me back towards her. "I know she took what happened to Rachel really hard. Nicole told me she made an appointment with the school therapist for this coming week. I spoke to her before she left for class yesterday."

"What did you talk about?"

"She wanted to come home this weekend. I told her we couldn't come up here to get her. She called me back later in the afternoon to tell me she found a ride with one of her friends."

"Do you know when she was supposed to leave?"

"Her friend was going to meet her this morning."

"Do you know who this friend is?"

"No, she never told me their name."

That was disappointing. I hoped to learn who Nicole was catching a ride home with to question them. Maybe they would have had some insight into Nicole's state of mind prior.

"Thank you," I said while patting Mrs. Sherman's arm gently. "I'll be in touch if I have any further questions."

Mr. Sherman continued to block the door. There was a tear trickling down his right cheek. "If my daughter was murdered…" More tears spilled out. "You better find the asshole who did this to her."

I nodded my head before exiting the room. I closed the door and leaned against the wall away from the window. I was more confused than I was when I left Esopus last night. I was still on the fence.

Was this suicide, or did someone kill Nicole Sherman?

"What happened?" Rodney asked as we marched down the hall together. I did everything possible to contain my emotions and not let it show how bothered I was by the case.

Before I could answer him, my phone started buzzing. I held up a finger to silence my partner while I took the call.

"This is Ryan."

"Ah, detective," the man said. "I need you to come down to my office. I have something important to show you."

The voice was familiar, but I had no idea who called me. I pulled the cell away and stared at the unknown number. "Who is this?"

"It's Fred…I mean Dr. Wu."

"Hi," I replied. I was not expecting a call from the M.E. and I had no clue how he knew my number. "I'm kind of in the middle of something. What can I help you with?"

"I have found something interesting while examining Miss Sherman's body. I think it will help your investigation."

"I can be there in an hour." I hung up the phone and stared blankly at my partner. "We need to get to the M.E.'s office. Dr. Wu has something to show us."

"Okay, I'll meet you over there."

I badged my way into the building and walked up to the receptionist's desk finding the same young girl from the other day.

"Detective Ryan," she squeaked. "It's good to see you again." She reached for the phone and called to the back. "Dr. Wu is all set; you can go right in." She got up from the desk and used the keycard to open the door. "Can I ask a question? What's it like being a cop?"

I stared at the girl. "It's the most interesting, exhilarating, risky, and heart-breaking job I've ever worked. Your personal life takes a backseat to your career. And you worry about everyone you love while they wonder if today's the day they get the dreadful call."

She straightened up instantly. Her face had expression of surprise and intrigue. It was the same look most people have when they join us on a ride along.

"D-do you think one day I could…" Her voice trailed off as fear took over. I didn't know if she wanted to join us for a field trip or if she wanted my opinion about joining the force. Either way; I was happy to help.

"Give me your information and we'll talk more."

The girl ran back to her desk and jotted down her name and phone number on a lime green Post-it. I glanced at the name; Meghan Grimes.

"Thank you," she said.

"I'll give you a call when I'm done with these cases." I placed the note in my pocket and smiled at the girl before following her to see Dr. Wu.

I entered the cold darkness of the exam room. It was eerie to be in there, especially when a large spotlight hovers over a body lying on a table. It was a setup right out of a bad horror movie. All we needed now was for the killer to pop up behind us with some sort of knife or gun or some other weapon to attack us with.

"Hello, it's good to see you again." Dr. Wu stepped into the light causing me to jump back a little. "I didn't mean to startle you." He pulled down the blue mask with a grin plastered on his face. "I'll be with you in one minute."

Dr. Wu ripped off the latex gloves and deposited them in the trash as he clicked on the overhead lights. He grabbed a folder from a nearby counter and handed the file to me.

"What's this?" I asked.

"That has the photos I took of your victim, Nicole Sherman, right after we took down her body. The second half of the pictures show her bruises hours after her death."

I flipped through them; reliving the horror of seeing a young girl's lifeless body. The first set of pictures showed Nicole Sherman hanging from the shower head. I could only assume the RA was told not to touch the body until someone got there. The next set of photos showed our victim lying on the cold tiled floor of the bathroom. There were stills of the marks around her neck. A large red ring appeared on Nicole's throat indicating her skin had been ripped raw from the noose.

Dr. Wu had been watching me go through each shot. He smiled and pointed to the next picture. "Here's where it gets interesting." His finger tapped on a larger purplish bruise around and underneath the earlier red ring.

"Where did this come from?"

"Precisely; it's not consistent with our initial review. The markings indicate something much larger wrapped around her neck prior to the noose. It could have been a belt, some sort of strap, or a collar." Dr. Wu let out a chuckle. He turned to me and must have seen the anger brewing in my eyes. "Sorry, I've seen a lot come through here."

"What else can you tell me about our victim?"

"There's a chance the marks came from a previous suicidal attempt. Maybe she was testing the water to see if she could go through with it, or what would work best."

"Could someone else have done it to her?"

Dr. Wu paused and tapped a finger against his lips. "It's possible; maybe more than possible." I wondered what he meant, but he was already on his way to answer my question before I had a chance to ask it. He handed me another file. "I remembered your conversation with your partner. So, I checked under the victim's nails for any sign of a struggle. I didn't find *anything*."

I nodded my head as Dr. Wu explained his finding. I thought he was going to deliver some sort of compelling evidence, but he found nothing. I looked up at him again and noticed the expression on his face was telling me to listen more carefully. I replayed his words in my head again.

"Wait, you didn't find *anything*?"

"No, there wasn't a single fiber. Curious; isn't it?"

That was the proof I needed to show someone else was behind Nicole Sherman's death. Anyone hanging themselves has that moment where they struggle for breath as the noose tightens around their throats. They dig and claw at the contraption. If Nicole had committed suicide, there should have been rope fibers under her nails.

"Is there any way I can get copies of the photos and your report?"

"What do I look like; CVS?" He let out a laugh while taking the files from me. "Give me an hour and I can have everything ready for you."

"Thanks; I owe you one."

Dr. Wu scratched an invisible goatee. "I might need to take you up on that. How do you feel about sushi?"

I exited the office and waited with the receptionist while Dr. Wu prepared my to-go order of evidence. *I'll take a report of possible foul play with a side of gloating.*

When I emerged from the building, I found Rodney leaning against my car. "Where the hell have you been?" I asked.

"I've been busy covering your ass." He opened the passenger side door of his squad car, picked up a beige folder, and handed it to me with a raised eyebrow. "You can thank me later."

"Thank you for what?"

"For getting my hands on this before the Lieutenant saw it." I opened the folder and found a list of items recovered from Nicole Sherman's room. "Morgan messaged me to let me know the evidence log from last night was ready."

I skimmed through the three pages detailing the clothes Nicole wore, the ones on the floor and in her hamper; the list of books found on her desk, a backpack, her bedding; and other items that could be considered potential evidence. I had ordered everything to be collected that night before Rodney took me home.

"What were you looking for exactly?" Rodney asked.

I used my finger as a guide tracing every item listed on each line, but I couldn't see the one thing I was searching for.

"Her student ID isn't on the list." My voice cracked with excitement as I bounced on my feet. "Do you know what this means?"

"Don't tell me you're still harping on that shit?"

"Rodney, there were two bodies found dead within a week of each other. Both girls were missing their student IDs, yet they needed them to access the rooms where they were found.

"Ali, there hasn't been any evidence supporting your theories."

"Actually…" I handed Rodney the files Dr. Wu had just given me. "I have something that might direct us down that path."

I reviewed the information with Rodney and told him everything Dr. Wu said earlier. I pointed out the different marks around Nicole Sherman's throat before finally bringing up the lack of evidence under the victim's finger nails.

"This isn't much to go on," Rodney said.

"It's enough to keep this case open a little longer."

Rodney cupped a hand to cover his face. "Ali, I tried to keep you out of trouble, but I don't think there's anything I can say or do to stop your pursuit of the truth." He patted me on the shoulder. "Just remember; I tried to warn you."

I got back in the car and followed my partner back to the station. I was more than determined to make the lieutenant see my point of view, but I knew there was much more to uncover before bringing it to him with a request to keep the investigations open. When we got back, Rodney and I quickly made our way back to our desks and slipped into our chairs.

"So, other than causing trouble; what are you doing tonight?" Rodney asked with a chuckle.

"Matthew and I are taking Amanda and her punk-rock boyfriend out on a double date."

"He's meeting the family? This is getting serious, Ryan. Maybe I should go with you guys to chaperone."

"Don't you dare. He's a good guy. I don't need you scaring him off."

It didn't take long for the lieutenant to notice we had returned to the station. I heard the door open and the angry voice calling my name.

"Detective Ryan…my office…now!"

I gathered the folders Dr. Wu and Rodney had given me and clutched them in my arms as I marched to the lieutenant's office. I expected him to rip them away the moment I entered the office. He had to have known I was involving myself in the Nicole Sherman case, and it was my only shot to convince him it needed to remain open.

I entered the office and took a seat in the uncomfortable pleather chair across from Lieutenant Esposito. I didn't dare make a sound until he gave off clues to how mad of a mood he was in.

The lieutenant ran his fingers through his unkempt gray hair. His eyes were locked on me. I swear he didn't even blink since I walked into the room.

"Why do you insist on disregarding everything I say?" I opened my mouth to speak, but he held up a hand with his palm facing outward; silencing me before I could plead my case. "I told you to leave the Rachel Walker case alone, and you fought me every step of the way. I purposely put your partner on the new one and you somehow weasel your way onto something that should be another open and shut case."

"How did you know?"

"Mr. and Mrs. Sherman stormed into the station demanding answers for their daughter's death after being questioned by a Detective Ryan. Apparently, you suggested their girl was killed."

I should have expected that backlash, but Dr. Wu's call diverted my attention. "Before you flip out; I have evidence supporting my theory."

"Oh really?" he said sarcastically. The anger lingered in his voice as he dared me to prove him wrong. "Okay, let's have it then."

I presented everything to the lieutenant. I walked him through Dr. Wu's findings and pointed out everything shown in the pictures. I told him about the lack of fibers under the nails, and the conversation I had with Mrs. Sherman about Nicole making plans to come home for the weekend. Finally, I told him about the missing IDs thinking that they would seal the deal.

"What do ya think?" I asked.

"Look, Detective; I can sit here and look over this report from now to next year, and it still won't convince me either death was a homicide. One girl died from drinking too much. The autopsy and toxicology reports confirmed it." Esposito could see the determination in my eyes and held up his hand before I could interrupt. "Our second victim believed she was partially responsible for her roommate's death. She tried living with the guilt; stayed in her room for most of the week and even called to make an appointment with the school therapist."

"Don't you think that's a little suspicious?"

"Yes, but anything could have sent her over the edge. The marks on her neck could have been a failed attempt earlier in the day before she decided on the noose. And then there's a little matter of the suicide note. Now have you found any evidence that contradicts anything I said?"

"No sir, but-"

"Then there you have it. It's an open and shut case."

"What about the missing student IDs? There's no way Rachel got into her room without it. We have proof Nicole was in class all day. She came back and supposedly hung herself; again, we didn't find her card. Our men searched that room from top to bottom and everything Nicole had on her. They still couldn't find it."

The lieutenant's brows narrowed at me. His cheeks flustered with a heated red glow. "I don't give a rat's ass about some stupid college IDs. Some punk kids probably found them and used whatever money was left on them to grab some food. I'm not wasting any more time, money, or personnel because you're worried about a card. These cases are closed."

"Yes, sir," I replied.

He pointed an accusatory finger at me. "That means no investigating on your own either. If you do, I'll see to it the Chief busts you down to school crossing guard; permanently."

Every officer in the station stared awkwardly at me as I exited Esposito's office. I wanted to slam the door in anger. My frustration grew to new heights over the Lieutenant's stubborn demands to leave the cases alone. Then again, he was probably more pissed off at me for telling Nicole's parents that I suspected their daughter was murdered without proper evidence to support my theory.

Rodney rushed to my side. He put his massive arm around me and escorted me back to our desks. "What the hell happened?"

"Let's just say I poked the bear with a beehive."

"That bad huh?"

"You heard him. He's threatening to demote me to a crossing guard if I keep investigating either case."

"I tried to warn you, Ali. I told you it wasn't a good idea. At least now you're finally gonna listen to reason."

I shook my head and opened the copy machine; taking each page from the folder, placing them inside and hitting the green copy button.

"What are you doing?" Rodney asked; snatching a page from my hands.

"What does it look like?"

"It looks like you're about to risk your career on a hunch."

I pulled Rodney closer. "I'm more than sure those girls were murdered, which means there's a killer on the loose. I'm not willing to wait around for him to strike again, especially with Amanda walking around campus."

"Ali, I love you and your sister. I'd do anything to protect both of you, but I can't risk my career for this case. I got a family to take care of."

"I don't expect you to. Just keep this between us for now and I'll handle the rest." I watched Rodney nod his affirmation. "No one can know what I'm up to."

"You have my word; just be careful."

Chapter 14-Ali

Nervous energy coursed through my body as I paced around my living room. Matthew was due to arrive at any moment for our double date with Amanda and her boyfriend. It was the first time I let him meet anyone I cared about. Truthfully, he was the first guy since high school I even contemplated introducing to anyone in my family. The last guy was Joey Peters in twelfth grade, and my father scared him off with a shotgun because I was twenty minutes late coming home. I moved away to college shortly after, and I never really got into a relationship until now.

The headlights beamed through the living room. I nearly jumped out of my skin. There was a knock on the door moments later. With a shaky hand, I turned the knob.

"H-hi," I managed to squeak out.

Matthew crossed the threshold and planted a kiss firmly on my lips. He pulled away with a smile. "I've been wanting to do that all day."

That was a perfect way to get out of the double date. "Well, we could always stay in and do a little more of that instead of going to dinner."

Matthew took a step back. "I would love to take you up on that offer, but I was looking forward to meeting your sister tonight."

"Do we really have to do this?"

"Why don't you want me to meet her?"

"My sister can be a bit nosey. She already grilled me the other day about our date, and I'm sure she'll do the same to you."

"I'm sure she's not that bad."

"Oh, just wait," I told him. "She'll put you in the hot seat whether or not I'm around to save you."

"I'll take my chances." Matthew put his arm around my waist and ushered me out the door. "Come on; it won't be as bad as you think."

We walked to his car where he held the door open for me. I climbed into the passenger seat and silently prayed for the night to be over quickly. I stared out the window as Highland passed by us. It didn't take us long to cross the border into New Paltz, but it wasn't until we turned into the parking lot of Pasquales Pizza and Italian Restaurant that my anxiety took over.

My leg bounced up and down in the passenger seat. Matthew's big strong hand caressed my knee. The touch of his skin on mine calmed me down instantly. He looked me in the eyes as if he was asking if I was okay.

"I'm better now; thanks," I told him.

"Good, then let's go inside and meet your sister."

We entered the restaurant, which didn't seem like much had changed since the last time I walked in their doors about three years ago. The red booths were still scattered around the dining area. Matthew was a little overdressed for the occasion. A suit and tie weren't typically worn by their customers unless they were picking up food to go. I wore a jean skirt and v-neck shirt with a pair of sandals. We approached the younger couple at the counter.

My sister and her boyfriend looked like the usual college kids. She was wearing skinny jeans and a teal tank top with her hair hanging just over her shoulders. Sean had on a pair of camo shorts with a black t-shirt with some band I had never heard of. His dirty blonde hair made it look like he hadn't showered in a week, and his facial piercings made me cringe every time I looked at him. There were two hoop-style earrings in each eyebrow, one on his lip, large plugs in each earlobe, and a hoop in his nose connecting each nostril.

"Whoa, what's with the suit, man?" Sean asked.

Amanda smacked his arm and stared him down. She muttered something to him to make her boyfriend step back and hide behind her.

"Hey, sis," she said. "I'm sorry about Sean. He's not used to people dressing nicer than a pair of jeans."

I let out a chuckle and tried to ignore her idiot boyfriend's comment. I gave my sister a hug and introduced her to Matthew. I looked up and nodded to Sean. I barely said hello to him before we grabbed a booth for all of us to fit in.

"So, Matthew," Amanda began. Our butts hadn't even touched the seat yet, and I could already sense she was about to launch into a series of questions. "Tell me about yourself."

Matthew grabbed a menu to look over. His eyes were focused on the items listed instead of looking at Amanda. "There's really not much to know. I grew up in Albany as the oldest of three. I have a younger brother and a sister."

"What made you decide to move down here?" she continued probing.

"I traveled around a bit after college and decided I liked the Ulster and Dutchess Counties the best. I found a place to suit my needs and the rest is history." Matthew pushed the menu in front of my face. "How are the ribeyes here?"

You've gotta be kidding me. I knew the sign said restaurant, but we were at a pizza place and Matthew was thinking about ordering a steak. I shook my head and pointed out the regular items people ordered. "I think you should forget about the ribeye and get either a pizza or a Panini."

I saw the look of disappointment on his face. I wanted to tell him to suck it up; we were on a date with two college students.

"Okay, can you get the waiter or waitress's attention when you see them?" he asked.

Poor guy, he really wasn't used to eating at a college town. "You have to go up and order the food," I replied.

Matthew stood up and pulled out a wad of money held together with a gold money clip. Sean's eyes grew larger at the sight of it.

"Dude, where'd you get all that cash?" I saw my sister nudge him with her elbow to stop Sean from being more of an ass.

"My company does very well for itself," Matthew replied.

"What kind of work do you do?" Amanda questioned.

That was something I wanted to know as well. I was curious to see how he was going to skate around that topic since he couldn't shut her up with a kiss.

Matthew raised an eyebrow but shrugged off the question. "What kind of pizza does everyone want?"

He completely ignored it as if my sister had not spoken. I was ready to jump in to bring the topic back from food, but Amanda's boyfriend decided to dig his hole a little deeper.

"I could go for a few meat lovers slices."

I got up to walk Matthew to the front counter. "Can we get two large pies; one meat lovers, and one with chicken and broccoli?" he asked.

The woman behind the register asked if we wanted any drinks. I told her four, and she handed me medium cups colored in the Italian flag.

"So, what are your intentions with my sister?" Amanda asked as she pushed her way between Matthew and me. I didn't even see her get up from the table. I glanced back and her idiot boyfriend was still there.

"Excuse me?" Matthew replied seemingly taken aback by Amanda's direct question. I tried to warn him. Knowing this would just get worse; I decided to step in to intervene.

"Amanda," I snapped.

"What? I'm simply curious about your boyfriend. I wanna make sure he's not just using you to get laid."

"Matthew, would you excuse us?" I grabbed my sister by the arm and marched her out the door. "You're way out of line."

"I'm just looking out for you, Ali."

"I appreciate it, but I'm the older sister. Whatever is going on between Matthew and I is none of your business." Hell, we hadn't even approached the whole putting a label on it conversation. I didn't need my sister scaring off my man with talks about sex and relationships statuses.

She folded her arms and stared me down. "Fine, I'll tone it down on one condition; you need to be nicer to Sean."

"Deal," I replied. I looked back inside the restaurant and saw how he looked again. "But can you do something with his wardrobe; like burn it?"

We laughed and rejoined the table. Sean was already digging into the food before we had a chance to sit down. I decided to play nice like I promised, and thankfully Amanda backed off Matthew. The night seemed to get better until I heard a commotion from another table. I glanced over at another young couple sitting at a lone table.

"You're sorry," the boy barked at the girl.

Nearly every head in the building turned towards them. He must have realized how loud he had been because he leaned forward to finish his argument with his date. I couldn't hear anything else they said. I considered walking by just to make sure the girl was okay, but Matthew put a hand on my lap.

"You're not on duty tonight, and she's not in any danger."

"Yeah, sis," Amanda added. "College relationships break-up and get back together all the time. It's about as bad as high school."

I was sure they were right. I settled back down in my chair and focused on enjoying my pizza. A few minutes later, I looked over at my sister.

"Do you wanna come with me to freshen up?"

We got up from the table and walked around the dining area and headed towards the bathrooms. The girl from earlier was sitting alone at her table. The boy she was arguing with was nowhere to be seen.

I guess Amanda was right; college kids break-up all the time and I guess she was just dumped.

<u>Chapter 15-CK</u>

Mark stood in the darkened hallway outside a familiar paint-chipped door. It had been months since he had last stepped foot in the abandoned building. The last visit took place after one of his meetings, the same one where he decided to kill Rachel and Nicole. He walked around it late at night and broke one of the planks of wood that boarded up the entrance.

Take what you want, he thought.

He did just that. Two of the people who ruined his life were now dead. The thought brought a sadistic grin to his face as he reached above the frame to retrieve the key. Mark remembered the layout and moved to the wall where a flashlight sat on a dresser. With a flick of a switch, a beam of light lit the way to his destination.

Home sweet home!

His eyes focused on the dusty white sheets that covered an old desk. Inside a drawer was a key he'd stashed during his last visit. He took it to the closet and removed a panel of the wall revealing a small brown box with two lion head handles. Using the key, he unlocked the box. His hand swept the inside feeling the red velvet lining. Mark took the two New Paltz IDs from his pocket and held them under the light.

Rachel Walker...Nicole Sherman...it's time to put you in your rightful place...in a box and forgotten.

He removed the false-bottom and tossed the IDs inside before sealing them within the confines of the box. After putting everything back in their places, he snuck out of the building and fixed the entrance to make it look like no one had been there. It was his secret sanctuary, but it was time to go back to the real world.

Two down and two to go! It's time to go hunting!

He returned to his apartment without running into a single person. No one noticed him or questioned his new look as he climbed the two flights of stairs to his door. He slipped inside and shut out the rest of the world as he sat at the rusty old metal desk. He did his best to silently open the drawer, but the screeching noise could not be avoided. The folded piece of paper was within grasp. He removed it and stared at the list. Using a red marker, Mark crossed off Nicole Sherman's name.

The plan was working perfectly. He felt on top of the world. Two of the four responsible for his year of misery were dead from his hand. The police were scrambling to figure out what happened to the girls, but he made sure to cover his tracks well enough to avoid suspicion. Rachel's death was believed to be an accident. Thanks to the planted search history and fake letter, Nicole's death was most likely ruled a suicide.

Mark placed the paper back into the drawer and closed it before getting up to look at himself in the mirror. He admired the man reflecting back him. The new version had succeeded in doing things he wouldn't have normally accomplished. It gave him the confidence to go after one more thing he wanted; Jess. Unfortunately, he couldn't flaunt his new look around her the way he did on campus.

With a little bit of water and his brush, Mark flattened his hair and pushed it to the side. He took his contacts out and replaced them with his black-rimmed glasses. In a matter of moments, he had transformed back into the geeky version of himself.

Mark pulled out a long brown sleeve shirt from his dresser and pulled it over his head before making the trip across the hall to Jess's room. With a deep breath, he knocked on the door. She pulled it open and smiled.

"Hey, buddy; what's up?"

He drank in how cute she looked wearing nothing but a tank top and shorts that threatened to show a little too much. She had her glasses on as well.

"I'm thinking of running out for some pizza. I wanted to see if you wanna go."

Jess placed a finger to her lips as if her decision was going to be a life altering event. "I could go for a slice or two. Is anyone else coming with us?"

Mark knew his neighbor was so close to saying yes, but one question pending a response stood in the way of taking Jess on a date. He wondered if telling her the truth would change her mind.

"No, it's just the two of us."

"Yeah, I'm down for it. I just need a few minutes to get ready."

"Take your time," he told her.

The door closed. Mark was sure Jess was changing into something more appropriate to go into public wearing. He didn't really care what she wore. He was ecstatic she agreed to go out with him. He pumped his fist in the air in silent celebration. He stood inside his bedroom with the door open waiting for Jess to emerge.

"I'm all set," she finally said while entering the hall.

Mark locked up his room and walked with Jess downstairs and out to his car. They drove into town and parked in an open spot outside of Pasquales.

Mark held the door open in an attempt to show chivalry to the girl he wanted to call his own. They moved to the counter and placed an order to dine-in.

"Let's grab a table while we wait." Mark led the way to a single table with two chairs. "I'm really glad you decided to come out with me tonight."

Jess's cheeks glowed with a grin. "I never mind grabbing a bite to eat with a good friend."

That was not how the night was supposed to go. Mark considered their dinner to be a date, but Jess was pushing him towards the friend zone. They sat in awkward silence while Mark tried to think of another way to break down Jess's wall and cross into her dating world. As he opened his mouth to speak, a woman called out.

"Number forty-two…number forty-two; your food's ready."

"That's us," Jess said sounding slightly relieved. She stood up at the same time as Mark. "Relax, I got it." She pushed in her chair and darted to the front counter.

Mark watched her walk away. The smile he had earlier in the night faded fast. He was on a downward spiral which would take a miracle to recover from. His fingers drummed nervously on the table in anticipation for his neighbor's return. This was his one and only chance to make a move, and he was going to do it whether he was ready or not.

Jess came back to the table holding a tray with four slices of pizza and two cups. It was set down between them. Mark reached for her hand, which Jess reluctantly allowed him to grasp. Her eyes had an uneasy look to them.

"Jess, you know how you were saying we were good friends?"

"Yeah," she replied.

Mark saw her eyes dart around the room. He could almost hear her thoughts; *don't do it. Please don't make your big confession. Don't ruin our friendship.*

"I've been thinking things over, and well…I've liked you for a long time. I was kinda thinking maybe we could go out on a real date sometime; like as a couple."

"I'm sorry," she said. "I don't really think that's a good idea."

Mark replayed the summer nights of Jess knocking on his door at night; the hours of watching T.V. and movies together; the staying up late eating popcorn and talking. All of it suggested there were more than just feelings of friendship.

"You're sorry," he snapped. Every head in the restaurant turned towards them.

Jess pulled her hand away. "Look, you're a great friend, and I like you a lot. I just don't think of you like a boyfriend. You understand; right?"

Mark couldn't comprehend what was happening. Everything he did since the spring semester; the meetings; the transformation; the newfound confidence was all meant to lead up to the moment where he got the girl. He finally confessed his feelings for her only to be rejected in a pizzeria with strangers watching the most embarrassing moment of his life.

"Yeah, I get it," he lied.

Anger filled his body as he sat there staring at the woman who he would have done anything for, but she didn't want him. Mark shoved the pizza down his throat; gobbling up as much as he could to end the miserable night. He already finished one slice when the regret of telling Jess how he felt consumed him. He excused himself and walked up to the counter to ask for a take-home box. That's when he noticed two women walking towards him.

He recognized one of them as a girl from campus. Mark was sure they even had a class together last semester. But it was the older woman who drew his attention. The long, black curly hair was a memorable feature of the woman he saw in Esopus the morning Rachel Walker's body was found dead. He was staring at the detective assigned to investigate the deaths on campus. She was in charge of bringing him to justice, but that was something she hadn't discovered yet.

Mark grabbed the box and hurried back to the table. "Hey, something came up at work and they need me to go in tonight."

Jess looked guilty. "A-are you sure? If this is about before-"

"No, we're good." It was outright lie, but he couldn't tell his neighbor why he was in such a rush to get out of there. "I just really need to get going." He finished packing up his food as he downed his drink. "I'll meet you at the car."

Mark rushed outside and breathed a sigh of relief the moment he sat behind the wheel. His paranoia forced him to make a rash decision, one which confirmed his third kill; his friendship and romantic feelings for Jess.

Chapter 16-Ali

It has been two weeks since the passing of Rachel Walker and Nicole Sherman. October rolled in quicker than I imagined, bringing a chill to the air. My case load had been slow, so I kept doing busy-body work to keep myself out of the lieutenant's doghouse. No matter what I did; he was still watching me like a hawk. I could feel his intense stare everywhere I went. I could see the blinds in his window pried apart as if he thought we had no clue he was spying on us. It was almost like he was begging for someone to slip up, and I was the focal point of that obsession.

Rodney noticed it too, but he used his size to capture moments of my time. His tall and bulky frame blocked the lieutenant's view whenever Rodney stood over my shoulder. He leaned in and brought his voice to a whisper.

"Have you found any new leads on those cases you're working on?"

I was shocked to hear my partner ask me about something which could get me in serious trouble. Rodney wasn't the type of person to defy a superior. His question made me wonder if this was his way of telling me he found something I could use.

I turned my head slightly and placed a finger to my lips. I nodded towards the lieutenant's office. Okay, I was being a bit paranoid, but I wouldn't put it passed Esposito to bug my desk. It was highly improbable and downright illegal, but he would do it if possible.

I pointed to the entrance. "Not here," I whispered. "Let's talk outside in five minutes."

Rodney moved away and grabbed a cup of sludge, our station's version of coffee. I waited a minute before grabbing my jacket and headed to the parking lot. Rodney showed up two minutes later as if it was part of his normal routine.

"I think we're good," he said.

We walked towards my car and leaned on the hood. "I've been racking my brain trying to figure something out, but I haven't turned up anything to support my theory." I pinched my thumb and forefinger to the inside of corners of my eyes massaging them gently. "And thanks to the lieutenant being on my ass; I haven't been able to talk to anyone at the dorms or the New Paltz campus. All I have to go on are the files I copied from the initial reports."

"Yeah, Esposito has been monitoring everyone. I guess he thinks one of us will do the dirty work to get you whatever answers you're looking for."

"He knows me better than that. I wouldn't ask anyone to put their necks on the line for me because of a hunch. I just wish he gave me enough time and space to investigate freely. One week is all I need."

Rodney chuckled and walked back to his car. He opened the rear driver's side door and pulled out a black workout bag. I was about to make a comment about him finally making the decision to go back to the gym. Then, he unzipped it and showed me the contents. There were a stack of folders inside.

"You can thank me later," he said while handing me the bag.

"Thanks, but what exactly are all of these files?"

"I called in a favor. One of my buddies hacked Nicole's web history and printed out everything she did in the last month. I figured this could keep you busy for a while. Hell, you might even get a lead or two."

I zipped up the bag and tossed it in the back of my car. "Rodney, you're amazing; thank you." I gave him a big hug. He came through for me without asking him. I loved him being my partner. There's no one in this world I would ever want to replace him with.

"Just don't let the lieutenant catch you with those. He will have both of our asses for it."

"I won't say anything." I wanted to run home and start reviewing the files, but there was still too much time left on my shift. Thankfully, I didn't have any plans once I clocked out; that was until my phone rang. The call came from a number I didn't recognize. "Ryan here," I answered.

"Ah, Detective Ryan," Dr. Wu's monotone voice said. "I was wondering what you're doing for dinner tonight."

Crap, so much for going over those files. I wanted to make up a lie to stop any chance he had to ask me out. Unfortunately, I owed him for helping me with the Nicole Sherman files. "I'm pretty much free; why?"

"I was wondering if you'd mind meeting me for some sushi. I know a great place in Poughkeepsie."

"I don't know, Dr. Wu. I don't like to mix my personal and professional lives together," I replied with a hint of uncertainty.

"Please, call me Fred."

Rodney nudged my arm. "You owe him," he reminded me again. "We don't need the M.E. pissed at us."

"Sure Fred, what time?"

"Meet me at Osho around seven."

He hung up rather abruptly. I was very confused by what happened, but of course my partner had to be annoying and turn it into something more.

"Aw, looks like someone's gotta crush on you, Ali."

I shoved Rodney as we walked up to the double doors. Lieutenant Esposito was waiting for us; tapping his foot impatiently.

"Where the hell were you two?"

"We went for a smoke break," I lied. There was no way I could let him know what we were *really* talking about.

"Neither of you smoke," he stated. The bass in his voice increased the volume of his annoyance.

"Consider it a fresh air break," I blurted out.

Lieutenant Esposito's face was burning red. He was about two seconds from ripping us a new one. "There's no such thing as a fresh air break."

"You mean to tell me smokers can get a fifteen-minute break to light up a cigarette but two non-smokers can't go outside for a few minutes for some fresh air? If I didn't know any better, I'd say you were discriminating against non-smokers." I was poking the bear with a beehive again, but it had been a couple of weeks, so I felt it was needed.

Esposito reached his breaking point. The vein was about to burst out of his head. "You keep running your mouth and I'll have you working as the precinct janitor. Now get your ass back inside and get to work!" He liked to threaten me with demotions, but he never followed through with any of them. Maybe it was because I hit the brakes before crashing into that brick wall.

I spent the rest of the day wondering what Dr. Wu wanted. Was this a date? If it was, I needed to find a way to let him down gently, so this way he wasn't upset or thought I led him on in some way. After work, I went home and placed the bag of files on my bed. They would need to wait until after my dinner with Dr. Wu. I didn't want him to think this was anything more than two colleagues having a bite to eat, so I stayed in my work clothes and headed out to Poughkeepsie.

I met Dr. Wu in front of Osho. He was standing outside the restaurant wearing a pair of jeans and a dark colored hoodie. He didn't look like his usual self. In fact, he seemed jumpy and nervous. I noticed him glancing over his shoulders and around the corners as if he was expecting to get busted by a cop for pedaling drugs.

"Hi, Dr. Wu; is everything okay?"

"Please, call me Fred," he replied. "Come with me." He laced his fingers with mine and pulled me into the restaurant. His palm was sweaty as it pressed against my skin. "Two please," he told the hostess before quickly following her and dragging me with him.

We sat down in a small booth facing each other. Fred was quiet and stared a hole through me. *Was this how he treated all of his dates? It would explain why he used a favor to ask me out.*

"Thank you for coming out tonight." He tried to reach for my hand again, but this time I pulled it away.

"I don't know what's going on or why you asked me out, but I need to tell you; I have a boyfriend."

I waited for his response or even a change in his demeanor. Instead, my words had no effect on him. His eyes weren't even looking at me. His head was bobbing around; turning in every direction as if he were looking for something or someone. He was acting just as squirrely as he did outside the restaurant. I snapped my fingers twice in front of his face to bring his attention back to me.

"I'm sorry; did you say something, detective?"

"I said I have a boyfriend."

Fred let out a chuckle. "Did you think I was asking you on a date?"

I was completely confused. "Then, why did you ask me to dinner?"

He leaned forward and brought his voice to a whisper. "I need your help. I think someone is following me."

"What? Why would someone be following you?"

"I don't know, but I swear someone is stalking me. Every morning I leave for work and see the same blue van parked either across the street, next door or down the block from my house."

"Maybe it's a neighbor and they got a new car. It could also be a new boyfriend or girlfriend spending the night at your neighbor's place."

"No, I asked around. No one knows who it belongs to and they don't recall seeing a blue van."

That was a bit concerning. "How long has this been happening?"

"A few weeks," Fred replied. "The first time I noticed it, there was a guy sitting in the front seat. He was some big muscular blonde guy."

"I'll look into it. Maybe I can send a patrol unit to keep an eye on you or swing by your house on occasion to make sure everything is okay."

Fred sunk back against his seat. "You think I'm overreacting."

"No, not at all," I replied. "Tell me everything you know about this van. What time do you see it? Do you see it when you get home? Do you see it throughout the day?"

"No, I only see the van when I leave in the morning."

The situation presented gave me an idea. It wasn't something I wanted to share with Fred just yet. I needed to flush out some more information first. Before I could ask another question, Fred's head tilted to the side. He was staring at the entrance. I looked back and saw there was a man with bulging muscles standing in the doorway.

"That's him; he's here."

"Are you sure that's him?"

"Yes," Fred replied. "I'm positive. What do we do?"

"Stay here; I'll handle it."

I rose to my feet and reached for my badge. I stared down the muscular man as he pushed the door open and let a small Asian woman enter.

Fred pushed me out of the way and ran to the entrance. "Hannah, what are you doing here? What are you doing here with this…" he couldn't find the words, but it was obvious what happened.

The small Asian woman's mouth hung open in disbelief. She took a step back and hid behind the muscle-bound gorilla.

The big man stepped up to Fred. "You better back off, buddy. She's with me."

"Hannah is my wife." Fred was trying to stand up to the man, but he was picking a fight with someone more than twice his size.

The muscular man flexed as the vein stood out against his fake tanned skin. I could tell he was someone who used self-tanner to alter his appearance.

"She's done with you. She found herself a real man."

Fred lost all composure and shoved the guy as hard as he could. Unfortunately, he didn't even budge. The big man grinned and punched Fred squarely on the jaw. My colleague was knocked to the ground. His black-rimmed glasses skidded across the wood surface next to his face. I ran to Fred's side just as the big man hovered over with a fist still clenched.

"Get the fuck away from him," I growled.

"Keep out of this lady," he snarled. "This is none of your business."

"I'm making it my business." I stood up and flashed my badge. "You're under arrest for assaulting this man."

"You're a cop?" The tone in his voice while asking the question was insulting. It was like he was saying there's no way someone who looked like me could be a police officer. Then his eyes looked me up and down. "You should come down to my gym. I can help you stretch and work you out *real* good, baby."

"I'll pass; mostly on the count of you being in jail. Plus, I don't work out with low-life douchebags."

I still had my handcuffs on me since I never got changed when I came home from work. I reached for them, but the big man quickly shoved me to the ground.

"Fuck you, bitch," he called out as he ran out the door.

I guess I have to really work for my dinner tonight.

I jumped to my feet and took off after him. There was no way I could take on a guy that size if he squared up to me. I had to work smarter, not harder. I dove at his legs and smashed my shoulder into the back of his left knee. He dropped to the ground but he tried to struggle back to his feet. I quickly kicked out the right knee with the heel of my shoe.

That'll teach him not to make a woman run in heels.

He tried to shove me away and knocked me back a few feet. I could tell he wasn't going to do this the easy way. Unfortunately, my only options were to let him go or to get physical. He grabbed me and tried to throw me into a parked car. That made my decision clear. I placed the cuffs around my knuckles and clocked him in the jaw. The big man was down and out on the ground.

"You have the right to remain silent." I snapped the handcuffs around his wrists and rolled him over. The big man's eyes were shut. "Well, I guess you'll be silent for a while."

I whipped out my cell and called it in. I told them my name, my badge number, and that the suspect was in custody for assault, assaulting an officer, and resisting arrest. They had a unit out there in five minutes to pick up the scumbag.

Fred appeared moments later holding a bag of ice to his jaw. He pointed at the big man. "Did you do that to him?"

"You wanted my help," I joked. "Come on; I'll take you to the station so you can make a statement."

Fred glanced back at the restaurant. His wife stood at the entrance. "What do I do about her?"

"For starters; I'd get a good divorce lawyer. I might actually know someone who can help. And I suggest getting a jump on it first thing tomorrow before your wife tries to spin the story in her favor."

Chapter 17-CK

Mark spent the last couple of weeks hiding in his room. He hadn't seen or heard from Jess since their disastrous date at Pasquales. It wasn't even a date. She'd considered it two friends having some pizza. The "Friend Zone" confirmation fueled Mark's anger. His emotions were getting the better of him, and it was time to unleash them on another victim.

No more waiting. It's time!

Mark opened a dresser drawer and retrieved a black sweatshirt and ball cap. He grabbed a backpack with some books to help blend in as a student. There was a specific target in mind, and he needed to conduct a stakeout to find her.

He checked the peephole to make sure the coast was clear. Jess's door was still closed and there wasn't any light shinning under the opening at the bottom. Mark took that moment to make a run for it. He wanted to get out of the house before running into any of the other occupants, not like any of them would recognize him.

The glowing sun disappeared behind a wall of darkness as Mark drove towards campus. The street-lamps flickered on to provide just enough light to illuminate a path, but there wasn't enough for someone to catch onto his plans.

Sitting outside of the dorms was a risky move. Half of the students on campus believed there could be a killer on the loose. There had been a buzz since someone claimed a detective told Nicole Sherman's parents she suspected foul play in their daughter's death. The campus police were patrolling the areas around the dorms more than usual. It didn't matter; they had no idea who or what they were looking for.

Mark left his car in the commuter lot across from Esopus. His eyes stared up at the building with a grin on his face.

I never have to step foot in there again.

There were no more targets living in that dorm. His sights were now set on a bigger fish. His eyes shifted to the larger building in the distance. The path from the parking lot took him to a small wall of stones layered knee-high. It was surrounded by a cluster of trees. It provided the cover he needed to keep him hidden from most students and campus police patrols. It also gave him a visual on another dorm, Lenape Hall. It was the largest of the housing for on-campus students, one that everyone wanted to live in. It was the newest, cleanest, and most up to date dorm created in New Paltz.

Mark settled in on the wall. His psychology textbook sat open on his lap to chapter four, but his eyes never glanced at the page. They were too busy combing the walkway for anyone walking to or leaving

Lenape. The wait wasn't long. A young man in his late teens turned the corner onto Loop Road and headed right for the dorm.

The book was placed back in the backpack. Mark pulled a small cell phone from his pocket and pretended to be on a call as the student passed. He followed the kid to the back door of the dorm, staying close behind him. A swipe of the ID, and the entrance was unlocked. Mark allowed the door to swing closed, but he managed to stop it just before it locked.

Great, now that I'm in; how the fuck do I find her?

Mark hadn't considered how to locate his next target. He only knew she moved into the new building after being placed on the waiting list. The dorm had four floors of rooms to check, which wasn't going to be easy to check. It would take forever to go door-to-door, and it wasn't like he could ask someone for help. That would definitely tip off police if someone claimed to be looking for a girl who turned up dead a few days later.

Mark walked through the first floor and passed several rooms on the way to the lobby. It was big enough to be the size of a small house. Blueish-gray couches lined the walls while high-rise tables and pub chairs filled in the gaps. It was impressive.

Damn, maybe I should have applied to be on the waitlist. He tried to remain inconspicuous as he moved around the lobby. He needed to find a way to locate students without making it obvious he was searching for something. *Where is it?*

He noticed the wall of mailboxes near the front entrance. It was his best shot at figuring out what room his target lived in. He bent down thinking names would be listed but only found numbers instead. It was another dead end. His plan was thwarted by the New Paltz education system. His attempt to locate the next person on his list was foiled by a mailbox.

A loud ding echoed through the lobby. Someone was about to get off the elevator. Mark was in danger of being seen. Quickly, he ran to one of the couches and ripped his text-book out of his backpack. He hid behind the theories of Sigmund Freud as a curly haired brunette approached the same mailboxes which outwitted him moments before. She took a key from her pocket and dropped to her knees.

You're making this so easy for me.

Mark did his best to contain the cackles of laughter threatening to blow his cover. The girl exited the building through a set of glass doors. Little did she know; she had just given the man hunting her the information he had been desperate to obtain. With a grunt of pleasure, Mark counted the columns and rows until he located the mailbox the girl had just opened. The room number was set in his mind, but now he had another item on his agenda for the night.

Where is she going this late?

Mark hurried outside and followed the girl. Her curls bounced off the gray New Paltz sweatshirt with every step she took. He kept a discrete distance to avoid suspicion. Their travels took them to the other side of campus. Mark rounded the corner and followed his target up the concrete steps until they reached the Lecture Hall.

What the hell is she doing here?

Most classes ended before six. There were very few which began later, but none were tempting enough for most students to drag themselves out late at night, especially when they were three hours long.

Mark entered the large communal area filled with hard wooden benches and tables. Bright orange and dark blue chairs were scattered over a beige and light-brown checkered carpet. His target walked through a cherry-wood door, which led to the classrooms. He followed but maintained his distance until he saw her stop in midway down the hall. She stood outside a room talking to a tall bald headed man with piercings in his eyebrows, nose, ears, and lips.

Oh, this should be interesting. It's time to say hello to old friends.

Mark entered the classroom with his head turned slightly to avoid eye contact with his target. He rushed to the last desk of the second row. His head rested on the psychology book he had been using as cover. Conversations continued around the room until a smiling couple entered holding hands. They closed the door and cleared their throats.

The rugged looking red-headed man was clean cut wearing cargo shorts and a green polo shirt. "Alright, guys; welcome to the Outdoors Club. We're keeping this meeting brief. We wanted to touch base with everyone." His eyes scanned the room with a smile on his face. "I see we have some new faces here tonight. Welcome; we look forward to getting to know you better."

Mark, the leader of the club, had noticed him as well, but he doubted any of them wanted to get to know him.

The girlfriend remained at the front of the room. "We typically meet Wednesday nights at eight. I hope you can make it to next week's meeting since we will be planning our first trip."

Another girl raised her hand. "Where are we going?"

"Typically, we go to Mohonk Mountain for the weekend. We're waiting to finalize the details and should have more information next week." The girlfriend walked to the teacher's desk and sat down while her boyfriend conducted the rest of the meeting.

Mark's focus remained on his target. She leaned in to speak to her friend. "Are you coming back?" she asked.

"I'm not a big fan of camping or hiking."

"Come on; it'll be fun. Please, just come back next week and hear what they have planned for the first trip."

"You know I'm not really an outdoors type of person," he replied.

"Please, Kevin; it would really mean a lot to me."

"Fine, one more meeting."

Mark listened intently. His tongue rubbed the tip of his tooth with anticipation. *Well, I know where I'll be next week.*

Chapter 18-Ali

The lieutenant refused to speak to me for the rest of the week. His only form of communication consisted of grunts or nods when he passed me; otherwise he ignored me all together. I stood outside his door for what seemed like hours, but in reality it was less than a minute, before knocking on his door. My anxiety was anticipating his wild temper. It almost caused me to hesitate knocking on his door.

"Hey, lieu; do you have a minute?"

He rolled his eyes at me while his face turned redder than a tomato. "What do you want, Ryan?"

"I know it's short notice, but I was hoping to take a few days off."

He almost fell out of his chair after hearing my request. "Let me get this straight; you want time away from here?" The lieutenant took a moment to think it over. Then, he did something I rarely got to see; he smiled. "Take as much time as you need."

His expression was priceless. I swore it was going to be the first night he went home to his wife and didn't start drinking because of me. I was happy he didn't ask why the sudden decision to take time off. The lieutenant would have exploded if he knew the reason was to investigate Rachel Walker and Nicole Sherman's cases.

The lieutenant was so eager to get rid of me; he actually gave me the rest of the afternoon off. I decided to go for a drive into New Paltz to enjoy a cool brisk day while sipping coffee. I ordered my grande soy latte and sat at a table overlooking Main Street. My eyes were set on my favorite spot; P&G's Bar and Restaurant. It had been a place I had known since my time in college. I spent many nights bar hopping in New Paltz with P&Gs being my go-to spot. Their food was delicious too. I was getting hungry just thinking about the place.

"Care for some company?" a familiar voice asked.

I turned my head to see Amanda and Sean standing next to me. I quickly suppressed my annoyance at the sight of my sister's boyfriend. He stood there wearing baggy jeans and a white tank top guys referred to as wife-beaters.

I guess she didn't convince him to burn his wardrobe.

I took my feet off the chair across from me and sat up straight. "Hi, what are you guys doing here?"

"Our class got out early and we thought it would be good to go for a walk and get some coffee. Sean and I have a test tomorrow. We need all the fuel we can get for our cram session."

There were too many words used that put bad thoughts in my head. I hated the idea of my sister spending a lot of time in Sean's room to "study." It usually meant the guy wanted to get his girlfriend alone to make-out or take things up a notch while his roommate was in class. Add in my sister talking about a cram session, and I almost lost it. I could feel the vomit rising; resting at the base of my throat. I faked a cough and held a napkin to my mouth.

They were about to go inside, but I decided to put my skills as a detective and big sister to use. "Hey, since you guys are here; do you mind answering a few questions?" Technically, I wasn't poking around campus. I just happened to have two students who may have interacted with the victims meet me for coffee.

"Oh no," Amanda replied. "You're not suckering us into helping you work one of your cases."

Sean's eyes lit up. "Wait, you mean; I can be a part of an official investigation?"

"Not quite," I replied. I kicked out a chair towards him. "But I do need some help. What do you know about Rachel Walker and Nicole Sherman?"

Amanda shoved the seat back to the table. "I already told you; I didn't really know them."

"Ha, why would you want to?" Sean smirked.

"What do you mean?" I could tell he knew more than I originally thought. Hopefully, he could shed some light on the girls.

Sean pulled another towards the table and placed it next to me. Truthfully, he was sitting closer to me than I would've preferred. But if he was willing to give me some answers, it might be worth it.

"I've run into them a few times, mostly during my freshman year. I had English with them." I watched Sean look off in the distance for a moment as if he was reliving the memory of his time with them. He shivered as his focus returned to our conversation. "I couldn't wait for that class to be over."

"Tell me about them?"

"Nicole was a little know-it-all. She was always butting into everyone's conversations. It was like she was right no matter what, and everyone else was wrong."

"What about Rachel?" I asked.

"You mean Two-Face?" He must have seen the confusion on my face. "Rachel was always nice to people, but she talked so much crap behind their backs."

It was beginning to sound like there was a lot more suspects than I originally realized. "Would you say they had a lot of enemies?"

"No idea, but I wouldn't doubt it. Those two just rubbed people the wrong way." I could tell by Sean's flaring nostrils they had crossed him at some point. Unfortunately, I couldn't dig deeper into it with my sister around.

"Ali, do you really think someone did this to them?" Amanda asked. I could see the fear creeping back in her eyes. It was the same fear I saw when the police prowled around Esopus.

I decided to come clean. I moved closer and brought my voice to a whisper. "To be honest; yeah, I think someone killed them." I watched them sit back in horror. "Look, I can't go into specifics, but I found evidence which could contradict the suicide theory.

"Then, why not bring it up to your boss?"

"I tried, but his mind is set on the initial decision. Either he really doesn't believe there's a killer on the loose or he's in complete denial."

Sean sat rigid in his chair. "Wait, you mean to tell me you're going rogue?" He held his hand up in the air. "Way to stick it to the man."

I hesitantly connected with his high-five. "Thanks; I guess. Listen, I need your help."

"Yeah, you got it; whatever you need."

I wasn't really directing the question at Sean, but I liked his enthusiasm. Amanda seemed to not like her boyfriend voicing his willingness to help. Her eyes had daggers pointed in his direction.

My sister glanced back at me. "What do you need us to do?"

They were going to be my eyes and ears on campus. "I need you call me if you see anything or anyone suspicious."

"Do I get a badge or something?" Sean asked.

Amanda smacked his arm to shut him up. "You got it, sis." She tugged on her boyfriend's arm. "Come on; we gotta run."

I nodded and took a sip of my latte. Amanda and Sean stood up to go inside for their coffee, but I grabbed her boyfriend's arm.

"I need you to keep an eye on my sister for me, and make sure nothing happens to her."

"Trust me, Ali; I'd do anything to protect her." He pulled his arm free and took my hand. "I'd die for her."

I was happy to hear Sean say that. It actually made me like him a little bit. I just hoped he would never have to lay his life on the line for Amanda.

I took the afternoon to walk around town, savored my lunch from P&G's and eventually went for a late afternoon run. I needed some me-time to distress, *even* for a short time. It wasn't until I got home later that everything started to hit me at once. Weeks of death, investigations, and being screamed at circled my head as I lowered myself into the white porcelain tub. The hot water and soothing bubbles covered my body as I stretched my long legs. My feet dangled over the side. I wanted to let go of everything bothering me, but I couldn't; not with a possible lunatic on the loose. If I was right, someone was killing innocent girls and staging their deaths to look like suicides.

Why doesn't anyone see it like I do?

I was the only one who believed there was something more to these deaths. I wanted to ask why; why was the lieutenant hell bent on closing the cases? Why couldn't he see things from my perspective? In the short time I worked for him; he'd never once stifled me or kept me from acting on my hunches. Going out on a limb was one of the reasons he chose me to be a detective for his station.

Despite his orders, I was compelled to keep investigating the Rachel Walker and Nicole Sherman cases. I needed to know there wasn't someone out there killing students, especially when my sister was going to school there.

The bubbles slowly disappeared. I could see my legs peeking out through the cloudy water. It was time to get out of the tub; maybe watch a little T.V. or call it an early night. I sat up and pulled the plug. The water slowly drained until there was nothing left. I stood up to grab a towel feeling droplets run down my naked body. There was an eerie feeling running through my body. I quickly pulled on a forest green bathrobe. I wrapped the belt tightly as a sense of danger continued. It was almost like someone was watching me. I stood on my tiptoes and looked out the small window into the backyard.

It's nothing; I'm just being paranoid.

I got out of the tub and stepped into a pair of fuzzy slippers. Something urged me to check outside. I felt like someone was prowling around my yard. I threw open the cabinet doors and pulled a spare Glock from under my sink. My back leaned against the wall. Slowly, I reached for the gold handle and ripped my bathroom door open. I knew the sound came from outside, but I needed to ensure my house was safe.

I cut across the hall. Shit, where's my phone?

I wasn't about to call the police. I was the police, but I still needed someone to have my back. The only person I trusted was Rodney. I quickly slipped into a pair of sweats and pulled on a tank top. I crept out of the room to begin my search for the trespasser.

"Damn it," a man's voice growled. It was accompanied by a loud thud. It sounded like it came from the front porch.

I had no time to reach out to Rodney or anyone else. My phone was still missing, and the person was at my front door. I gripped my gun and marched up to the peephole. A large man was bent over with a plastic bag at his feet. I flung the door open.

"Freeze, asshole!"

The man spun around and fell back into the banister. His hands raised into the air to surrender. The mocha clean-shaven face turned ghastly white.

"Shit, Ali; are you trying to give me a heart attack?" Matthew's chest rose and fell rapidly. His eyes settled on my gun. "Do you mind putting that away?"

"Sorry," I said while placing the Glock on the end table next to the door. "What are you doing here?"

"I tried your cell a few times, but you never picked up. I reached out to the station and someone named Rodney told me you were taking some time off. I figured I'd surprise you with some dinner, drinks, and a movie."

I glanced down at my deck and found a six pack of Bud in a broken plastic bag. Next to it was a small stack of DVDs and a large white pizza box.

"You're lucky I called out a warning and that I didn't call this into the station." I helped pick up the movies. "I really thought someone was trying to break into my house."

"I'm sorry, Ali. I just figured you're always busy taking care of everyone else; I thought it was time someone did the same for you."

"Come on inside." I helped Matthew inside the house. "I'll get us some plates and napkins. Do you want a glass for your beer?"

I watched him slip off his suit jacket. It was placed neatly over a chair. He grabbed a can of beer and popped the top.

"No, this is good."

I never really pictured him as a beer drinker. I pegged him for a wine guy. I mean; he always ordered it whenever we went out to eat. To see him kick back and relax with a beer was out of character. But watching him loosen his tie and opening the top three buttons on his shirt was a bit sexy. My eyes devoured him instantly.

"You know; that's a good look for you."

"What is?" he asked.

"The way you look right now. You seem so relaxed." I placed the plates on top of the pizza box and walked over to him. I straddled him on the couch, pulling his tie away from the collar. "Maybe next time we can get you into a pair of jeans."

That thought sent me over the edge. I used the opening of his shirt to pull him upright and into a hot passionate kiss. His hands started rubbing my back gently. My breathing quickened. I wanted him to take me right there; on the couch; the bedroom; anywhere as long as I was his. I fumbled with the rest of his shirt. It took every fiber in me not to rip the shirt completely open.

His large hand gently pushed me back. "Wait," he whispered.

I had waited long enough. This should have happened the night he took me to the Italian restaurant, but a death got in the way. I wasn't letting anything stop us tonight.

I cupped my hands against his cheeks. "I want you."

He pulled me away. "I was just going to say; I don't think our first time should be on your couch."

I jumped off his lap and pulled him to his feet. "I know just the right place." I led Matthew down the hall to my room. The door closed the moment we entered.

His hands grabbed my waist as his lips smothered my neck. It tickled at first, but it felt right. My knees got weak. I wanted to lose myself in his arms. He spun me around and guided me towards the bed. His lips moved down my neck to my collar bone. My tank top was cast aside, and Matthew's large hands explored my body.

We inched closer to the bed. I tripped and fell onto the mattress. Matthew smiled and began tugging my sweatpants off. I was completely naked. He managed to drop his pants before I had a chance to make a move. Then, he pressed against me. I could feel his girth plunge deep inside. I moaned in ecstasy as we rocked back and forth. It was everything I'd wanted; everything I needed. It was the perfect night.

Chapter 19-Ali

"Good morning, Hudson Valley," a loud voice said. The sound came from my alarm clock. "We're coming up on nine on this beautiful October morning. It is currently forty-six degrees out." I refused to open my eyes. I didn't want to admit the night was over. "Today will be partly cloudy; a high of fifty-five with a chance of showers this afternoon. Tonight will cool off with the overnight temperature going down to a low of forty."

My hand smacked the alarm clock; silencing the annoying DJ as they continued to ramble on about something pop-culture related. I really didn't want to hear any celebrity gossip or what happened on T.V. that week. My only concern was the man in my bed.

I reached back to where Matthew slept. The warmth of his skin was gone. There was nothing there but cold pillows and sheets. The smile I had last night was gone; replaced with a feeling of being used. I sat up in the bed and held the sheets to my chest. I could feel the emotions building up; ready to break free from my eyes. I went to search for my phone but found a note hanging from my lampshade.

Good morning, beautiful;

I hope you slept well. I'm sorry I wasn't there when you woke up. My office called this morning to drag me away. I promise to make it up to you. I left the movies on the coffee table. Maybe next time we'll actually spend some time watching them. I put the pizza and beer in the fridge last night after you fell asleep. I'll call you when I get done with work.

Matthew.

Every thought of being used or last night being a hook-up vanished from my mind. The smile I fell asleep with returned. Matthew was an incredible man. He always made me feel like I was the only woman in the world who mattered. I was stupid to think he would be anything less than the perfect guy.

I put my head back on the pillow and gazed at the window. I wanted to just lay there and wait for Matthew to call, but my eyes flickered to the alarm clock. It was already nine-thirty. A half hour had already been wasted on thinking about last night.

Get your ass out of bed, Ali, I thought. *You need to get up and get started on this case.*

The first thing I needed to do was clear my head. Going for a run was the best way to do just that. I went to my drawer and pulled out a pair of workout pants, a gray tank top and a New Paltz sweatshirt. With my hair tied back and my pink sneakers on; I was ready to take on these cases at full speed.

I parked my car in the dirt lot and headed up to the Walkway Over the Hudson. I put my earbuds in and set my music to my running playlist. I started out with a brisk walk while listening to "The End of Heartache" by Killswitch Engage. The first line was almost like my mind begging to find the answers. "Seek me; Call me; I'll be waiting."

My pace quickened in time with the music. I began jogging a minute later. It was the same speed I maintained for a quarter mile. The next song queued up. It was a faster paced hard rock/metal song, which triggered my feet to break into a full run. Three miles didn't seem so long when my mind was focused on the drums and lyrics in each song on the playlist.

I was halfway done with the return trip when I decided to take a small break. Sweat dripped down my face as the cool autumn air whipped a gentle breeze against my body. I stood near the rail and stared at the Hudson River. The sun glistened on the water. It was beautiful. I spent every morning for the last two years walking or jogging up the same path, and yet I never stopped to take in the picturesque scene surrounding me. It gave me a sense of peace and relaxation I hadn't felt in quite some time. It provided the clarity I needed to finally dive into the case files.

I walked the rest of the way back to the car and drove home. I went straight to the fridge to make a protein shake instead of making coffee. The files I "borrowed" from the station sat in the gym bag Rodney gave me. The answers I had been searching for were hidden somewhere within their contents. It was time to uncover the truth.

I separated them by each case with my ottoman being the divider. Rachel's files were placed on the left; Nicole's were moved to my right. I glanced through everything within the first hour, but nothing seemed to be jumping off the pages at me.

Come on, girls; give me something to work with.

I took to reviewing the crime scene photos. Rachel was lying in a perfectly made bed. Her lifeless eyes started at the ceiling. I thought back to my initial thoughts.

Someone who was drunk would climb into bed and pull the sheets over them.

I stared at the photo. There wasn't a single crease in the comforter. It was almost as if someone had placed her perfectly in the center of the bed. Then, I grabbed a set of pictures taken after Nicole's body had been found. I wasn't interested in the crime scene photos yet. I wanted to see the ones taken showing her side of the bedroom. The pink comforter had minor wrinkles. Her books and purse sat at the foot of the bed. I knew it was circumstantial, but both sets of pictures didn't match up to the circumstances surrounding their deaths.

No one would make their bed if they were thinking of committing suicide. Why would she even go to class?

I was certain neither girl died the way we thought. Someone else was with them. I just needed to know more. The pictures of the bodies were placed next to each other. Nicole's initial set of photos showed the noose marks. It was easy to jump to the suicide conclusion. If it wasn't for Fred pointing out the inconsistencies in the bruising, I wouldn't have known the difference.

Maybe if there was something overlooked on Nicole, there could be something we didn't notice about Rachel.

I examined the pictures of Rachel's body. She was fully clothed from her night out. There were grass stains on the knees and mud caked to the bottom of her ballet flats.

Questions began to form. Where did she fall? Was it earlier in the night? Did it happen on the way back to the dorm?

I remembered my conversation with Dr. Wu where he confirmed the findings of the BAC level and how Rachel would not be able to walk on her own after drinking that much alcohol. I needed his help in proving my theory. It was time to give the good doctor a call.

"Detective Ryan, this is a bit of a surprise." His voice wasn't his usual chipper self. It sounded like he had been replaced by a depressed, sleep-deprived version of him.

"I need your expert opinion on a case I'm working on, but I need you to keep it under wraps for now."

"You're referring to the two dead girls from New Paltz?"

The man had known me for only a couple of weeks, and he seemed to understand I wasn't going to let either case go as easily as my partner did.

"I know you said Rachel Walker's BAC level was two point six, and that she wouldn't have been able to walk or stand in that condition. Would she have been able to crawl?"

"If she could, our victim would not have made it far." He took a deep breath. "I know you think the second girl's death may not have been suicide. Are you thinking something similar for the first victim?"

"Do you think I'm crazy for thinking someone might have staged their deaths?"

"I am not a detective. I only use science to tell me what happened. Based on what you've said and what I observed; I think it could be a strong possibility."

Finally, someone who admitted my theory was more than just me trying to be a pain in the butt. It gave me hope that I could find a way to overturn the initial decision and get the cases re-open.

"Is that something you would be willing to tell my lieutenant?"

"I don't like to get in the middle of workplace discrepancies, but I will voice my opinion if you need me to."

I believed knocking out and arresting his wife's boyfriend caused Dr. Wu's opinion to lean in my favor. Just thinking back to that night made me feel bad for him all over again.

"How are things on the home front?" I asked.

"Hannah took everything and moved out. She told me she wanted to be with a real man."

"I'm so sorry, Fred. Did you get in touch with my friend?"

"Yes, she already put the paperwork together to be filed on Monday."

I guess that sealed the fate of his marriage. She already walked out on him, and he has everything ready to move forward with a divorce.

"You deserve better than this." I really meant it. He seemed like a nice guy who led with his heart. No one should have it stomped on and thrown away by the person they loved. "If you need anything, I'm just a phone call away."

"Thank you," he replied. "Let me know if you need my expert opinion again."

I sat in silence after my call with Dr. Wu. It felt good to know someone had my back and was willing to stick up for me against the lieutenant. Then again, my partner had tried to do the same. He looked out for me and gave me warnings not to get caught messing around with the case files. That's when I remembered the one last report Rodney obtained for me before I decided to take time off.

I searched for the one folder I hadn't reviewed. It contained Nicole Sherman's web history for the week leading up to her supposed suicide. There was nothing from the weekend of Rachel's death. I didn't see anything out of the ordinary on Monday either. Tuesday, Nicole had looked up the school's counseling center. This matched the time frame in which her phone records showed she had made a call to them. It was the only indication something may have been wrong up until the day she died. I went back and reviewed each line of her browser history, but nothing showed any signs of depression or suicidal thoughts.

I snatched my phone from the ottoman and called Rodney. "Hey, it's me. I think I just found a way to prove Nicole Sherman was murdered."

"That's great, Ali; how?"

"It's a combination of everything I pointed out, add in Dr. Wu's findings and his opinion, and top it off with Nicole Sherman's browser history you gave me."

There was an uncomfortable silence. "I'm happy for you, Ali; really I am. But do me a favor; when you talk to Esposito about this; leave my name out of it."

I knew Rodney did his best to help me, despite the possible consequences for digging into a closed investigation, which we had been given explicit orders to stop pursuing. I had no problem putting my career on the line to prove I was right, but there was no way I would drag Rodney down with me.

"As far as he's concerned; I did this on my own."

"When do you plan on confronting him?"

"Is he there now?" I asked.

"You couldn't let us have more than a day of happiness at the station; could you?" Rodney let out a laugh. We both knew my time off was just temporary. We just didn't think I would figure it out that quickly.

I rushed to the station with renewed determination. I ripped open the double doors and marched straight to Lieutenant Esposito's office. I was ready to go toe-to-toe with the lion himself, Mr. King of our jungle.

I knocked on the door and stepped inside. "Sir, we need to talk." The lieutenant glanced up from a pile of papers on his desk. His eyes met mine with a look of disbelief. "I have proof Nicole Sherman's death was not a suicide."

"Not this shit again. Ali, we've been over this a dozen times, and you were ordered not to poke your nose into either investigation again. I guess I have no other choice-"

"You need to stop cutting me off and listen for once," I barked. My outburst caused the lieutenant to sit up straight in his chair. I quickly shut the door before anyone else heard us. "I have evidence which points to this being something other than suicide. If I'm right; that means there is a killer on the loose, and I am not about to wait for them to strike again for you to finally see my perspective."

"You have five minutes, and you better convince me."

I definitely overstepped this time. I was sure a suspension was coming my way unless I proved I was right. I slapped the thick folder of information on the desk and towered over the lieutenant as I reviewed the information. I revisited my previous points about the missing student ID cards and the mismatched markings on Nicole Sherman's neck. Then, I pointed out the BAC level along with the grass stained jeans and mud-caked shoes.

"I spoke with Dr. Wu earlier. There was no way Rachel Walker could have made it far with a BAC level of two point six even if she was crawling. In his opinion, there is a strong possibility of someone else being involved with both deaths."

"And he is willing to go on record confirming your theory?"

"Yes, sir."

"Do you have anything else?"

I knew the M.E.'s opinion might not be enough to change the lieutenant's mind. So, I pulled out my secret weapon. I flipped to the last few pages of the file, where I had the browser history. I pointed out the two days showing any indication of potential depression. The lieutenant of course pointed to the Friday log where there was a Google search on *how to make a noose.*

"I think this day speaks for itself and disproves your little theory, detective." He was ready to dismiss me again.

"You're not seeing the big picture. These cases were too neat and clean. It was like everything was handed to us on a silver platter to make it an open and shut case, including the searches done on the same day Nicole Sherman was found hanging in a public bathroom outside of her room. But did you look at the time stamp of the searches?"

The lieutenant bent over and read them again. "They were all done between ten-thirty and two in the afternoon."

"Did you know Nicole Sherman was in class during that time?"

"How do we know for sure?"

"For starters; her mother confirmed it based on conversation with Nicole that morning. We can also obtain a copy of the attendance logs for her classes." I pulled out another page with a list of items entered into evidence. "We also have a copy of her course schedule and her notebooks to review. I'm sure she took notes since everyone I talked to said she was a bit of a perfectionist."

Lieutenant Esposito sat back in his chair. "Say we confirm she was in class; what does that prove?"

"It means someone killed both girls."

"How do you figure that?"

"Someone had to be in Nicole Sherman's room while she was in class to conduct those internet searches. Our victim obviously had her ID card on her when she left for class. Without it, she wouldn't have been able to get back into the building or her room. So, whoever was in the room needed access some other way. The only other card with that access was Rachel Walker's. Her ID has been missing since the night of the party.

Esposito got up from his desk and paced the room. "Let's say I believe you. If we're wrong and this leaks out, our station will be under a hail-storm of shit."

"So, let me continue my investigation; off the record; at least until we turn up a solid lead."

His head snapped back with a satisfied smile. "Fine, you and your partner have the green light." I couldn't hold back my smile. "Wipe that smirk off your face Detective. You have work to do and you better get it done fast."

I exited the room; collapsing against the door; breathing a sigh of relief; thankful the Lieutenant finally decided to listen to me.

Rodney hurried over to me. "Are you okay?"

"Never better," I replied. The wide smile on my face told him I got what I wanted. "We got some work to do partner."

The campus security patrols seemed to decline over the next week. Their spot checks were done to check for parking violations. It was almost as if they were hoping to see a student doing something wrong. But they never saw anything out of the ordinary, not even Mark Thompson sitting on the stone wall outside of Lenape Hall.

He had been stationed there all week. With the heightened alert downgraded; he was free to stalk his next victim, Christina Tyler. His stakeout last week allowed him to find her room number, but he needed to plan his attack carefully. She wasn't an easy mark like Rachel Walker was, or even had a way of using her roommate to get close to her like he did with Nicole Sherman. The Outdoors Club was his best chance. He just needed to ensure Christina showed up.

The backdoor to Lenape opened. The crack of orange light broke into the night, disturbing the darkness. It also allowed Mark Thompson to see his victim as she began her journey across campus. He waited for her to pass. His head tilted towards his text-book to maintain his cover; yet his eyes watched Christina like a hawk. She made it twenty feet before Mark followed her.

Get a little closer, his brain told him. *She won't recognize you.*

The makeover was designed to disguise him from his victims. It worked with Rachel, but she had been heavily drinking all night. Nicole called him out for looking familiar, but he lucked out. She wasn't able to put everything together in time. His next two victims were going to put his disguise to the test. Joining the same club would require them to interact more than just passing by them while walking through campus.

He rounded the corner to the Lecture Hall. Christina was standing outside talking with the same bald headed man she met last week, Kevin Graham. He knew they would be joining the rest of the group any moment, and he had no need to follow them at that moment. He ripped open the door next to them and made his way to the same classroom he entered last week. He darted for a desk in the back of the room and kept his head down in another book.

His targets entered the room moments later. They continued mumbling something to each other until Christina Tyler stopped short. Mark glanced up to see her staring at him. She quickly sat down and kept her focus on the front of the room.

Mark's heartbeat quickened. *Shit, she made me.*

He leaned back and watched her as she whispered something to Kevin. He glanced back but shook his head. It escalated Mark's fear that she recognized him.

"I'm pretty sure it's him," she said. Her voice was barely audible.

"No way," Kevin replied.

"Well, when was the last time you saw Nick?"

"Not since he moved away. I heard that asshole transferred to a place back home."

Mark nervously bounced his knee up and down. His eyes were locked onto the back of Kevin's bald head. He needed to do something to shut them up. They had to die before Christina or anyone else figured out the truth.

He drifted off into a daydream; imagining how he would kill his two remaining targets. *His hand gripped a knife concealed in his bag. He pulled Kevin's head back and slit his throat. Then, he ripped Christina to the ground and stabbed her over and over again until she bled to death.*

Mark glanced down at his bag. *Not here; not now.* Even if he decided to act on impulse, he didn't have a weapon at his disposal. There were also too many witnesses. He would be in jail before the night was over.

More students filed into the classroom along with the red-headed man from last week. He stood at the front facing the rest of the club members.

"Okay, guys," he said. "It's time to start tonight's meeting." He motioned to the girl at the professor's desk. "Marie will pass out the sign-in sheet while we discuss this weekend's trip to Mohonk Mountain." He took out a green notepad from his satchel. "We'll be meeting in front of the administration building at nine. If you are not here by nine-fifteen, we *will* leave without you." His head was on a swivel and made eye contact with everyone in the room to make sure they were paying attention. "It is supposed to be in the mid-fifties during the day. We plan to camp out for the night. I suggest you pack something warm."

A girl's hand shot into the air. "What if we don't want to spend the night up there?"

Mark rolled his eyes at her. *If you don't plan on camping out, then why are you going in the first place?*

Marie finished putting the sign-in sheet on the first desk closest to the door. "Anyone who does not wish to camp out is free to leave whenever they want." She glanced back at the man at the other club leader. "However, Marty and I will lead a group at two. Those wishing to leave should do so at that time."

"Basically, don't go off on your own. You should wait for us to bring you down. It's extremely easy to get lost in the mountains."

Those pieces of shit really think they're better than us. Mark saw Marty with a grin plastered on his face. He wanted to knock that stupid look off the red-headed asshole. He saw one of the other students turn around to hand Christina the sign-in paper.

"Are you gonna go?" she whispered.

"You know I don't like that shit," Kevin replied.

"Come on; it'll be fun. Besides, who else will I talk to for two whole days up in the mountains?"

Oh, I'll talk to you Christina, Mark thought. *And then I'll cross your name off my list.*

Kevin let out a sigh. "Do we really have to camp out there?"

"Why not?" she asked. The smile on Christina's face made Mark think there was something more going on. She reached over and placed her hand on the back of Kevin's arm. "I'll make it interesting." She winked at him before passing the paper back.

"Fine, I'll go," he reluctantly agreed. "Hey, before I forget; I'm having people over on Sunday for a Halloween party. You should come by."

Mark heard every word. The mountains would be difficult to eliminate both of his victims. But the trip combined with the party would help set his new plan in motion.

Who knew camping would be such a great idea?

Mark waited patiently for Saturday morning. It started out as a bright beautiful sunny morning with a slight chill in the air as the students arrived at the base of Mohonk Mountain. Twenty-two college students followed the trail guide up to the top with brief breaks to take in the sight of New Paltz from high up. It wasn't surprising to see Christina join the Outdoors Club. Mark recalled conversations with her where she talked about going up to the lighthouse one day. She wondered what it would be like to look down on their town. When asked why she never went up there; Christina said there was no one to go with her.

Mark remembered her not wanting to do anything the rest of her housemates weren't going to do. All of that changed the year when she was taken off the waitlist and was able to move into Lenape Hall. It forced her to be more social, but she still seemed to cling to her former housemates; at least she did with Kevin.

"Alright, guys," Marty called out from the front of the pack. He led them to a large clearing. "We're going to set up camp here." He put his gear down next to Marie's and faced the group again. "Anyone who does not plan on camping hang tight for now. Marie and I will bring you back down the mountain in a few hours." He pointed to the trail the group stood on. "This is Spring Farm Trailhead. This is the main path we'll be using. You will want to stick close to it so you do not get lost."

The group walked into the clearing where most of the group threw down their bags and camping gear. Several students began working on their tents, while others stood around talking with their friends.

Christina bent down to unload her bag. "Should we get started on ours?" She sounded excited to go camping, but Mark could see the happiness fade when she looked at Kevin.

"Yeah, I guess," he replied.

Mark put his tent up quickly and watched his targets struggle to get set up. Kevin wrestled with the silver poles as he tried to place them inside the lining of the tent walls. The outside shook with each attempt to place the poles in the right spot only for the whole thing to collapse on top of Kevin.

"Do you want some help?" Christina asked.

"No," Kevin snapped. "I've got this."

Mark watched Christina take a step back. Kevin's anger had caused a lot of problems in the past. It was one of the reasons why he and Kevin did not get along. The slightest annoyance would set him off. He would snap at everyone nearby, which was why most of his housemates left after living with him for one year.

"Does anyone need help setting up their tents?" Marty called out as he walked up and down the rows of students. He stopped outside of a pink tent and smiled. "Good job," he told Christina. Then he looked down at the gray tangled mess Kevin had been trapped in. "Do you need some help?"

"I'm fine," Kevin growled. "I almost had it." The tone in his voice pushed the club leader away.

"Suit yourself," Marty replied. "But if you change your mind, let me know." He walked off to check on more students.

Christina placed her hands on her hips. "When was the last time you went camping or set up a tent?"

"Never," Kevin noted.

"Then, maybe you should've let him help you."

"I don't need any help." He reached into the tent and pulled the poles back out. "I just need to figure out how to get these damn things to stay in place." He threw the sticks down without trying again.

Christina grabbed his hand. "Maybe you just need to relax for a bit. We can try again later."

Kevin pulled away from her and passed by Mark's tent. He was heading back to the path, but found Marie standing in the way.

"I see you're having trouble getting set up."

"Ya think?"

Mark wondered if Marie was biting her tongue to stop herself from putting Kevin in his place. Her eyes shifted from Kevin to Christina and back to the prick standing in front of her.

"I'm about to take a small group up to the Lemon Squeeze. You guys should come with us. It'll help take your mind off the tent for a while."

"Yeah, but what about the-"

"Forget it," Marie interrupted him. "It can wait until we get back. Plus, you should have some fun while we're here."

"Let's go," Christina urged as she clasped her hand around Kevin's.

"Fine," he mumbled. He stomped his feet to follow the girls. "Wait, what the hell is a lemon squeeze?"

Marie smiled at him. "You'll find out soon enough."

Mark was curious too. He slipped into the group unnoticed as they began the uphill hike. Marie led them up the path to a large section of rocks and boulders sitting at the base of a cliff.

"I think we went the wrong way," Kevin stated.

"No, we're right where we're supposed to be," Marie replied. She started climbing over the rocks and looked back at the rest of the group as they stared in disbelief. "That up there is the Lemon Squeeze."

"And we're supposed to do what exactly?"

"Hope you're good at climbing." Marie made her way to an opening to a large wall. The group was hesitant but quickly followed.

"She's joking; right?"

"Stop being a baby." Christina climbed over the rocks and tried to keep up with the others. "You coming or you gonna chicken out?"

Kevin shook his head and followed Christina. His long legs took bigger strides while Christina struggled with her shorter steps until they reached the wall.

"Is everyone here?" Marie asked. She placed a foot on the wall and stood up to take a head count. "It looks like we're all set. I'll go up first and help you guys."

Mark watched in amazement as Marie scaled the wall with ease. She didn't have any kind of ropes or climbing gear. She did everything free-handed. She dug her fingers into chunks of the wall using it for leverage. She moved swiftly like a cat climbing a tall tree.

I may have underestimated that one, Mark thought.

"Okay, who's next?" she called down.

A boy took a running start up the wall and made it halfway up before being told to stay put. He was placed there to assist the students who had a harder time making it up the Lemon Squeeze.

Kevin waited until the group dwindled down to only a few people left. He entered the opening and began to claw his way up the wall.

"Just put your foot on that rock to your left," the boy called out from the mid-way point. "Come on; move your foot and swing your body to the right so your hands and feet are on both walls."

Mark stifled a laugh. He knew Kevin hated taking orders from anyone, especially if he had no idea what he was doing. But he had no choice. Kevin was stuck. His only choice was to take their help and get to the top or fall to the bottom once his arms and legs became too tire.

Kevin did as he was told. Slowly, he made it to the mid-way point where the boy calling out the directions stood. He grabbed his hand and listened as he was told how to make his way up to the top of the wall.

He peered down at the remaining students. "That was awesome."

"Hold on," Christina yelled up to him. "I'm up next." Her shorter limbs made it harder to reach both sides like most of the group had done.

Mark darted behind Christina. "Here, let me help you." He considered helping her to a certain point. Once they were high enough; Mark would let her fall as if it was an accident. *No, I better not. There are still too many witnesses.*

Mark decided to go through with helping Christina. He believed the kind act would help ease their minds about his identity. He needed them to feel comfortable around him just long enough for their guard to drop.

"Thank you," Christina said once they reached the top. She took a few deep breaths before turning to the man who helped her. She gulped down a large intake of air at the sight of Mark.

"No problem," Mark replied.

He kept his contempt hidden, but that didn't stop him from staring down Kevin. The look in his eyes reflected the man who just saw a ghost.

"Come on," he urged Christina. "Let's go check out the view." Kevin led Christina away. His arm wrapped around her shoulders as they moved further up the hill.

Christina removed her backpack and took out an SLR camera. She moved towards the edge of the cliff.

"This is so beautiful," she noted. "I'm really glad we did this."

Kevin took her by the hand and stared deeply into her eyes. "You know what? I'm happy to be here with you." He leaned in for a kiss.

As far as Mark knew; this had been the first time their lips had ever touched. It was so touching to see them act on their attraction to one another, but it also made Mark's anger bubble up to the surface.

Why should they be happy when they made my life miserable? He considered doing something drastic. *Two birds; one stone; it could still look like an accident.*

Before Mark could do anything, the new couple trotted back to the group with big smiles on their faces.

"Hey, I don't know if anyone's interested," Kevin began. "I'm having a party tomorrow night." He looked down at Christina. She gave his hand a little squeeze urging him to finish. "I'd like to invite everyone to my place."

The group crowded around them in excitement. Everyone was clamoring for the details. Mark stood at the back of the group. His plan to attack during the hike had been thwarted, but a new opportunity had risen.

I'm coming for both of you.

<u>Chapter 21-Ali</u>

It was another crisp Saturday morning bringing cold air to the Hudson Valley. Winter was around the corner, which meant morning jogs were going to get harder to do. I had to enjoy them while I could. After scrambling out of bed, I pulled on a pair of workout pants, a t-shirt, and an orange zip-up sweatshirt. Coffee was calling my name, but I let it go for now in favor of a protein shake.

Since the lieutenant had me working the case unofficially, I went back to work after taking a solid three days off. The rest of the week was spent at the station tying up some loose ends on a break-in case I was about to put to bed. There was little on my plate, and I wanted to focus my weekend on reviewing the Rachel Walker and Nicole Sherman cases.

I ran out to my favorite jogging spot to clear my mind before launching my investigation. Instead, I found a surprise waiting for me at the entrance. Rodney stood next to his navy blue truck wearing an old pair of Adidas pants. They clung to his legs indicating he hadn't worn them in quite a while.

"What are you doing here?" I asked.

"I figured I'd join you for your morning run."

"You…run…when was the last time you did that?"

"Laugh it up, Ali." Rodney didn't seem amused by my comments. He didn't really seem like he wanted to be there at all. "So, what if it's been a while?"

I began stretching in the parking lot by pulling my foot towards my back; doing lunges; and bending to touch my toes. I glanced over to find my partner clumsily trying to copy everything I did. This was not like Rodney. Something was up.

I placed my hand on his back. "Why don't you tell me why you're really here before you hurt yourself?"

Rodney stood up straight. His eyes searched the parking lot. "I talked to Esposito yesterday about the cases. He specifically said he wants to keep this under wraps."

"I know; he told me the same thing."

"No, I mean he doesn't even want us working on it at the station. We're not to involve any other officers or even let them know what we're working on. We're only allowed to talk to him, the forensics team, and the M.E. about it, and only if we have questions. We can't bring it up to the D.A. unless we need a warrant for something."

The lieutenant was going overboard on this being an unofficial case. Was this really about keeping the public calm and not causing a panic? Was it to stop the victim's families from storming the station like he said? Or was the lieutenant worried about his boss finding out about his screw-up and punishing him for closing investigations when a murderer was still on the loose?

"So, how are we supposed to work these cases if we can't do it at the station?" I asked.

"That's why I'm here. I figured we could talk things over while getting into shape."

Rodney had a spare tire around his waist. Married life and patrols caused him to pack on some weight over the last few years.

"You have a long way to go before you're back in shape, partner."

Rodney pushed out his bottom lip before breaking from his attempt to make me feel bad about my comment. The corners of his mouth turned into a large grin.

"Hey, round is a shape."

I laughed at his lame attempt at a joke. "You do realize this is a three-mile run; right?"

"Three-miles?" he repeated.

"Yup; are you ready to get started?"

"Uh, do you think we can start out slow?"

"You wanted to join me for my run. Now, it's time to keep up."

I walked the first quarter mile but jogged the rest of the way. It didn't take long for Rodney to hunch over. He was gasping for air before we made it a third of the way down the bridge.

"No more, Ali; I can't do it."

"Come on; you wanted to get back in shape."

"No more; please," he begged.

I patted him on the back. "Fine, we can take a break, but nothing more than a couple of minutes. We don't want to waste our adrenaline."

"Yeah, that would be terrible." Rodney dropped to his knees and sprawled out on his back.

"You shouldn't lie down if you're having trouble breathing. You need to get up and walk it off with your hands on your head until your heartbeat slows back down."

Rodney barely lifted his head. His eyes were red and glassy. "Shut up," he growled before dropping back to the ground. After another minute, he turned to his side. "So, what's the plan on catching this killer?"

I took a seat next to him. "We know enough that it was probably someone who knew Rachel and Nicole. It was most likely someone from school."

"What about the killer being a student in the Esopus dorm?"

"Possible, but something tells me the suspect doesn't live there. My money is on them using Rachel's ID to access the building."

"They may have just needed it to get back into the room to go after Nicole," Rodney suggested.

"You could be right," I replied. "Let's not rule out that option yet."

"So, that narrows the list of potential suspects to a few thousand people. We don't have much which can narrow it down."

"It has to be someone who has been around them enough to know their routines; their habits; and their friends."

"Are you suggesting it's one of their friends?" he asked.

"It could be, but I would bet it was someone they *used* to be friends with; a person they had an argument with, or they just stopped talking to them."

"Ali, that's two and a half years worth of students who may or may not have known them. There are people who might know Rachel and not Nicole or vice versa."

"I know, but that's our pool of suspects. I think we need to start off with their known friends. Maybe one of them can tell us if the girls had a mutual falling out with a friend; a roommate; or a boyfriend."

"This is insane," Rodney replied. "There's no way we can catch the killer like this. Even if we figure out their identity, that person will be long gone by then."

"And that brings me to my next suggestion. I think we should question the professors at the college, too. They might be able to pinpoint an irregularity in attendance or a student who hasn't shown up in class lately."

Rodney's eyes lit up. I could see the lightbulb turn on in his head as he was struck with an idea. "Why don't we start with the attendance records for the days Rachel Walker and Nicole Sherman were murdered?"

I liked where he was going with it, but both victims were killed on a Friday night. Most students didn't have class on that day, so it was unlikely we would be able to find anything based on that information. I explained it to my partner before piggy-backing off his idea.

"I think examining the attendance logs and class rosters would be good for us to review. Maybe they could turn up a possible lead." I patted him on the shoulder. "I'll place a call to the D.A. and get the warrant first thing Monday morning."

"Why wait?" he asked. "You got a hot date this weekend?"

I know he was trying to joke around, but it was a bit of a sore spot for me. I turned around and started back towards the entrance.

"As a matter of fact; no, I do not. Matthew has been…out of town."

My partner followed me. "What the *hell* does that mean?"

I really didn't want to discuss with him, but I had no one else to talk to about it. "Matthew and I hooked up last week. I woke up on Saturday to an empty bed and a note telling me he was called away on business. Apparently, the issue had taken him away on some business trip. I haven't heard from him since."

I felt Rodney's hand grip my shoulder. "Do you want me to hunt him down and beat some sense into him?"

"No, I can do that myself. I just wish he would have been straight with me. If I was just a hook-up, then let me know. Don't write some note telling me all this crap with a made-up excuse. I'm a grown woman. I can handle it if he told me the truth."

"Guys are assholes," Rodney said with a laugh.

"Um, you're a guy," I giggled.

"I'm the exception." We looked up and saw the entrance was almost in view. "I'm done with this walking and jogging crap. How about we grab something to eat?"

"Now, that sounds like the partner I know and love."

We drove to the diner down the road from my house on Route 9W. He scarfed down his breakfast consisting of eggs, bacon, toast, hash browns, and pancakes. I took my time with my egg white omelet with spinach and feta cheese. I was still stuck in my head about our last conversation about Matthew. I don't know why it was getting to me. My partner must have noticed it too. Rodney insisted on making sure I got home okay. He even walked me to my door.

"Cheer up, detective," he whispered in my ear. "We have a case to solve. So, don't let that asshole get to you. There are plenty other guys out there."

"Thanks, partner." I hugged Rodney tightly.

As I opened my eyes, I saw a handsome hunk of a man park his car across the street. He stepped out of the driver's seat and started walking towards my house carrying a bouquet of flowers.

"What the fuck?" Matthew called out.

I let go of Rodney and rushed towards the street to meet Matthew at the curb. "What are you doing here? I thought you were away on business."

"I was," he snapped back rather coldly. "I finished up earlier than I expected and came here to surprise you." His head turned towards Rodney. "But I show up here and see this." He pointed at my partner.

"You mean Rodney? There's nothing going on between us. He's my partner. We went for a run this morning and he was making sure I got home okay."

I don't know why I had to justify anything. Matthew and I were dating but he wasn't my boyfriend. He had been M.I.A for a week, and now he pops up and accuses me of messing around on him?

"And I'm just supposed to believe he's just your partner?" Matthew asked. His eyes were locked onto Rodney. One hand gripped the bouquet of flowers tightly while the other had a fist clenched.

Rodney must have heard everything. He walked back to his vehicle and pulled out a small object from his glove box. He stomped towards us holding up his badge.

"Believe her now, asshole?" Rodney slipped his shield back inside his sweatshirt pocket and turned towards me. "I'll call you later." Then, he leaned in close to Matthew. I could see he was trying to appear even more intimidating. "If you hurt her in any way; you'll answer to me."

I watched my partner drive away in his truck leaving Matthew dumbstruck. He'd stumbled on something innocent and blew it way out of proportion.

"Ali, I'm sorry; I did't-" his mocha skin had a tinge of red rushing to his cheeks.

Now, it was my turn to be fueled with anger. I faced Matthew with my hands on my hips. "Yeah, you didn't think." I stared him down. "You left me with only a note about taking care of something for work. Then, you let me know you're running out of town on some supposed business trip. I haven't heard from you in a week. And now, you show up at my house and have the balls to accuse me of messing around on you?"

He lowered his head with pouty lips. His hand extended the bouquet of flowers. "I'm sorry, Ali. One of our large clients was dangerously close to leaving us. I had to rush out of town for emergency meetings to keep them. As soon as I was done, I rushed back here to spend the weekend with you."

There was sincerity in his eyes. The brief moment of anger he displayed told me how much Matthew cared about me. I couldn't fault him for misinterpreting me hugging a guy he didn't know in front of my house so early in the morning. I was guilty of jumping to conclusions earlier by insinuating Matthew used me for just a hook-up.

I accepted the flowers and smelled the scent of lilies and roses. I decided to put the situation behind us. I gave him a kiss to let him know we were okay.

"Do you wanna come inside for a bit?"

"I thought you'd never ask." His hands grasped my waist and pulled me in for a deeper more passionate kiss. He lifted me off the ground in a massive embrace. We moved towards the front door refusing to break our intense lip-lock.

I fumbled with my keys and unlocked the door. "You're not gonna leave me again?" I asked.

"I'm yours all weekend."

I dragged him into the house and closed the door behind us. Every worry I had was left on the front lawn vanishing into thin air.

I spent most of the weekend in bed with Matthew. It went against everything my mother told me when I was growing up. But for once, I had a damn good reason. My eyes lifted to the blackout curtains desperately trying to keep the sun from entering the room. I felt Matthew's long arm drape over my left shoulder. His hand reached for mine as he pulled himself closer.

A euphoric smile crept over my face as his body pressed against mine. "Someone's ready for another round."

"Sorry; I can't help myself," he whispered into my ear. "You're too tempting to pass up." His lips pressed the back of my neck causing me to bite my lip playfully as I anticipated his next move. Then, my phone rang. "Don't get it," he told me. "Whoever it is; they can wait."

I reluctantly stretched my hand out to tip my cell over enough to see the screen. Amanda's name appeared in green letters. I snatched it from the nightstand.

"Sorry; I have to take this; it's my sister."

A look of disappointment swept over Matthew's face. He fell onto his back. A loud puff sound emitted from the pillows as his body made contact with them. It was the same sentiment I felt, but I had to take the call. She was my sister, and she was living on a campus where a killer was on the loose.

"Amanda, hey; what's up?"

"Can you meet me for lunch later?"

I sat straight up in the bed. She never reaches out just to talk or just to go to lunch. Usually, there is some sort of hidden agenda. Either she needed or something happened.

"Yeah, I can make it. Is everything all right?"

She paused. That wasn't a good sign. "Sean and I have been checking around campus like you asked. We might have a couple of leads for you to look into."

I was relieved. I sunk back into the bed and turned to my side. Then, I felt Matthew's lips connect with the middle of my back. A pulsating shiver cascaded down my spine.

"Oh," I moaned. "I mean oh, okay; sure." He kissed the same spot yielding another moan. "G-give me a couple of h-hours."

Matthew's lips worked their way up my back while I kept the phone pressed to my ear. I tried swatting him away, but he was coming on stronger. It was getting harder to fend him off.

"Am I interrupting something?" Amanda asked.

I couldn't concentrate. I needed to get off the phone before things escalated and my sister heard something she shouldn't.

"No, not at all," I replied breathlessly. "I'll pick you up from your dorm in a bit. Bye!" I quickly ended the call. The cell dropped to the floor as I quickly turned to pelt Matthew with a barrage of kisses. Damn, he was hard to resist, and God help me; I didn't want to.

I got up from the bed a half hour later. Matthew continuously attempted to drag me back. "Please, don't go." It was playful, but I kind of liked him begging me.

"I have to get ready. My sister needs me."

I could see the look in his eye. He was wrestling with the urge to make a comment to convince me to stay put. Matthew knew my sister was the one person I would drop everything for, and I wasn't about to let anyone, including a guy, get in the way.

I got to Amanda's dorm less than an hour after and found her waiting for me outside. She was sitting on the stone ledge near the front doors of Esopus. She was bundled up in a large black hoodie with the band name Revolution on it. I recognized the name from a show my sister forced me to go to last year. Sean happened to be the lead singer o the group.

I pulled along the curb and rolled down the window. "Hey, what are you in the mood to eat?"

"I can go for anything other than campus food." Amanda jumped into the passenger seat and buckled in.

"Great, I know just the place." I drove away from the college and onto Main Street.

We traveled down a steep hill and followed the road to the end. There was a large ranch house with a parking lot in back. No one would know it was a restaurant if they were driving by, except for the green and gold sign standing out front.

We're going to the Gilded Otter?" Amanda asked.

I parked the car with a smile knowing it was one of my sister's favorite places to go. She was about to push the passenger door open to get out, but I quickly hit the auto-locks.

"Not so fast; what did you find out?"

"Can we wait to talk business until after we put in our orders?"

"No, I can't risk anyone overhearing us. We can eat after we talk shop. I need to know what leads you uncovered."

"I overheard a few girls talking about Rachel. They were saying how no one was surprised to hear she died from alcohol, and that she was drinking like a guy the night of the party."

"What's that supposed to mean?"

"She was out back doing keg stands and participating in drinking games all night. I overheard them say Rachel was either looking for trouble or some action."

Finally, there were some other witnesses other than Rachel's friends. I hoped they would be able to tell me more about that night.

"Did you get the names of those girls?"

Amanda shook her head. "You told me to be careful. I didn't want anyone thinking I was poking my nose into the case or their business. I did my best to listen to their conversation without being caught."

I slammed my hand on the steering wheel in frustration. "Damn it; I need to know who she was hanging out with that night."

"I thought you had a list of her friends."

"We do, but the two girls she was with said Rachel took them back to their dorm before going back to Esopus. They said she was fine."

"But you don't think that's the truth?"

"I have a few pieces of evidence telling me these girls were murdered. I need a solid lead to prove it before the lieutenant hangs me out to dry."

"I thought you were doing this off the record?" Amanda asked.

"I am, but now I have some support from him." I could see her confusion. "There was a suicide note found on Nicole's computer along with a browser history indicating she had suicidal thoughts. The same time those searches were done; Nicole was in class."

"So, there really *is* a killer on campus?"

I pursed my lips together and stared at the windshield nodding my head. "I need you to promise you and Sean will stay close to each other and keep out of trouble."

"I promise."

"Good, and if you see anything suspicious or out of the ordinary-"

"I'll call you right away," she finished my statement. She turned towards me in her seat. "Now, do you mind telling me what was going on this morning when I called you?"

My cheeks flushed with embarrassment. *How do you tell your little sister you were moments from having sex while she was on the phone with you?*

"I was…uh…working out."

"Uh huh, sure you were." She reached for the door handle. "And tell your man I said hi." Amanda made a gagging face to let me know she knew what was really going on. "Ugh, I really don't want to think about that one. Can we go inside before I lose my appetite?"

Mark waited in a car around the corner from a house of Grove Street. His time on the mountain was over, but his fun was just beginning. His eyes searched the cold dreary night for any sign of the Outdoors Club's arrival. It was foolish to go into the house alone. It would only allow Kevin and Christina to focus their attention on him. The safety of the group would be like his camouflage; concealing his identity.

He noticed a small group approaching the house. Mark exited his car and slipped behind the students without alerting anyone. They walked up the path to the house. By the looks of it; no one was home. The windows were boarded up with sheets of plywood. No one could see what was going on inside the house.

Feels like home to me. Mark rubbed his hands together excitedly in anticipation of the night's events.

The front had the appearance of someone decorating for Halloween. Spiderwebs were strewn across the porch, hanging from the awning and over the door. Everyone cautiously inched closer. The planks of wood creaked with a single step. A large black spider dropped down in front of a girl. Her high-pitched scream caused the group to jump back, but the girl tripped and fell onto the lap of scarecrow in a rocking chair. Everyone laughed, as did the girl until the body she sat on sprang to life. The man wrapped her in his arms. The poor girl was terrified. She cried to be let go and for others to help.

The front door opened revealing a bald headed man holding a pitchfork and wearing devil horns. His make-up gave him an ashy-looking appearance as if the man had stepped straight out of hell.

Fitting since he used to act like he was devil worshiper.

Devil Kevin put a hand on the scarecrow's shoulder. "Okay, Jason; I think she had enough."

The man's arms dropped to the side allowing the girl to scramble away quickly. "Assholes," she hissed while walking back to the group.

"Sorry, everyone; I go all out for Halloween parties. Come on in and have some fun." Devil Kevin waved for his guests to follow him inside.

"Hey, when can I come inside?" Jason asked.

"In about an hour," Kevin replied. "We still have some people who should be showing up soon."

Mark entered the house with the rest of the group. His eyes darted around as they passed through a long hallway to the kitchen. He expected any number of ghostly or spooky things to pop out at them along the way. Doors to a couple of rooms remained closed, which made Mark wonder what was behind them.

"Hey, you guys made it," Marie called out to the group. She was standing near the entrance with Marty with a couple of beers in hand.

There were a few other members of the Outdoors Club already there attempting to mingle with the other guests. They were the ones who drew Mark's attention. He knew them from the parties Kevin threw the previous year. They were his friends from Westchester, the same ones who only showed up for the biggest parties where everyone gets wasted. Mark needed to stay away from them in order to avoid suspicion.

Christina pranced around the kitchen in a sexy cat costume consisting of a leather corset, booty shorts with a tail, and a pair of fishnet stockings. Her face had make-up for the nose and whiskers. A pair of cat ears sat on top of her head. She smiled at the new arrivals and grabbed a tray filled with paper cups.

"Anyone want a Jell-O shot?" Christina asked.

"What's in them?" a girl questioned.

Christina pointed to each color. "The orange ones have vodka; the red ones are rum; and the green were mixed with tequila." Her head turned back to the counter and saw half of the tiny paper cups were missing. "I think you need to hurry if you want more of the green ones. It looks like those are going fast."

Mark's eyes lingered on Christina's outfit. He wanted her dead. She deserved it for the way she had treated him. But Mark had a new thought, one that viewed her in a different way. For a moment, he considered pursuing her for the night. It would be a cheap thrill; a night of taking what he wanted before ultimately taking her life. It was risky, especially with Christina and Kevin being so close, which seemed to grow during the camping trip. It was better to leave and find another way to eliminate his targets.

"Excuse me," he said while slipping between Christina and another couple blocking the entrance. His hand grazed against her upper thigh. It was an urge he needed to fulfill.

"Hey, hold up," she called out over the loud music.

Shit, I need to get out now.

Mark chose to ignore Christina and continued down the hall. He felt a hand grip his wrist and tug it back. He turned and saw Christina staring into his eyes.

"You look really familiar. Where do I know you from?"

Dozens of sarcastic replies fluttered through Mark's head, but he maintained his composure. He bit down on the inside of his cheek trying to think of his next move; the next lie to tell. He needed to say something to throw her off his scent. His eyes had dropped to the top of

Christina's corset. Her breasts were nearly popping out of it as her chest rose and fell rapidly.

"Uh yeah; we're in the Outdoors Club together; right? You were on the trip up the mountain yesterday."

"Yeah, but…" Christina paused. Mark could tell she knew who he was but didn't want to accuse him of anything. "Kevin and I swear we met before the last couple of meetings."

Say my name, bitch.

Mark's desires were clashing. He didn't know what he wanted to do more but toying with Christina was part of the fun.

"Sorry, but I would remember meeting someone as pretty as you." Mark used the one line he knew would throw her off his trail. Even in a darkened hallway, he saw her cheeks blush a rosy shade of pink.

She twirled the cat's tail. "What did you say your name was again?"

"Marcus, but my friends call me Mark."

"It-it's just so weird; you remind me of our old housemate."

She knew it was him. There was no doubt she was fishing for the truth. Mark was tempted enough to play along. He forced a smile as he moved closer and leaned a hand against the wall.

"Did you have a thing for this housemate?" Her eyes looked away for a moment. "I take that as a yes?"

"It was complicated," she replied.

"How about we have a drink and you can tell me all about this complicated housemate of yours." He noticed her hesitation, but Mark made a move to return to the kitchen.

"Sure," Christina replied.

Mark placed a hand on the small of her back as they returned to the party. They grabbed beers from the fridge and moved to the counter. Five paper cups remained on the tray.

Mark grabbed one of them and downed the contents. "So, tell me about this guy I remind you of who you may or may not have had thing for."

"His name was Nick and he was a decent guy."

"You make it sound like a bad thing."

"He spent more time with his girlfriend then the rest of us."

"Isn't that what a good boyfriend does?"

"Yeah, but then he would complain that we didn't include him in our group outings."

"So, you guys cast him out because he was more about his girl than hanging out with his housemates?" Mark was trying hard not to make it sound like he was against Christina, but he wanted to make her see how they were ones in the wrong. "I mean; the guy sounds like he wanted to be your friend but wasn't given much of a chance to do it."

"We did what was best for us."

"That's a bit harsh; don't you think?"

"We couldn't wait around for him to show up before making plans to go somewhere." She was getting defensive. Her chest was heaving up and down rapidly as she got worked up.

"Did you want him there?"

"The house decided not to invite him."

"But did you want him there?"

"I did at first. He seemed like a great guy who cared about his girlfriend. But then, I couldn't sit around watching him cater to her."

Mark's brain was working fast to process the new revelation. "So, you were jealous?"

"No...yes...maybe."

"Did you want to be with him?"

"No, not really," Christina replied. "I just wanted someone to treat me like he did his girlfriend."

Mark used the new information to piece together what happened next in the story without needing Christina to tell him anything more.

"What ever happened to this housemate, Nick?"

Christina took another paper cup and downed the shot. "He and Kevin had gotten into a bunch of arguments, which led to the whole house shutting Nick out. After a few months of the silent treatment, he moved out around April. We haven't seen or heard from him since."

"So, now it's just you and your boyfriend?"

"Kevin?" The tone of Christina's voice got higher as if she was surprised to hear him being thought of in that manner. "We're just friends. I just stay here on the weekends so I can hang out and party without having to walk back to my dorm."

Mark wanted to dig into their relationship a little more, but the light bulb in his head gave him another idea. "I don't really plan on drinking more than this tonight. I can give you a ride back when you're ready."

She took another shot. "Thanks, but I'm gonna crash here tonight. I already have a bag with my clothes in Kevin's room."

Mark was done playing around with Christina. She claimed to be only friends with his bald headed target, but Mark could see she wanted more.

Enjoy one more night together.

Mark put his hand in his pocket and set off his cell. "Sorry, I need to take this." He pretended to talk on the phone as he disappeared behind a group of people. His eyes remained on Christina to make sure she wasn't watching him.

He located a small wooden door about ten feet from the fridge. Mark remembered a few nights hanging out on the other side of that wall.

When parties at Grove Street ended, the remaining guests and housemates typically hung out in the kitchen or in Kevin's room. That was where he had his fun. He let the drunks act like fools while he captured everything with pictures and video. There were a few more hours before the Halloween party ended, but Mark was ready to get out of there. There was one thing left for him to do.

His hand gripped the knob and twisted it until he was able to push his way inside the bedroom. The room was dark. Mark turned the flashlight on his phone and used it to search for Christina's bag. The peach colored satchel sat on top of Kevin's black comforter. Mark shoved his hand inside. He could feel the silky fabric of Christina's bra and underwear against his skin as he searched for her jeans or purse. Inside the back pocket was a piece of hard plastic. He pulled it out and held the card up to the flashlight to see the image of his next victim staring back at him.

This is just what I needed.

He pocketed the ID card and closed up the bag before hurrying out of the room. He made sure no one saw him and no one, including Christina, followed him out of the house. He walked back to his car with pep in his step. His hands clapped together excitedly as he sat in the driver's seat.

Tomorrow, we're gonna have some fun.

<u>Chapter 23-Ali</u>

I strutted into Monday morning more relaxed than ever before. I had a smile on my face, a spring in my step, and a desire to jump right back into work. My partner was already at his desk with a small stack of paperwork he had left over from the weekend.

Rodney looked up at me as I took my seat. "Someone's in a good mood this morning." He must have noticed my ear-to-ear grin. "I know *that* look."

"What look?" I innocently asked.

Rodney leaned over the desk and whispered to me. "Someone got lucky this weekend." He started laughing immediately.

I took a swipe at him but he sat back in his chair. "Cut the crap."

"Hey, I'm just sayin' if you're in this good of a mood on a Monday, then I think I need to have a talk with Matthew. We need to make sure he takes care of you every night."

"Rodney, sex isn't everything, and it definitely doesn't equate to happiness."

"No, but it sure put you in a really good mood this morning."

"You're such a jerk," I replied. "Can we please focus on actual work? We need to get some new leads on these cases before the lieutenant blows another gasket on me."

"One, we're not supposed to be talking about that here. Two, there's not much for us to go on."

"We have the attendance records."

"No, we need to *get* the attendance records. That still doesn't mean it'll give us anything useful."

"It's a long shot, but it's a start."

I grabbed my desk phone and dialed the number for the D.A.'s office. I needed to book an appointment. I only let the secretary know we were asking for a warrant for attendance records at the New Paltz campus. I expected more questions, but I don't think she wanted to get too involved. I put down the receiver and smiled at my partner.

"We have a meeting set for a half hour to convince her to grant us the warrant we need."

"Damn it, Ali." He threw his pen down on the desk. "You had to get the first available meeting; didn't you?"

I looked at the pile of paperwork. It was probably going to take Rodney half the morning to finish it. Neither of us really expected to get the appointment that early. I already had to plead my case to the lieutenant, and he was more stubborn than anyone I ever met. The D.A. shouldn't be too difficult to convince.

I stood up from my desk and turned to find the lieutenant standing in his doorway. He remained silent, but his eyes were staring daggers at me. He stretched out two fingers, pointed them at Rodney and me, and then signaled for us to follow him. I knew this was his way of asking about the case without drawing attention to us.

Rodney walked in first with me following behind. He took a spot leaning against the window. I closed the door and sat down across from the lieutenant.

"I want an update on the case," Esposito quietly demanded.

There wasn't much to tell him. I relayed our theories that the suspect was someone who knew the girls, most likely a former friend or roommate. I furthered the point it could also be an ex-boyfriend, but we would need to talk to their friends a little more to get a list of potential people of interest. Then, I announced Rodney's suggestion of reviewing the attendance records and our meeting set with the D.A.

"I know you wanted Rodney and I to work these cases on our off time, but if we want to make any progress, we need to put in effort during our regular hours as well."

The lieutenant nodded. "I'll call the D.A. and let them know of our situation. I'll ask for the warrant to be expedited, but you need to get me results. It won't be long before the media gets wind of this once you start poking your noses around the school and the victims' friends."

I knew Lieutenant Esposito was right, but my bigger concern was the killer had already left town. Two deaths within a week painted a large target on everyone who knew the girls, especially anyone with a sordid past. If the suspect left town, any chance of us arresting them was thrown in the trash. The alternative scenario was far scarier than the original fear. The suspect could be lying in wait; stalking their next victim; ready to strike at any moment.

"Thanks, Lieu; we're heading to the D.A.'s office now."

I rushed Rodney from the station. We took his squad car, even though this was supposed to be unofficial police business. We both had issues with the other person's driving ability. He thought I drove like a maniac, and I reminded him to drive the actual speed limit. I let him win more. It was senseless to argue over who should be the one behind the wheel unless we needed to get somewhere quickly.

Thanks to my partner's Sunday driving; we showed up ten minutes late for our scheduled appointment.

"I'm sorry, but she had to rush out to court," the secretary told us when we arrived.

"We were only ten minutes late," I replied. "How long was she planning on giving us to present the information?"

"I can't help you with that information. I just know she was on a tight schedule this morning. When you didn't show at your appointed time, she hurried out of here for a court case."

"Do you know when she'll be back?"

"Her schedule has her blocked off for the next couple of hours. She could be back sooner than that, or court could hold her up longer. You can sit and wait around if you'd like."

I couldn't take a chance of missing another opportunity to speak with the D.A. We needed the warrant as soon as possible. I didn't care how long we had to wait for her.

"We'll hang around here until she gets back." Rodney had a look of disbelief on his face. He obviously didn't want to wait no matter how long it took. So, I tried to make it a little more bearable for him. "Is there somewhere we can grab something to eat?"

The secretary gave us directions to the nearest cafeteria. Rodney stomped his way towards the destination.

"I really don't have time to sit here all day," he growled when we were far enough away from the secretary.

"Hey, if you had hit the gas a bit more, we would have been here on time." I brought Rodney to the cafeteria. "At least we can grab some food and relax for a bit."

"Yeah, but I have so much paperwork to go through when we get back to the station."

Truthfully, that was his fault for putting it off until that morning to complete it. I wasn't about to tack it on to the list of things he should have done.

"Hopefully, this won't take long and you can go back to it."

Unfortunately, it took three hours for the D.A. to return. She allowed us a half hour to speak about the cases and why we needed the warrant while she ate her lunch.

"Okay, we'll talk it over with a judge," she advised.

We went to the courthouse with the D.A. where we spent forty-five minutes repeating everything we just spoke about in her office. The judge didn't seem keen on the idea, but the D.A. spoke up on our behalf and argued enough to change the judge's mind. Finally, we had what was needed to kickoff our investigation.

"So much for expediting the warrant," Rodney mumbled as we walked back towards the squad car.

"Hey, at least we have the warrant. We can get back to the campus and get the files we need." I glanced down at my watch. "Let's just hope there is someone still there who can help us." I ripped the keys from Rodney's hand. "Sorry, partner; I'm driving this time."

I jumped behind the wheel and revved the engine. My partner's face turned pale. He made the sign of the cross before getting into the passenger seat. Rodney quickly buckled up as I flipped the switches for the lights and siren.

"Why do I get the feeling I'd be safer in the back?" He pointed to the cage separating the front and back of the car.

"Stop being such a baby, Rodney. I'm not *that* bad of a driver."

I shifted the car into drive and slammed on the gas. Our heads jerked back against our seats. Rodney's hand gripped the door handle tightly as I sped out of the parking lot and onto the main road. His eyes grew wide with terror as I weaved in and out of traffic. I was thoroughly enjoying the ride. It was a rush to fly through the streets of Kingston making it seem like just a blur. Cars swerved to get out of our way; some pulled onto the shoulder of the road.

"Ali, the light…the light…" Rodney stiffened his body as we ran through an intersection just as our light turned red. "You're gonna get us killed."

I glanced at my partner from the corner of my eye. "Do you really wanna be pushing papers all week, or do you wanna help me take down some murderous asshole?"

"You know I want to bring this bastard down," Rodney began. He inhaled deeply and closed his eyes as I crossed the median into oncoming traffic to pass another driver. He exhaled just as we moved back into our own lane. "I also wanna get home safely to my wife and kid."

I slowed down as we approached Route 299. I could hear Rodney whispering to God under his breath. It really wasn't as bad as he made it out to be.

I pointed to the clock on the dashboard. "See, we made excellent time thanks to my great driving skills."

"Pull over," he moaned. I laughed it off at first. "Ali, I'm not joking; I'm gonna be sick."

I moved to the shoulder and stared at my partner. He looked like a ghost compared to his normal dark complexion. "Okay, you win," I replied. "I'll take it slower."

The car came to a halt. Rodney shoved the door open and just made it ten more steps before spewing his guts all over the side of the road. He started to walk back to the car but quickly turned for another round.

"I guess you don't do well with rollercoasters," I called out to him.

My partner responded with the one-finger salute while dry heaving. A minute later, he stumbled back to the car with sweat pouring down his face.

"Don't ever do that shit again."

"Come on; it wasn't *that* bad."

Rodney wiped the sweat from his face and buckled himself back into the passenger seat. "Let's just get down to the school in one piece."

We arrived twenty-five minutes later. It would have been less time if my partner hadn't been such a baby. As we showed up to the administration building, I thought back to my conversation with my sister from yesterday when she mentioned the conversations she overheard. Unfortunately, she couldn't tell me the names of those students talking about Rachel or Nicole. That didn't mean I couldn't reach out to the other three girls I interviewed the morning after Rachel was found. They were the last ones who claimed to have seen her alive.

"Hey, can you go in and collect the attendance records?"

"Where are you going?"

"I want to check into another possible lead."

"Is it something you want to share with me? I mean; I'm supposed to be your partner in this investigation."

"I want to reach out to Rachel's three friends to see if they can give me any information on who would want either girl dead."

"Are you sure that's a good idea, Ali? You heard the lieutenant this morning. Once we start poking around; this will hit the media, and then we'll be facing a shit-storm."

"I'd rather them come knocking on our door than to let a killer go free." I left Rodney at the administration building and walked back to Capen Hall.

I walked through the front door and flashed my badge to the RM who sat in the front office. I told him who I needed to speak to, and he reluctantly agreed to bring me up to their rooms. Marci and Jodi were in class, but Lucy was still around.

"Hi, detective; what can I help you with?" she asked.

"I need to ask you some follow up questions."

"I'm on my way out, but I can talk while we go to my class."

It wasn't much time, but I was happy to get what I could. "How well did you know Rachel's roommate, Nicole Sherman?"

"We hung out a few times. She wasn't much of a party girl, so we usually just met during lunch or dinner."

"Did you know any of her other roommates?"

"I didn't know of any before Nicole. She had one other one last year."

"So, Nicole had moved out for a period of time?" I asked.

"No, all three lived in the same room. I don't really remember her name. She didn't really hang out with the rest of us."

"Do you know why she wasn't living with them this year?"

"I know there were some arguments between the three. Rachel complained about her situation. Rachel and Nicole were planning on living together just the two of them this year. Luckily, the girl decided to transfer at the end of last spring. It made their decision easier."

"Do you think the other girls might remember more about this third roommate?" This was the first time there was anyone specifically mentioned to have issues with Rachel and Nicole. Finding out her name was my best shot.

"No, but I can text them to call you when they're out of class. Maybe they can get you more information."

"Thank you, Lucy."

I broke away and headed back to the administration building. Rodney stood there with a stack of folders in his arms.

"It's about time you showed up." He lifted the pile up. "These are all yours, partner. I have to get back to the station to finish up the rest of my work."

Monday mornings were the most hectic school day. Students were still recovering from the weekend of parties, hanging out with their friends, or returning from a visit home. Everyone with morning classes scrambled to get up or finish up their homework five minutes before it was due. Mark Thompson was not concerned with any of those trivial matters. He was focused on one thing.

He sat in his car around the corner from the Grove Street house, the same one where Kevin had his Halloween party the night before. Neither of his targets had left for school. It was the determining factor in plotting his attack. He needed to know when they left for class and hope to learn how much time he had before either returned.

The moment the front door opened he noticed the curly hair holding open the screen while Christina's bald-headed companion locked up the house. Mark knew she needed to return to the dorm. Christina didn't have any of her books for Monday's classes, not unless she had them sitting in Kevin's car. Mark sped back to the dorm; doing his best to make sure he arrived before they did.

Mark walked up the path from the commuter lot and watched as Kevin's beat-up looking red Honda pulled up to the front of Lenape Hall. Christina emerged from the passenger seat. Her hair was a curly mess. She tried to tie it back, but strands fell out around her ears. She reached into her pockets. He knew exactly what the confused look on her face meant. Mark knew what she was looking for because the missing item was in his possession.

Mark swiped the ID card to access the backdoor and walked through to the front of the building. He arrived just in time to take a spot on a couch where he hid behind one of his books. He could hear someone banging on the window and pressing the buzzer to call the office.

A woman came out of a small room and opened the door enough to question Christina. "Can I help you?"

"Yeah, I can't seem to find my ID card and I need to get up to my room to get my books. I have class in an hour."

The woman held the door open and walked Christina to the room. "I need your name, room number, and some form of ID."

"My name is Christina Tyler, and I'm in room three-twenty." She reached into her back and retrieved her wallet. She took the license out and handed it to the woman.

"Why didn't you just call your roommate?"

"I don't have one right now."

"Fine, I'll let you in, but I'll need you to fill out some paperwork first." The woman made Christina sit inside the room where she was presented a form to complete.

Mark placed his text-book into his bag and inched forward like a child checking to make sure his parents weren't watching.

Go now, he thought.

Mark darted for the stairs and rushed up the three flights. The elevators on campus always seemed to take too long, and he couldn't take the chance of Christina seeing him. He located her room and knocked twice. He heard his target say there was no roommate, but he needed to be sure before barging into the room. There wasn't a single sound made in reply. It was the green light he needed to swipe the card and enter.

His eyes observed how everything looked. A lavender area rug stretched across the middle of the room between two twin-sized beds. The large wooden closets were pushed together against the wall opposite the window. There were boxes on the floor next to one of the desks. Realizing there wasn't much time before Christina came up to the room with the woman, he began searching for a place to hide.

"Remember, we're only going to do this once," the woman's voice said from the hall. "You need to get down to the Student Union and get a new ID card."

Mark opened one of the closet doors. It was large enough for him to step inside and hide, but it looked cramped and he didn't know if the doors would close. His heart was beating faster. He was almost out of time. The only options were the bathroom or under the bed. He hurried to push himself along the floor until his body was concealed by the pink comforter and the nearby boxes.

"Thank you," Christina replied as the lock buzzed. The door opened and she was permitted access to the room. "I'll try to get down there this afternoon. I have class and then work."

"Just make sure you get down there before they close at five," the woman reminded her before closing the door.

That didn't give Mark a lot of time to plan out his attack. With Rachel and Nicole, he had weeks where he plotted each aspect out. He ran through multiple scenarios of how to kill them and how to cover the murders up. This time, he had a few hours before his opportunity was lost.

He saw her sneakers approach and heard Christina dump the contents of her bag on the bed. She had picked up another backpack next to the boxes and rummaged through the contents. Papers fell to the floor as she frantically searched for the only thing Mark knew she was missing, the ID.

"Shit," she hissed. "I don't have time for this." Christina's fingers reached to pick up the papers from the floor. Her hand was a foot from Mark's face as she scooped them up. "Where the hell is it? I know I had the card yesterday."

The stiletto heels she wore the night before dropped onto the carpet. The sexy cat costume joined the pile. Mark remembered how she looked in the outfit. He wondered how many other men had hoped she would get drunk enough for them to have their way with her, or if Kevin had played with the kitty. Before his mind could drift too far off course, Christina let out a sigh bringing him back to reality.

"I really don't have the time for this. I need to get to class."

Mark positioned himself to see what his victim was doing. He saw her grab a pair of black flats, a pair of dark dress pants, and a white button-down shirt. They were placed into her peach satchel, which Christina draped over her neck and shoulder. She grabbed the books she needed and headed out the door.

Mark waited two minutes before sliding out from under the bed. There was no sign of anyone else in the room. He even checked the bathroom to make sure Christina didn't deviate last second to fix her hair or make-up.

It looks like the coast is clear.

Mark pulled out his leather gloves from his bag and placed them on his hands as he took a seat at the desk. Christina's laptop sat on top.

I wonder if I can still break into this without her knowing.

He opened it and typed a few passwords into the space provided. He gained access after the third attempt.

Time to get this party started.

Mark exited the room and headed back to his car. He grabbed a toolbox from his trunk and headed back up to Christina's dorm room. He sat at her desk and began crafting her goodbye message to the world. It took him some time to prep for his next attack, but he was ready by the time the sun set and the night sky took over. He looked down at the time and noticed the time hit eight. He closed the laptop and set the room just the way it was when Christina had left for class. He took his place under the bed where he was able to watch for the right time to strike.

Her bubbly voice could be heard approaching the room. "Hey, I was wondering if you were gonna call." The low buzz let Mark know his target was entering the room. "Tonight? Yeah, I'm free. Give me an hour to shower and get ready."

Christina put her bag down on her bed along with her cell phone. She turned and rummaged through her drawers. She grabbed a pair of black jeans and a low-cut long-sleeve silk shirt and held them against her body.

"This'll be perfect."

She slipped out of her flats before shimmying out of her tight dress pants. Then, the button-down shirt dropped to the floor. The pile of clothes rested at her bare feet, inches from Mark's face. He felt the urge to peek out from under the bed; to see her amazing curves and the rack he'd always wanted to see.

His eyes glazed over as thoughts of living in the same house as Christina came floating back through his mind. *He walked down the stairs just as she exited the first-floor bathroom wearing nothing but a baby-blue towel. Mark wished it would have been caught on something or it fell to the floor; anything which would have left him with a front row-seat to her little show. It never happened. Christina was always too quick as she darted back to her room and closed the door.*

The bra hit the floor waking Mark from his dream-like state. He was so close to getting what he wanted. His inched towards the pile of clothes, but Christina's feet carrier her away. The sound of faucet handles turning and the rush of water spraying from the shower head broke the silence. Mark wanted to pound his fist against the floor. It was a missed opportunity to get everything he wanted, but he was willing to settle for the main reason he broke into Christina's dorm.

He pulled open the laptop and searched for a recent playlist. It was one he remembered her listening to last year when they lived together. It was the distraction he needed to put the final pieces of his plan in motion. He grabbed the toolbox and began tampering with the window. He smashed a hammer in the handle of a straight-slot screwdriver; aiding in breaking the locks. He had just enough time to push the window open before the sound of the faucet handles squeaked again letting him know his target was about to come out of the shower.

Mark placed the tools back in the box and slid under the bed. He moved himself into a better position to see his victim as the pair of bare feet came dancing into the room.

Does she really think she turned the music on? Oh well, I might as well enjoy the show.

Mark inched a little closer to the bed frame. He caught the white fluffy towel fall into a heap around Christina's ankles. He was finally able to see his former roommate the way he always wanted. It was better than expected. His eyes traveled up her legs and focused on her curvy ass.

Come on; turn around.

It was almost as if she heard his thoughts and complied with the orders. Christina pulled a pair of underwear from her drawer and put them on. She turned to reach for the towel to dry off a bit more.

Mark wore a grin of satisfaction as he retrieved his phone. He was quick to snap a few pictures to capture the moment. He knew it was pervy, but that was the only chance he would ever get to see Christina Tyler naked again. He wanted something to remember her by.

How could I kill a woman that beautiful, especially after seeing her like this? The second thoughts caused him to teeter on the edge of aborting his mission.

He continued to watch her slip on the bra, then the jeans she'd laid out before her shower. It was becoming a voyeuristic version of foreplay to Mark. His heart was beating faster. He wanted Christina. He wanted to take her in the room, but an unsettling thought tore him from the lustful ideas. She was getting ready to go out, most likely with Kevin. Christina Tyler would never be his romantically, but she would be his next victim.

Christina grabbed the silk top from the bed and pulled it over her head. She danced her way over to the mirror by the bathroom to check out how she looked. Mark took the moment to slither out from her bed and quickly crossed to the vacant one across from it. He ducked under it knowing Christina would eventually go to her desk to turn off the music.

She sat down and scrolled to another song. Mark watched her stare at the screen. He knew Christina was reading the note he left for the police to find. His moment to strike was at hand. He crawled out from the bed and positioned himself behind her chair.

"What the fuck is this?" she mumbled to herself.

"Your suicide note," he whispered in Christina's ear.

His arm curled around her throat and pulled his target towards him. Christina attempted to scream for help, but her cries were silenced by the crushing of her windpipe. Her hands flailed in the air as she desperately tried to smack her assailant. Every attempt to scratch, claw or gauge her way out of the choke hold failed. The only thing left was to use her legs. She kicked backwards and connected her feet against Mark's shins. His grip loosened momentarily, but he cinched it tighter immediately.

Christina began to fade. She was starting to lose her fight to survive. Her final defensive maneuver was to place her foot between Mark's legs. She drove her heel into his groin causing her attacker to let out a low groan, but he refused to let go.

Christina's arms fell limply to the side as Mark lowered her gently to the area rug. He stood over the body massaging his bruised body parts.

"It's really such a shame things had to end this way. We could've had a lot of fun together."

Mark retrieved the toolbox from under the bed and began prying open the screen in the window. He pulled it inside just as he heard a woman cough. He knew Christina wasn't dead yet. He wanted her to know who did this to her.

"Wait, I know you," she said while gasping to get air. "You're not Mark." Her eyes flashed open. "Oh my God; you're-"

She was seconds from screaming for help. Mark needed to do something quickly before she said his name. He placed his lips on hers to silence her. Then he covered her nose and mouth with a hand.

"Sorry, sweetie; your window of opportunity has closed."

Mark pulled Christina onto his shoulder and carried her to the open window. He shoved her through it and watched as she fell three stories. Her hands clawed the air as if she they could grab some invisible rope to save her at the last second. Her eyes were filled with tears as Christina Tyler's body smashed into the cold hard concrete outside of Lenape Hall.

"OH MY GOD," someone shouted from below. "I NEED HELP. SOMEONE CALL 9-1-1; A GIRL JUST FELL OUT OF A WINDOW.

Chapter 25-Ali

I conned Rodney into coming back to my place after work so we could review the attendance logs together. We were trying to compare them to the class rosters, but there were too many for us to go through.

"This is useless, Ali," Rodney said after his third cup of coffee. "How are we supposed to pull a suspect out of this pile of crap?"

I had to agree. It was hard to stay focused. Plus, trying to find a person of interest from the information we obtained was more like throwing shit at a wall and seeing what stuck.

"You're right," I replied.

Rodney sat straight up in his chair. "I-I don't think you've ever said those words to me before." A wide toothy grin spread over his face. His eyes were largely expressive. "Say it again."

"Sorry, partner; you only get that once a decade." I was almost ready to admit defeat, but I decided to give into hunger instead. I entered the kitchen and rummaged through the junk drawer. "Hey, do you wanna order Chinese?"

"Yeah, I could eat. Did you wanna have it delivered or go out for it?"

I picked up a menu and brought it to the living room. Just as I rounded the corner, the doorbell rang.

Who the hell was that?

"Were you expecting company?" my partner asked.

"Maybe the people at the Chinese restaurant got your order telepathically and sent their delivery person to my house."

"Ah, if only it was possible," Rodney said as he relaxed in the chair with his hands folded behind his head.

I opened the door and found Matthew standing on my doorstep holding a large pizza and a six-pack. It was déjà vu from the other night.

"Hi, um, what are you doing here?"

He flashed his sexy smile which made me melt every time I saw it. "I thought we could try that movie night again. Maybe we could *actually* watch the DVDs this time.

I glanced back at the living room where Rodney sat. "I really wish you would have called. This isn't the best time."

Matthew entered the house and looked over at my partner. Rodney was sitting there with his shirt half-buttoned and his tie hanging loosely around his neck.

"I see; I guess I'm interrupting you guys."

I brushed the stray locks of hair from my face. "We were looking over the college attendance records and class rosters. We're hoping we can somehow find a suspect using this information."

Matthew looked to be defeated. "Oh, I guess I'll get out of your way then." He turned to walk out of the house, but Rodney stopped him.

"No, it's okay; I'll go. I should be getting home to the wife and kiddo before they think something happened to me." He grabbed his jacket from the chair and walked towards us.

There was a wave of relief which seemed to wash over Matthew. He glanced down and saw Rodney extending a hand. They shook on it as my partner walked out the door. He glanced back and nodded at me as if he was telling me to thank him later.

"Look, I didn't mean to get in the way of-"

I lunged forward and kissed my guy to shut him up. "We weren't getting anywhere with that heaping pile of crap." I led Matthew into the house and closed the door. "I'm starting to think our suspect has been watching too much C.S.I."

Matthew chuckled as he took my hand and pulled me closer to him while we slowly moved towards the couch. "I'm sure you'll figure a way to take this asshole down."

Matthew leaned in for another kiss. A loud vibration on the counter stole the moment. I rolled my eyes thinking it was the station.

"I should get that," I told him.

"Let it go to voicemail," Matthew urged. "You're off the clock." His hands grabbed my waist and pulled me to where I could feel a bulge in his pants. He smiled as the phone stopped. "I think it's time I take you to my interrogation room." His head jerked in the direction of my bedroom.

"Am I under arrest?" I asked seductively. "Are you gonna pat me down?" I placed my hands on the wall and looked back at Matthew with an evil smile.

"No, but a strip search is definitely in order."

I felt his hands on my back. They pulled my button-down shirt out from my pants. His fingers pressed against my skin. It was a tease, and I was at his mercy.

"Do your worst," I told him.

"That might require us to call out of work tomorrow." Matthew's hands reached around to pull at my belt.

The phone interrupted us again. Its violent vibration on the counter top was starting to piss me off. "Just let me put it on silent." I grabbed my cell and saw Amanda's name. "On second thought; let me take this." My sister had a knack for the worst timing. "Hey, sis; it's not really a good time."

"Ali, you need to get down here right away. There's been another one." I could hear people surrounding Amanda. She wanted to tell me more; I knew it by the sound of her voice trembling.

"Where are you?"

"I'm outside of Lenape. It's across from my dorm."

"I'll be there in a few minutes."

I hung up the phone and fixed my clothes. "We need to get down to New Paltz now. Someone's been killed."

"Another one?" Matthew asked. "Is your sister okay?"

"I think she's fine, but Amanda sounded really afraid. I need you to come with me and bring my sister to Sean's dorm. Stay there with them until I come back for you both."

"Don't worry about Amanda; I'll keep her safe."

I called Rodney the moment we got in the car. I told him how frantic and worried Amanda sounded on the phone. He agreed to meet me on campus, although he probably knew I would be there before he arrived.

Three dead bodies, I thought as I gripped the steering wheel tightly. *This asshole killed three innocent women.*

Matthew put his hand on my lap causing me to flinch at his touch. Thankfully, I wasn't speeding like I did with Rodney earlier in the day.

"It'll be okay, Ali. Your sister is fine."

Yeah, she was for now, but who knew what the killer was planning. It was bad enough Amanda was going to school with some sick bastard who was killing women on campus. The part tearing at me from the inside was how we let the suspect take another innocent life because we weren't able to stop them.

I made it to New Paltz within fifteen minutes. Police cars had already sectioned off the road with a perimeter surrounding the dorm. I parked on the side of the road and walked up with Matthew at my side. I began searching for my sister. I called her cell a couple of times and finally met up with her in a sea of students.

"Ali," she croaked out as she threw her arms around my neck. Amanda hugged me tightly as if she were petrified what would happen if she let go.

"We'll talk later," I advised. "Go with Matthew; he's bringing you to Sean's room until I come and get you."

"But-"

I couldn't tell if she was trying to object or say something important. It didn't matter. I was there to do a job. My sister being a witness complicated matters and jeopardized my role in the investigation.

"Trust me; you need to go now."

Matthew put a consoling hand on her shoulder. "It's for the best." He led her away from the crowd.

Amanda glanced back at me. Fear hid behind her eyes. Who could blame her? There were two girls from her dorm found dead within a week of each other. Now, a third girl died across the street. The body was lying on the ground for everyone to see. If there was any doubt before, there most certainly wasn't anymore. New Paltz had a serial killer on the loose.

"I'm sorry, miss," one of the campus police said as he attempted to stop me from ducking under the yellow crime scene tape.

I immediately held up my badge and introduced myself. "I'm with the Ulster County P.D." I waited for him to step aside before crouching low enough to cross under the tape. "What can you tell me about the crime scene and the victim?"

"I really don't know much," he replied. Yeah, like that was helpful. Hearing that was not how I wanted to begin an investigation. "The victim was a female in her early twenties. I'm guessing she was a resident." Guessing wasn't going to help me to identify the girl, and it definitely wasn't going to help catch the killer. "It appears she fell out of the third-floor window and probably died on impact."

I glanced up and saw a light shining brighter than the other windows facing me. I could already tell where the victim fell from, but I wasn't seeing any glass or screen fragments on the ground.

"I need you and the rest of the campus police to maintain a tight perimeter. I don't want anyone to go in or exit the building."

He agreed and called it over his radio. It was now onto one of my least favorite jobs as a detective, checking out the dead body. The girl was pretty. She was definitely in her early twenties. She was curvy and had curly light-brown hair.

I clenched my fist at the sight of the lifeless student lying on the ground. I viewed her death as my failure. It was my fault for not pushing harder to keep the other cases open. But I wasn't the only one to blame. The lieutenant was too busy trying to play his political games than worrying about a potential killer being on the loose. If he had just listened to me from the beginning, we might have stopped this lunatic before claiming a third victim.

A young boy broke free from the crowd and rushed towards me. One of the officers grabbed him, but I heard him shout for me.

"I need to speak to the detective; it's important."

I walked over there and told the officer to let him go. "Who are you and what do you want?" I snapped. I wasn't in the mood to deal with some murder fan or groupie. I had a lot of work to do and wasn't about to entertain some guy who probably wanted to tag along while I reviewed the crime scene.

"Are you Detective Ryan?"

"Yes, now, what do you want?"

"Your sister told me to find you. I was the one who saw the victim fall and called for help."

I pulled the boy away from the crowd. "I need you to leave my sister's name out of this and tell me everything you know."

"The girl's name is Christina Tyler."

"Did you know the victim?" I asked.

"No, I met her this morning. She showed up claiming to have lost her ID card. She needed me to let her into her room."

"What happened next?"

"Nothing really; I had her fill out some paperwork and told her to get a replacement card before the Student Union closed for the day."

"Did you notice anyone suspicious lurking around the dorm or anyone go near her room?"

"Not that I'm aware of," the boy replied.

"Do you know if Christina got the replacement card today?"

"I couldn't say for sure, but it would be pretty hard to get back into her room without it."

"Was it possible?"

"Well, yeah; but only if someone let her into the building. Then she would have had to keep the door to her room unlocked so she didn't need the card to get back in."

I already had a hunch the killer had stolen the ID sometime before this morning and used it to access the room before Christina showed up tonight. It would have meant the suspect had been lying in wait all day for their victim to return.

"I need you to come with me and keep quiet about this for now. I'll need access to Christina Tyler's room and all surveillance videos showing hallways, exits, and common areas of this dorm." I put my hands on the small of the boy's back and pushed him towards the building. Then, I saw our medical examiner approaching. "Wait here," I told the boy. I ran towards Dr. Wu. "I need you to make sure no one else but you goes near that body/"

"Uh, nice to see you too, Ali," he scoffed.

"I mean it, Fred. I am a hundred percent sure this girl is tied to the other deaths from the dorm across the street."

"Okay," he said defensively. "You have my word; no one else goes near the victim but you."

"Great, and if you see the C.S.U. team, send them upstairs to find me. We've got a lot of work to do."

Dr. Wu reached into his bag to get his camera. He began to snap pictures of the victim and of the crime scene. I was about to escort the boy into the building, but I noticed my partner parting the crowd as he approached the crime scene. He ducked under the tape and hurried around the outer circle to catch up to me.

"Hey, where are you off to in such a hurry?" he asked.

"We're about to head up to the victim's room."

Rodney's eyes flickered to Christina Tyler's body. "Ali, I'm sorry I didn't believe you sooner. You were right."

Normally, I would joke about always being right or I would chastise Rodney for not having more faith in my instincts. There was nothing I could say other than words of regret.

"For once; I wish I had been wrong."

The boy brought us inside and grabbed the room information. He escorted Rodney and I up to the door belonging to Christina Tyler. He inserted a keycard and reached for the handle.

"Don't touch it," I snapped.

There had probably been a hundred different prints on it, but I had hoped the handle had been recently wiped and the killer made a mistake. I needed to preserve it from being contaminated by anyone else's print.

"I got this," Rodney said as he slipped on a pair of latex gloves. He opened the door and let us in. The room was a little messy with clothes littering the floor. Rodney bent down and picked up a leather outfit with his pinky finger. "Someone had something kinky in mind."

I almost cracked a smile, but then I noticed something at Rodney's feet. "Don't move," I cautioned. "There's a towel a few inches from your feet." I hurried over to it and used the back of my hand to test if it was wet or dry.

"Well?" Rodney asked.

"It's still damp. Our victim must have just gotten out of the shower." I pushed the boy out of the room along with my partner. "I need you to take Officer Johnson downstairs and check all of the security footage." I grabbed my partner by the arm. "Call the lieutenant and get me a crime unit here ASAP."

Rodney escorted the boy away from the room while punching numbers into his phone. I was left to survey the room. I tiptoed around and noticed the window was wide open. It was obvious the suspect wanted Christina Tyler's death to look like a suicide, but the room wasn't as organized as the first two murders. The crime scene looked sloppy and impulsive, as if there was no plan this time.

I wanted to take notes; check the call and message logs on the victim's phone; go through her computer to make sure there wasn't anything out of the ordinary. Unfortunately, I needed the C.S.U. team to show up and do what they do best.

The first few people showed up a half hour later. "Right on time," I said sarcastically.

Two men with large bags and cameras walked down the hall accompanied by a young officer I met a few weeks ago.

"Give us a break, detective," one of the men wearing a navy-blue jacket said. "We got here as fast as we could."

I tapped my foot impatiently as they reached the door. "It's fine; I'm just wasting time waiting around for a couple of knuckleheads to get here so I can start reviewing evidence."

They stared me down and entered the room to begin their work. I stood outside and watched while occasionally pointing out something I wanted them to add to their evidence collection.

"Such a damn shame," the young officer said. "Isn't this the third girl in about two months?"

Hearing him point that out; almost made me break out in tears. I could feel my lips quiver. "Yeah," I grunted.

"Man, I hope you bring down the son of a bitch soon."

"Thanks, but we have a long way to go. Maybe we'll be lucky and the suspect screwed up."

"Is there anything I can do to help?"

"Just keep everyone without a badge away from this room." It was a cold response, but the last thing I needed was some fresh-meat rookie messing up the case over a minor detail, and it be used against us when we bring the killer to trial.

I stood by and waited for the C.S.U. team to finish their preliminary review of the crime scene. I was primed and ready to tear through the room.

"It's all yours, detective."

Access was granted. I walked around barking out more orders. "I need her cell phone before you take it away." I grabbed a notepad and started jotting down the last five numbers in the call history. "Take her charger too. I don't want this thing dying on us when we need it."

I looked around the room again. There didn't seem to be any sign of a struggle. I was sure the suspect left some sort of clue or piece of evidence behind this time. Then, my eyes zoomed in on the windowsill.

"Did you guys get a good look at this?" I pointed to the sides finding tiny scratch marks. "Someone tampered with this window." They looked at me with confusion in their eyes. "These are not meant to open this much." I unlocked the second window and lifted it up. It rose halfway compared to the one our victim fell from.

"Maybe the victim did it?"

"I really doubt that one," I replied.

"What? Chicks can use tools too, detective," the member of the C.S.U. team joked.

"Thank you for enlightening me on gender equality in the world of using tools, but I don't think our victim was the type to keep a toolbox in her room."

"Hey, you never know."

I could see they were pushing my buttons, but I was willing to put them in their place. "Fine, find me the toolbox and drinks are on me tonight. If you can't, then you owe Rodney and me a steak and lobster dinner."

Both men turned away from me refusing to make the deal. They focused their cameras on the windowsill and continued taking pictures. I decided to focus my attention to one other area before heading down to check on the second part of the crime scene outside. During our investigation into Nicole Sherman, the killer had typed up a suicide note to reinforce the theory she killed herself. I wondered if the suspect did the same for Christina Tyler.

I sat down at the desk and moved the mouse on the laptop. The screen came to life instantly. There was no password blocking my access, which meant we were supposed to find the note.

This is the end. I can't live without him anymore. I loved him for too long only to get rejected the moment I put myself out there. I can't face him. I can't face anyone after making such a fool out of myself. So this is it, my final chance to show Kevin how much he means to me. Maybe now he'll know what he lost out on.

I printed a copy of the letter and closed the laptop. "Guys, I need you to bag this too."

There was no doubt in my mind there was a killer roaming New Paltz campus and that person was making it look like their victims committed suicide.

I left Rodney to talk to the boy who brought us up to Christina's room. I had someone a little more important to speak to before he packed up and left for the night.

"Dr. Wu," I called out as I approached. He was already putting his camera away. I quickly pulled him aside. "Please tell me you have something for me."

"I definitely believe this was a homicide."

"I agree, but what are you basing your opinion on?"

"Mostly, it's the position of the body." He pointed up to the third-floor window, the same one I had the C.S.U. team taking pictures of just ten minutes earlier. "It's safe to say our victim was dropped from that opening."

I looked at Dr. Wu curiously. "Wait, you said dropped; not thrown?"

"If our victim was thrown, she would most likely have landed on the side of her face or she would be looking up at the sky. If she killed herself, she would have done a swan-dive and smashed her face into the ground. Another factor would be the direction in which she fell. The top of her head would be pointed at the street."

I review the body and thought about what Dr. Wu said. Christina Tyler's body was flat on her back with the top of her head angled towards the parking lot.

"What if she tried to grab onto something in a last-ditch attempt to break her fall?"

"It's possible but very unlikely. It wouldn't take long for a body to hit the ground after being dropped from the third floor. Plus, I don't see anything she could have been reaching for on the way down."

I stared at the body. There was no way the suspect could have killed her the way Dr. Wu explained without the victim putting up a fight or without being subdued first. It was reminiscent of how Nicole Sherman died.

"Was there any additional physical trauma done to the victim's body that wasn't caused by the fall?" I asked.

Dr. Wu bent down and pointed to a red mark around Christina Tyler's throat. The indication showed there had been some sort of strangulation prior to the fall. Then, he pointed out a bruise developing on the bottom of her right foot.

"It looks as if she got in a few good shots on our suspect before he killed her." He checked the other foot to show the difference. "She either kicked her attacker or she connected with a heavy object."

"Thank you, Dr. Wu. Hopefully, we can figure out more with the evidence collected and the information in your report."

I got all I could from the crime scene. There wasn't much else to review without a deeper analysis of the evidence and the victim's body. Both would have to wait at least until tomorrow before we could dive deeper into them. I called Rodney to let him know I was done.

"Hey, were you able to get anything from the video?" I asked.

"No, we couldn't find anyone suspicious looking and the cameras on the third floor didn't have an angle where we could see room numbers."

"So, we have nothing…again?"

"That sounds about right," Rodney replied. "All the kid was able to tell me was how he let the victim into her room this morning."

"Okay, let him go and head back out front. I need you to run everything here while the body is taken and the C.S.U. team finishes up."

"Where are you going?"

"I need to go check on my sister."

As much as I wanted to take the rest of the night off, I needed to debrief Amanda. I walked over to Sean's dorm and called her from the entrance. She came down a few minutes later, and I took her back to my house for the night.

There wasn't much to discuss. Amanda told me how she saw something falling from a window in the distance. She was about to turn towards Esopus when she heard someone scream.

"I ran towards Lenape," she told me. "When I got there, the girl was dead on the ground. Another girl was standing over her screaming. A boy showed up a minute later. He was freaked out and said he had just met with her that morning. So, I told him to wait for you."

"Thank you," I replied. "He was able to bring us up to the room and saved us some time. Unfortunately, he wasn't able to find anything on the cameras to give us any leads."

"I'm sorry, Ali."

"Don't be," I told her. "You did everything right. This suspect has been exceptionally good at covering his tracks."

"You think it's a guy?"

"It's possible the suspect is a strong woman, but my suspicion is it being a male. Whoever is behind it hoisted Nicole Sherman up using a noose and dropped Christina Tyler out a window. It's very possible they carried Rachel Walker back to her room, but we don't really know where that would have been from."

"Ali, what the hell is going on? Why is this person killing women on campus?" It was a question I kept asking myself.

"I don't know. As far as you and Sean have said, Rachel and Nicole rubbed people the wrong way. There are a lot of possibilities for potential enemies. Now that there's a third victim, we have to figure out the connection between the three girls. Maybe then, we can narrow the field of suspects."

The rest of the night was spent marking Detective Ali Ryan off-duty and stepping into the role of big sister. I spent hours consoling my sister until she fell asleep next to me in the bed. Matthew didn't bother to stick around. He knew there was nothing he could do for either of us.

When sunrise hit, I was already up and dressed for work. I decided not to venture out for my morning run to make sure my sister was okay with staying at my place for the day. We both agreed she would be safest there, and she felt more comfortable being away from other students.

I got to the station about a half hour before my shift began. I couldn't help but think about the three young girls whose lives were cut short because of some maniac.

What is the link between these three ladies?

"My office, now," the lieutenant growled as he walked by. It was weird not to hear him yell out my name in front of everyone. This was the nicest way he had ever called me into his office.

It had to be the calm before the storm. Word of a third body on New Paltz campus already hit the news. It was only a matter of time before the media began banging down our door for answers. They would definitely twist the story to paint us out to be incompetent police who let this asshole kill three girls.

I entered the lieutenant's office and stared at him. The poor bastard looked like he hadn't slept in days. His tie was already loose around his neck, the top two buttons on his wrinkled, white shirt were open, and his graying hair stood on end.

"You wanted to see me, sir."

He ran his fingers through his hair while pacing the room. "Where are we with the Campus Killer Case?"

"We still don't have a suspect, but I've established enough information to create a profile."

"Great, I want you to brief the squad in ten minutes. That should give you enough time to get ready."

"Me?" I asked. "I've never led a briefing before."

"This is your case, Ryan. You're running the show."

The lieutenant usually led these meetings. He had the officers in charge of the investigations brief him, and he spoke to the rest of the station. Now, I was in the spotlight, and I had no idea what to say. There was no substantial evidence to present to the other officers. All I had were my theories and suspicions I had obsessed over for the last two months.

I ran back to my desk and pulled the files from the Rachel Walker and Nicole Sherman cases. I pinned their pictures to the corkboard the lieutenant wheeled out to the pit.

"Can I have everyone's attention," I began. No one paid any attention to me. They ignored me, which I usually preferred.

"Hey, listen up," the lieutenant shouted forcing everyone to look his way. "Our own Detective Ryan will lead the briefing on the Campus Killer investigation. Make sure you give her your full attention."

Great, now every cop in the station was staring at me. My hands felt sweaty. I wiped them on my black slacks. I was nervous, but it was something I had wanted to do for years and it just felt right.

"I was originally assigned to the Rachel Walker case, where it was believed the victim had died in her sleep from the after-effects of binge drinking. We have since learned; Ms. Walker was the first in a series of murders. It is believed our suspect set each one to appear as if the victims died accidentally or by way of suicide. I'll admit, the first two were very convincing, but they made one mistake. Both Rachel Walker and Nicole Sherman were missing their student ID cards. My theory is our suspect had stolen Rachel's as a way to get back into the dorm to kill her roommate. They took Nicole's as a trophy.

"What about the third victim?" one of the officers asked.

"Christina Tyler had reported her ID missing yesterday morning. We have not confirmed if she obtained a new one later in the day, but we did not see one during our initial sweep."

"Do we have any potential suspects?"

"None at this time, but we have gathered enough information to piece together a criminal profile. We believe the killer is male and most likely in his early twenties. Based on the age of the victims, the suspect is a junior and either a current student or had been a student at New Paltz."

"What are you basing this profile on?" someone asked.

"All three girls are about the same age. The suspect had a working knowledge of how and when to enter the dorms. He knew where Rachel Walker lived, the building and room number. He was able to locate Christina Tyler's room and avoided being seen by any of the security cameras."

Lieutenant Esposito moved back into view and leaned on a desk next to me. "We need all hands-on deck with this one. Detective Ryan will be your point person for the investigation. All information should be brought to her attention first. I want to set up patrols in and around campus. This son of a bitch killed three young girls, let's not give him a chance to claim a fourth victim." His head swiveled to make eye contact with every officer watching us. "Dismissed," he barked causing the rest of the staff to scatter.

I waited until the lieutenant and I were alone before pulling him aside. "I was wondering if you could reach out to some of your old contacts to get some new cameras installed at the school, especially the dorms. Maybe we can even have some dummy ones put up in an effort to force the suspect to slip up."

"I'll see what I can do," he replied. "You just better get me a solid lead before the media shows up on our doorstep and eats us alive."

I braced myself for the media onslaught expected to face. We didn't have anything concrete, and our station was about to jump into a tank of sharks who were looking for their next meal. Mentally, I was prepared to walk out of the building to a mob of reporters, photographers, and residents of Ulster County demanding answers. Instead, a bald headed man with facial piercings stormed the entrance and barged inside.

"Who the fuck is in charge?" he shouted. One of the officers stood in his way. "I need to talk to whoever is investigating Christina Tyler's murder."

"Calm down, sir," another officer said. "What can we help you with, sir?" He inched closer to the bald headed man.

I saw the man clench his fist and raised it level with his chest as if he was about to strike. "I don't want to talk to you, idiots. I only want someone who can give me answers."

"Just relax, sir; and we can sit down peacefully."

"Don't tell me what to do," the man spat. "If you jackasses knew how to do your job, then Christina would still be alive."

I watched as more officers approached the bald headed man. They had their hands on their batons. "Sir, if you don't quiet down, then we'll have to restrain you."

"So, you'll arrest an innocent man for speaking the truth, but you won't admit there's a killer on the loose in New Paltz. Maybe I need to go after this guy since you fat slobs won't."

I was sick of hearing their horrible attempt to de-escalate the situation and decided to step in. "Enough," I called out while pushing my way through the sea of officers. "I'm Detective Ali Ryan, and I'm in charge of Christina Tyler's investigation."

"Great, a chick who thinks she's a big shot. Look, lady-"

"No, you listen," I snapped. I pointed a finger at his chest and pushed him back an inch. I really wasn't in the mood to deal with some sexist bullshit. "I'm the one in charge. So, unless you have some important information or a lead to give us; I suggest you shut your trap and get the hell out of my station before we throw you in a holding cell for the next twenty-four hours."

The man looked like he was about to argue, but he closed his mouth. His eyes looked down at the floor. Then, he spoke in a much softer tone.

"Christina was one of the few friends I had here. I just wanna help find her killer." The anger which once filled his eyes was now replaced by a red glassy stare.

"Come with me," I said sternly while motioning for Christina's friend to follow. I took him back to one of the interrogation rooms. I pointed to one of the uncomfortable cushioned metal chairs and instructed him to have a seat. I positioned him in front of the long mirror so the lieutenant could hear and see everything the man had to say. "Let's start over. How about we begin with your name?"

"My name is Kevin…Kevin Graham," he choked out.

"Okay, that's better. Now, how do you know Christina Tyler?"

"We were housemates and became really good friends. She wanted to live on campus and finally moved off the waiting list this year."

"How often did you speak with her?"

"When we lived together; we talked every day and had dinner every night. We started to drift apart after she moved out, but we reconnected after the summer."

"Earlier, you insisted she had been murdered. Why do you think someone killed her?"

"Isn't it obvious? Three girls have been found dead under suspicious circumstances in the last couple of months. It doesn't take a genius to figure it out."

Try telling that one to my lieutenant.

"When was the last time you saw Christina?"

"I dropped her off in front of her dorm yesterday morning." Kevin took a deep breath and launched into the weekend he spent with Christina Tyler. He told me all about their trip with the Outdoors Club up to Mohonk Mountain on Saturday. Then, he brought up the party at his house on Sunday night and how Christina spent the night at his place."

"Can you describe her behavior during the trip?"

"She was happier than I had ever seen her. It was almost infectious."

"What do you mean?"

"Christina had a very bubbly personality and was incredibly friendly. She could meet someone and be best buds within an hour. In fact, she talked to a bunch of people from the trip and even convinced me to invite them to my party."

"I'm going to assume everyone there was of age." I watched his eyes shift from side-to-side after my comment. It was as if he was trying to decide how to respond. "I'll just take that as a yes." He squirmed in the chair. That's what I wanted. Making the person being interviewed uncomfortable helped me get a better read on them, which caused them to let something slip. "So, Christina spent Sunday night at your house, and you dropped her off in front of the dorm yesterday morning. Can you tell me where you were last night?"

Kevin slammed his fist on the table. "Are you insinuating I had something to do with her death?"

"I'm just trying to rule you out as a potential suspect."

"Why would I show up here on my own if I killed Christina or any of those other girls?"

I maintained my composure. "You tell me; why would you want to kill Christina Tyler?" The last question was crossing the line, but I needed him to break and tell me something useful.

"I'd never hurt her," he replied. "I love Christina." He cupped a hand over his mouth as he blurted out the words. I could tell he had never said that to anyone before, and I suspected he never told Christina either.

I leaned forward and dropped my voice to a whisper. "Just tell me where you were last night, so we can get on with the investigation."

"I was home getting ready to pick Christina up for our date."

Did he say a date? I guess he made a move at some point to transition from friends to something more.

He must have noticed the indifference in my eyes. "Everything changed this weekend. I had never been camping before, but Christina convinced me to go." He told me all about his reservations about going and how she made him go hiking with the rest of the group. "When we got back, I was calmer and tried to set up the tents again. I asked for some help and managed to get her tent up, which was big enough for both of us."

"And then what happened?"

"We sat up when everyone else went to sleep. We talked and eventually made-out. We put our sleeping bags together inside the tent and slept next to each other."

"Was this why she stayed at your place Sunday night?"

He nodded. "She stayed the night once before when I had a small party over the summer. This time was different. We weren't living together, and this was the first time we share a bed."

I could see Kevin was genuine. His eyes were filled with love for Christina. But the more he thought about what they'd shared, the more he realized he was never going to have another moment like that with her again. His expression changed, and I could see the pain and sadness in his eyes.

"Can you tell me about the people who came to your party?"

"A bunch of them were friends from Westchester. A couple of them were my current roommates. The rest were friends of roommates and people from the Outdoors Club. I really don't know much about them."

"Did any of your current roommates know Christina?"

"No, everyone who lived with her moved out already, so they were all new people. I didn't really talk to their friends."

"What about the Outdoors Club; do you remember any of their names? Was anyone acting suspicious?"

"I really don't know who showed up from the club. A lot of people were dressed up in costumes. The only people I really remember being there were the club leaders Marty and Marie."

"Do you know their last names?"

Kevin shook his head. "I really didn't care enough to ask that information. I was only part of the club because Christina asked me to be there."

I jotted down the names Marty and Marie and left a note next to them staying Outdoors Club. I racked my brain to think of any more questions for Kevin, but I wasn't getting much out of him.

I placed a card on the table with my contact information. "Take this and call me if you can think of anything else that could help us."

Kevin took the card and stood up. "So, that's it; I'm free to go?"

"Yeah, you're all set; unless you have something else to tell us." I waited for Kevin to respond, but he shook his head. "Then, I suggest going home and leaving the investigation to the police." I got up from the chair and moved towards the door. "Oh, and one more thing; I plan on taking the son of a bitch who killed Christina and the other girls down."

Chapter 27-Ali

Lieutenant Esposito pulled me aside the moment I left the interrogation room. "I want you to find out who Marty and Marie are and convince them to hand over the names of everyone on that trip."

Apparently, the lieutenant and I were on the same page. We both had a hunch the killer had posed as a member of the Outdoors Club. My money was on the suspect using the party as a way to steal Christina's ID card to break into her dorm room.

"I'll grab Rodney and head down to the school now."

I could easily have gone by myself, but my partner was tall, muscular, and possessed an intimidation factor which could force people into giving us information we wanted.

I waited for Kevin to leave the station before signaling Rodney to follow me. "The kid gave us a lead to look into. He went on a hiking/camping trip with the school club on Saturday and invited that same group over for a party on Sunday. We need to head over and find out who runs it and get the list of people who went on that trip."

"Okay, let's go." Rodney stopped short and turned towards me. "But I'm driving this time."

I wasn't about to argue after my partner puked out his breakfast the last time we rode together. "Fine, but you better not drive five miles an hour."

"Well, you're in luck; I now drive fifteen miles an hour," he joked.

We got in the squad car with the New Paltz campus set as our destination. We parked in front of the administration building and entered the lobby. Rodney held up a finger as if he was using it as a laser pointer on the directory board.

"The registration office is downstairs," he advised.

We saw the stairs to the left and took the short flight down to the basement level. A few quick turns placed us in front of the school store. We continued down the corridor until we arrived at a series of window-panes and a door marked for the registrar. I walked inside holding out my badge as I approached an older woman with thick glasses and white hair.

"Good morning, I'm Detective Ryan, and this is my partner Officer Johnson. I was hoping you could help us. We're investigating the deaths which occurred on this campus."

"Well, it's about time someone did something," she mumbled under her breath just enough for me to hear her. "How can I help you?"

"I need the names of the students who run the Outdoors Club. We know their names are Marty and Marie, but we need their last names, or any other students associated with the club."

"I'm sorry; I can't help you with that request. Even if I could, that information is confidential and would require a warrant." The woman went back to the paperwork on her desk as if Rodney and I weren't there.

This was our first substantial lead, and we were being held back by a cranky sixty-year-old woman. A minute earlier, she was acting as if the police hadn't done anything to investigate the murders. Now, she was standing in the way of our case.

I nodded to my partner. He leaned more to the sympathetic and compassionate side of requesting information. I was always the one being called ma'am, sweetie, honey, hot stuff, or getting hit on to be taken seriously. So, I of course always took a more blunt approach to going after what I wanted.

Rodney stepped forward. The woman looked like a toddler compared to my partner. "I know you're just doing your job, ma'am, but I think the college would be willing to cooperate with the police since there have been three deaths on their campus." Rodney leaned over the counter and stared the woman down.

She bit her lip nervously. "I-I'll see if my boss can help you." Her attitude completely changed in a manner of seconds. She was no longer making comments under her breath or being uncooperative. She was too busy scrambling out of her chair to get her boss for us.

"Yeah, you do that," Rodney muttered just enough for me to hear.

The older woman returned a minute later with a tall blonde in a knee-length gray pencil skirt, black flats, and a white-button down which had been tucked in tightly to accentuate her boobs. She was in her late thirties or early forties, but this woman was good looking enough to be a model. She was a complete knockout, one who even made me want to say *Damn!*

"Close your mouth, Rodney," I whispered while nudging my partner. He quickly brought his hand up to his mouth and faked a yawn.

The woman glanced over at us. I could tell her focus was on Rodney by the way she stared. She turned to her office for a moment and returned a second later with her blouse missing the top two buttons.

She strutted over to the counter and extended a perfectly manicured hand with French tips. "Good morning, detectives; I'm Anna Rutowska." She shook our hands with a firm grip. "Betty says you need access to our student records."

"We don't need to see them," I corrected her. "We just need to know who is in charge of the Outdoors Club and where we can find them. We need to ask them a few questions about the trip they took this past weekend and who went with them."

She glared at me. "Don't you need a warrant for something like this?" Her question was laced with an anger directed at me. I could already tell this bitch had it out for me and I had no idea why.

Rodney must have noticed the tension too. He stepped forward to push me out of the way. He cleared his throat and turned on his charming and sexy-man voice that he uses to get a woman to cooperate.

"We were hoping you could help us get around that issue." He leaned on the counter and placed a finger next to Ms. Rutowska's hand. "I would be very appreciative if you could help save us a bit of time so we can hunt down this killer and stop them from hurting anyone else."

I watched as the woman's eyes devoured my partner as she stroked his hand gently. "I think something can be arranged." Ms. Rutowska strutted back towards her office. She stopped in the doorway and turned back to stare at Rodney. "Are you coming?" She wiggled her eyebrows at him. I started to move around the counter, but she held up a hand. "No, detective; you can stay put. I only want your partner."

Rodney gulped down a breath of air. His eyes open wide as he took baby-steps towards the open office door.

"Just remember; you're a married man," I whispered while patting him on the back. I watched him enter the office and close the door. I took a seat across from Betty's desk to wait patiently for my partner to return. "So, how long have you worked here?" I got no response except an evil glare.

Great, this is going to be super awkward, I thought. I was stuck waiting with some miserable old woman who stared daggers through me; while Rodney was behind closed doors doing God knows what to get us the information we needed. I just hoped he wasn't about to cross a line he couldn't come back from.

Shortly after the door closed, I heard loud noises coming from the office. It sounded like something was being slammed against filing cabinets. The sounds continued for several minutes ending with a woman's voice squealing with delight.

"Yes…yes…that's it; right there."

I looked back at Betty. "You don't happen to have some ear plugs in that desk; do you?" She didn't even look up from her work. She gave a lighthearted chuckle and kept typing away. *A simple no would have sufficed.*

The door opened a few minutes later. Rodney stepped out with his uniform looking like a wrinkled mess. His shirt was un-tucked. Ms. Rutowska appeared in the doorway a moment later with an exasperated look on her face. The buttons on her shirt were open more than they already were previously. I shook my head disapprovingly at my partner as we exited the registrar's office.

"What; I got the information," he stated with a sly smile. His hand gripped the small piece of paper.

"Yeah, at the cost of your marriage," I replied.

Rodney took a couple extra strides to get ahead of me before turning around. His massive hand pushed against my shoulder to hold me back.

"What are you talking about?"

"I'm talking about the wild sex you just had with that office slut." We never held back our comments to each other, especially if either of us thought the other was doing something to hurt their life or someone else's. "We could hear you guys in there."

"Whoa," he replied. "I didn't…we didn't…that's not what happened." Rodney wiped a bead of sweat from his face. "Anna wanted help moving the filing cabinet out of the way, so she could hang a painting on the wall."

"Really; I'm supposed to believe that load of bull?" My partner nodded his head in response. "Then, why was she squealing like that? I mean; the only times I've heard a woman make those kinds of noises were in pornos."

"Ali, she was happy the painting was finally up in her office. It was a picture of where she grew up as a child in Poland." Rodney turned around to go back down the hall towards the stairs but spun around to stare me down. "Wait, when and why were you watching pornos?"

I could feel the heat rising in my cheeks. That was something personal, which I didn't particularly want to share with my partner. Instead, I snatched the paper from his hands and took off down the corridor to the stairs. I made it up to the first floor and out the doors before Rodney got halfway up the steps.

"What's the matter, old man; can't keep up?"

"You…got…a…head…start," he gasped.

"Oh please; I was faster than you and I did it in heels."

"And you run every day for the fun of it." Rodney doubled over with his hands pressed on his knees. "Can we just check out the people on the list before I'm the next person found dead on this campus?"

That was a bit morbid even for us. "Don't ever joke like that again," I warned him. Our humor could be dark at times, but that comment was a little too much.

We took a few minutes for Rodney to catch his breath before heading off towards the southern end of campus. Our destination was a fifteen-minute walk, not something I was fond of doing in three-inch heels going up and down steps and small hills. As we started our journey to find Marty and Marie, I heard a woman's voice calling my name. We turned to see my sister jogging over to us. I was surprised to see her there considering our plans were to have her stay at my place for the day. I guess she decided classes were a better way to forget about what happened.

I could see the concern in her eyes. "Ali, what are you doing here?"

"We're here on official police business," I advised.

Amanda brought her voice down to a whisper. "Please don't tell me there was another death."

"No," I replied. "We're here to speak with a couple of students about one of the victims." I couldn't tell Amanda anything more than that with Rodney standing there. He wouldn't rat me out to the lieutenant, but I liked to give him as much deniability as possible. "Where are you going?" I asked.

"I need to run to the library for a book before my next class."

Rodney took the moment to be a cop more than a family friend. "Can you tell us anything about the girl from last night?"

"I've hung out at Lenape a few times. I don't really know anything about the girl except for her name. From what I've heard; she was well liked."

Amanda and I didn't go into too much last night other than what happened at the crime scene. Rodney had done me a favor by opening the door to questioning my sister, and I had a couple of my own.

"What else do you know about Christina Tyler? What have you heard from other students?"

"I just know she transferred to New Paltz last year as a sophomore and lived off-campus."

"Do you know where?" I asked.

"Not really," Amanda replied. "I overheard her once telling people it was hard living in a house full of guys."

My mind replayed the conversation with Kevin. He had told me about living in the same house with Christina Tyler prior to her moving into Lenape Hall. He mentioned other housemates had stayed there too, but they had all moved out. It was a small fact I overlooked.

"Do you know if one of those guys she was complaining about was Kevin Graham?"

"Was he a dorky looking guy?"

"No, I would say he belonged to the Goth scene."

"I have no idea who that is," Amanda replied. "I just remember her saying there was guy who moved out earlier than the rest and it made everything so much better at the house. Based on what I overheard, it doesn't sound like Christina or her housemates like this kid."

I heard Rodney ask if my sister knew the guy's name, but I was thrown off by the eerie feeling I was being watched. I stopped short and felt someone smack into me from behind. It was a boy in his early twenties. Books scattered on the grass around us.

"I'm so sorry," the boy mumbled as he quickly tried to gather his belongings. He pushed the text-book open. "Are you okay?"

"I'm fine," I replied. "Are you hurt?"

"What? No, I'm just in a hurry. I have a test in a half-hour and I need to cram a little more." He propped open the book on his arm and hurried off reading it again as he rushed towards the buildings where most of the classes were held.

I brushed off the grass from my dress-pants. I stepped back into my shoe and stared at the boy as he kept going without looking back at us.

I turned to my sister. "I really need you to be careful but still keep your eyes and ears open for me. People have no problem talking except when it comes to police. No one says anything to cops, which makes it harder to catch the bad guys."

"Gee, I wonder why," Amanda laughed. "Maybe it has to do with badgering us for answers when we don't know anything. I mean; I'm your sister and I always feel like you're interrogating me."

"That's because I'm the older sibling and I have to look out for you."

"I'll remember that the next time I want the scoop on your relationship," Amanda warned. "You know; just so I can make sure you're okay."

I lightly shoved my sister. "Get your butt to the library and then to class." We dropped Amanda off at the entrance and said goodbye. I looked over at my partner. "Come on; we have some leads to follow up on."

Chapter 28-CK

Mark walked the New Paltz campus after grabbing lunch at the Student Union. He needed to keep up appearances to ensure no one viewed him as being suspicious. It was also a celebration of sorts since he knocked off three of the four people on his list. He felt great until he noticed two people and he recognized the cops who were working all three cases. The duo was walking with another girl, with a striking resemblance to the female detective.

What the hell are they doing here?

Mark continued walking towards small group. It was foolish of him to pursue the trio. He was tempting fate, but he needed to hear what they were talking about. Then, he realized the two ladies were sisters.

Well, that puts an interesting little twist on things.

Mark moved in closer in hopes of hearing a discussion about the dead girls. He pulled out his psychology text book and opened it up to chapter ten. He kept it steady in his arms as he continued to keep pace with the officers while staying far enough away to avoid suspicion. He was within earshot of them as they started talking about knowing Christina Tyler.

He heard every little word the younger one spoke. It was being implicated as a potential suspect without any of them knowing his name. Mark's heart started racing. Panic had set in. The police were getting closer to discovering the truth. He thought they were still looking at each death as a suicide or accident. His latest may have been the tipping point, and now he didn't know what to do.

Mark stared at his text book too long. The detective stopped short causing him to collide with her. He dropped everything while knocking her off her feet; out of her shoes; and to the ground. His hands braced for impact; stopping him before his face hit the sides of the detective's pumps.

"Sorry," he quickly said with a mix of urgency, panic, and anxiousness in his voice. Mark tried desperately to hide his face from the trio he was stalking. "Are you okay?" He didn't want to ask it, but knew it was the only way to cover up what really happened. If he had just run off, he would look suspicious.

"I'm fine," the detective replied. "Are you hurt?"

"What? No, I'm just in a hurry. I have a test in a half hour and I need to cram a little more." Mark gathered everything back into his arms and positioned the text book to look like he was studying again while rushing off.

What the hell did I do? It's only a matter of time before they figure out who I am and my connection to those dead bitches. And now, I literally ran into the cops hunting me while spying on them.

He walked at a quicker pace until he made it to the steps between the Lecture Hall and the library. Anger took over after realizing he had been foolish to think he could eavesdrop on two cops without alerting them. He kicked the metal rail out of frustration; repeating it until his foot began to throb.

Thankfully, there was no one around, but Mark heard voices approaching. They sounded like they were coming from the same direction he had just left, which meant the trio was headed his way. Mark fled down the steps to the parking lot and took the loop back around to look for his car.

That fucking bitch knows. They all know, and it won't be long until they find me.

He rushed to get home. It was time to put his backup plan into action before it was too late. He reached his apartment and slipped inside without anyone seeing him. It was time to purge everything and figure a way out.

He began by pulling every duffle bag he owned out from under the bed. The desk was his first objective. It was the only place with evidence from the murders; even though he only had one ID and the list sitting in the top center drawer. There was also a spare cell phone with prepaid minutes. He grabbed it and dialed the only person who he felt could help him go into hiding.

"Hey, it's me," Mark said on the voice message. "Shit is starting to hit the fan and I need to get out of New Paltz for a while. I could really use your help. Please call me back when you get this; it's an emergency."

Mark hung up the phone and kept it in his back pocket. Once the computer and the contents of the desk were packed up, Mark began throwing his clothes into bags. He was in a rush to get out of the apartment, but he was determined to grab everything to ensure there was nothing the police could use to identify him. After the room was stripped bare, Mark took bleach and other cleaners to all the surfaces. He refused to let anyone find a single drop of his DNA in the room.

Suddenly, there was a soft knock on his door. Panic set in. *Was it the police? Did they figure out it was him already? Did that detective follow him back to the apartment?*

"Hey, I know you're in there," a woman called through the door.

Mark knew it was Jess. Part of him wanted to let her in to talk, but it would only delay his escape. She knocked again and called out his name. Mark needed to silence her before she drew attention to him or his apartment.

He stripped off the gloves and opened the door. "What's up?" he asked as his eyes drank in the sight of a hot brunette wearing tight yoga pants.

Her head tilted to see the bags on the bare mattress. "Um, are you going somewhere?"

"Yeah," Mark replied. He ran a million different excuses through his mind but settled on the simplest reason. "I need to go home for a few days."

"Oh," Jess replied. His response left the conversation open for follow up questions digging into a cover story. She looked back at him. "When are you leaving?"

"Tomorrow," Mark said.

"Wait, what about your classes?"

"I'm taking some time off." He knew Jess was already becoming more inquisitive. She was getting more suspicious by the moment. He needed to say something to throw her off. Mark put on his sad puppy dog eyes. "My aunt passed away last night. I have to get back for her wake and funeral."

Jess pulled him into a tight embrace. "I'm so sorry," she said sympathetically. "If there's anything I can do…"

"Thanks," he whispered into her ear.

Mark held her tightly against his body not wanting to let go. Jess was his hope for the future. She was supposed to be his once he got rid of every name from his list. But then, he remembered how she turned him down; put him in the friend zone; and took away his last chance for happiness. The anger was rising again causing Mark to break their embrace. He pretended to wipe invisible tears from the corners of his eyes.

"I need to get back to packing and cleaning."

"Do you want some help?" Jess asked.

"No, I just need some time alone."

"Did you let Val know you're leaving?"

"No, everything happened today. If I don't see her before I go, I'll leave a note under her door in the morning."

Jess grabbed his hand with a quick squeeze. "Call me if you need anything." She wrapped her arms around Mark one more time before exiting the room.

"Thanks," Mark mumbled.

He considered using the cover story as a way to get something out of his neighbor. Sympathy sex crossed his mind. It was the one thing he wanted before going into hiding. He considered going across the hall to go after Jess but remembered the last time he was turned down and how horrible he felt.

Snap out of it, he thought. *You need to stop this love-sick puppy bullshit and focus on getting out before the cops find you.*

Mark stood at the entrance of his room staring at his neighbor's closed door. He was about to listen to the voice inside his head but changed his mind at the last second. He stormed across the hall and knocked on the door.

Jess opened it and looked at Mark seemingly confused to see him again. "Hey, did you forget something?"

"Yeah, there's something I need to do before I go…in case I don't come back." Mark saw she was about to ask what he meant by it, but he decided to shut her up.

Mark grabbed Jess by her waist and pulled her towards him. His lips smothered hers in one quick motion. He pushed her against the door frame.

A minute later, Jess pushed him back. "Wow," she said slightly breathless. Mark felt the same way and wanted to continue. He moved in to kiss her again, but Jess stopped him. "That was intense, but I think we should hold off until you get back from your trip."

"I will try to get back as soon as I can."

"You better," she replied.

Mark went back to his room as they both lingered in their separate doorways. He closed the door, but took everything in him to fight wanting to stay. He was willing to risk his freedom for a chance with Jess. He glanced around the room and saw how much he had packed and cleaned. The reality of what he had done and what was needed weighed heavily on his mind. In that moment, he knew there was no other option which let him live free with Jess at his side.

It was time to pull a little disappearing act.

<u>Chapter 29-Ali</u>

Our remaining objective was to locate Marty and Marie. Based on their schedules, they were done for the rest of the afternoon. It would have been a lost cause, but I had a few ideas thanks to my sister being so nosey.

"Why are you so happy?" Rodney asked. I reached for my cell and stabbed at the numbers. "Who are you calling?"

I held up my finger to silence my partner. The call instantly connected to the D.A.'s office. "Hi, is Ms. Colon available? This is Detective Ali Ryan."

"Weren't you just here?" the woman asked.

"Yes, and I need to speak with Ms. Colon about another request."

"Hold please," she replied. The line went silent until another woman picked up two minutes later.

"Hello, detective; how can I help you this time?" Yvette Colon's voice was stern; sassy; and had a bit of sweetness when she spoke.

"I need another warrant to conduct a search at the New Paltz campus." I was sure my request was going to be met with some pushback, but I had a few ideas on how to catch our killer.

"Another one?" she asked. "We just issued one the other day. Why do you need another search warrant?"

"Actually, I need a few," I replied knowing the D.A. was about to flip out over my latest favor. "I need one to search the guest logs at Esopus, one for Lenape Hall, and one to check the administration building for students reporting lost ID cards."

"And what exactly are you looking for, detective?"

"We know the killer is either a current student or recently left the university. We know this same person had history with all three victims, one of which told the RM at her dorm about losing her ID over the weekend. I believe the suspect has either stolen other cards to break into the dorms or had been very familiar with the dorms and where the girls lived."

"What about the dorm logs? Why do you need them?"

"In case the killer needed to get in after hours and was forced to sign-in when he showed up. That one is a long shot, but I think we might find something useful."

"Do you have any proof?" she asked.

"No, ma'am," I replied.

"So, this is just another random theory you're hoping will lead you to some credible piece of evidence?"

"With all due respect; this son of a bitch murdered three young women on a college campus in their own dorms. They cleaned up the crime scenes well enough to make each appear like an accident or suicide. We need to do whatever it takes to find out who did it and bring them to justice."

"While I admire your determination, Detective Ryan; it will be hard to convince a judge to grant several warrants without any shred of proof." She took a long pause as if she were mulling things over before rendering her decision. "When do you need them by?"

"I'll take whenever you can get them."

"Fine, meet me at the courthouse in an hour, and I'll see if we can get a judge to grant you the warrants."

I hung up the phone and turned towards my partner with a smirk on my face. He shook his head instantly. "I know that look," he said. "You want me to go down there and get your warrants; don't you?"

I folded my hands and batted my eyes playfully. "Please, Rodney; it'd be a real big help."

"How is it you're the detective and yet I'm the one doing all your grunt work?"

"It's because you love me."

"Fine, I'll go." He sighed heavily and started to walk off. Rodney came to a halt and spun on his heel. "Wait, why aren't you going?"

"I'm gonna track down Christina Tyler's housemate, the one who barged into our station demanding answers. Maybe he can clue us in about the other guys who lived with them."

"Do you want me to drop you off at the station?"

"No, I want to walk around campus for a bit. I can have someone pull his address and call a cab if it's too far."

"You're gonna pay for it later." He raised an eyebrow and tilted his head to glance down at me shoes.

Yeah, I didn't take the heels into consideration. "Don't worry about me; I can deal with them for a bit. You need to get down to the courthouse. It'll take you the whole hour or longer driving at your speed."

I watched Rodney walk back to the north side of campus. I knew I should have taken him up on the offer, or even gone to the courthouse myself to ensure we got the warrants. But hearing my sister mention Christina had an issue with one of her former housemates made me think one of them could be a potential suspect.

I called the station and asked them to run the name Kevin Graham. They managed to pull an address, which wasn't far from campus. It was pointless to call a cab. By the time someone showed I could have made it to my destination and back. So, I decided to hoof it over a mile and a half to Grove Street.

I really need to bring a pair of sneakers with me when I leave the station, I thought as blisters began to form on the bottom of my feet. It took me twenty minutes, but I finally arrived at my destination. *This can't be the place.*

It was an average looking ranch style home which had seen better days. The blue painted siding had begun to fade. The boarded up windows and door made me think I had the wrong house. I decided to approach with caution and check out the home just in case I was wrong and someone really was staying there. When I reached the porch, I realized there were tons of fake cobwebs, an old rocking chair, and a large stuffed spider hanging near the entrance.

I guess someone loves Halloween.

I moved towards the wooden barricade and pulled it aside with ease. It uncovered the front door. I gave it a loud knock. No one answered at first.

"Mr. Graham, this is Detective Ryan. Mr. Graham, I may have a lead on Christina Tyler's killer, and I could really use your help."

The door swung open instantly with Kevin standing inside the house with a look of anger and sadness in his eyes.

"What did you find? Do you have a suspect in custody?"

I didn't really want to talk about it in the open. Our conversation could have been heard by anyone walking by or a neighbor. Anyone could be our suspect. I also knew the end of the semester was approaching, which meant the killer could be looking to make a run for it. I didn't want Kevin's anger and accusations to alert him and send him into hiding sooner.

"Can we speak inside?"

Kevin stepped aside allowing me to enter his home and into a narrow hallway next to a staircase. He escorted me to a small, brightly lit kitchen. He removed a wooden chair to sit in and kicked another out for me.

"I guess you're not here to tell me you caught the son of a bitch. So, what do you want?"

"We need to discuss your former housemates. How many lived here with you and Christina?"

"Two other guys," Kevin replied.

"What were their names?"

"Why? Did they have something to do with this?"

Kevin was already jumping to conclusions, which was not what I wanted. He could easily give me nothing to work with and then go after one or both of his former housemates on his own.

"I'm trying to eliminate as many potential suspects as I can. I figured you would be the best person to help me; unless you don't want to catch Christina's killer."

Kevin had an angry glare to his eyes. My comment was designed to get under his skin and insinuate his failure to cooperate would result in his girlfriend's murderer to slip away.

"There was Brian Rivera and Nick DeFalco." Kevin grimaced as he uttered the second name.

I jotted down both names and put an asterisk next to Nick. "Did they get along with Christina?"

"We all did…for a little while."

"What changed?"

"Brian was a heavy drinker. He came home from class and popped open a beer the moment he walked through the door. He hung around the house for a few hours before walking into town to go bar hopping. We'd find him passed out on the couch, the porch, on the kitchen table and even the floor. We thought he had an alcohol problem. It went on for a few months until we decided to call him out on it. He, of course, denied it and stormed off. We figured he went to the bars to drown out our comments."

"Did he ever get violent?"

"No," Kevin said immediately. "Brian was the complete opposite. Yeah, he would argue with us, but he would always get really quiet and disappear for a while. He just wanted to be left alone."

"When was the last time you heard from him?"

"I wanna say it was in July. He moved out of the house in May and said he wasn't coming back. Then, he called me over the summer to say we were right about him, and he was going into rehab."

"So, there were no hard feelings?"

"No, in fact, Brian told me he was going to take Christina and me out to dinner when he was done with rehab to thank us."

"Do you know where he was going to rehab?"

"No clue, but I know his family lives in Nyack. They would probably have a better idea."

The rehab could have been a cover story to make people believe he was out of town when all the murders happened, but it didn't seem like Brian Rivera had any anger or resentment towards his housemates.

"Okay, what can you tell me about Nick?"

The anger in Kevin's eyes came back into an icy cold stare. It sent a shiver down my spine.

"Nick was a decent guy when he first moved in," Kevin noted. "He got along with everyone and even helped out around the house."

"And then what happened?"

"Nick became obsessed with his girlfriend, Brianna. I mean; I don't blame him. She was hot. Who wouldn't want to spend all their time with a girl like that?"

Kevin's statement led me to believe he viewed Brianna differently than the other housemates. "Did you get along with his girlfriend?"

"Everyone did," Kevin replied. "Everyone liked hanging out with her, but not when Nick was around. He was too overprotective and was overly paranoid."

"In what ways did he show this behavior?"

"Nick insisted on driving Brianna everywhere. He picked her up and dropped her off at every class. If she made plans to hang out with her friends, Nick had to go too."

"Did you witness this first-hand?"

"No, Brianna told me how Nick treated her."

"Did you and his girlfriend speak often?"

"I would say a few times a week through IMs or texts."

I was seeing multiple patterns forming. Kevin seemed to get in the middle of a lot of his housemate's affairs; first Brian and now Nick. I was beginning to think Christina Tyler might have played a similar role.

"What did you witness when Nick and Brianna were around?"

"In the beginning, they were both cool to hang with and talk to. She started sitting in the kitchen with us more than spending time with Nick. He might have been jealous because he would come down and order her up to his room. They'd hide there for hours until they had to go somewhere, or they argued."

"How often did this happen?"

"This was normal behavior that went on almost every day until Nick stopped bringing her to the house."

I jotted down more notes. "How was he with the rest of the housemates when Brianna wasn't around?"

"After he became controlling with her, we barely saw him. Then, we just stopped including him in house gatherings like parties, club nights, or going to the movies. He started to throw hissy fits over it because no one asked if he wanted to go."

"So he was cut out of your lives completely?"

"We were sick of him," Kevin replied. "We wanted him out of the house. So, we chose to ignore him and pretended like he wasn't there."

"I'm sure that went over well with Nick." Hearing the statement come from my mouth surprised me. I had meant to think it, not say it out loud. Then, I noticed Kevin fidgeting in his chair awkwardly.

"It kind of worked out better than we expected." Kevin took a deep breath and recapped the last month Nick spent in the house. "He tried to pick fights with us hoping to get someone to respond and acknowledge him. We did our best to stay silent. He made some sort of arrangement with the landlords and started packing his room up. He kept cursing and yelling the whole time. Brian, Christina, and I went out to a movie, so we didn't have to hear him. When we got back, almost three hours later, Nick was gone and the whole house was trashed."

My notepad was filled with every detail Kevin provided. "Do you know where he went?"

"I heard he moved to some studio apartment owned by our landlords."

I got the names of the owners for my own records and people to possibly follow up with once I learned more about Nick DeFalco.

"Have you heard from him since then?"

"No, and I would rather keep it that way. I did hear from Brianna a few times since he left. She broke up with him at the end of last semester."

"Do you know how Nick reacted to being dumped?"

"She wouldn't say, but Brianna wasted no time moving out of town. In fact, she left the state just to get away from him."

"Did she say it was because of Nick?"

"Yeah," Kevin admitted. "Brianna told me she didn't want to deal with Nick once they split up and needed to get far away from him."

"Where did she move to?" I asked.

"Last I heard; she was somewhere in Connecticut."

Nick's ex-girlfriend was the next best person to give me some insight into what happened with the housemates and in her own relationship with him. I was already moving Nick up to the top of my suspect list.

"What is Brianna's last name?"

"Cataldi," Kevin replied.

Everything was logged in the notepad. I had a new lead to follow up on, and another person to speak to about Nick DeFalco. I just needed the proper authorization.

"I think that's everything for now," I told Kevin. I stood up from the table and flipped my notepad closed. "If you can think of anything else which might help our investigation, please don't hesitate to call."

I strutted out of the house feeling more satisfied than I had when I started my day. I had one person with a connection to Christina Tyler, who had issues with her. I just needed to find a way to connect Nick DeFalco to the other victims.

My cell buzzed as I walked down the street. "Hey, partner," Rodney said as I picked up the call. "I'm on my way back."

"How did it go with the D.A.? Were you able to get the warrants?"

"No dice, Ali. The judge required evidence or to know exactly what we hoped to gain from the guest logs. Without a name, he wasn't giving us anything."

I was pissed about the warrants, but those needed to take a backseat to my news. "That doesn't matter now," I told him. "I need you to hurry back to campus and pick me up."

"Why? What's wrong?"

"I have a lead on a potential suspect. Hurry up and meet me in front of the administration building. I'll fill you in when you get here."

I hung up the phone and marched back to campus with renewed energy. Unfortunately, my feet did not feel the same way. Twenty minutes of walking put more blisters on them than I was willing to endure. I sat on the steps with my heels off and set to the side until Rodney showed up.

He opened the driver's side door and chuckled at me sitting on the ground. "Maybe next time you'll let me drop you off at the station to get your car instead of walking."

"Shut up and help me to the car," I snapped.

Rodney walked over and scooped me up with one arm carrying me to the passenger side. "Now, besides being unable to walk; why have you summoned me?"

"We have our first possible suspect," I grunted while throwing myself into the passenger seat. I waited for Rodney to close the driver's side door before continuing. "His name is Nick DeFalco. He is a former housemate of Christina Tyler."

"Was that the kid your sister was talking about?"

"I think so. Let's head back to the station for now. I need to run his name through the system. I'll fill you in on everything along the way."

I told my partner everything I'd discovered during my time with Kevin Graham, especially the part about Nick's girlfriend and the way he left the house."

"I think you're definitely onto something, Ali. Where do we go from here? I wondered if my partner was itching to get back behind his desk for a while, or if he was looking for me to order him around some more.

"I need to work on learning everything we can about our suspect. I also need to track down his ex-girlfriend so we can question her. In the meantime; I'll get a picture of Nick and send it to your phone. I want you to check with the Esopus and Lenape RAs and RMs to see if anyone recognizes him."

"What about the warrants you were asking for?"

"I'll reach out to the D.A. again and tell her what we uncovered. I might be able to get them now."

"Good luck, Ali."

I couldn't wait to arrive at the station. The moment Rodney put the car in park, I shoved open the door and hurried into the station. I did my best to ignore the blistering pain in my feet as I walked barefoot up the steps and through the double doors.

"Hey, Ryan," one of the officers called out. "What happened? Did you break a heel?"

"Fuck you, Thompson," I shouted back.

I made a beeline for the lieutenant's office. He appeared busy, but what I had to say was more important. I knocked on the door jam.

"I'm in the middle of something, Ryan," he barked from behind a pile of papers on his desk. "Come back in an hour."

"But sir-"

"But nothing, detective. Unless it's life or death; I don't wanna hear about it."

My blood was boiling red hot for being dismissed again. I had enough of his crap. I wasn't going to be ignored. To me, there was nothing more important than taking down the asshole who killed three college girls.

"Fine," I snapped. "I just figured you'd wanna know we have the name of our first potential suspect." I turned on my heel and slammed his door shut.

I took a deep break and painfully peeled away from the lieutenant's office by walking on the sides of my feet. I made it three steps before I felt a hand grab me by my shoulder.

"You have my attention," the lieutenant said. "Tell me everything you got on the son of a bitch."

I hobbled into one of the chairs inside the office and walked him through the day's events. By the time I repeated my conversation with Kevin Graham, Lieutenant Esposito had pegged Nick DeFalco as the killer.

"Who else knows this DeFalco kid?"

"Rodney is going to check with the RAs and RMs at the dorms once I get him a picture. His ex-girlfriend used to go to school there as well. I'd like to talk to her."

"Good; bring her in for questioning."

"That's easier said than done, sir. She moved to Connecticut at the end of the spring semester. We need to conduct a search for her and probably get their local police involved."

"Don't worry about them. I'll put in a call and get you the authorization to bring her in. I want you focused on learning everything about this DeFalco kid."

I was a little shocked to hear the lieutenant practically give me free rein to run the investigation as I saw fit. I think the third victim proved there was a killer targeting college aged women. His daughter was almost their age. I was sure it fueled his desire to bring down the sick bastard.

I limped back to my desk and began my research. I typed Nick's name into the system. There were no prior records or tickets. In fact, there was nothing turning up on him at all. I had to run a full background check on our suspect. Unfortunately, it was something I had to wait on for any kind of results.

"How did it go?" Rodney asked.

"I have the green light to go after DeFalco and bring in the ex-girlfriend for questioning. I just can't find anything on him."

"Do you still want me to go back to the school?"

"See what you can get from your girls at the registrar. Maybe they can get you a picture of the suspect."

"Are you sure you want me to go back there? You know; I could be putting my marriage at risk." Rodney's sarcastic humor wasn't wasted on me, but I also didn't care for it in that moment.

I glared at him. "I don't care if you have to fuck every cougar or hag in that place; I want a photo of our suspect and I want you checking those dorms."

Rodney took a couple steps back. "Have you checked for an online profile?" He sat down at his desk and opened up a few websites. "Got it," he said. Rodney turned his monitor around so I could see him.

"Are you sure that's the same kid we're looking for?"

"It's his name; his college is listed; and he even has a friend named Brianna Cataldi."

I let out a smile. "I guess there's hope for you yet."

It was time to hit the gas pedal on the investigation. It was time to rip open Nick DeFalco's life and bring that asshole to justice.

Chapter 30-Ali

I spent hours waiting for the D.A. to call me back, and for Rodney to report on what he found out at the dorms. I was set at my desk doing research on our suspect. Google didn't pull up anything on Nick DeFalco, and our databases weren't populating any information. The only saving grace was social media sites.

I was able to see his favorite bands, which was mostly rock music. He had his favorite shows, movies, and books listed on the page. All of it provided a little insight into what our suspect liked, but nothing too personal. His relationship status showed; *It's Complicated.* I could only assume it was his way of still being with Brianna without mentioning her by name. The biggest problem I noticed was he had not posted anything since June.

After spending so much time at my computer, my eyelids drooped, my arms fell to the sides of my chair, and I felt a sudden urge to crawl into my bed and pull the covers over me.

"Ali," a hoarse voice said. A melon-sized hand grasped my shoulder and shook me awake. "Ali, wake up."

I sat upright in my chair as if woken by the sound of thunder. Rodney was back and staring at me with a massive grin.

"Tell me you found something," I yawned.

He placed a stack of papers on my desk. "Those are the guest logs since the beginning of fall semester for Lenape and Esopus."

"How'd you get them? We haven't heard back from the D.A. or obtained the warrants."

"I asked them if they could provide the information. I guess the RAs and RMs want us to catch the bastard just as much as we do."

"This is great; I can get started on them tonight."

"I already reviewed the lists. DeFalco's name never showed up on any of them."

That was a blow to the gut. The logs were a bit of a long shot but knowing the suspect's name gave me hope we would see him appear somewhere on the logs. Then, I saw Rodney's toothy smile.

"Why are you so happy? This was a dead end."

"I showed the picture to the staff in Esopus. One of them remembered Nick, but he hadn't seen him recently. The last time the RM saw our suspect was last year when he was visiting his girlfriend Brianna."

That confirmed DeFalco had knowledge of Esopus Hall; the layout of the rooms; where the cameras were located; and the times the staff monitored the lobby at the end of the night.

"This is great news," I began. I started to get up from my chair to run to the lieutenant's office, but Rodney pushed me back down.

"It gets better. The RA you spoke to after Christina Tyler's death said he thinks the picture looked like someone loitering around in the common area that morning. He didn't know the student or ask him for a name at the time, but he was there the day Christina died."

"We got him, Rodney." I jumped up to celebrate, forgetting how much damage I had done to my feet earlier. I sat back down immediately wincing in pain. "We just need to find the son of a bitch."

Rodney tried to hide his enjoyment over my discomfort. He did a bad job concealing his delight. "Okay, before you go hurting yourself anymore; I have one more thing to add. I talked to a few people at the administration building. They couldn't give me any records, but they did look up our suspect's name. He is still a registered student at the school, but he wasn't enrolled in any classes this semester."

This was a bit surprising. I figured our suspect would still utilize the cover of being a student to blend in with the rest of the crowd at New Paltz. Maybe he was and just didn't attend any classes. It was possible he used that free time to stalk his victims.

"Okay, we need to find out if Nick was using an alias. We can begin by interviewing Marty and Marie from the Outdoors Club. They can get us the list of the people who went on the trip, and they could also help identify if DeFalco was at any of their meetings or with the group that weekend."

"They both have the same class tomorrow morning."

"Perfect," I replied. "That will give us some time to relax and think of the right questions to ask." I reached for my bag and pulled out my cell. I had three missed calls from Matthew and a voicemail.

"Hey, Ali," his message began. "I thought we had plans for dinner tonight. Maybe I got the days mixed up. I'll try again later."

I glanced at the time. It was already seven o'clock. It was much later than I thought it was. *How long was I asleep at my desk?*

I painfully slipped on my heels and shuffled my way out of the station. I called Matthew while driving home. He didn't pick up. I didn't blame him. I blew off another date. This time it was because I fell asleep at my desk.

"Hey, I'm really sorry," I said in my message. "I got caught up at work and lost track of time. I even fell asleep at my desk, which is why I didn't know you called until now. Please call me back so I can make it up to you." A message popped up on my cell a few minutes later.

Matthew: Dinner...tomorrow night...and wear something sexy.

It put a smile on my face as I tried to walk into my house. I didn't even attempt to cook when I got home. I hurried to the bathroom and sat in a tub full of hot water to soak away all the pain.

The next morning, I needed a change-up to make it through the day. I threw on a pair of black jeans with a white polka-dotted blouse. I doubled up on my socks and slipped my feet into a pair of boots to help stabilize me for walking around New Paltz. I called the lieutenant to let him know Rodney and I were headed to campus to question the Outdoors Club leaders.

Cold winds swept over Ulster County along with blanketing us with a dusting of wet slushy snow. It was a sure sign winter was rapidly approaching, which mean there were only a few more weeks until the end of the fall semester. Our time to catch the killer was running out. Rodney was already standing outside the Lecture Hall when I arrived.

"You're late," he growled. "And here I thought you're supposed to be the early bird."

"You try getting around with blisters covering your feet."

"I warned you yesterday, but you wouldn't listen."

"Shut up and get moving," I snapped while holding onto his arm as we ascended the snow-covered steps.

We entered the Lecture Hall and searched for the room number listed on the information Rodney got from the cougar the other day. We located the class halfway down a long narrow corridor. I took the lead and knocked on the door. A woman in her sixties greeted us with a large textbook in her arm. She stared me down through her bifocals. I had the feeling she wasn't happy we were interrupting her lecture.

"Can I help you?" the woman snapped.

I held up my badge and introduced Rodney and me. "We need a word with two of your students."

"Can this wait until after class?"

"I'm afraid not, ma'am. We need to speak with them immediately." I was sure the professor didn't like us. I'd already interrupted her, and now I was pulling two people from her room whether she approved or not.

Rodney pushed his way into the room decked out in his uniform. He cleared his throat to get everyone's attention. "Marie Kennedy and Martin Song; please come with us."

Two people stood up with confused expressions on their faces. They stepped towards the front of the room. Rodney escorted them into the hall and closed the door. I could hear everyone in the room rushing to eavesdrop on the conversation. Their professor was yelling at them to get back in their seats.

I whipped out my notepad and paid no attention to the growing crowd. "As I understand it; you both run the Outdoors Club." They nodded to confirm. "Good, we are looking for information on one of your members."

Rodney slipped out his phone and pulled up the picture of Nick DeFalco. "Do you know this man?"

Marie's face switched from a worried expression to jaw-dropping terror. "Do you think that's the Campus Killer?"

"He's a person of interest," Rodney replied. "We need to ask him a few questions pertaining to the recent murders. We haven't been able to locate this person. We were hoping you could help us."

Marty inched closer to stare at the picture. "Yeah, he looks like one of our members. The guy I'm thinking of has shorter hair and it looks a blonde instead of brown. He was thinner and I don't recall him wearing glasses."

"Do you remember his name?" I asked.

"I think his name is Mark. If you give me a minute, I have the club folder in my bag inside my class." Marie darted inside of the room and came back out a moment later clutching an orange folder. She flipped it open and pulled out an attendance sheet. "Here it is; Mark Thompson."

I glanced over the sign-in page. "How many meetings did he attend?"

"I only remember him showing up for two meetings and our trip last weekend to Mohonk Mountain."

"Do you have a way to contact him; a phone number or an email?"

Marie shook her head. "Everything we have is on that sign-in sheet. It has a space to enter contact information, but it's not required."

I remembered Kevin's party and how everyone on the trip had been invited back to his house. "Do you know if Mark Thompson showed up to the Halloween party?"

Marty rubbed the back of his head. "To be honest; I don't remember much of the night. There were a lot of people there, and half of them were wearing costumes."

I looked to Marie. "Do you recall seeing him there that night?"

She had a guilty look on her face. "I-I just remember drinking a lot. We played a few games, and I hung out in another room with a few other people." Her eyes were filled with tears trying desperately to contain a secret.

I grabbed Marie by the hand and escorted her down the hall. "What happened in that room?"

"I-I really don't want to talk about it."

"Please, we need to know everything that happened that night. We believe the killer was at that party."

"There's a lot that's still a blur. I just remember being in a room with Kevin and a few other people. We were joking around; laughing; listening to music. The next thing I knew; the girl next to me was sitting on a guy's lap topless. For some reason, I thought it was a good idea. I flashed the group until I felt someone grab me. It made me realize what I was doing, and I ran out crying. Marty found me outside and took me home.”

“Does he know any of this?”

“No, and I want to keep it that way.”

“Okay, this will be just between us. But if you remember anything else, especially pertaining to Mark Thompson; I need you to call me immediately.”

I walked Marie back to her class. Rodney and I thanked them both for the information. They turned and walked back into a den of wolves waiting to pounce on them over our conversation. I knew the rumors would make their rounds. It wouldn’t be long until Nick DeFalco or Mark Thompson knew we were asking about them.

“What now?” Rodney asked.

“We get our hands on that background report and find out where our suspect lives. Then, we turn the dogs loose on his apartment and rip it apart. Hopefully, we find something linking him to the murders.”

<u>Chapter 31-Ali</u>

The lieutenant was chomping at the bit to speak to us once we arrived at the station. His hair was a mess and had sweat dripping down the sides of his face.

"Ryan…Johnson…my office, now!"

We didn't even have time to put our stuff down. We were beckoned by our *king*. I shut the door and took a seat across from him.

"You wanted to see us?" I joked knowing how frantic our lieutenant appeared when we walked in.

"Cut the shit and tell me what happened."

Rodney handed him the paper from the Outdoors Club. "We showed Marty and Marie the picture of Nick DeFalco. We never gave them his name, but they called him Mark Thompson. He joined their club a couple weeks ago and was on their trip last weekend."

"Great, so we know his alias," the lieutenant said. "Do we have anything connecting him to the murders?"

"Kevin Graham invited everyone from that trip back to his place for a Halloween party. Marty and Marie advised there were people there dressed in costume. We believe our suspect was there that night."

"How are you sure if no one says he was there?"

"Kevin Graham said our third victim, Christina Tyler, spent Sunday night at his house. He dropped her off the next morning. The RA claims she reported her ID missing and had to be let into her room."

Rodney interrupted to add what he learned. "The same RA recognized our suspect as someone loitering around the lobby the morning Christina Tyler died."

"And there was evidence of the window being tampered with prior to her death. This all indicates the killer had access to Ms. Tyler's room and may have entered it repeatedly while she was in class. I believe our killer used this same move to murder Nicole Sherman."

Everything was fitting into place. We just needed to know the motivation for targeting the first two victims, and how they were connected to Christina Tyler.

"Good work, team," the lieutenant said. That was about as much praise as he could muster. Then, he picked up a file from his desk and handed it to me. "I believe you were waiting for this."

I opened it to find the full background check I ordered on Nick DeFalco. IT contained his date of birth, his social security number, where he was born, what schools he attended, where he worked, and all his previous residences including his current address.

"What's wrong?" Rodney asked.

I pointed to the last known place of residence for Nick DeFalco. "I know this house."

"Great, let's get over there and drag his ass out."

"We can't," I replied. "He doesn't live there anymore. I was there yesterday when I questioned Kevin Graham."

The lieutenant's smile faded quickly. He inched closer to my face and spoke in an angry whisper. "Find the son of a bitch. I don't care what it takes; just get him and bring him in."

"That's easier said than done," I relied. "Kevin told me Nick moved out before the end of the spring semester. He hasn't heard from him since."

"Who else could help you track this DeFalco punk down?"

"Maybe his girlfriend, but she broke up with him around the same time as his departure from the Grove Street house."

"I don't care; you're going there in the morning to question her."

"I told you yesterday; she lives in Connecticut. We need permission."

"I'll get you the damn clearance, and I'll send one of our officers with you as backup."

"Wait, what about Rodney? Why can't he go with me?"

"I need him to stay behind in case we need to follow up on anything here. I don't trust anyone else to handle this case."

"Fine, I'll go by myself."

"No, you're taking an assigned officer to keep you out of trouble. If needed, he can run interference with their local police while you talk to the girlfriend."

It wasn't a bad idea, but I didn't like another partner being forced on me, especially when working a case like this one. I could see the lieutenant was digging his heels into the ground on this one. There was no way I could talk him out of this decision.

"Fine," I sighed heavily.

I got up and stormed out of the office with Rodney following closely behind me. We sat down at our desks, and I stared at my blank monitor.

"Just tell me what you want me to do, Ali."

"Remain on standby in case I get anything useful out of the girlfriend. I need the D.A. and a judge on standby for a search warrant."

"Don't worry, Ali; I got it covered."

I reviewed my notes for hours along with DeFalco's background report. Before I knew it, the sun was setting on Ulster County and the killer spent another night walking around freely. I wondered if he had gone into hiding or if he was sitting around planning his next attack.

It was the only thing on my mind, even while I drove back from the station. I was so lost in thought; I almost crashed my car into a vehicle parked in my driveway. I lifted my eyes and noticed a man sitting on my front porch. It was Matthew. His eyes were cold and distant. His left leg was draped over his right with the foot tapping the air impatiently.

I parked next to his car and walked up the path to my front door. "You know; you really can't keep showing up here unexpected." I reached for my handcuffs. "I might have to arrest you for trespassing." My fingers barely touched the cold steel.

"Cut the crap, Ali. You forgot about our dinner plans; didn't you?"

I let it completely slip my mind. Matthew's text last night felt like a distant memory. "Shit, I'm so sorry. Give me twenty-minutes to get ready and we can head out." It didn't give me a lot of time to dress sexy like he requested, but I figured I would do my best.

"Forget it; we already missed out reservation." I knew he was pissed about it being canceled, but I really couldn't remember us setting a specific time to meet.

"Matthew, I'm really sorry. I've been so caught up on this case. We finally have a suspect in mind and-"

"I don't care, Ali," he snapped. "I don't care about your cases; your suspects; or even how much time you put in at the station. None of that matters as long as you make the time for me."

"I do," I protested. "It's just-"

"No, you don't; at least you haven't been. I'm the one coming here to surprise you. And every time you brush me off or disappear the moment we have some alone time."

I grabbed his hand. Mine were much smaller than his, which were filled with warmth. "I'm here now, and it's just you and me. We can do whatever you want."

I slid his fingers between mine and pulled my hand to his lips. "I haven't felt this strongly about anyone before. I just need to know you feel the same about me, and not like I'm some runner-up to your career."

"Matthew, I take being a cop very serious." I knew it wasn't the answer he wanted, but it was the truth. "My career is my life, but it won't always be. My only purpose right now is to bring down the piece of shit that killed three college girls. But when this case is over, you will have my undivided attention."

He gave me a half-smile in return and leaned in for a kiss. "Maybe we can forget about going out to eat and order some takeout instead."

"I'd really like that." I planted a big kiss on his lips and took a nibble while I pulled away. I was about to pull him inside the house when I heard my phone ringing.

"Just let it go," Matthew whispered. His breath was like a cool breeze hitting my ear. I wanted him to desperately throw me over his shoulders, bring me inside the house, and have his way with me. Unfortunately, the ringing cell phone was a constant reminder that there was always something else pulling at me for my attention.

"This'll just take a moment." I retrieved my cell and saw the lieutenant's name flashing on the screen. I could see the anger and defeat in Matthew's eyes as I answered the call. "Hey, lieu; this isn't really a good time."

"I won't take up too much of your time. I just wanted to tell you a squad car will pick you up in front of your house in the morning. I'm sending Reyes."

"Reyes…the rookie?"

"I think he could be helpful, and I want him to shadow one of my best officers." That was a great compliment, but it happened to come at a bad time.

"Okay, just send him over in the morning. I'll be ready."

"Great, he'll be there by seven-thirty."

I hung up with Lieutenant Esposito and caught Matthew getting into his car. "Wait, where are you going?"

"Home," he replied.

"I thought we were getting takeout?"

"You're obviously busy, and I have to leave early tomorrow for a flight to Atlanta."

"You're leaving?"

"Yes, Ali. There's an important meeting I should attend. I'll call you when I get back."

I rushed my boss off the phone so I could spend time with Matthew only for him to walk out on me. I guess that's what I usually did to him. Instead of begging him to stay; I watched Matthew pull out of the driveway and down the road. He was gone, and I was left standing in front of my house feeling more alone than when I was single.

<u>Chapter 32-Ali</u>

I woke up the next morning not wanting to get out of bed. Last night was too fresh in my mind. I barely got any sleep knowing Matthew was about to walk out of my life if things didn't change. It had only been a few months, but I was already falling for the guy. He was smart, funny, very handsome, and he was patient enough to deal with me. Matthew was pretty much the perfect man, and I was dumb enough to push him away. It wasn't intentional. I had something bigger than us to worry about; like a killer on the loose who had murdered three New Paltz girls on campus. That thought was the only thing dragging me out of bed.

I grabbed a dry-cleaned pair of black dress pants and a navy-blue blouse. Thankfully, my feet were in much better condition to allow me to put on nude heels. I wasn't about to face a repeat of the other day, so I snatched a set of flats from my closet as well to take on the trip.

The patrol car pulled up in front of my house five minutes before the designated time. I quickly poured myself a cup of coffee, grabbed a small bag with the things I needed, and locked up before greeting my babysitter.

Despite the reasons Lieutenant Esposito gave me; I knew Officer Reyes was there to make sure I didn't get out of line or piss off the local cops meeting us at Brianna Cataldi's home. We all called him the rookie, even though he had been on the force for about two years. He was the youngest in our station, and he seemed very wet behind the ears when it came to being a cop.

"Morning," I said as I opened the passenger side door.

"Hello, Detective Ryan," Reyes replied. "Did you need to grab anything for breakfast or make any stops before we hit the road?"

I held up my coffee. "No, I'm good."

"Thanks for letting me come with you."

It wasn't like I had a choice. I stared out the window and rolled my eyes so he couldn't see. "Yeah, the lieutenant and I thought it would be good experience for you."

Reyes pulled away from my house and navigated us back to Route 9W. "So, why are we driving out to Connecticut to interview this girl?"

I guess the lieutenant failed to clue the rookie in on what we were doing or that we had a suspect in mind for the murders. "She is the ex-girlfriend to a potential suspect on the Campus Killer case."

"We finally have a lead?" he asked with an increased excitement in his voice. "I was one of the first officers on the scene when the first two victims were found."

I was curious what he thought and decided to pick his brain. "What did you think when you viewed the crime scenes?"

"The first girl looked like it was a pretty simple case. I really didn't know why there was a big fuss made over a girl who died from choking on her vomit. I read somewhere there are about fifteen hundred deaths each year related to alcohol consumption."

"Are all of those from asphyxiation?"

"It just said related to alcohol. There wasn't a breakdown of each type of death." Reyes was trying to show he could hold an intelligent conversation with me.

"It's definitely a good statistic to know for a death like hers, but I suggest digging a little deeper to pinpoint the total number per year for a specific category." I was still impressed by his ability to pull that data and was curious to see what he had to say on Nicole Sherman's death. "What about victim number two?"

"Well, I knew she was the roommate of the first girl who died. Seeing her death by suicide made sense to me. She might have felt responsible for her friend and roommate. She may have been depressed after the first victim's personal items had been removed from the room. There could have been any number of items triggering depressive thoughts, with a culmination of her hanging herself that night."

"Interesting," I replied. "What about the location of where her body was found? Did it seem odd she would choose the bathroom?"

"Yes, but it could have been chosen for two reasons; the first being a cry for help. The victim may have known that bathroom to be frequently used, and therefore someone would have stopped her from going through with it."

"And what is the other reason?"

"There is little opportunity to hang oneself in the dorm room. Truthfully, I would have thought the stairwell leading to the back exit would have been the ideal choice."

We discussed the case for a little while longer. His approach and viewpoint of the first two crime scenes was a bit refreshing. He was able to see things I ignored because my sister lived in the same building. I was blinded by the urge to make sure there wasn't a killer targeting women in the Esopus dorm. So, I continued discussing how I figured out the girls were murdered, and then I reviewed the findings of the third crime scene.

"So, do you really think this girlfriend will be able to tell us to find this Nick DeFalco kid?" Reyes asked.

"Yes, but I need everyone else to stay out of the conversation. The last thing I need is for her to feel overwhelmed or attacked."

"I'll do whatever you need me to."

We got to Brianna Cataldi's house a little after nine that morning. There was no sign of any other police presence, which meant we were not permitted to begin the interview process. I stared out the window at the cozy two-floor house with bluish-gray siding. I wanted to go in with or without the local police being there to oversee my questioning. Every minute wasted waiting around was another moment the killer had to plan another attack or go further into hiding.

Five more minutes past and my patience had already run out. "I'm done sitting around." I shoved open the passenger side door and stepped onto the street.

As I glanced down the road one more time, a white police car with blue and gold striped sides slowly approached from the other end of the block. It pulled up behind our squad car with a heavy-set man behind the wheel. He slid out of the driver's seat and stared us down.

"Detective Ryan?" he called out. Apparently, he didn't know the meaning of the word discrete.

I gritted my teeth; wanting nothing more than to rip this cop a new one for shouting my name for the whole block to hear. Giving him a quick once-over; I knew he was a desk cop. His hair was combed too perfectly to be on the street or a detective. His uniform was also pressed as if he was trying to impress his superiors. I glanced at Reyes and noticed his uniform had a few wrinkles in it.

I choked down my anger and extended my hand. He raised his arm to return the gesture. I could feel his fingers trembling as they wrapped around my hand.

"Officer Tremont," I said while reading his name badge. "It's nice to meet you. This is Officer Reyes."

Reyes and Tremont exchanged pleasantries while I eyed up the house with focus on the aqua shutters and doors. It looked like a nice house, perfect for a small family. I guessed it to be a two-bedroom home with a full-sized living room and kitchen.

"So, can someone explain why we're all here?" Tremont asked. It was apparent his supervisor didn't feel the need to provide any information to him. He was probably just told to show up to chaperone us.

"We are here to interview Brianna Cataldi. Her ex-boyfriend is the prime suspect in an ongoing homicide investigation. We need to question her without drawing too much attention to ourselves." I shot Officer Tremont a dirty look to remind him of how he acted moments after arriving.

"Then, why am I here?"

I inched closer to bring myself nose-to-nose with the West Haven officer. "You're here out of courtesy. Our lieutenant didn't want to step on any toes by walking into your backyard unannounced." Tremont was already pissing me off. Maybe it was a good thing I had Reyes with me to stop me being a raging bitch to him. "Furthermore, if our suspect decided to pay his ex a visit or is using her to hide out, we will need the help of your department to bring him in."

Tremont's eyes resembled a scared little dog who was scolded for peeing on the carpet. His pudgy face turned whiter than a ghost. His lips quivered as they tried to form words.

"L-lead o-on, d-detective."

I walked up to the aqua colored front door with Reyes and Tremont flanked at my sides. I knocked loudly calling out Brianna Cataldi's name.

"Open up; this is the police."

Two minutes later, the door creaked open. A short Italian woman with light-brown hair stood in the open space. Her eyes darted between the three of us.

"Um, can I help you?" she asked.

"Are you Brianna Cataldi?" The girl nodded her head in response. At least we had the right house. "Ms. Cataldi, we're with the Ulster County Police Department. We need to ask you a few questions about the recent murders on the New Paltz campus."

"I haven't been there since May," she defensively admitted.

"We understand," I replied. "But we would like to speak to you about a person of interest. Any information could be extremely helpful in bringing a killer to justice." I let my statement register as Brianna had a look of shock on her face. "May we come in?"

She led us into the house and through the living room to a small square kitchen table. I stopped Tremont and Reyes and asked them to let us have a moment to discuss the case. They sat down on the couch, which didn't provide much privacy.

"So, I don't understand how I can help," Brianna told me with a confused expression.

I glanced back at the two officers to ensure neither were eavesdropping. "Do you know anyone by the name of Mark Thompson?"

"No, that name doesn't ring a bell."

"We believe your ex-boyfriend, Nick DeFalco, has been using that as an alias. We have reason to believe he may have something to do with three deaths in New Paltz. We need your help to find him."

"You think Nick killed someone?" Brianna laughed at the suggestion, which drew the attention of the two chaperones in the living room. "He would never hurt anyone. That man is a wuss. He ran away from everyone who tried to pick a fight or argued with him."

"Maybe he was tired of running," Officer Reyes added with a smirk.

I snapped my head back to give him a disapproving look. I was sure he was right, but I needed him to stay out of the conversation.

"Nick was the most passive aggressive person I knew," Brianna added. "He purposely agreed with people just so they wouldn't be mad at him. Plus, he couldn't stand the sight of blood. There's no way he could see it without almost puking."

That was probably a factor for his method of killing. It would explain why there weren't any cuts found on any of the victims. "All three victims were subdued prior to their deaths."

"Detective, I dated Nick for a few years. I know him better than most people, including you. There's no way he would kill anyone."

"With all due respect, Ms. Cataldi; there are three dead New Paltz students found in their dorms. One of the victims had a direct connection to Nick. We are trying to establish a connection to the other two."

Brianna sat back in her chair. She rolled her eyes while muttering something under her breath. It was lower than a whisper, but I couldn't hear what was said.

"Fine, I'll try to help you. Who were these three students?"

"Rachel Walker, Nicole Sherman, and Christina Tyler," I replied without hesitation. "Each crime scene was staged to make it look like an accident or suicide."

Brianna's eyes grew wide. She was frozen in her chair. The happy-go-lucky expression was now replaced by complete and utter fear.

"No, please tell me it wasn't them."

Based on her reaction, I was sure Brianna knew each of the three victims. "How do you know them?"

"Christina was one of Nick's housemates." She choked back tears and wiped her blotchy red face. "Nicole and Rachel lived next door to me in the Esopus dorm. They were my best friends."

"So, Nick would have known them too." I waited for Brianna to confirm, but water-filled eyes did that for me. "Did he get along with the girls?"

"Fall semester, we all got along just fine. It seemed like he was as close to them as I had been."

I could see there was a lot more to the story and I needed the information. "What changed?"

"Nick and I kept getting into arguments. The girls kept blowing me off whenever we made plans. I didn't understand why until Rachel told me the truth. She said they couldn't stand Nick and the way he treated me. They said he was controlling and hated how he had to tag along every time we went anywhere. Nicole started to give me relationship advice. Once Nick found out, he freaked out. He kept going on about how they didn't know anything about relationships because the girls had never been in one."

"What issues did you have with your relationship with Nick?"

"He was always complaining about his housemates. He had major trust issues with one of them and the rest just shut him out."

"Which housemate did he not trust?" I asked.

"We had multiple arguments over his belief Kevin wanted to hook-up with me, and he was purposely trying to break us up."

That was something important Mr. Graham left out during our conversations. The news didn't surprise me at all based on the tone in his voice and the way he described Brianna.

"Why would Nick think Kevin was looking to hook-up with you?"

"I don't know," she replied. "I hung out with his housemates a lot when Nick was working. Kevin and I talked through texts and IMs a few times, but I never showed any of them to Nick."

"That doesn't mean he didn't find them some other way." I began to worry if Nick DeFalco had one more name on his hit list. I feared for Kevin Graham's safety. "Ms. Cataldi, when was the last time you heard from your ex?"

"Not since I moved. He called me several times a day throughout the month of May. Every call, voicemail and text begged me to take him back. So, I decided to leave New Paltz and I changed my phone number."

"Do you know where we could find Nick?"

"He moved prior to our breakup to a studio apartment on Oakwood. I can give you the names of his landlords and his house number."

Brianna gave me the information. The names matched the ones Kevin Graham provided me during our conversation. I just prayed they were able to let us know if Nick was still living there.

"Is there anywhere else he would go if he went on the run?"

"Maybe back to his parent's house." She wrote down the address underneath the one for the Oakwood apartment.

"Thank you, Ms. Cataldi. If you hear from him or you can remember anything else that can help us, please call me immediately." I handed her one of my cards and rejoined the officers in the living room.

I was in a rush to get back to New Paltz. Tremont barely had time to ask any questions or to say goodbye before I hurried Reyes to get in the squad car. I grabbed my cell and called it in to Lieutenant Esposito.

"Hey, I have a possible lead on the current address of our suspect."

"Great, are you on your way back?"

"No, we are just about to leave the house."

"Good, give me the info and I'll put in a rush for a search warrant. Maybe, we'll get lucky and find something linking him to the murders. Or better yet, maybe we'll find him."

I smiled at the thought of barging into Nick's house and finding the missing IDs. That would be the final nail in his coffin. We would have him dead to rights as the murderer of three innocent college girls. I wanted to be there when it happened. I wanted to be the one to take him down; to throw his ass in jail; and break his silence during the interrogation.

I snatched the keys from Reyes. "Forget it; I'm driving."

I sped through I-84; weaving in and out of traffic with ease. Officer Reyes held on for dear life with his arms bracing against the center console and the passenger side door. I exited onto Route 9W and hit the gas again until we reached Route 299. I made it in record time, an hour, and two minutes. I guess a loud siren and flashing lights helped get most of the people out of the way. I cut them off as I rounded the corner and pulled into the station parking lot as if I were a street racer seeking refuge from the cops. The squad car came to a screeching halt in a spot near the entrance. Reyes shoved his door open; falling out onto his hands and knees. I swore he kissed the concrete in an attempt to thank God for letting him return in one piece.

I got out and stared at him. "Welcome to the force, rookie," I joked while grabbing my bag from the car and hurried inside the station.

It was quiet as I entered. I could hear the sound of my heels clicking against the tiled floor as I made my way to the crowd of officers standing around my desk. They were already suiting up with Kevlar vests. Esposito stood in the middle of the group. He had tossed his jacket over the back of my chair and grabbed a vest. He seemed just as ready for battle as the rest of the officers.

"Are we all set?" I asked.

The crowd parted allowing me to pass. The lieutenant smiled and held up the search warrant. "We're ready to head out as soon as you're ready."

"You're joining us in the field?" I questioned.

"Hey, why should you get all the fun?" The lieutenant's smile was something none of us were used to. It was kind of like an eclipse; exceedingly rare to see, and everyone loved to catch a glimpse of it. "I wanna see this bastard in cuffs just as much as you do."

"Then, what are we waiting for?"

The lieutenant grabbed Rodney's hand to help him stand on top of my desk. "Ladies and gentlemen," he called out. "We're about to move out to the Oakwood house. This is a search and seizure for any evidence linking the suspect to any of the three murders. You also have a picture of what Mark Thompson; Nick DeFalco; or whatever he's calling himself these days. If you see him, I want you to take the son of a bitch down, but do not use deadly force. We want him brought in alive. In the meantime, we need to secure that house and rip apart his studio apartment."

The group of officers marched out of the station and took to their squad cars. One-by-one they pulled out of the parking lot and sped down Route 299. It took us fifteen minutes to drive into New Paltz and make the turn onto North Oakwood Terrace. It was surrounded by squad cars. Some were parked in front of the house; others sectioned off the intersections; and more on Grove Street and Prospect Street.

I stood in front of the towering three-floor home watching as more officers lined up all around me. The lieutenant stood on the curb and cleared his throat.

"Johnson, I need you to take a few officers with you to the backyard in case the suspect is here and makes a run for it. We have patrols on the next couple of blocks as well. Anyone you encounter is to be detained until Detective Ryan, Officer Johnson, or I have spoken to them."

Rodney motioned for three officers to follow him through a cluster of bushes and passed through a tall wooden gate. I hated to be ordered around. I wanted to barge into the house and run up to room fourteen immediately, but I knew the lieutenant wanted to ensure the building was secure and that no one got out.

"Okay, detective; you take the lead."

"What?" I was shocked to hear him tell me to be the point person.

"This is your investigation. You're running the show."

I looked around the group of men and women who swore to protect and serve the people of Ulster County. There were some I didn't like, and I was sure there were a bunch of officers who weren't a fan of mine. But that day, we stood together as one looking to take down the Campus Killer.

I separated the group into two. "I want Alpha to come with me. Beta team will take the first floor. I want every room swept for our suspect in case he is hiding out somewhere else." I wasn't willing to take any chances. "We go on my mark."

I walked up to the front door and stood ready as everyone else filed in line behind me. The lieutenant stood at my side as I raised three fingers into the air. I counted them down slowly; *three...two...one.*

I pushed the door open with my gun clutched tightly in my hand. My intended destination was the second floor. I raced up the stairs as a sea of officers invaded the house. I checked each door and saw black numbers etched on each. I followed them until I saw the two at the end; neither had anything indicating which room they were.

"Which one is it?" I asked.

The lieutenant shrugged. "You take one and I'll get the other."

He waited until there were more officers at his side before kicking down the door. His intrusion was met by an ear-piercing scream.

"Who are you?" a woman shrieked. "What do you want?"

I heard the lieutenant trying to calm the woman down and explain everything to her. I chose to ignore and breached the room across the hall from them. The door broke from its hinges. I ran into the room only to find it stripped down to its basic necessities; a dresser, a desk, a table, and a bed completely void of any sheets or pillows.

"He's not here," I called out.

"Where's Nick DeFalco?" the lieutenant barked at the woman across the hall as he brought her to our room.

"H-he left a few days ago," she replied. "He told me he was headed back home for a family emergency. I think he said an aunt died."

"Damn it!" the lieutenant snapped. He grabbed his radio. "The suspect is gone."

I slammed my fist into the wall outside of DeFalco's apartment. "Get me a C.S.U. team down here right away. I want this place turned upside down. I want anything linking him to the crimes; his DNA; I'll take a damn fingerprint."

"I had them on standby," the lieutenant told me. He grabbed his cell and called the C.S.U. team. "They'll be here in less than five minutes."

"Gloves on, people," I ordered.

Everyone holstered their weapons and did as they were told. One person ripped through an old metal desk. Another started on the dresser. More went through the cabinets. Every response was the same; *everything's gone.*

I bowed out of the room and let the C.S.U. team take over the apartment. The lieutenant advised most of the officers to head back to the station. The blockades at both ends of the street were sent away.

"Are you coming back to the station?" the lieutenant asked.

"No, I'm going to stay here for a while in case they find something."

"Ali, look at this place," Rodney said. He had joined us shortly after the C.S.U. team arrived and stayed out of the way until now. "DeFalco knew what he was doing. He took everything from the apartment. The place reeks of bleach. We're not gonna get anything useful from it."

"I don't care," I growled. "I'm not going anywhere until the team is done, and I've interviewed every tenant in this house."

The lieutenant nodded towards Rodney. "I had a few officers ask around. No one knew him by name or face except for two people."

"Then, we need to grill them for every bit of information they have on him. We can't leave any detail behind."

The lieutenant put a hand on my shoulder. "You've had a long day. Rodney can take over for now and fill you in tomorrow morning."

"So, you're ordering me to go home? What happened to this being my investigation? What happened to; you're running the show?"

"Ali, you are the best person we have on the case. I need you at your best, and right now; you're like a ticking time bomb. You're pissed off, and rightfully so. I think it's just best for Rodney to handle things here while you cool off for a bit."

I looked to my partner for help, but he nodded in agreement. They were leaving me with no choice. I missed out on my chance to bust Nick DeFalco, and now I was being sent home.

"Fine, I'll go."

I stormed out of the house and sat on the front steps. *The son of a bitch must have gone into hiding right after killing Christina Tyler.* It was taking everything in me not to shed a tear out of pure anger. I had let down all three girls. Their killer was on the loose and I couldn't do anything to stop him.

I felt a hand press lightly on my shoulder. "It's not your fault, Ali," the lieutenant whispered.

"My fault…you think I feel like this is my fault?" The lieutenant quickly removed his hand. I stood up and stared him down. "Why the fuck would I think this was my fault? I was the one pushing for this investigation since we found Rachel Walker's body in her dorm. You were the one hell bent on closing the first two cases, and for what?" I waited for him to reply, but he had no response. "Exactly; there was no reason to shut me down except to make our closed case ratio look good."

"You're right; I should have listened to you sooner."

"You're damn right; you should've. We might have actually caught this asshole instead of standing around looking like incompetent morons."

Rodney hurried down to meet us. "Can you quiet down? I can hear everything upstairs."

"So what?" I snapped.

"That means all the neighbors and all the tenants can hear you too." His statement was enough to smack some sense into me for a brief moment. "Look, we won't get anywhere playing the blame game. That's what this piece of shit wants us to do. He wants us to fight each other and stop focusing on finding him."

"Fine, how do either of you plan to catch a guy who has been one step ahead of us this entire time?"

"For starters," the lieutenant said. "You will be in charge. You call the shots. Whatever you need; I'll get it for you."

I heard that one before, and then the lieutenant ordered me to go home. "I want round the clock patrols at the New Paltz campus. I want a car here at all times watching this house in case the suspect comes back." I looked up at the windows above us. "Rodney, stay here and monitor the C.S.U. team. I want you to interview the girl across the hall and the landlords when they return. They need to know if they hear or see the suspect; they are to call us immediately."

"You got it, Ali."

I turned to Lieutenant Esposito. "You need to track down DeFalco's parents and see if they've heard from their son. We also need the police in North Carolina to be on alert for him. Send over his picture and any information we have on the suspect. I want an A.P.B. out on him for all of Ulster and Dutchess County as well."

"I'll head back to the station now and get started on it. Is there anything else we can do for you?" The lieutenant's tone was filled with concern. He had to know how hard I was taking this loss.

"No," I replied while shaking my head. "I'll see you both in the morning." I opened my car door and ducked inside. "I want a full report of your conversations with the neighbor and the landlords in the morning."

I tried to go home and forget about our massive failure. I dropped my bag the moment I entered the house and left it right outside the living room entrance. The anger only increased during the drive. I took my heels off while walking down the hall and threw them across my bedroom.

This was our big chance to nail DeFalco and we were left looking like fools. The lieutenant was right; I was partially blaming myself for it. I should have pushed harder to take over the cases. I could have found ways to convince him to let me look into them. In the end, we lost the suspect. We had no other potential leads to find DeFalco.

I paced my house for a couple of hours. I tried cooking; I tried cleaning; I did laundry; I looked for anything possible to keep my mind off the case. Nothing seemed to work. Every thought seemed to be consumed by the man who killed three college girls. The only possible distraction left town on a business trip. I tried calling Matthew and even sent him a few text messages, but he never responded. My only other option was to drown the thoughts at the one place I considered *my spot.*

I was sick of wearing my work clothes. I changed into a pair of jeans, a white shirt, a forest green jacket, and I pulled on a pair of brown suede ankle-boots. It made me feel like a normal person, which was really needed even though I slipped my badge in my back pocket. I grabbed the keys and headed back to New Paltz.

I drove down Main Street where crowds of students and people in their early twenties began to form around the bars. I wasn't in the mood to hang out with a younger crowd or be hit on by someone who barely made it through puberty, but I needed a distraction. With a flick of my hand, I hit the turn signal and turned down Plattekill Avenue. I took the first available spot and walked up the hill to P&Gs.

I walked to the end of the bar and sat down on one of the stools. "I'll take a beer tower and three shots of tequila," I told the bartender.

He took three shot glasses and lined them up in front of me pouring Jose into each one. Then, he filled up the tower with whatever was on tap. It was set down next to the shots before the bartender reached for glasses.

"Are your friends meeting you here, or do you need me to bring this to a table for you?"

"No, this is all for me," I replied. I knocked back all three shots in succession without any salt or lime. I snatched the glass from the bartender's hand and filled it with beer. "I'll take another three shots."

"Rough day?" he asked.

"More than you can understand."

The DJ finally finished setting up. Neon lights swirled around the bar as music pumped through the speakers. It was exactly what I needed. The alcohol and deafening sounds drowned all my thoughts. I lost track of time, but I had enough sense to know I had been there for a couple of hours. Six shots and two beer towers were the limit.

"I'm done," I called out to the bartender.

He came over and tried to show me the bill. I didn't care how much it came to. I handed him my card and let him cash me out. I could feel my body swaying from side-to-side on the barstool.

"Do you need me to call you a cab?" the bartender asked.

"No, I'll be fine." I had no intention of driving home. I planned on sleeping it off in the backseat of my car until I heard a man's voice trying to get my attention.

"Hey there, hot stuff; care to dance?"

Normally, I would turn down strangers at bars. I wasn't the hook-up type and I used caution when meeting new people. But the alcohol had already messed with my head too much. I had already climbed to the top of a water slide of bad decisions and was about to hurl myself down it.

"Sure," I finally mumbled while taking his hand.

I stumbled off the stool. I heard the bartender call out, but I had no idea what was said. The stranger wrapped an arm around my waist and directed me to the dance floor. My body complied. Before I knew it, we were in a small crowd of people. The man had one hand on the small of my back and the other low on my hips. He kept me close enough to feel his body rubbing against mine. My heart began racing. I lost all control. My arms rested on top of his shoulders bringing his face closer to mine. His nose matched mine. Our lips were inches from touching.

This wasn't going to end well. Everything in me was screaming for me to stop him; to run and get out of there. Unfortunately, my mind was on pause and my body was on auto-pilot. Hours of drinking clouded my judgment, and now I was locked in an embrace with an unknown man whose face I couldn't see.

I felt his hands slide down south firmly cupping my ass. He squeezed tightly and pulled me towards him until I could feel how stiff he had become. His lips kissed my collarbone; hit sensitive spots on my neck; finally making their way up to my ear.

"How about I get us one more drink and then we take this party back to my place?" The air blowing from his lips to my skin excited me.

"God, yes," I moaned as he lifted my leg to wrap around his. I could feel him pressing into me, grinding against my body on the dance floor. My cheeks flushed with heat from embarrassment, excitement, and desire. "Let's go now," I said breathlessly.

His arm was around my waist as he escorted me back to the bar. I could feel my eyes getting heavy. A glass was pushed into my hands, which I instinctively chugged down as if someone handed me water while spending hours outside on a hundred-degree day. It was taken away from me a moment later.

I found it harder to stand on my own. I couldn't see the neon lights swirling any longer. I was almost ready to drop, but a familiar voice calling my name brought me back.

"Ali, what are you doing here?" The woman pulled me out of the arms of the stranger. I stumbled, but thankfully she caught me. I could see the motherly stare down; the one where you know you messed up big time.

"Hey, sis," I replied sounding incredibly happy. I placed my arms around her neck and hugged her tightly.

"Oh my God; how much have you had to drink?"

"I lost track. I'm having a shitty day. I happened to run into this nice guy who bought me a drink." I thought I sounded like a laidback smartass who was throwing the same reckless attitude Amanda usually reserved for me back at her. My sister didn't even flinch. Maybe she didn't hear me, or maybe I didn't actually formulate coherent words. I was later told I said, "La track; I'm winding a shitty day. Happened to run a drunk guy."

"Yeah, you definitely had enough." Amanda wrapped her arms around me and tried pulling me away from the bar.

"Hey, where are you taking my girl?" the stranger asked. "I thought we were about to take this party to the next level."

Drunk Ali wanted to take the guy up on his offer, but my sister was the voice of reason. "She says thanks for the drink, but we need to get going."

The man rushed to get in front of us. "Come on; just stay for one more drink. I'll get you one too. What would you like?"

I was already reaching for an invisible glass but Amanda swatted my arm down. "Sorry, buddy; it's not happening…not tonight, and definitely not with us."

The stranger seemed to match our movements. "Come on; I'm not a bad guy. I'm just looking for a girl to dance with and talk to for a while."

I could feel a hand reaching into my pants pocket. Amanda retrieved my badge and held it up enough to scare off the stranger.

"If you don't get the fuck outta my way, I'll take your ass to the station and make you spend the night with our favorite inmate, Bubba."

The bartender must have caught the argument and decided to step in on our behalf. "Is there a problem here?"

The stranger put his hands in the air and backed into the crowd. "I'm good. There's no problem." He disappeared, and I still had no idea what the guy looked like.

"Do you need some help?" the bartender asked. "I tried calling her a cab earlier, but she refused and snuck off for a while."

"Help me get her outside," Amanda said. The two of them held me up and took me to the exit. The cold air hit me immediately and I became a little more alert. "Did you bring your car?"

"Yeah, it's down the block," I mumbled.

Amanda pressed me against the side of the building and tried searching my pockets for my keys. I pushed her away and took them out for her. The two sets of hands grabbed me and escorted me to the car. They placed me in the backseat while Amanda got behind the wheel. She revved the engine and slammed on the gas. She made a sharp right turn making my stomach do summersaults.

"Slow down," I whined.

"Hey, you like driving fast." I tried to protest but couldn't muster the words to reply. "Just remember; it's your car. If you puke, you're cleaning it."

"I really hate you."

"This is the only time I'll get to do this, so I'm gonna enjoy every minute of it." The car screeched as my sister made a left turn onto Route 299. We were on our way to Highland, but my world had gone black.

What seemed like minutes was in fact hours ticking away until the sun brought on the harsh consequences of binge drinking. The blurry bright light beamed on my face. My hand rose to shield myself from the blinding sunshine coming through my window.

What the hell? This is why I have blackout curtains.

"Rise and shine," Amanda said loudly as she entered the room. Her voice sounded like it was being magnified by a large speaker sitting next to my head. "Time to get up, sis."

"What the hell are you doing in my room? Why are you here, and how did you get here?" I was so confused.

"You don't remember anything about last night; do you?" She laughed while I rubbed my eyes. I used a pillow to block the sunlight as I tried to sit up. "You got trashed last night at P&Gs."

"I only had a few drinks." It was a blatant lie. I'd kicked off the night with the worst combination. My spiral had taken me down a path which required my sister to take care of me.

"Look, I don't know how many you had or what you drank, but I found you around eleven last night and you could barely walk." Steam billowed from the top of a mug as Amanda handed it to me. "So, who was that guy you were hanging out with?"

I stared at my sister while raising the mug to my lips. "What are you talking about? I was with some guy?"

"Um, yeah; he was all over you on the dance floor. I only noticed it was you when he brought you over to the bar for another drink."

"Please tell me I didn't do anything with him." My mind raced to recall anything from last night. There were fragments being pieced together but nothing substantial.

"I only saw you for like a minute, but he seemed to have it bad for you. I don't think anything happened, but another couple of minutes and you'd be waking up in someone else's bed."

I was panicking. "Tell me everything you saw."

Amanda recapped her going out with her friends and then dancing together. She noticed a guy getting aggressive with a woman who looked like she was about to have sex right in the middle of the crowd. Then, she realized that woman was me and decided to put an end to it. Amanda told me how she used my badge to back the guy off and how the bartender came to our rescue to make sure the guy stayed gone.

"So, why were you there last night?" my sister asked. "And why did you need to get that wasted?"

I felt like I was seventeen again when my mother grounded me for being out all-night drinking with friends. I had the same urge as I did then; to pull the covers over my head and go back to sleep.

"I had a bad day," I mumbled in reply.

"And that made you think it was a great idea to piss away everything good in your life?" I turned my head and stared at her in confusion. "I'm, talking about your love life; your career; hell, you could've hurt yourself or someone else. Not to mention; that guy could have been some psycho."

"Thanks, mom; but I wasn't going to drink and drive. I planned to sleep it off in the car by the bar."

Amanda shook her head. "What the hell sent you over the edge that badly last night?"

I told her about learning the identity of the killer and where to find him. Then, I rehashed our breaking down the door to an empty apartment. My sister's amusement died down and turned into fear as I told her everything that happened.

"W-what was his name?" she asked.

"Nick…Nick DeFalco." I saw my sister's horrified reaction. She cupped a hand to her mouth and let out a gasp. "What is it? Do you know him?"

"Sort of," she replied. "He dated a girl from my dorms. I think her name was Brianna. I'm fairly sure she lived next door to Rachel and Nicole."

"I met with Brianna yesterday. That's how we knew where to look for Nick. We just happened to get there too late." I grabbed Amanda's hand and made her sit down next to me. "You are not to go anywhere alone. I want you to stay with Sean until we catch DeFalco." I didn't like endorsing her to stay with a boy, especially one I didn't approve of, but I needed her to remain safe. DeFalco proved he could get into Esopus, and he had two ID cards to give him the access. I wasn't about to take any chances. I pulled my sister in close and gave her a huge hug. Then, I said something I normally never told people. "I love you."

Chapter 34-CK

It had been days since Mark Thompson went into hiding. There wasn't much choice. Mark had to make a run for it after running into the detective on New Paltz, her partner and her younger sister. He was sure it was only a matter of time before she spoke to Kevin, Brian, and eventually Brianna, which meant she would figure out where his studio apartment was located.

His decision to leave was the right move, but he couldn't leave town. There was nowhere to run. His parent's house in North Carolina would be closely watched, not like they would do anything to protect him. They seemed thrilled when he had told them about going away to college and urged him to stay during the summer. It was when he had reached his lowest point and decided to make a change. It was when he decided to eliminate the people who hurt him the most, and there was still one more name on that list.

Mark took out the folded-up piece of paper. Three names had been crossed out in red ink. His finger circled around the only one left creating an invisible bullseye on Kevin Graham's name.

I saved the biggest asshole for last.

Too many people had been hurt by Kevin's actions. He claimed to be a good guy; a loving boyfriend; a decent housemate, and a friend. Mark knew Kevin was none of those things and was nothing more than a liar.

The first time Mark realized Kevin wasn't the man he claimed to be happened after the Halloween party from the year before. Kevin had been in a relationship with a goth-emo chick name Angie. Mark knew she deeply loved her boyfriend and would do anything to make him happy. It took no effort for him to convince her to have a threesome with one of his friends after a night of drinking.

The second infraction showed him being a scumbag to his friends and his housemate. Christina Tyler didn't recall the night, but Mark had been sober and saw everything. Kevin Graham had used another big party to lower everyone's guard. They sat in his room when most of the guests had gone home. Somehow, he had convinced a girl he was friends with to flash her breasts while Kevin sat there taking pictures. Christina Tyler had joked about doing it too, but only showed them in her baby-pink bra.

The final straw was when Kevin had targeted Brianna. He'd wanted to sleep with her. Mark did his best to find out why. The only answer he ever received was *because I want to.* He didn't like anyone messing with his relationship. He checked Brianna's phone while she slept to see her text messages and logged into the computer to view her IMs. He saw everything Kevin sent her; telling her to leave the loser; how he would treat her right; how they would all be better off without her boyfriend. Mark did everything to keep Brianna away from Kevin, but it only drove her further away from their relationship. The plan had worked. She left him. Mark was sure she hooked up with Kevin before she left town. Mark wanted him dead for that reason alone.

The Outdoors Club had been the perfect way for him to get close to his targets. It proved to be a wealth of information while giving him cover. The trip up to Mohonk Mountain allowed Mark to see how close Kevin and Christina had become. It was also the perfect setting for the last name on the list to die.

Mark managed to hack Marie's email and used it to create a fake memorial for Christina Tyler. It was sent to Kevin as a blind copy to ensure he believed they were protecting everyone's personal information.

Subject: Christina Tyler Memorial

Dear Outdoors Club Members

We are saddened by the loss of our friend and fellow member, Christina Tyler. Though our time with her was short, we would like to honor her memory at the place where we felt closest to her. We will be holding a brief memorial at the lighthouse on top of Mohonk Mountain. It would be great if you could all make it. We will be meeting there at noon tomorrow.

Let's unite as one in Christina's memory.

Marie

Mark hoped the email was enough to get Kevin to make the trip on his own. He knew his target wouldn't reach out to the other club members, because Kevin didn't talk to any of them without Christina being the one encouraging him to do it. Giving little notice made sure his target didn't seek out the club leaders to give them a piece of his mind. The only options left were to show up to provide some validity to the sham of a memorial, or to look like the jerk who didn't want to honor his friend's memory.

Mark left the security of his safe house and drove to the mountain early Friday morning. He had a few supplies to help set his plan in motion, including using a few items he stole from Christina Tyler. He ascended the mountain using the same trail Marty and Marie had shown him during their trip. Once he was done, he walked down the path and hid in the bushes waiting for his target to arrive.

Mark couldn't help but continually check his watch. Then at eleven-thirty, the sight of Kevin's bald head came into view. The sweat coated skin greatly amused Mark. Then he heard the other man mumbling low.

"I can't believe I have to hike up a mountain to honor my friend," Kevin complained.

The comment was even funnier because Mark knew Kevin would have to keep hiking since the Lemon Squeeze was the only way he knew of to arrive at the lighthouse, the supposed destination.

Mark looked on from a distance until he saw his victim enter the space between the two cliffs. He was going to attempt it by himself. Even though Mark wanted to be the one responsible for Kevin dying, it would be amusing to watch the douche die by his own hand. But the risk was too great. Mark needed to make ensure he was ready to attack his victim the moment he stumbled onto his little setup. Mark trotted off hastily to the dirt path, the only other way up to the lighthouse.

He crouched down and waited for Kevin to arrive. He could see a pink tent sitting in the open field in the distance. The door to it was open and facing the world below.

"Hello," Kevin's voice called out. "Is someone here?"

Mark made sure to stay silent. The only reply came in the form of an icy-cold wind hitting him in the back. He walked into view. Mark knew his victim expected there to be a few people there. It was already a few minutes after twelve. He turned towards the tent and looked around.

"What the fuck is this?" he barked.

The distraction was working. Kevin appeared confused by Christina's tent; the same one they shared the night of the camping trip. There was a note inside lying on a single pillow. Kevin entered through the open door. It was that moment Mark decided to strike.

He rushed towards the tent and tackled his target, trapping him inside. Mark reached for the zipper and quickly closed it. Kevin tried to fight back against the silhouette of his attacker.

"Nick, you son of a bitch," Kevin called out. "I'll kill you."

Mark slammed his fist against the side of his target's head knocking him back to the ground. He kicked him a couple of times to ensure Kevin stayed down long enough for him to grab something to help subdue his victim.

Mark picked up a large rock he left lying near the tent. His eyes watched Kevin crawl to the door and pull on the zipper to free himself from the trap. Mark used that moment to deliver another shot to the side of Kevin's head. This time he used the rock as a weapon to render his victim unconscious.

"You know; all of this could have been avoided if you had just left Brianna and me alone." Mark grabbed the pieces of pink fabric by the entrance of the tent and began to drag it towards the edge of the cliff. "I wanted to be your friend. We were cool with each other for a little while. I even ignored the shit you did to Angie and your friends. But going after Brianna crossed the line." Mark struggled to move the tent to the edge. "Damn, you're heavy." He kicked the lump trapped under the pink material to inch forward a little more. "At least you can be with Christina again."

Mark got on his knees and rolled Kevin and the tent over the side of the cliff. It tumbled down the mountain, smashing against the rigid rock walls. He watched it until the pink material disappeared.

He pulled the piece of paper and the red marker from his pocket and crossed out Kevin's name from his list. A wave of relief washed over him as a cold breeze circled around his body. He let out a cackle of laughter as his phone began to buzz. He glanced down at it and nodded.

"Looks like it's time for the real fun to begin."

<u>**Chapter 35-Ali**</u>

I barely made it the station before noon. My hair was a curly mess, which needed to be pulled back into a ponytail to keep me from looking like I just rolled out of bed. I wore a pair of black sunglasses to hide my red, glassy eyes. There was nothing that could hide the amount of shame I felt coming into work after a horrible night of binge drinking and bad choices.

"Where the hell have you been?" Rodney asked as I took my seat across from him. I put my head down on the desk. My partner came over and placed a hand on my shoulder. "Are you okay?"

"Go away," I moaned. "I'm not in the mood."

"What's the matter?"

"I had a shitty night I'd like to forget about."

I could feel Rodney's fatherly stare. He patted me gently on the shoulder and whispered in my ear. "I don't know what happened last night, but I'm here for you if you need to talk."

"Thanks," I sighed. Truthfully, I didn't know what to say about what I did at the bar. I barely remembered anything, and Amanda filled me in about the ending.

"Well, now that you're here; the lieutenant wants us to meet him in his office before briefing the rest of the squad on the Campus Killer case."

I sunk deeper into the crevice of my arm while whining like a little kid. "Do we have to do this now?"

"It won't be that bad," he reassured me. Rodney grabbed me by the elbow and brought me to my feet. He knocked on the lieutenant's door and opened it. "Hey, look what the cat finally dragged in."

I hurried to the nearest chair and threw myself into it.

"Ryan, what the hell happened to you?" the lieutenant asked. "You look like crap."

"Thank you for such a great compliment." Damn, even my sarcastic humor took a hit due to the hangover.

"Officer Johnson, please brief Detective Ryan about your talks with the neighbor and the landlords last night."

I had completely forgotten Rodney stayed behind to oversee the C.S.U. team and talked to the people who interacted with Nick DeFalco the most.

"The landlords weren't much help," Rodney began. "They didn't even know he left town. Leonard didn't talk to Nick at all. His wife, Valerie, handled most of the issues our suspect had. She confirmed the story of Nick asking to be let out of his lease at the Grove Street house. In return, he would move into the studio apartment for the next year."

"Did she provide you with any reasons why Nick asked to get out of that house?" I asked.

"She only said he didn't get along with the housemates and they were interfering in his personal life. She didn't have specific examples, but Valerie did indicate she had multiple conversations with him and discussions with the rest of the house. The decision was based on a mutual agreement by all parties to remove Nick from the situation."

That pretty much confirmed what Kevin Graham had told me, with the exception of the landlords speaking to Nick's housemates about it.

"What about the neighbor? What was she able to tell you?"

"The girl's name is Jess Davidson. She and Nick got along pretty well and hung out several times during the summer. They mostly watched movies and T.V. shows late at night together."

"Did she notice anything off about him?"

"She said he came back right before the semester started with a few bags full of new clothes. He got a haircut, and she noticed his eyes looked a bit different."

"So, our suspect had undergone a complete makeover before going on a killing spree," I noted. "That explains why some people said the picture we had looked like Mark Thompson but advised he had a different appearance."

"She also told me he asked her out a couple of times. The girl tried to set him straight by saying they were only friends. But right before he left, Nick said his aunt died and used it to kiss her."

"So, we're looking at this Jess girl as a potential name on his lit list or someone he might come back for to take with him."

"I'll have someone keeping an eye on her," the lieutenant added.

"I don't want them tracking her while in uniform or in their patrol car," I replied. "If she represents anything for Nick, we need to use her as bait to lure him out. Any police presence will keep him far away."

"Anything else?" the lieutenant asked.

"No, sir," Rodney replied.

"Okay, then let's brief the team and hand out some assignments."

The lieutenant exited the office and called everyone over. "I wanted to update everyone on the status of the Campus Killer case. As of last night, our suspect is still on the loose. We do not know about his whereabouts at this time. We have canvassed the surrounding blocks of his last known address and spoken to everyone who lived in his building. Most of the community doesn't know who the hell this kid is, which is going to make the task of finding him that much harder. It is very possible the suspect has left town."

It made sense for DeFalco to go into hiding. He had killed three people and knew enough about our investigation to get out of his apartment before we raided it. He had been a step ahead of us this whole time. Despite that knowledge, something felt off about him running away. It was as if his mission was incomplete.

"He's hiding somewhere here in Ulster County," I blurted out. Everyone's head turned towards me. *Crap, why did I say that out loud?* My comment meant more work for the squad, which is something the lieutenant was already considering.

"Did you have something to add, detective?" The lieutenant asked. I could tell he wanted me to speak my mind. After all, I was the one who pushed to run the investigation.

"In your office we discussed the possibility of DeFalco coming for his neighbor, Jess. She could be another target or he may consider running away with her as his endgame." I watched everyone stare at me as they waited for me to finish my thoughts. "What if he had another person in mind for his hit list?" I ran through the people who we knew wronged him in some way. There was Brianna, his ex-girlfriend; Brian, one of his housemates; and Kevin, the one who he blamed for his breakup. My head snapped up with my eyes wide open. "It's Kevin…Kevin Graham is his next target."

"Come on," an officer called out. "That kid is long gone by now."

Rodney stepped forward with his hands out. "We need to listen to Ali and hear what she has to say."

"Why should we listen to her?" another officer griped.

"Because she's the only one who said these cases were homicides when everyone else called them suicides. I trust her judgment and you should too."

The lieutenant nodded his head. "He's right; you should be listening to her. It was my mistake we didn't in the first place." He gestured towards me. "The floor is yours."

"I talked with Kevin and know DeFalco didn't get along with his roommates. Nick's ex, Brianna, also confirmed he believed there was something going on between her and Kevin, or at least that his housemate was trying to break them up. If he went after Christina Tyler for not including him in house activities, then he would definitely target Kevin Graham."

"Then, we need to warn him," Rodney suggested.

"You're right. We should head over to the house now."

Rodney and I took a ride over to Grove Street. It was different from the last time I had been there. All of the Halloween decorations had been removed and put away. I walked up the porch and banged on the front door. After the fifth knock, Rodney grabbed my arm.

"Maybe he's not home," he said. My partner looked me in the eyes and probably saw the worry reflecting back at him. "Do you have his number? We can try calling him and ask him to meets us at the station."

"I have to look it up. In the meantime, we need a car stationed here and following Kevin until Nick is caught."

Rodney and I walked back to the car. Dispatch called in a ten-seventeen over the radio…a homicide. The location wasn't far from where we were. We were about ten minutes out. My heart was lodged in my throat. I prayed the victim wasn't Kevin; prayed it wasn't someone else on Nick's list of victims. This nightmare needed to come to an end.

Rodney sped down Route 299 until we saw a line of police cars, ambulances, and traffic blocking our way.

"Looks like we have to do the rest of this on foot, partner." I let out a lighthearted laugh.

Truthfully, I wasn't in the mood for a long walk. I was still hungover from the night before. I was just thankful I decided to wear a pair of boots to work instead of heels.

"How about I wait here, and you go check it out?" Rodney asked.

"Nice try, but you're coming with me."

We left the car half a mile down the road. The fear in me wanted to run down to the crime scene to make sure it wasn't Kevin, but Rodney wasn't up for another jog. The last time we tried that; he nearly collapsed in front of me. Instead, we walked at a brisk pace down the road and badged our way through the secured perimeter near Mohonk Mountain. An officer led us up the dirt path to where a pink tent lay broken at the foot of the cliff.

Rodney was the first of us to put on a pair of gloves and peek inside. He gagged at what was inside. His eyes told me this wasn't just another one of DeFalco's victims. It was the one we needed to catch the killer.

"Don't go over there, Ali," he warned as I approached. "Trust me; you don't wanna see it."

I pushed my partner aside and looked at the victim. It was Kevin Graham's battered, bruised, and mutilated body lying on two small pillows. His clothes were ripped and shredded from the fall while bones broke through the skin on his arms and legs.

I looked away in disgust. "Get the C.S.U. team down here now. We need to know exactly where our victim fell from."

"Tell me you're joking," Rodney said as he glanced up the mountain. His eyes returned to me staring in disbelief. "There's way too much ground to cover. It'll take forever to find anything, and it'll be compromised by the time we do."

He was right. It would take weeks for us to comb through every inch of the mountain hoping to find where Kevin fell from and any potential evidence that could have been left behind.

"We need Marty and Marie down here. They were on the trip with Kevin and Christina. They can show us the path they took with the rest of the club. It should help us narrow down the search." I bent down and looked at the body one more time. I was sure there was an injury which wasn't caused by the fall. "Make sure Dr. Wu sees this."

"Why?"

"Nick messed up this time. He used a weapon to do his dirty work. He may have actually left us some evidence."

<u>Chapter 36-Ali</u>

I sent Rodney and Reyes to pick up Marty and Marie. They returned with only one of the leaders from the Outdoors Club. They partnered up with me and a team of analysts as we climbed up the mountain. She led us up the same path she and the rest of the club took during their trip. The first location was a clearing where they camped out.

"Spread out and look for anything out of the ordinary," I ordered.

The analysts and I scoured the area for over an hour. Unfortunately, we only found sticks and leaves covering the grounds.

"Was this the only place you and the rest of the club went that day?" Rodney asked.

"No, we went up to the lighthouse too," Marie replied.

She led us up the trail to a bunch of rocks. I knew the area as the Lemon Squeeze. It was possible for Nick to have killed Kevin and sent him over the edge from there, but it was unlikely to have included the tent.

"Let's save us some time and take the walking path up to the lighthouse," I suggested.

Marie led the group up the long way to another open field. The only thing in view was a tall building. Rodney and I directed everyone where to go. I moved towards the edge of the cliff where I believed Kevin had been sent plummeting to his death. I could see Ulster County in its purest and most serene form. It was a place where I had gone a few times just to clear my head and relax. It was now and would forever be tainted by the broken lifeless body of Kevin Graham as he became victim number four.

"Ali, we might have something over here," Rodney called out. There was a tone of hope in his voice.

I hurried back to where my partner stood over a patch of dirt leading from the lighthouse into the grass. "What did you find?"

"Drag marks," an analyst replied. "It's possible the victim had been inside the tent and dragged along this path where he was inevitably shoved over the cliff."

"Okay, I want the lighthouse, this path, and everything from that trail leading up to this point reviewed extensively. If there is any evidence left behind, I want to get it before anyone contaminates this crime scene."

Rodney joined them and bent down by the side of the lighthouse. There was a piece of plywood leaning against it. Under it was a large stone that seemed to have broken off the building. He called the analysts over to dust for prints, but they shook their head.

"What about checking for blood?" I suggested.

They reached into their kits and sprayed the stone with a clear liquid before turning a UV light on over it. "Sorry, detective; there's just a few droplets of water leftover from the morning dew."

"What do we do now?" Rodney asked.

"Let's keep looking for any evidence. We'll need to work with the C.S.U. team to see what evidence they collected from the crime scene down there. After that, we'll have to wait on Dr. Wu's findings."

"And in the meantime; we just sit around and let this guy slip through our fingers again?"

"We just need to increase our patrols and keep watch over certain people of interest to see if Nick makes a move against them."

We spent hours combing through the trail and found nothing to help us. I spent even more time at the station waiting on the evidence log to come in. Eventually, I got what I needed and went home around eight that night.

"Hi, honey; I'm home," I said mockingly knowing no one would hear me. The house was empty. Matthew was gone. The only way I heard his voice was by hearing his outbound message every time he ignored my calls. To be honest; I think he did it on purpose to show me how it felt to come second to the job.

I kicked off my boots at the door and headed straight for my couch with a stack of papers contained in a folder. I held it tightly in my hands.

"It looks like it's just you and me tonight." I put it on the end-table before walking into the kitchen. I pulled three beers from the fridge and headed back to my homework assignment. "This should help me get through the night."

I sat down and reclined the seat while pulling the first page from the folder. It was the one I was most eager to review. It listed everything found at the crime scene and in the car, we learned belonged to Kevin Graham.

It was a short list. There were two small pink pillows, a pink sleeping bag, two tent poles, and four tent stakes with traces of blood on them. It was odd to see the last item listed as inside the tent, considering they would be used to hold the structure up on a windy day. It was a clear indication our killer had set this up. The stakes were left inside to inflict more damage to Kevin Graham as he fell from the mountain. It could have potentially killed him had the fall not finished him off.

The color of the tent was the next thing to catch my eye. It was labeled as pink. When I flipped through to see the picture of the crime scene, it had more of a magenta appearance. It definitely didn't seem like anything Kevin would have purchased. I grabbed another folder which contained the contents of Christina Tyler's room. I flipped through those pictures and the list. There was nothing showing a tent. That's when it hit me.

He planned this attack even before he killed Christina Tyler. How much had he plotted prior to targeting Rachel Walker? When did he start?

There was so much to figure out. I thought back to my conversation with Kevin Graham. He told me about the party the night they came back from the trip. He didn't know if Nick had been there. I was almost sure he had been there. If Christina Tyler spent the night, then Nick most likely stole the ID that night and used it to break into her dorm room. It made me wonder where the tent had been stored; the house; Kevin's car; or Lenape Hall.

I decided to go back to the evidence listing for Kevin Graham's case. A red 2003 Toyota was noted on the page. The items recovered from it contained a black and red lighter; a pack of cigarettes; the car registration; and several notebooks and textbooks. The trunk contained a green tent and sleeping bag.

Well, we know he had one of his own, which was most likely used during the camping trip.

Then I saw the listing of items found on Kevin Graham when they searched his pockets. One cracked green lighter. I was sure the fluid had leaked over everything, which could have made for a fiery ending if Nick realized what happened. There was a crushed pack of cigarettes. Then, there was a wallet with Kevin's credit cards, license, car insurance, and a small picture of him and Christina Tyler.

He didn't have his student ID on him. How the fuck did Nick manage to steal that one?

It was possible he rendered Kevin unconscious and took it from the wallet prior to shoving him off the cliff. I wondered if it had been taken from the house, or maybe it was still there.

I grabbed my cell to call my partner and tell him my idea for the next morning. "Hey, I was going over the evidence log and noticed something missing."

"Let me guess; the ID wasn't there?"

"Yeah, I think we need to-"

I lost my ability to speak as headlights beamed at my living room window. They seemed to be getting closer. I was frozen in fear as an out of control car sped towards my house. I expected it to come crashing through at any moment. I screamed and dropped the phone while taking cover. I could hear tires screeching and my window shatter. I glanced over the couch and saw fragments of glass littering the floor with an object lying in the wreckage.

The incident lasted a few short seconds, but everything felt like it happened in slow motion. It took me another minute to realize I was fine, and what came crashing through my window wasn't a car.

Rodney's voice shouted from the phone. "Ali…Ali, you there?"

I pulled my gun and cautiously walked towards the window to make sure no one was around. I hurried to my door and swept the area, but the car was long gone. I noticed skid marks directly in front of my house where the driver must have made the last second turn. I returned to the living room where Rodney had apparently hung up and kept trying to ring me back. I picked up after the third missed call.

"Hey, I'm okay," I told him.

"What the fuck happened?" he snapped.

"I don't know; maybe it was a bunch of stupid kids pulling a dumb prank." Whatever it was; it bothered me more than I was willing to let on.

I put on shoes to sweep up the mess and retrieve the object which was hurled through my window. I figured it was a rock. Instead, it was a small red brick with a piece of paper wrapped around with a rubber band. Protocol would have dictated not to touch the evidence without gloves, and I should have waited for the crime scene analysts to dust for prints. But in that moment, I wasn't a detective. I was a woman who had her window bashed in for malice reasons.

I took a tissue and removed the rubber band from the brick. The note coiled together and fell to the floor. The only words I saw were typed in blank ink saying *Hello Detective.*

A shiver ran down my spine as I grabbed the phone to call Rodney back. "You need to get over here now and bring a C.S.U. team."

"Seriously, you want me to call them over a little prank?"

"I don't think it was a bunch of kids. I think it was DeFalco." I told Rodney what I saw leading up to and after the crash. He wasn't sold on it being the man we referred to as the Campus Killer, but he wasn't taking any chances.

Rodney was at my house ten minutes later. It was a new record for him. It usually took him twenty or more to show up. I guess the circumstances allowed him to break his rule about speeding. The C.S.U. team showed up a few minutes after my partner. I was sure he called them from the road and told them to haul ass to my place. Their faces were relieved and annoyed when they saw me standing there visibly shaken yet unharmed. They didn't ask questions about what happened. That was never their goal. They showed up and did their job, which meant dusting the brick, the rubber band, and paper for any fingerprints. Another pair went out to the street to examine the tire marks.

Rodney had put his massive arms around my neck, draping them across the top of my shoulders. "I'm so glad you're all right."

"I'll be better when you stop smothering me."

He released me from his tree trunk-like arms. "Did you get a good look at him or the car he was driving?"

"No, he positioned the car where his headlights were pointed right at my living room. The brights were turned on, so I couldn't see anything."

"Did you reach out to anyone else other than me?"

"Are you asking if I called the lieutenant?" We locked eyes for a moment before I shook my head. "No, I don't want to involve him in this tonight."

"We can't exactly keep this from him," Rodney reminded me.

It was obvious Lieutenant Esposito would learn about it when he got to the station. We had a C.S.U. team at my house. There wasn't a way to keep that under wraps.

"I'll talk to him about it in the morning. Right now, I wanna know what that note says, board up my window and get some sleep."

"Fine, but I'm calling in a favor to have someone watch over your house in case that son of a bitch comes back."

"I don't need protection." I held up my gun. "I've got everything I need right here."

"Ali, you might think that will stop him, but this sicko knows where you live. He was here tonight just to send you a message. He could come back here at any time and mess with your gas line while you're asleep. You'd be dead without ever facing him."

My partner had a point. Nick DeFalco killed four people and made each one look like it was an accident or suicide. But something about the drive-by didn't make sense to me.

"I really think this was a way to scare me off."

"And what if it wasn't?" Rodney asked. "What if this was his way of telling us you're next? We can't afford to lose you…I can't afford to lose you."

"You better not start getting all sappy and sentimental on me."

Rodney dapped at his eyes in an attempt to make it look like he was wiping sweat from his face. "Hey, I just don't wanna break in a new partner."

"Aw, you love me, and you know it." My partner tried to look away. I placed my hand on his shoulder and leaned in to kiss his cheek. "I know you're looking out for me." I considered Rodney's request to have someone stationed outside of my house. "Fine, you can send an officer over for now, but they better not get in my way."

Rodney smiled. "I'll make the call."

Just as my partner went to ask for protection detail, one of the analysts called me over to look at the note.

Hello, Detective Ryan.

I won't apologize for the things I have done or begin to explain why I killed those four pieces of shit. This isn't some big confession. I'd like to look at this letter as a peace offering. Kevin Graham was my last victim. I plan to leave this town and get far away from here. I promise you'll never hear from me again, as long as you stop investigating these terrible accidents.

I re-read the note again with Rodney standing next to me. "Does he really think we're going to stop hunting him down just because he claims to be done killing people?" he asked.

I really didn't know what this psycho was thinking, but I wasn't going to stop until I put his ass in jail. I looked over at the C.S.U. team who seemed to be done. They were packing up their equipment.

"We'll put a rush on everything and start working on the tire tracks once we get back to the lab."

I thanked them and walked the team out to their van. I glanced over at my partner. "Are you heading home too?"

"No, not until your babysitter gets here," Rodney joked as he led me back inside the house.

We sat around for another half-hour telling stories and laughing. Despite the drama, it was nice to talk with someone about anything other than work. It made me miss what I had with Matthew that much more.

Chapter 37-CK

The strike against Detective Ryan's house was meant to throw her off balance. It was supposed to make her afraid for her life and possibly go into hiding. She was getting too close to the truth. She already knew the real name of Mark Thompson, knew who he dated, and searched his apartment. It was only a matter of time before she found him. The note was a warning. He wanted her to think he was done and was leaving town, but he knew she wasn't going to give up the fight. It was why he decided one more attack was needed.

Mark had shown up on campus earlier in the day and located Marie as she got into her car. She drove to a baby-blue house located on Church Street. It was one he'd overlooked many times. Most of the building had been hidden by a large tree which sat in the front yard. It was late afternoon. No one seemed to be home. It was a perfect opportunity to strike. But the attack would have to wait until the night sky concealed his identity.

He waited and returned when the sky darkened, and the orange glow of nearby streetlamps lit the street. Mark grabbed a pair of binoculars from the backseat and watched his victims through the window. They were cuddled on the couch watching something on T.V. An orange plastic bowl sat between them. Their hands dug into it at the same time spilling popcorn over the sides.

Fuck, it's only nine, he thought while sitting in the car.

He peered through the binoculars again and saw a shadow move from the couch and across the living room. The image from the T.V. flickered to a bright blue screen causing Mark to pull his head away.

Those fucking assholes!

He rubbed his eyes and re-opened them hoping to adjust to the light. He continued to watch the house intently until his cell phone vibrated in the center console. He glanced down at the text message and dismissed the person reaching out to him. He returned his attention to the house where the bright blue light had been extinguished. The room was shrouded in darkness.

"It's showtime, folks," he said excitedly to himself.

He exited the car and popped open the trunk. There were twin five-gallon containers of gasoline sitting inside. He picked them up and carried them to the side of the baby-blue house in a hurry. Every step had his head turning in different directions to ensure there were no nosey neighbors watching his every move. One container was set down next to the side of the building. The other was hurled through the window into the living room he had been spying in.

The sounds of shattered glass disrupted the silence on Church Street. Someone was bound to look out their window to see him. If that wasn't enough, Marie let out a high-pitched scream moments after the crash. The noise was worth the risk. Marty and Marie were the last two people who could pick Mark Thompson out of a lineup. Once they were gone, there was no one to link him to the trip.

He hid under the windowsill as the lights in the living room sprang to life. They were sure to find the broken glass and the gasoline container any second.

"Stay back," Marty called out.

"What the hell happened?" Marie questioned.

Mark managed to peek over the ledge enough to see the pair inching their way into the room. Marty clutched an aluminum ball bat in his hands as if he was ready to take on an intruder or animal with it.

"Just stay back, Marie."

Mark watched as the tip of the baseball bat nudged a few items if there was anything else in the room. Then, his eyes fell on the red object.

"What the fuck?" he snapped. "Someone threw a gas container through our window."

"Who-who would do such a thing?"

"It was probably some stupid kid trying to act cool in front of his friends. It's no big deal."

"But what if it's him?"

"Will you stop, Marie? No one is out to get us." Marty approached the window as the cold air blew through hole.

Mark dropped out of sight to ensure no one saw him.

"I don't care; I'm calling the cops anyway. Someone needs to pay for this window, and it definitely won't be us."

"Do whatever you want. I need to find something to cover the window so we don't freeze our asses off all night."

Marty poked his head through the opening. It was a stupid move; one Mark had planned for. He picked up a red brick and smashed it against his target's head. The body fell limp. His neck dropped onto the jagged edges of the shattered window.

"Marty…Marty, are you okay?" Marie called out in hysterics. She rushed over to her boyfriend to check on him. She shook his shoulders as fear seeped into her mind. "Please stop playing around; this isn't funny."

From where he hid, Mark could almost picture the panic overcoming the woman. He smiled with glee as her boyfriend's death hit her. Seconds later he saw her hand poke through the broken glass of the window to place two fingers on Marty's neck, searching for a pulse.

Mark snatched her wrist and pulled Marie until her head smashed against the broken window. A crimson stream poured from her face with droplets of blood falling onto the back of Marty's head. She let out a moan while trying to use her other hand to stop the bleeding.

"Still alive, huh?" Marked laughed.

He gripped the brick tightly while repeated hammering Marie's head until her body collapsed onto her boyfriend's back. Blood dripped down the side of the house leaving a crimson pool on the grass below.

Mark leaned forward and checked for a pulse. "It looks like we're all set for the big finale."

He lit a book of matches and tossed it inside the opening into the living room. The carpet caught fire; burning the happy home as the flames inched closer to the can of gasoline. He grabbed the second container and dumped the contents over his victims, the windowsill, and the area underneath it.

Mark wedged the second can between the two lifeless bodies before taking off to the car. He sped off just as a neighbor's light turned on.

They woke up just in time for the fireworks.

Chapter 38-Ali

The call came around ten-thirty that night. The sound of the phone ringing and incessantly buzzing on the nightstand ripped me from a peaceful dream. It was one where Matthew had taken us on vacation. We were away from everything; friends; family; our jobs; nothing was going to rip us away from that place. We were on a beach holding hands as the sun beat against our bodies. We were wrapped in a cool, gentle breeze as waves crashed along the shore. It was exactly where I wanted to be, but it was only a dream. The phone vibrating on the top of the table next to my head made sure I knew it was all in my head.

In a sleep-depraved fog, I reached for my cell. "Hello," I groaned.

"Ali," Rodney's said. I could hear the panic in his voice. "A call just came in. There was a fire at a house on Church Street in New Paltz. We need to get down there now."

"A fire?" I questioned while rubbing my eyes. "Shouldn't that be the arson team's problem?"

"Normally, you would be right, but there were two bodies found in the window burned to death. We found out from their landlord they were students at New Paltz."

I sat up feeling a bit more curious. "Do we know their names?"

"There hasn't been an ID on the bodies, but the tenant names matched Marty and Marie from the Outdoors Club."

Hearing their names was like being attacked with daggers. But they weren't stabbing me; they were poking holes and cutting up our investigation against Nick DeFalco. I knew it was his way of tying up loose ends. They were the only people left who could have matched Mark Thompson's name with the description of Nick.

"Give me forty-five minutes to get ready and head down there. I want a shot at that crime scene before anyone contaminates it any further."

I quickly jumped out of bed and grabbed a pair of jeans and a sweatshirt to change into before running out the door. I drove out to New Paltz where black smoke filled the sky. Police cars and fire trucks sectioned off the block as neighbors lined up along Church Street to watch the fire consume what was left of the two-story home. The flames signaled another two lives lost; two families torn apart by tragedy; and a town kept in fear wondering who would be the next victim.

I parked at the end of the block and jogged my way towards the crowd. I snuck around the spectators to see most of the fire had been extinguished. All that remained was the charred home with smoke rising from the ashes.

"Ali," Rodney called out. "I'm over here."

I pressed a finger to my lips signaling for him to keep quiet. I didn't need the crowd to notice the detective in charge of capturing the murderous son of a bitch was among them. They would turn to me demanding answers I wasn't prepared to answer. I grabbed my partner by the arm and led him over to another familiar face, Dr. Wu who was with a few analysts and a woman I had never met before.

Fred stepped aside and let me into their circle. "Hey, Ali…I mean detective." He glanced at the house as more firefighters emerged from the smoke-filled doorway. "We should get the all clear soon."

I caught the unknown woman staring at me. I returned it while wondering who she was. Her hair was long but tied back exposing her breathtakingly, light-green eyes. I didn't know if she was a new tech or a higher ranked official taking interest in the case because they weren't seeing results.

I nudged my partner. "Who's she?" I asked while nodding towards the mystery woman.

Rodney smiled and placed a hand on the small of my back. "Ali, let me introduce you to Mallory O'Hara from arson."

I reached out to shake her hand. "Hi, I'm Detective-"

"I know who you are," Mallory quipped. She turned towards the house just as a firefighter crossed the street to speak with our group. "How are we looking, Luke?"

"The fire is out, and the building is clear. You should be set to go in shortly. I'll send one of the guys to let you know when it's safe and they'll walk you through it."

She thanked the fireman before turning back to our group. Her face was stern-looking and very business-like.

"I'll take the C.S.U. team in first to conduct our arson investigation. Once we're done, then you can do whatever you need to do." She walked off with a smirk on her face while waving the analysts to follow her.

"Is it just me, or was she purposely trying to be a bitch?"

Rodney shrugged his shoulders. "I think she's annoyed we're walking all over her turf."

"That's why I was shocked you called."

"The lieutenant heard about the fire and started making some calls. He found out it was the two students and lost his shit. He sent instructions to leave the bodies alone. No one was allowed to touch them until we looked them over."

"I know O'Hara," Dr. Wu said. "I've worked with her before. She's genuinely nice, but strict and professional. She does everything by the book. So, I must agree with Officer Johnson; she probably thinks you are stepping on her toes."

I had my hands digging deep into my sweatshirt pockets. "Do I really look like I wanna be here right now? I was sleeping in a nice, warm, cozy bed before being woken up for this. I'd rather be back there than standing around in the freezing cold waiting to go inside a burned down house."

"Look, the lieutenant wants us here, and that's all that matters."

Knowing Rodney spoke to the lieutenant caused me to think about what happened earlier in the night. "Did you tell him about my house?"

Dr. Wu craned his neck to look at me. "Wait, what happened to your house?" he asked.

"Nothing, don't worry about it." I didn't want to involve Fred or have to relive the story, but Rodney decided to include him.

"The Campus Killer threw a brick through Ali's living room window tonight warning her to back off."

"He did what?" Dr. Wu asked. "Ali, are you okay?"

"I'm fine," I replied. "It's not a big deal." I mentioned the note and brought up how Nick said he wasn't going to kill again as long as we stopped pursuing him. He was going to leave town.

"So much for that happening," Rodney said sarcastically.

"Maybe this was his final farewell. Marty and Marie were the only two left who could tie him to the trip which would point him as the lead suspect."

"Do you think he's really gonna leave town now?" Rodney posed a good question. I didn't have an answer for him other than shrugging my shoulders.

We stood around talking for another twenty minutes before Mallory O'Hara finally entered the house. All of us let out a deep and annoyed sigh knowing it was going to be a while before we were allowed to take over the crime scene. Rodney volunteered to get us coffee. We leaned against one of the squad cars drinking it until the piping hot liquid lost its heat.

After an hour and a half of waiting, I chugged the last quarter cup of what was now cold coffee. "So, do you think she actually found something, or is she taking her time just to be spiteful?"

"Or maybe she's being very thorough with her crime scene," a woman snapped from behind us. We turned and saw Mallory O'Hara standing there with her clothes covered in ash and soot. Her hair was messy and dripping with sweat.

Another great first impression, Ali, I thought. "Sorry," I quickly replied in a blatant attempt to cover up my mistake. "The cold was just getting to me."

"Did you find anything?" Rodney asked. He obviously knew Mallory and I were not getting along, and it would not be beneficial to our investigation to piss her off.

"I found lots of stuff," she replied. "Both bodies were found in the broken living room window. Their bodies were doused in gasoline, as well as the side of the house, and the ground beneath the window. Whoever did this wanted to make sure every bit of evidence was burned beyond recognition."

"What about inside the house?" I questioned. "Was there an accelerant used in there as well?"

"Yes, we located the remains of a gasoline container on the opposite side of the window where the bodies were found. There was enough to engulf the house in flames but not cause an explosion."

"Were you able to determine how and when the fire began?"

"I am guessing the killer used the first container to break the window before killing the victims. Then, he set fire to the living room. I believe a book of matches would probably do the trick."

I was shocked at the lengths Nick DeFalco went to cover his tracks. He'd burned down a home with his victims in it, while risking the lives of the neighbors. I was sure we were wasting our time at the crime scene. Collecting any shred of evidence seemed pointless. The destruction of the fire and the fire department inadvertently contaminating the crime scene ensured anything we collected was useless.

"Are we cleared to enter?" Dr. Wu asked. He was probably looking to getting out of there just as much as we were. There was a tall order ahead of him tomorrow once the bodies were sent for autopsy.

"Yeah, just be careful. The building is unstable. The fire severely damaged the support beams."

That was my signal to haul ass and get my review done quickly. I thanked O'Hara and took off towards the house knowing there was a limited amount of time before the place came crashing down on us.

Chapter 39-Ali

The alarm rang at six the next morning. The loud obnoxious chorus of music blasted from the clock next to my bed. There was a violent, pulsating ache, which felt like someone was beating a drum on the back of my head.

Damn and I didn't even drink last night.

By the time Rodney and I finished up at the crime scene on Church Street, it was one-thirty. We decided to grab a bite to eat at a diner before heading home. I walked in the door at three, stripped down to take a shower, and passed out the moment my head hit the pillow. I had the option to come in late, but I had forgotten to turn off the alarm. Now, it was maliciously summoning me to get up. I turned it off and tried to go back to sleep, but there was no way I could close my eyes again without thinking about the two new victims we saw burned in their own home.

I decided to get up for my morning jog hoping it would help to clear my head. I slipped on my running gear and headed out the door to another cold Ulster County morning. I drove to the dirt lot where I typically parked my car. I was used to seeing one or two others, and they were always the same. There was one more I didn't recognize. It was an old clunker with black paint chipping off the sides. I tried to look inside from a distance, but the windows were tinted and were too dark to see anything. My curiosity pulled me towards it, and I wondered if there was someone new going for a run, if someone needed to ditch their vehicle due to mechanical problems, or if they needed to sleep somewhere for the night.

I approached the driver's side door and knocked on the window. "Is anyone in there?" I asked. There wasn't any movement or sound coming from inside the car. I knocked again, but there was no reply. I considered calling it in and having an officer come by to see who it belonged to. In the end, I decided to wait until after my run. What could one more hour of sleep hurt?

I walked up the dirt path to the fence and stretched. I had a weird vibe someone was watching me. I turned my head quickly, but didn't see anyone. I continued my stretches only to feel the eerie presence again. This time, it felt like there were eyes gawking at me.

Maybe it was just the person in the car waking up.

I couldn't blame the vagrant for staring me down. They probably needed some sleep, and I woke them up. Hell, I could have used some extra bonding time with my pillow and comforter this morning, too.

I decided to worry about the black car later and start my morning jog. The first two minutes were a brisk walk designed to get my blood pumping. Then, it turned into a jog. This was typical of my routine. Five minutes in; my adrenaline kicked in as my feet pounded the pavement of the bridge. The speed intensified every couple of minutes as if someone pressed a button on a treadmill. I let my thoughts consume me. Each case, each murder swirled around inside my head.

Why? Why did Nick kill each of these students? What did they do to him to make him snap? Was it really because they didn't like him, or was it because his housemates didn't invite him to hang out? Was it a control issue which spun out of control once Brianna left him? Or was there more to the story we had yet to uncover?

I had to believe the last theory more than the others. It was hard to think Nick would snap over neighbors or housemates giving relationship advice. Although, there have been plenty of stories where boyfriends with jealousy and control problems go off the deep end and hurt the ones they felt betrayed by. The only murders which made any type of sense were Marty and Marie's deaths. It was a blatant attempt to mess up our investigation and cover his tracks. But it wasn't done like the others. They were killed and the crime scene staged to look like suicides.

Every victim's name and image flashed through my mind. A rage had been building up for weeks until it finally unleashed its aggression against my own body; punishing it for not finding their killer sooner. It brought me to the point of exhaustion as I reached the halfway mark on the return. I finally slowed to a walk. My heart was beating too fast. My lungs were working too hard against the cold air making it impossible to catch my breath. My vision blurred as I hunched over clutching at the pain in my chest. That's when I felt a hand touch my shoulder.

"Are you okay, miss?" the man asked.

"Y-yeah, I think so," I gasped. "I just need to rest."

"You need to stand up so the air can get through your body. If you hunch over, it'll make it harder to breathe."

This was something I already knew, but my body was too busy reacting to the pain. I tried to ignore the man until I felt his hands touch my lower back and shoulder. They pushed and pulled until I was forced into an upright position. Then he took my hands and placed them on top of my head. I was too weak and out of breath to stop him.

"There; isn't that better?" he asked.

The cold air hit my body as I tried to inhale deeply. I nodded in agreement. "Thanks," I muttered between gasping breaths.

"No problem," the man replied. "Here, let me help you over to the rails and I'll go get you some water."

I nodded in agreement and allowed this stranger to guide me to the side of the bridge. It was weird to put my trust in a guy I just met. It was weirder my blurred vision had not cleared, and I was still unable to see his face. Slowly, my world came back into focus. I could see we were approaching the rails. I could see the water down below. I shuddered to think what would have happened to me if this man had not shown up when he did. I was grateful for him until I felt the hand on my lower back drop down to grab my ass.

"I appreciate the help, but I don't think your assistance requires you to grope me." I tried to move my hands to swat him away, but his grip on my wrists tightened. He held them over my head rendering me defenseless. "Hey, let go of me."

I struggled to get free, but the stranger became increasingly aggressive. This time the hand on my ass grabbed my inner thigh. He hoisted my body off the ground and leaned me over the rails.

"It's been nice knowing you, detective."

Those were his final words before shoving me over the side of the bridge. My body smacked hard against the water. which emitted a big splash. It felt like a thousand knives were piercing me all at once. The frigid waves slammed against my body forcing me under multiple times. I tried to fight it. I tried to swim back to the docks I saw in the distance. It was getting harder to breathe; harder to stay above the water.

There was hardly anyone out at that time other than the two other cars in the parking lot. I doubted anyone saw me thrown off the bridge. There was nothing I could do to save myself. I was about to die. I would never see my friends, my family, or even Matthew again. I sunk into the Hudson knowing I was the Campus Killer's final victim.

The next time I opened my eyes; I was surrounded by a bright white light. I thought I was about to step up to the golden gates or meet my grandfather's spirit. I couldn't see anything. I was still blinded but something shining in my eyes.

"Ali…Ali," a soft voice said in the distance. "Ali, can you hear me?"

I wanted to reach out and grab the woman's hand; praying she could pull me to safety. I tried to raise my arms, but a surge of pain coursed through my body with every move I made.

"Detective Ryan," a stern male voice called out. It was forceful, familiar, and yet oddly comforting.

Am I dead? Did that son of a bitch kill me?

The blinding light turned off. Now, a shadow of a man slid into view.

"Get away from me," I shouted.

My arms sprung alive trying to push, punch, and claw at anyone around me. I felt two set s of hands pin me down.

"Nurse, get the Propofol."

"Relax, Ali," another voice said. I recognized it immediately. It was Rodney. "It's okay; you're safe now."

Hearing him put an end to my resistance. If he was telling me to calm down, I was somewhere safe, and the people around me were not there to hurt me.

"Rodney?" I called out.

"Yeah, it's me." I felt the person holding my right arm down release me. My partner's big strong hand grabbed mine, and I knew everything was all right. "You gave us all a big scare."

The rest of the room started to come into focus. I could see the doctor and nurses staring at me with a look of panic and concern. One of them was holding a syringe in her hands. I guess that was supposed to calm me down. The doctor waved her off and said it was no longer needed.

"W-what happened? Where am I?"

Rodney pulled a chair closer to me and sat down. "You were attacked on the bridge this morning and thrown into the Hudson."

I replayed the end of my run, and how I was bent over in pain. I remembered a guy helping me, but I never saw his face, but I heard his voice.

"It was him," I cried out.

"Who was it; Nick?"

I pushed myself up in the bed against the doctor and nurses objecting. They were already trying to check me over and shoo out my partner. I refused to listen to them. Thankfully, Rodney didn't either.

"I'm sure it was him."

"Did you see him?" the stern voice from earlier asked. With clear vision, I was able to see it was the lieutenant.

"No, I-I couldn't see anything. I pushed myself too hard when going for my morning run. I almost collapsed on the bridge and some guy helped me up. I thought it was just someone seeing another person in distress and wanted to help. He brought me over to the rails and said he was going to get me some water. Next thing I knew; he was shoving me over the side of the bridge." All the pain I felt was a reminder of what happened. It fueled my anger for Nick DeFalco. This was the second time the asshole targeted me. "How did you guys find me?"

"It wasn't us," Rodney said. "Matthew pulled you out of the water."

"What? Why was he there?"

"Does it really matter? The man saved your life."

I was beyond grateful for him to show up when I needed him the most. There were so many questions needing to be answered, and so much I had to tell him. It was to be put on hold until I took care of the Nick DeFalco situation.

"Where's Amanda? I need to make sure she's okay."

"She's fine, Ali." Rodney said as he stood up from his seat. "We have a uniformed officer standing guard outside of her dorm room."

I swatted him away. "That's not good enough. This son of a bitch knows more than we give him credit for. He knew where I lived; he knew where to find me this morning and that I went out daily for a run before my shift. He had to have been stalking me for a while. He's probably been following her too."

"Tell us what you want us to do, Ali."

"You can start by helping me out of this bed."

The lieutenant approached the other side of my bed. He placed a hand on my shoulder. "You can't leave the hospital. You were almost killed. You're lucky to be alive right now."

"I'll be fine; I just need to see my sister."

"You plan on rushing out of here to do what; collapse in front of her?" The lieutenant applied a gentle amount of pressure to make sure I stayed in bed. "Ali, your body was already fighting off exhaustion. The fall alone could have killed you. Instead, you have some bad bruising. The water sent you into hypothermia. The doctors have spent most of the day warming you back up to a normal temperature."

I had no idea I had gone through so much. It felt like only a few minutes had passed since Nick DeFalco had attacked me on the bridge. By the time I saw a clock; it had been more than twelve hours.

"But-" I tried to reply.

"I don't want to hear any arguing or complaining. I don't care if I have to handcuff you to the bed. You're not leaving this hospital until the doctors medically clear you."

I wasn't about to let the lieutenant dictate what I could and couldn't do when it came to my health or my sister's safety. I pushed his hand away and tried to get out of the bed. A second later, I felt the cold steel snap around my wrist.

"Rodney, what the hell are you doing? Let me go."

"Sorry, partner. You heard the lieutenant."

"I need to get Amanda away from this craziness."

"And take her where?" the lieutenant asked.

"I can put her and Sean on a train back to my parent's house. They can keep them safe until we take down the son of a bitch who put me in this bed."

We spent another ten minutes arguing over me getting out of the hospital. They were hell-bent on keeping me there and threatened more restraints or sedatives unless I cooperated. I reluctantly agreed as long as they helped to get my sister out of town. The next hour was spent going over the plan. I put the lieutenant in charge of overseeing the operation and coordinating with the Glen Falls police department to set up a watch on my parent's house. I wanted to get her out of town safely, but I also needed to ensure Nick DeFalco didn't follow her. Rodney's role didn't need to be spoken. He would be escorting Sean and Amanda out of town. He and Lieutenant Esposito were the only two people I trusted to protect my sister. I just prayed everything worked out.

<u>Chapter 40-Ali</u>

It had been a few hours since Rodney and the lieutenant left my room. I was on edge and was chomping at the bit to get out of the hospital. I still had no T.V. I really didn't want it since I'd planned on getting out of there the first chance I had.

"How are we doing tonight?" a nurse asked as she walked into the room. She was in her mid-forties with curly blonde hair. I caught a few streaks of gray mixed in, but I wasn't about to point that out to her.

"I feel great," I lied. "When can I get outta here?"

"Let me take your vitals first." She reached over and placed the cuff for the blood pressure machine around my arm. Then, she placed a thermometer under my tongue until it beeped. She reviewed the other monitors and jotted down the information onto my chart. "Well, so far everything looks good. I can check with the doctor, but I'm sure you'll probably get released sometime tomorrow." She must have noticed me rolling my eyes. She let out a chuckle. "Don't worry about it. Just get some rest and it'll be morning before you know it."

"That's going to be impossible. I need to get out of here to take down the piece of shit who put me in here."

"Well, I hate to break it to you, but you're not going anywhere tonight. I *can* get something to help you sleep if you'd like."

I really didn't want anything. I was awake and alert, which is what I needed to be to go after DeFalco. The nurse exited the room and came back a few minutes later with a paper cup filled with two pills. She ordered me to swallow them and get some rest. I did as I was told, mostly because I wanted it to be morning so I could get out of the hospital. Part of me was grateful for the nurse. She was kind and caring; the kind of way my mother used to be when I was home sick. The nurse waited with me until I started to drift off. My eyelids became heavy; my arms became numb; my body felt weightless as my mind took a first-class trip to paradise.

I opened my eyes to the sight of crystal-clear waters of Saint Lucia, a place I dreamed of going to one day. My body was sprawled out on the beach with the hot sun radiating against my bikini clad body. I plunged my hand into the warm sand and let it sift through my fingers. It felt so real, and I wanted nothing more than to be there with Matthew.

A tall dark shadow stood over me. I held a hand over my eyes to block the sun. There he was,; my hunk of a man standing in front of me holding two drinks. He smiled at me while placing a blood-orange margarita in my hands. I lunged forward, almost knocking him and the drinks over, and pummeled Matthew with kisses.

"I guess someone missed me," he laughed.

I didn't care if this was real or a dream. I was happy to see Matthew; to hear his voice. "I'm so sorry we fought. I'm such an idiot. I never want you to feel neglected. I should've-"

He placed a finger to my lips and waited for me to quiet down. Then, he placed his lips lovingly on mine for a passionate kiss.

"I say we finish these drinks and jump in the water for a bit."

He chugged down his Jack and Coke before sprinting down the beach. I knocked back the margarita as if it was a shot of tequila. I jumped to my feet and felt a little dizzy, but nothing was going to stop me from being with my guy.

He was already waist deep in the water by the time I dipped a toe into the cool refreshing water. It was clear-blue and felt great to let the waves wash over my feet. Matthew ran over splashing me in the face. I laughed and chased after him.

"I'm gonna get you for that," I declared.

He took off down the shore with me running after him. But the more I ran, the more our scenery changed. The warm sand and cool water weren't there anymore. Instead, I was in sneakers running along a bridge, one I knew too well.

I ran down the concrete path feeling like someone was coming after me. I glanced over my shoulder, but there was no one there. I wanted to stop and look around. My feet seemed to have a mind of their own and carried me further away. The eerie feeling of being watched continued. I looked behind me again. This time, there was a man dressed from head to toe in black. He was running after me. I could feel him nipping at my heels within moments. Finally, he slammed into my body knocking me to the ground. My hands and knees scraped against the concrete. His hand gripped my arm and pulled me to my feet. I tried to strike him, but my arms were too heavy to lift. The faceless man laughed as he picked me up and threw me over the bridge into the water below.

I felt the waves knocking me under as I struggled to stay afloat. I was desperate to get somewhere safe, but I grew tired and inevitably sank to the bottom of the river. I had to remind myself it was just a dream. Once I woke up; everything would be fine. I opened my eyes and breathed a sigh of relief to be back in the dark hospital room.

"Thank God that nightmare's over," I whispered.

"Oh, it's only just begun," a man's voice replied.

I tried to sit up and click on a light. I needed to see who was in my room. The cold steel from the handcuffs kept me locked in place.

"Who's there?" I called out. "Show yourself."

"Come on, detective; you know who I am." The man stepped out of the shadows of the room. I could see a black shirt and pants underneath a white doctor's coat. I tried to scream for help, but he muffled the sound with his hand. I could hear him ripping a piece of tape as he placed it over my mouth. "There; that's so much better." He paced around my bed letting out little cackles of laughter. "You're at my mercy again, detective. Now, what should I do to you this time?" His hand skimmed my leg. I tried to kick him away. "Feisty; I like it. You don't want to go down without a fight." I tried to kick him again. "Don't worry, Ali; I'm not going to kill you, not yet anyway."

I kicked and thrashed in the bed; doing everything possible to keep this man at bay. I dropped my head to my chest and struggled for my fingertips to catch the edge of the tape. I was able to rip it from my mouth.

"HELP! HELP! THE KILLER IS IN HERE"

He rushed to my side and placed another hand over my lips. "If you keep that up, I'll really give you something to scream about." His words sent a chill up and down my spine. "Oh, don't worry; you're not my target, but I might enjoy spending some intimate time with your sister."

I bit the man's hand forcing him away. "If you touch her, I'll kill you." I was at his mercy, but my threat was very real.

"Keep talking, Ali; that's all you can do. But I have killed six people, and I will enjoy watching your sister die next."

I continued to fight against my restraints while screaming and cursing at the man.

"Ali…Ali wake up," another man said. His hands shook my shoulders pulling me from my nightmare.

"I'll fucking kill you."

"Ali, it's just a dream. You're safe."

I opened my eyes and saw Matthew sitting on the edge of my bed. Sweat poured down my face as my eyes searched the room for any sign of the man who haunted me in my sleep.

"Where is he?" I asked.

"Who are you talking about?"

"I don't know," I replied with uncertainty. "Someone was in here. I was handcuffed to the bed and…" I glanced down at my wrists. There were no restraints keeping my hands at bay. "I swear someone was in here a few minutes ago."

"No one's been in or out of your room in hours," Matthew reassured me. "I've been sitting outside of your door since eleven."

The red digits on the clock told me it was now three in the morning. I had been asleep for more than five hours.

"Amanda," I gasped.

"She's safe. Rodney has three officers monitoring her room, patrolling the hallway, and watching the building. No one is getting anywhere near her."

"Where is he, and where's my lieutenant?"

"They went home to be with their families and to get some sleep. They've been busy all night making the arrangements to get Amanda and Sean out of town." Matthew wiped some of the sweat from my head. Then, he brushed a tendril of curly hair behind my ear. "Ali, I-"

I didn't let him finish his statement. I could care less what he had to say. Matthew was the reason I was alive. I pulled him towards me and kissed him just as passionately as I did in my dream.

"Stay with me tonight. Just hold me and don't ever leave me again."

<u>Chapter 41-Ali</u>

I woke the next morning to the scent of fresh flowers. My room was filled with colorful bouquet arrangements and get well wishes from friends and family. I loved them all, but they were overshadowed by the oversized card signed by all the officers from my station. My hand sat comfortably on my stomach. When it rolled to my side and touched the cool fabric of the hospital sheet, I began to panic.

"Matthew," I called out hysterically.

He barged through the door instantly and ran to my side. "What happened? Are you okay?"

I wrapped my arms around him and squeezed tightly. "Yeah, I'm fine. I just…you weren't here, and I freaked out."

"I was just outside. You have a few visitors who have been impatiently waiting for you to wake up."

I wiped my eyes before running my fingers through my hair. "I probably look like shit right now."

"No, you look beautiful," Matthew replied in a charming manner. "Are you ready to see everyone?"

I nodded, which gave Matthew permission to open the door. He signaled for my visitors. Amanda was first into the room. Rodney accompanied her. My sister wasted no time in running up to my bed and hurling herself at me. She hugged me so tightly; I almost couldn't breathe.

"Don't ever scare me like that again," she whispered.

"I won't; I promise." I squeezed her a little more before releasing my sister. "Besides, I don't want you having all the fun of being an only child." She looked at me with a shocked expression before both of us broke into a giggle. "Did Rodney go over everything with you?"

The light in Amanda's eyes disappeared. She seemed depressed at the mention of the plan. "I don't wanna go. You need me here."

"No," I said flatly. "I need you to be somewhere safe. This psycho made this personal, which means you're a potential target. I can't chase him and keep an eye on you at the same time."

"I don't need you to protect me, Ali. I'm a big girl. I can handle myself. Plus, I've taken several self-defense courses."

Rodney stepped closer to the bed and positioned himself next to us. He placed his large hands on our shoulders gently.

"Your sister is right, Amanda. This guy is unpredictable. He already tried to kill your sister. He may come after you next. You'll be a lot safer in Glen Falls with your parents and an officer guarding the house."

Amanda looked like she was about to protest the decision again, but I cut her off immediately. "You're going and that's the end of the discussion."

Amanda got up from the bed and stormed out. Rodney started to chase after her. "Don't worry, Ali; I'll make sure she gets on that train." He hurried after my sister and left the door open as he made his exit.

The lieutenant appeared a moment later with a smirk on his face. "There's the big hero."

"Thanks, but I wouldn't call being overworked and dumped in the river by a psychopathic killer being a hero."

"I wasn't talking to you, Ryan. I was referring to your boyfriend; the guy who saved your ass."

I felt my cheeks glow. He was right. Matthew was a big hero. He rescued me from the freezing river, and I had yet to thank him.

"Matthew, I…uh…"

"You don't have to say anything, Ali. I'm glad I was in the right place at the right time. I don't know what I would've done without you in my life."

That warmed me up a little more. I was happy to hear Matthew wanted to still be with me despite our fight before he left for a business trip. There was still so much for us to discuss, but not with the lieutenant standing ten feet away.

"I really didn't come here for this mushy love story nonsense," Esposito groused.

"Then, why are you here?" I snapped.

There was something bothering the lieutenant. I could tell by the way he stopped looking at me. His eyes turned towards the floor as if he was counting tiles or fixated on his shoelaces.

"I really don't wanna do this, but I have no choice. I'm officially pulling you off the Campus Killer investigation."

"What?" I shrieked.

I was completely enraged at the news. I had been chasing lead after lead for months to track down a possible suspect. I'd worked even harder to convince the lieutenant there was a killer on the loose. And now, I was being removed from the case. I demanded to know why.

"I'm sorry, Ali; my hands are tied on this one."

"Why? Is it because this son of a bitch attacked me? That's no reason to pull me from this investigation."

"You were one of his targets, Ali. He tried to kill you. There is a bullseye on your back; on your chest; your family; hell, the whole station for that matter."

"That's all the more reason for me to be out there hunting his ass."

"I'm sorry, but I can't put you on the street until we catch him."

I wasn't just being thrown off the case. I was being benched. I would be held captive in my own home or someplace else under witness protection.

"I'm not going into hiding. You can't make me."

Matthew grabbed my hand, but I jerked it away instantly. "Ali, you can't continue to go up against this guy. He knew your routine; where you live; where you work."

I naturally assumed Rodney clued them about the brick being thrown through my window the other night.

"I don't care what he knows. It's not gonna stop me from taking him down." I was coming after Nick DeFalco with vengeance on my mind.

"Well, that's not your call or mine to make, detective." The lieutenant walked to the window with a scowl on his face. "Because of the attack on you, and the two other deaths from the house on Church Street, the police commissioner has called in the F.B.I. to take over the case. They'll be here sometime this afternoon to take your statement and review the case."

"Here? Are you telling me I'm not getting released today?"

"Ali, the doctors feel it's in your best interest to stay for another night or two," Matthew confessed.

"I'm healthy enough to go home now," I snapped. The lieutenant was already telling me I was being benched and would have to stay under police protection until DeFalco was caught. Now, I was being held captive in a hospital.

"It's for the best," Matthew replied.

Fuck you both. I flung the sheets off me and tried to stand up. "I don't give a shit what any of you say." My feet touched the cold tiled floor. I was about to storm off like a child, but Matthew grabbed the back of my hospital gown.

Then, the lieutenant stood in front of the door. "Where do you think you're going, Ryan?

"Ali, you need to get back in bed," Matthew advised.

"No, I'm getting out of here. Besides, someone needs to make sure Amanda gets on that train to my parent's house."

"Rodney and Spencer are taking your sister and her boyfriend to the train station. They're riding with them and will meet the Glen Falls P.D. at your parent's house."

"See, they're in great hands," Matthew reassured. "Now, get back in that bed before we tell the nurse you are freaking out and need something to calm you down."

"You'll need something more powerful than a sedative," the lieutenant joked. "I think a horse tranquilizer should do the trick."

There was no way I was winning the argument with them both in the room. I reluctantly climbed back into the bed and pulled the covers over me.

"Just get out and leave me alone," I ordered.

Matthew bent to kiss me, but I turned away. I wasn't going to act loving to a man who chose to go against me rather than take my side. He joined the lieutenant as they exited the room.

I truly felt alone. I was trapped within the confines of the hospital with no way out and no case to work on when I finally did get out of there. I sat like that for an hour before I heard a soft knock on my door. The person on the other side pushed it open and crept in.

"Get out," I barked. "I don't want any more visitors."

"Sorry," Dr. Wu said. "I'll come back later." I could hear the door closing behind him.

"Wait," I replied. Fred stood frozen to the spot. "Come in and keep the door shut."

Dr. Wu stood in front of the only thing keeping me in my room. "I just wanted to stop by and see how you were feeling."

"I feel fine, but they're keeping me here against my will. I need to get out before they realize I'm gone." I eyed up Dr. Wu while toying around with idea to break me out of the hospital.

"You're kind of scaring me."

"I need you to help me. Maybe you can sign off on release papers."

"Ali, I'm not that kind of doctor. I just can't sign a patient out of the hospital. I don't have the clearance."

"Fine, then sneak me out of here."

I could see Fred tossing thoughts around in his head; no doubt struggling with the ethics of following another doctor's orders versus helping out a friend in need. He knew what was at stake. I only had a few hours to catch a killer before the feds took over the investigation.

"If I help you, we need to make sure no one knows my involvement." I nodded my affirmation as Fred laid out his plan. "Just wait here and I'll be back in with a pair of scrubs for you. You're on your own from there."

"Thanks, Fred. I owe you one."

"Good, I like it when you owe me."

<u>Chapter 42-CK</u>

Mark Thompson watched as the squad car pulled up to the Poughkeepsie train station. He was aware Detective Ryan had survived the attack, and that she decided to send her sister away to live with their parents until the Campus Killer was caught. There were scheduled to be two officers accompanying Amanda Ryan and her boyfriend onto the train. It would prove to be difficult to take them out, but he was positive the plan would work.

He waited and watched as the two officers got out of the car and opened the backdoors for his targets to get out. Officer Johnson stayed close to the girl. He was like a big brother to her. There was no way Mark could get close enough to do anything with the man around. It was just as bad as having Detective Ryan there to thwart his plans.

"You got everything you need?" Johnson asked.

"No, I need to be here with Ali," Ali's sister replied.

"She has the whole police force watching her back. You'll have the same ready for you once we drop you off at your parent's house."

Mark watched as Amanda's boyfriend laced his fingers around hers.

"I'm sure it won't be that bad up there," the kid said. "Besides, you kept saying how you wanted me to meet your mom and dad."

"Not under an armed guard," Amanda replied. Although with my father letting you sleep under the same roof as me, we might need a cop to stop him from shooting you if we messed around."

Mark kept within earshot of the foursome, but remained out of their sight. He knew exactly where they were headed, but he needed to ensure no one deviated from their schedules.

"Stop messing with the poor boy," Officer Johnson said. "We don't need to be cleaning up any stains." He checked his watch. "Come on; we need to hurry or we'll miss the train."

"Oh darn," Amanda replied sarcastically.

Mark reached into his pocket and scrolled to the few contacts listed. He sent a text to one of his friends.

Mark: It's me. Do it now!

Unknown: Are you sure?

Mark: Yes. Go now!

He continued to follow the group inside the station and out to the platform. The plan needed to work. Time was running out. The train was sure to arrive within the next few minutes, and the officers were still with the targets.

Then the big man grabbed his cell. "Hey, Lieu…She did what?"

Mark stood there unsure of what was happening. There was no woman part of the plan other than to kill Amanda Ryan.

"Rodney, what's going on?" she asked.

The radio sounded off a moment later.

"Attention all units; we have reports of a possible suspect being spotted near the bus terminal on Main Street in New Paltz." The woman's voice on the radio continued to list the description of the man in question.

Officer Johnson turned back to his cell. "I might know where she's going. I just heard someone reported seeing Nick DeFalco at the New Paltz bus terminal." He held the phone away from his ear as the man on the other end shouted.

"Get back here and bring Ali in before she hurts someone."

"I can't go. The train is arriving any minute."

"Let Officer Spencer watch them. I need you to bring in Ryan. You're the only one she'll listen to."

"What's going on?" Amanda asked.

"Your sister broke out of the hospital and no one knows where she is. We also just received a possible hit on our suspect."

"You think Ali is going after him?"

"Yeah, and she'll kill him if she finds DeFalco before we do."

"Is that such a bad thing?" the boy asked. His question was met with glares from the two officers. "I'm just saying; the dude killed six people and attacked a cop. She'd be doing the world a favor by blowing a hole right through the guy's head."

I wasn't going to hurt you unless you got in my way, Mark thought. *Now, I can't wait to watch you die.*

"We need to bring the suspect in alive. We need to know why he did this. The victims' families deserve to see the bastard rot in jail for the rest of his life." Johnson whispered something to the other officer before turning away.

"Wait, where are you going?" Amanda asked.

"I need to stop your sister before she hurts herself or anyone else."

"Then, I'm coming, too."

"No, you need to get on that train with Sean and Officer Spencer. We need to stick to the plan until we have the suspect in custody." He stepped forward and took Amanda Ryan by the hands. "Everything will be okay; I promise."

Oh, Officer Johnson; you shouldn't make promises you can't keep.

Amanda gripped her boyfriend's hand tightly. Mark wasn't a mind reader, but the fear, plainly written on her face, was obvious. The time had come for the second part of his plan to take effect.

Mark Thompson found a teenager nearby. "Hey, kid; I was wondering if you could help me out with something."

"Get lost."

"I'll give you fifty bucks."

The teenager turned his head. "What do I have to do?"

"That woman over there took something from me and is hiding it in her purse. I need you to steal her bag and meet me in the bathroom inside the station."

"So, you want me to rob a chick for fifty bucks? Get real, dude. I'm not getting arrested for that."

"Fine, make it a hundred," Mark replied.

"Two hundred and you better make sure I don't get caught."

Mark rolled his eyes and took out his wallet. He paid the money to the teenager and told him to make his move. The kid walked at a brisk pace through a crowd. He bumped into the woman and snatched her bag. He was running before she knew what happened.

"Help," she cried out. "He stole my purse." It was enough to grab everyone's attention. The teenager was already darting into the station by the time the woman noticed Officer Spencer. "Please, help me," she begged. "Some kid stole my bag."

"Don't move," he warned his protective detail. "I'll be right back." Officer Spencer took the woman to find out where her mugger had gone. "Dispatch, we have a two-eleven in progress at the Poughkeepsie Train Station. I am in pursuit."

This was his moment. Mark Thompson's plan worked perfectly. The two targets were alone and vulnerable. He took a small black object from his pocket and approached them from behind. He used it to knock the boyfriend out.

Amanda dropped to her knees to check on him. Her eyes stared up at Mark, but she was unable to see his face through the black ski mask.

"Oh shit," she mumbled. "HELP!"

Mark snatched her by the hair and dragged Amanda Ryan away from her boyfriend's body. "I want you to deliver a message for me." He pulled her towards the tracks. "Tell her payback's a bitch." Using both hands, he shoved Amanda Ryan onto the tracks below the platform.

A few people tried to fight him over his actions. They stopped when the train whistle blew. It was the distraction Mark needed to break away from the group and make a run for it. His hand gripped the black object and used it to attack everyone who got in his way.

"Help," Amanda called out again.

"I'm coming, baby," Sean strained to yell. He scrambled to his feet and made it to the edge of the platform. "Can you stand?" There was no reply. "Hold on; I'll get you out of there."

Mark watched from a distance as Sean jumped down to the tracks. The train whistle blew again. It was getting closer.

"Please, someone help us," she cried out.

Sean pushed her up onto the platform into the arms of other passengers waiting for the train. The train blew one more time as it entered the station.

"I love you," Sean said.

The breaks screeched as they tried to bring the massive locomotive to a stop before colliding with the young boy. Everyone turned away as he was crushed and killed by the train.

"Sean," Amanda sobbed hysterically. She tried to reach for the edge of the platform but was held back.

Mark marched back towards the newest crime scene. He beat everyone out of his way with the weapon in his hands. He snatched Amanda Ryan by her hair again and forced her to stare into his masked face.

"I have something bigger planned for you."

<u>Chapter 43-Ali</u>

Dr. Wu dropped me off at my house after helping me escape from the hospital. My car was sitting in the driveway, which meant Amanda must have let Rodney or Matthew into my house to get the spare set of keys.

"Thank you for breaking me out of there," I told him. "I'll get these washed and back to you as soon as I can."

"Don't worry about it. I just want you to be careful."

I patted him on the back and entered my house without another word. Caution went out the window the moment I decided to sneak out against the lieutenant's orders. I had a limited amount of time before the F.B.I. took over the case.

I grabbed a police scanner from my room while changing out of the scrubs Dr. Wu lent me. I heard a voice advise officers of a possible suspect sighting at the New Paltz bus station. I quickly grabbed my Glock and stared into the mirror as I pushed my hair into a ponytail.

"He's mine," I spat.

I retrieved my car keys from the bag of personal items recovered after the attempt on my life. I took my badge from the dresser and headed out the door.

My foot slammed on the gas, propelling me forward at a speed I could only assume would be clocked in at over a hundred. There was no plan. I wasn't calling for backup, but I was sure they were headed to the same destination. I arrived before any other officers and saw passengers boarding. I parked on the block next to it and ran up to the bus.

I tapped my badge against the door as it closed. "Are you the only bus that's pulled into the lot in the last ten minutes?" The forty-year-old man behind the wheel nodded. "Good, don't leave this spot until I tell you to."

"What's going on?"

"There was a report of a wanted suspect walking around this area."

The diver took the key out of the ignition. "It's all yours, lady."

I boarded the bus and began searching for Nick DeFalco. I carefully moved along the narrow path to the back, but no one resembled the suspect.

Where the hell was he?

I stepped off the bus just as the first squad car pulled into the lot. The driver jumped out with his gun and pointed it at me.

"Stand down, detective," he called out.

I slowly reached for my weapon and held it up in the air over my head. "He's not here."

The officer hurried to my side to disarm me. He pulled out a pair of handcuffs and snapped them around my wrists.

"I'm sorry; this is the lieutenant's orders."

"You can restrain me all you want, but we need to find out who placed the call and figure out where the suspect went."

The officer directed me to the back of his squad car. He called back to the station to let them know I was taken into custody.

"Let her go," the lieutenant replied.

"Are you sure?" the officer asked.

"Did I stutter? I said let her go."

The officer unlocked the cuffs. "I'm sorry, detective. We were instructed to arrest you on sight."

"I get it. You were following orders. But right now, we need to canvas the area for the suspect."

I ran into the office to question the employees. I showed them the picture of Nick DeFalco. No one recognized him, which made me think this may have been a setup or a diversion to draw us away long enough for him to escape. Then, my cell phone rang.

"Ali," Rodney said. His voice was low and unlike his usual chipper self. "There was an attack at the train station. Sean is dead and Amanda is missing."

"Missing? What do you mean; she's missing?"

Rodney recapped what happened; how he was called away at the possible DeFalco sighting. When he got back, he found out Officer Spencer was pulled away from Amanda because of a purse snatcher.

"He's holding my sister hostage to get out of town." It was the only possible reason for kidnapping her and keeping Amanda alive. "We need all hands on deck. I want surveillance tapes from the train station immediately. I want-"

"Ali, we'll find them."

"You better; because if I find him first, I'll kill him."

I got back in the car and sped to the station. The lieutenant was pacing around the office talking frantically on the phone. His eyes locked on me the moment I walked through the doors.

"Ali, I'm so sorry," he began.

I slapped the lieutenant. "Why the fuck did you tell Rodney to leave my sister at the train station?"

"I heard about the DeFalco sighting right after you escaped from the hospital. I knew you were going after him. Rodney was the best shot I had to stop you from doing something stupid."

"You mean kill the son of a bitch who murdered six people, threw a brick through my living room window, and put me in the hospital?" There was a fire burning inside of me that I had never felt before. "I wasn't going to hurt DeFalco, but that changed the moment he went after Amanda."

"Ali, I know you want revenge, but you have to remember you're a cop first. We need to do everything we can to bring DeFalco in alive."

"I won't promise anything." I shoved the lieutenant out of the way and stomped towards my desk. There was a large manila envelope sitting on my keyboard. "What's this?"

The lieutenant approached cautiously and eyed up the item. "I didn't see anyone drop it off."

The envelope had my named etched in red ink. I quickly opened it. There was a note inside attached to a photo of a young dark-haired woman. I recognized the girl instantly. It was Amanda. She was sitting in a large tub; stripped down to her bra and underwear. My heart was racing thinking of what this monster could be doing to her. I ripped open the note and read it.

You know who I am, and now you have a choice. Save your sweet little sister or catch me. This is your only chance.

The picture fell to my desk.

"What is it? What's wrong?" the lieutenant asked. He picked up the photo pinching it between his thumb and index finger. "I need an analyst down here to dust for prints. I need someone to queue up the footage from the last two hours."

"Don't bother," I mumbled. "He's been too careful. We'd only be wasting time my sister doesn't have."

The lieutenant wasn't listening to me. Why should that be any different than any other part of this investigation? He walked to another desk to make the call to the C.S.U. team. With his back turned, I heard a low buzzing coming from a drawer. I opened it and found a prepaid flip phone. I retrieved the device and saw there were two text messages.

Unknown: To find her, you must go where I have been. To find me, we need to take our relationship to new heights.

Unknown: Tell anyone where you're going, and you will suffer the consequences.

The second text had a picture of a man dressed in black holding a knife to Amanda's wrists while she sat in a tub.

I jumped to my feet. "I need you to run Nick DeFalco and Mark Thompson's names through the system again. There has to be a house or an apartment he stayed in up here. Maybe check other locations his landlords own."

The lieutenant's facial expression was a mix of anger and shock due to me ordering him around. "You do realize I'm your boss and not your employee?"

My eyes burned a hole through him. "It's your fault my sister is missing. So, I don't give a damn about who has a higher ranking. You need to do what I say for once."

He knew I wasn't messing around. If he had listened to me in the beginning, then we could have saved a few lives and kept my sister safe.

I watched the lieutenant scurry off to his office. He had the most important task, finding Amanda. I had something much more difficult to do. I had to figure out the second part of his message.

How do we take our relationship to new heights?

I considered the possibility of it referring to Mohonk Mountain, but he wasn't stupid enough to bring me back to one of his other crime scenes. I considered other possibilities, especially ones which included DeFalco escaping.

The doors to the station opened, which broke my concentration. Rodney stormed over to my desk. His face was drained and more emotional than I'd ever seen him before. He wrapped his massive arms around me.

"Ali, I'm so sorry. I was just following the lieutenant's orders."

I hugged him and told my partner it wasn't his fault. "I need you to help the lieutenant. He's looking into possible locations that DeFalco stayed in while living up here or other properties his landlords owned. I have a feeling he's been using one of them as a safe house."

"Okay, we can figure it out together." I'd already started to walk away before he finished his statement. "Ali, where are you going?"

"I'm going to hunt the son of a bitch and stop him before he hurts anyone else."

"But you don't know where to find him."

"You worry about getting my sister. I'll worry about DeFalco."

Before I left the station, I managed to swipe a set of keys. My car was fast, but Lieutenant Esposito topped mine. I rushed out to the parking lot before he had a chance to stop me. I jumped inside the sleek black Corvette and peeled out. I really didn't have a destination in mind, but I knew sitting around the station wasn't going to help. And the moment Rodney or the lieutenant found the address; I would feel the urge to run out with them and save my sister. I had to figure out the second part of the message. I was the only one who could take down DeFalco.

I sped down Route 9W thinking of what the clue meant. Taking our relationship to new heights? I didn't have a relationship with DeFalco. But then, I thought about how close I had been to him before he threw me off a bridge. The Mid-Hudson was where he had attacked me. But he said new heights. There was only one other bridge it could mean.

I slammed on the gas to get down to Newburgh. I slowed up only for stop lights. I was in a hurry, but I wasn't about to kill myself in pursuit of the suspect. I made it to I-84 just as my cell started to ring. Rodney's name flashed on the screen.

"Tell me you found her," I barked.

"The lieutenant and I located another house used for rentals on Prospect Street. It was boarded up after a fire last semester. We breached the building and found your sister."

"Is she okay?"

"He sliced her arms, but the medics said the cuts weren't too deep or severe. It was like he wasn't even trying to kill her."

"I don't think that was intention at all. He was testing me to see what I would do." I was almost at the Newburgh Beacon Bridge when I pulled to the side of the road.

"What do you mean?" Rodney asked. "Where are you?"

"Don't worry about me," I told him. "You are not to leave my sister's side no matter what." The tone in my voice made sure Rodney knew my orders trumped everyone else's.

"You got it, Ali."

"I need you to do one more favor. Call the lieutenant and tell him to send a few officers to the Mid-Hudson Bridge, the Newburgh Beacon, and the airport."

"What the hell is going on?"

"Now that you have Amanda; I can tell you. DeFalco left a cell for me with clues on how to find him and my sister. He said I could only choose one. That's why I had you and the lieutenant track down the rental locations."

"Okay, but what did it say?"

"To find him; I had to take our relationship to new heights."

"And you think that means he wants to meet you at a bridge?"

"No, I think he's heading to the airport to make his big escape. But I need to make sure he didn't set a trap at either location." Before I could say another word, the prepaid cell began buzzing. "Rodney, I have to go."

I hung up with my partner and took a deep breath. I knew the lieutenant wanted me to bring DeFalco in alive. He wanted us to arrest him; to pay for his crimes; to let the families he hurt watch him waste away in a jail cell for the rest of his life. But I was one of his targets too, and so was my sister. All I could imagine was pointing my gun at him and pulling the trigger. I wanted to watch him writhe in pain; leaving him with just enough of his life to be saved for a jury to convict him.

I flipped open the phone and saw a text message just as a black car sped past me. It was the same one from the parking lot where I went for my run every morning.

Unknown: COME GET ME!

I shifted into drive and took off after the car. I was in pursuit and called the lieutenant immediately. I gave the direction we were headed in; believing the destination was the airport. The driver was doing everything to lose me as we pulled into the parking lot. I was right on his bumper before he made a quick turn. I had no time to react. I sped past the row of cars. Without hesitation, I threw the car in reverse and drove backwards to the row DeFalco ducked into.

"Where is he?" I searched the up and down the aisle unable to locate the black Civic I had been chasing. "Where'd you go?"

I drove down another two rows before finding DeFalco's car illegally parked. The driver was missing. He abandoned the vehicle and was now on foot.

I radioed it in. "This is Detective Ali Ryan." I read off my badge number to the operator. "I am in pursuit of a murder suspect fleeing into Stewart Airport. I am requesting backup immediately. He is possibly armed and extremely dangerous."

I rushed into the building where long lines sat at security and baggage. I knew there was no way he slipped through either line without alerting the officers. I held my gun at my side while scanning the crowd of people for anyone resembling my suspect.

"Nick DeFalco," I called out. Many of the passengers turned their heads, but only one kept his head pointed in the direction of the security checkpoint. I noticed him right away. "Freeze," I shouted. He spun around brandishing a knife. "Put it down or I'll shoot."

He had to know I wasn't bluffing. His eyes shifted from left to right while backpedalling. He grabbed the first person within reach. The tip of the blade pressed against a woman's carotid artery.

"I didn't do it," he spat.

I was surprised by the comment. "You didn't kill any of those people? It was just a pure coincidence they all knew you and had become your enemy in the last year?"

"Yes…I mean no."

"Which is it, Nick?" There was fear in his eyes, which most cold blooded men didn't have right before they killed. "Did you or did you not kill those students?"

"Rachel, Nicole, Christina, and Kevin deserved it," he replied. "I had to kill them. They fucked up my life."

I had him talking, which was beneficial. If I could keep it going, I might be able to stall him long enough for backup to arrive.

"They were the reasons Brianna left you; am I right?"

"Yeah," he admitted. "Rachel and Nicole got in her head and tried to tell Brianna things which weren't true. They were giving her advice on how to change me and to walk away. They were always jealous over what we had.

"What about Kevin and Christina?"

"You know about them. She was a tease and only pretended to be my friend, but she talked so much shit behind my back. She wanted me out of the house so Brianna would move in. Kevin…well, I could tell you about all the fucked-up crap he did to everyone, but we don't have time for it."

"We have all the time you need. Tell me about Marty and Marie."

"That wasn't me, and neither was the attack on you."

"What do you mean? Who killed them?"

"I can't tell you," he replied. I could see Nick was getting desperate. He was panicking, which wasn't good news for the hostage. "Please, just let me go. I don't wanna hurt her."

I wanted to ask Nick more questions knowing he would be tight-lipped once he was custody. I could see he was inching his way towards the doors. He was about to escape with the hostage. Instead, a man broke away from the crowd and tackled Nick to the ground. The woman ran away screaming as the two men wrestled each other on the ground. I lined up a shot, but failed to pull the trigger when I saw the face of the attacker.

"Matthew," I gasped.

Nick scrambled to the knife and jammed it into Matthew's shoulder. Blood spilled to the ground as it surrounded the blade. DeFalco jumped to his feet and ran towards the door.

Every fiber in my body was filled with rage. There was no hesitation this time. I pulled the trigger. The bullet flew through the air and pierced the suspect in the middle of his back. Nick DeFalco dropped to the floor and remained motionless.

I was frozen to the spot. In all my years of being a cop, I only fired my weapon at two people. And now, Nick DeFalco, the man known as the Campus Killer, was lying dead on the floor.

"Ali," Matthew gasped as he reached out for me with his blood hands. "Please, help me."

I ran to Matthew's side. "Don't move; I'm getting you help." I grabbed my cell to call for an ambulance. I told them about a suspect being shot and another wounded from a stab to the left shoulder.

"I'm sorry," he whispered.

"Don't be sorry; you're a hero again. You saved a woman's life."

It took several minutes before backup arrived. The lieutenant led the charge into the airport. He noticed the body lying in the entrance and then saw me cradling Matthew in my lap.

"Ali, are you okay?" He surveyed the crime scene. "What the fuck happened here?"

"I-I don't know. It all happened so fast. Nick pulled a knife on a woman. He was about to walk out with her, but Matthew stopped him."

"And then what happened? How did DeFalco get shot?"

"He stabbed Matthew," I replied. "He was about to get away. I had no choice. I had to stop him."

Medics arrived two minutes later and rolled a stretcher into the airport. One of them tended to Matthew and brought him out to the ambulance. The other checked on Nick's lifeless body.

Lieutenant Esposito threw his arms around me and pulled me in for a consoling hug. "Everything will be all right, Ali. You're safe; Amanda's safe; and Matthew will be fine. It's all over."

But it didn't feel over to me. There were so many answers I still needed. Nick swore he had nothing to do with the attack on me and someone else killed Marty and Marie.

Was he telling the truth? If so, who was responsible?

I omitted that information from my statements, even to the lieutenant. I didn't want to cause additional panic or make him believe I was about to launch into another crazy idea DeFalco having a partner. I kept the information to myself and let the lieutenant comfort me while we watched Matthew get taken away in an ambulance.

<u>Chapter 44-Ali</u>

I sat at Amanda's bedside for the next two days while she recovered. I actually alternated between spending time with her and visiting Matthew who was down the hall. It was a bit obsessive, but I refused to let either of them out of my sight. I came so close to losing two people I loved. Even though the man known as the Campus Killer was dead, Nick DeFalco's words still haunted me. I didn't know if he had a partner; if he was covering for someone; or he just didn't want me shoot him out of revenge.

I tried to push those thoughts out of my mind. Instead, I played couch commando in Amanda's room. I controlled the remote. It was my right as the older sister to watch whatever I wanted on T.V. I think she just tolerated it because it allowed me to spend more time with her.

As we laughed at a stupid commercial, the hospital room door opened letting Lieutenant Esposito poke his head inside.

"I hope I'm not interrupting."

"No, not at all," Amanda replied. "Come in and join the party."

The lieutenant had a guilty expression on his face. He had already apologized to Amanda and to me but seeing us sitting in a hospital must be like a knife twisting in his stomach. This time was different. There was a look in his eyes which said he was looking for me regarding business.

"Um, Ali; can I have a word with you in private?" He escorted me from Amanda's room and led me to a vending machine. "I know this is a rough time for you-"

"I already gave my statement to I.A."

"I know, and after careful consideration, the department has decided not to press charges against you."

Thank you, God.

A surge of relief washed away any doubts lingering in my mind. I was certain I was done for after the comments I made. I did exactly what I threatened to do; kill Nick DeFalco. At the very least, I expected to face suspension with the possibility of being fired.

The lieutenant leaned in close. "Off the record," he whispered. "I'm glad you killed that sick bastard. If I was there, I would've pulled the trigger too."

"I tried to bring him in alive." Despite the anger raging inside of me, I'd wanted to do the right thing. I had even been willing to let him get out of the airport with the hostage hoping backup would be able to take him down the moment he stepped outside. "Once he stabbed Matthew, I lost my ability to control the situation. I had to take him down to ensure Matthew and the woman were safe."

"Ali, I know you did your best under the circumstances. I promise, once you come back from your mandatory leave of absence, I'll try to listen to you and your theories a little more."

"Wait, mandatory leave? I thought I was cleared."

"You were of criminal charges, but you still fired your weapon and killed someone. You know the protocol. You are required to undergo a psychiatric evaluation and mandated to therapy until they determine you are cleared to return to the field."

I knew the lieutenant was doing his job, and he had stuck up for me to ensure I wouldn't be punished for bringing a serial killer to justice. At the same time; I hated the idea of sitting on administrative leave pending therapy and evaluations.

"Look on the bright side," he said. "You get to spend quality time with Amanda and your boyfriend. And *we* get the added benefit of not having you around for a little while."

I was unsure if he was joking or serious. I'm sure the lieutenant's blood pressure was going to be normal for the first time in over a year. It was also nice to know I wasn't going to be screamed at on a daily occurrence.

"Is it going to be paid leave?"

He took a deep breath and rolled his eyes. "I'll see what can be arranged. In the meantime, I suggest you stop worrying and relax a bit."

There was a smile on my face for once. You know what? I could use a nice vacation after all of this crap."

"Good, you can start by coming to my house for a small Christmas party. Bring Amanda and your boyfriend. Maybe we can actually talk without involving work."

"So, does this mean I have permission to raid your fridge this time?"

"Yes, but if you touch my car again, I'm throwing your ass in jail for a month." We both let out a laugh.

"Yes, sir," I saluted. I gave him a hug and thanked him again before walking down the hall. I located Matthew's room and snuck inside.

"Hey, you look like you're in a good mood," he stated.

"The lieutenant just told me I have to take a mandatory leave of absence." I sat down on the edge of the bed and held Matthew's hand.

"And you're okay with that?" he asked.

"I'm not thrilled with the idea I can't go to work every day, but I like having the option to spend a lot more time with you. I was thinking once you're all healed up; we could get out of town for a while."

"You want to go away together?"

It was a big move. We'd barely had time to talk since our fight. He showed up to talk things out with me the morning I was attacked. A day later, he ended up in the hospital after being stabbed. There was so much to discuss, but I couldn't think of a better way to kick it off than to sit on a beach for a couple weeks.

"I think it's long overdue."

"Then, my answer is yes. Where did you want to go?"

"I've always heard St. Lucia was really nice."

"Grab my laptop. Let's start planning."

<u>**Epilogue**</u>

The Ulster County and New Paltz police presence on campus vanished. The papers and internet spread the word the Campus Killer had been killed. There was no need for the additional patrols. Students were packing their bags to return home for winter break. The general consensus was a hope all the tragic events which took place could be forgotten. The very least, they all wanted to move on from all that happened.

The car arrived on Prospect Street where yellow crime scene tape surrounded the perimeter of a home. There were wooden planks scattered on the ground which once kept intruders at bay. It was a spacious three-bedroom home with a hidden driveway. It was the same place Amanda Ryan was found less than a week ago.

It's good to be home again.

The man parked along the hidden path and snuck into the house. He was the one who told Nick DeFalco where to go when he feared the police were closing in on him. Nick placed all his trust in one man, and it was that same person who set him up to fail. There was so much his little protégé hadn't known. One thing in particular was that he referred to himself as the Puppet Master.

Sorry, kid, but someone had to take the fall. You played the part well enough to get your revenge. But in the end; you were too much of a liability.

The Puppet Master walked up the stairs to the bedroom just off of the second-floor landing. He entered and walked directly to the closet. He was sure the police had searched it but wondered if they found the missing IDs. He removed the false panel and located the small box. There were four student IDs and a list of victims inside. They were the remnants to show who Nick was responsible for killing.

Good thing I convinced him to leave this behind.

Nick wasn't aware of the other deaths he had been framed for or the attacks on Detective Ryan. Those were meant to ensure he was killed instead of merely being arrested. It was the only way to guarantee his hands remained clean. It was why the final plan was for Nick to make the call about someone seeing him at the bus station in New Paltz before telling him to run for his escape flight out of Stewart Airport. Everything was done by design, and the poor bastard never saw it coming.

The Puppet Master added a few newspaper clippings to the box. One included an article of two students dying in a fiery attack at their home on Church Street. Another talked about a young man who died while saving his girlfriend from an oncoming train. The final page was a write up on how Detective Ali Ryan stopped the Campus Killer, a man responsible for seven murders.

The Puppet Master took out the folded paper with the names of the victims crossed out. He added two more to the list. Detective Ali Ryan and Amanda Ryan.

<u>The End</u>

Bio

Andrew Hess, the King of Cliffhangers, was born of Long Island, New York. His love of writing was discovered while studying psychology at SUNY New Paltz. He grew up an avid reader of fellow mystery and suspense authors such as James Patterson and Edgar Alan Poe. He designed his writing to be a combination of the two authors and added plot twists to his stories.

The cliffhangers began with The Phoenix Blade series, a government conspiracy series, which introduced a group of 22-year-old vigilantes hired by the government to eliminate people who were guilty of heinous crimes. Hess continued the trend while venturing into the world of crime fiction penning the Detective Ryan Series and the Detective Thornton Series. Readers have been glued to both book sets demanding the next installment from the author.

Hess has a love for multiple genres and has demonstrated this by penning several books in romance, thrillers, and psychological fiction with books such as; Learning to Love, #1 Fan, Finding Strength, The Kritana Contract, Trapped Inside: Living with Agoraphobia, and submissions in the Detours in our Destinations Anthology. He has also written two books of free-verse poetry with Chamber of Souls, and Hall of the Forgotten (an ode to Poe's Cask of Amontillado).

Hess won Indie Author Books Best Mystery Thriller Author (2015), and Indie Author Book Series of the year (2014) for The Phoenix Blade Series.

Hess was also nominated for Best Male Author, Best Mystery Suspense Author, Book of the Year, and Best Mystery Book (2015) for Campus Killer by Wickedly Devine Divas, The Three Bookateers, and SNSBAH Promotions. He received several nominations in 2016 from Summer Indie Awards for Contemporary (#1 Fan), Crime (Conviction; Deadly Games), Mystery (Campus Killer; Scorned; and Conviction), Romance (#1 Fan) and Anthology (Detours in our Destinations).

With more than twenty books to his name, Hess is not done yet. He moved to Georgia with his wife and son to spend more time with them. The area has filled him with more inspiration to branch into other genres including horror, psychological thrillers, children's books, and mid-grade books. With so much already accomplished and much more to come, keep your eyes on this author as he takes you on a literary journey you will never forget.

Social Media Links

FB
https://www.facebook.com/TheRealPhoenix13/

Team Phoenix
https://www.facebook.com/groups/andrewsphoenixstreetteam/

Twitter
https://www.twitter.com/Iamphoenix13

Instagram
https://www.instagram.com/author_andrew_hess13/

Amazon
https://tinyurl.com/AuthorAndrewHess13

Website
https://tinyurl.com/KingofCliffhangers1

Other Works by Andrew Hess

Poetry
Chamber of Souls
Hall of the Forgotten

The Phoenix Blade Series
The Phoenix Blade: Project Justice
The Phoenix Blade: Awakening
The Phoenix Blade: Pandemonium

Detective Ryan Series
Campus Killer (Detective Ryan Series Book 1)
Scorned (Detective Ryan Series Book 2)
Conviction (Detective Ryan Series Book 3)
Frantic (Detective Ryan Series Book 4)
No Way Out (Detective Ryan Series Book 5)
Escape (Detective Ryan Series Book 6)
Atonement (Detective Ryan Series Book 7)
Truth and Lies (Detective Ryan Series Book 8)

Detective Thornton Series
Deadly Games (Detective Thornton Series Book 1)
Manhunt (Detective Thornton Series Book 2)
Deception (Detective Thornton Series Book 3)
Chaos (Detective Thornton Series Book 4)

Sugar and Spice Mysteries
A Scream in the Night (Book 1)
My Deadly Valentine (Book 2)

Strength Hope and Love Series
Finding Strength

#1 Fan
#1 Fan
#1 Fan: Obsession

Veritas Series
Unraveled (Book 1)

Stand Alone Books
Trapped Inside: Living with Agoraphobia
Learning to Love
The Kritana Contract

Mid-Grade Books
Thornton Twins Detective Agency (Book 1)-Case of the Missing Purse

9 798349 376771